AMY
SNOW

AMY SNOW

TRACY REES

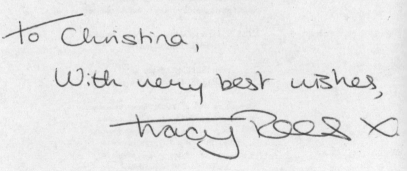

To Christina,
With very best wishes,
Tracy Rees x

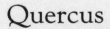

Quercus

First published in Great Britain in 2015 by

Quercus Publishing Ltd
Carmelite House
50 Victoria Embankment
London EC4Y 0DZ

An Hachette UK company

A CIP catalogue record for this book is available
from the British Library

PB ISBN 978 1 78429 145 7
EBOOK ISBN 978 1 78429 146 4

10 9 8 7 6 5 4 3 2 1

Typeset by Jouve (UK), Milton Keynes

Printed and bound in Great Britain by Clays Ltd, St Ives plc

To my parents, with love

Prologue

Aurelia Vennaway held her breath as she tiptoed from the stuffy parlour and stole along the hallway. Her mother and aunts had paid her no attention for the past hour but that did not mean she would be allowed to leave. Her mother thought that the weather would keep her inside, that for once she would sit quietly and decorously in the corner as a little girl should.

She jammed her fur hat over fat, drawing-room ringlets and stuck her feet into sturdy boots. Shrugging on her blue cloak as swiftly as she would shrug off her destiny if she only could, she heaved open the door.

It was the kind of day that glittered and beckoned like a foretaste of heaven. The snow no longer fell, but lay thick and silver-white on the ground. The sun dazzled and the sky was a rich, celestial blue. On such a day as this, the whole world might change.

Aurelia sank up to her knees, then squared her shoulders and considered her nonsense of skirts. Gathering them up in great bunches, she lurched like a staggering deer through the snow until her lungs flamed with its cut-glass brilliance.

Last week she had not seen her mother for five days. The metallic smell of blood and the screams that came from the bedchamber were only a memory now and her mother was back amongst the family once more – but harder than ever to please. Aurelia was not sure that she cared to try. The house was brittle and tense.

Sunlight could find no way into the woods beyond the house. Snow-laden branches of yew and wasted, straggle-thin fingers of oak reached for Aurelia. She laid her hands on them, greeting them like old and comforting friends. Her ringlets had loosened into snakes. Screeching jays made the only sound. She swung herself onto a low branch to listen and dream of the time when she would leave Hatville Court and never come back.

She nearly tumbled into the drifts when she heard an unfamiliar cry. It came in bursts, feeble yet grating, insisting she jump down and follow. She felt as though some other-worldly force were playing catch-me-if-you-can with her. It came again – goblin song – drawing her through the trees and into the sunlight.

Finally, she stood on the breast of a hill. Before her, something blue and hairless wriggled in the snow. For a moment the enchantment of the old woods clung to her and she feared to touch the creature. But curiosity broke the spell and she stepped closer. It was a human child, a tiny baby. She tore off her cloak and snatched the baby from the snow. Its skin was as chill as strawberry mousse. She wrapped it up and hugged it close.

Something was distinctly wrong, Aurelia decided, when a naked infant lay alone at the edge of a deserted wood.

'Hello?' she called, staring all around. 'Hello? I have your baby!'

Nothing but silence, and a crow lifting into the air on silky wings. The baby was very cold and weighed almost nothing. Aurelia turned and, as fast as her skirts allowed, she ran.

PART ONE

———❦———

January 1848

Chapter One

I know they are watching me go. The road out of the village is long and straight. It will be miles before it bends, carrying me out of sight of the upper windows of the grand house. I know what they see: a nothing, a nobody. A small, staunch figure, lonely in mourning black, stiff skirts rustling about my boots, cloak fast against the cold. A crisp black bonnet settled grim upon my head and ribbons whipped by the wind. What a desolate January traveller I must represent.

Frost on the fields and upon the road, the village empty and forlorn, my boots leaving a trail of prints that peter into infinity. That is what they hope I will do — vanish like a melted footprint. If I can, I will oblige them. My reason for being here, the only person I have ever loved, now lies beneath six feet of earth and thick, shadow-green boughs of yew in a quiet corner of the churchyard. She was laid there yesterday.

The air is so cold that the tears are flayed from my eyes, eyes I had thought to be finished with crying for all time. After the biblical floods I have shed in the last three days I thought there could be no water left in my depleted form. Yet it seems that life, and grief, and winter go on. My toes are numb as I trudge the miles that lead me away from Aurelia's grave and from Hatville Court, the only home, grudging as it was, that I have ever known.

Soon enough, it threatens dark. The sharpest sickle moon I have ever seen hangs razor-edged in a grey sky and ahead I see the silhouette of Ladywell, the next village. I have walked for hours.

I stop there because I know I must, although my needs are not the sort to be assuaged by food, or ale or fire. The chill in my bones is nothing to the freeze in my heart and no congenial company on earth could compensate me for the lack of Aurelia. But the next village is six miles yet further and the lanes are awash with shadow. It would be the height of folly to go on; a young woman alone has ever been an easy target for villains. And although I have little faith that my life will ever again feel worthwhile, I still do not wish to throw it away. Aurelia may be gone, but she is not done with me yet. I will carry out her wishes in death every scrap as faithfully as I did when she was with me.

I enter the Rose and Crown. With my second, secret legacy from Aurelia I could afford the White Harte Royal, a hotel of some repute. But news flows between Ladywell and Enderby. If it were heard at Hatville Court that Amy Snow was seen taking a room at the Harte, they would be after me tomorrow in their carriage like the hounds of hell. For then they would guess there is more to my legacy than meets the eye.

The Rose and Crown will suffice. The chat in the lounge may not be the most refined for a young lady with a mind to her reputation but then I am *no lady*; this has been made abundantly clear to me.

I hesitate in the hall. *What am I?* Respectable young woman or guttersnipe? Servant, sister or friend? My role in the tale of Aurelia Vennaway puzzles no one more than me, especially now that I am called upon to conclude it.

'May I help you, miss?' A soft-spoken landlord approaches, clasping his hands as though anxious that his very presence might cause offence. How well I know that feeling.

'Thank you, sir. A room for the night, if you please, and perhaps a little supper – nothing rich – and a warming drink.'

'Certainly, miss, certainly. BELLA!' His welcoming tone leaps to a bellow and a young maid pops into the hall like a jackrabbit from a hole.

'Bella, light the fire in the Barley Room and take the lady's bag there,' he instructs, resuming his normal pitch. 'Might I recommend, miss, that you take supper in the lounge tonight? I would not suggest it except there is a blazing fire there and it will take a while for your room to reach a comfortable temperature. The lounge is quiet – the cold is keeping many at home – and, if you'll forgive me, you look frozen to the bone, Miss . . . ?'

'Snow.'

He looks at me then, understanding dawning. Bella stands with my bag stretching her skinny arm almost to the floor, gazing with frank curiosity until he orders her on her way.

'Begging your pardon, Miss Snow, if the lounge is acceptable I will attend to you myself, ensure you are undisturbed. By the time you are fed, your room will be fit to receive you.'

His kindness brings fresh tears to my eyes and only a supreme effort keeps them there.

I take my supper in the lounge and though I can eat only a little, the warmth and flavour are somewhat fortifying. I do not linger but retire to a small, simple room which is, as promised, tolerably warm. I perform a rudimentary toilette in a daze.

Whilst I walked I conceived the idea to write an account of my time and travels, so as to feel that my life has some substance, some witness. Alone in the silence, Aurelia's absence presses down upon me but now is not the time to give in, not so very early on in my quest. I must be as strong as I need to be.

I begin to write. Really, there is nothing else I can do.

Chapter Two

I cannot help but begin with a reflection on beds. An unseemly object of consideration for a young lady, no doubt, yet why should it be so? A bed is a place where so much of life is played out – births and deaths and passions and dreaming – all the most fundamental moments of our fragile human existence.

In this story there are several important beds, not least the sick bed of my mistress, where she lay for the better part of three years. And my own, very first known bed, which was a bank of snow – a pristine white mattress that supported my tiny head, cradled my kicking limbs and chilled my poor infant flesh 'til I was blue to the bone. It also gave me my name. Indeed, it provides not just a convenient name but an apt symbol of my identity. My whole standing in this society we call the world is drawn from that unloving, white blank.

I would not have survived that soft, glittering, beautiful bed – was not intended to, let us not shy from the facts – had it not been for a headstrong child who rarely did as she was told.

That child was Aurelia Vennaway, only child of Sir Charles and Lady Celestina Vennaway, the first family of the county.

At a precocious eight years of age, Aurelia was her parents' treasure and their bane. Unimpressed by her own elevated standing in society, she seemed oblivious to the inherent differences in value that exist between human beings. I, in contrast, have never been ignorant of the fact that some children are infinitely more precious than others.

The day she found me, Aurelia wore a copper-coloured dress and sturdy brown boots with copper-coloured buttons. She was wrapped in a sky-blue cloak and wore a cream fur hat. I cannot remember this, of course, but she told me. Aurelia told me all the stories of my early life in painstaking detail as if to make up for my unknown identity with a richness of personal history.

That day, the tedium of the overheated, overpopulated parlour had quite engulfed her. Although the deepest snow in living memory lay upon the ground, the sun was shining and Aurelia breathed easiest out of doors. The four walls of any given room could not give her the horizons she longed for – horizons she could measure with her eyes and strive to conquer with her own two legs. She was like a wild animal, Cook always said.

She ran to the woods, where the jays knocked and shrieked with such heartfelt outrage it was a wonder she heard me at all. But she did, and though she lost her hat as she scrambled and slipped in the snow, she found me – skinny and frantic beneath an endless blue sky. I wonder, if I were even able to be conscious of such a thing, whether Aurelia in her sky-blue cloak appeared to me like a divine being condensed from the air.

Unlike the babies of cousins and acquaintances that had hitherto constituted her experience of the infant population, I was not red-faced and hearty but sliver-thin and blue. Nor was I smothered in yards of satin and lace; I was entirely naked. I screamed, she said, as though I would take on the whole world.

So she wrapped me in her cloak and ran for home. Neglecting all rules of decorum and boot removal, she erupted into the parlour, where her mother and aunts still sat talking and stitching and talking. Horrified gasps greeted the snowy tracks on the rug as Aurelia laid her bundle carefully before the fire and loosened the folds.

She could not quite understand why Lady Vennaway's response to my arrival was to cry '*Aurelia!*' as if she had done something truly dreadful. She could not understand why she was in disgrace (and it was clear that she was) for helping a living soul. Nor could she understand why her aunt Evangeline made such a fuss about the loss of the hat, as though a hat were more valuable than a baby.

In time they explained to her that not all babies are of equal value, that their worth depends upon many things, particularly the circumstances of their birth and the family into which they make their appearance. Indeed, that the world has room for an entire hierarchy of babies. I was a particularly worthless example, an unsavoury breath of disgrace – albeit not their own – that was simply neither welcome nor appropriate in the elevated Vennaway household.

Within moments of my arrival at Hatville Court I was banished to the kitchen. Not for me the roaring parlour fire and the rich softness of the Indian rug. No, the residual warmth of the stove and a bucket hastily emptied of potatoes had to serve. But Aurelia insisted on following me there and together she and Cook tended me, nursing me back to pinkness, and life.

Lady Vennaway was deeply shocked. Not at the atrocity that had been done to me, for she was well aware that mankind, outside the best families, was a seething pot of iniquity. But that the result of such immorality had presented itself on *her* property, encroached into *her* household – this was outrage. All she wanted that day (and her husband was in accord) was to get rid of me. There were orphanages, workhouses that existed to solve problems like me. But their cherished, adored Aurelia would not hear of it.

Hatville Court may be imagined as a sort of latter-day Agincourt, hosting a struggle that ebbed and swelled over two and a half decades. One army was composed of Lord and Lady Vennaway: powerful, respected, moneyed and always, incontrovertibly, *right*. They had history, authority and convention on their side. The opposing army consisted of Aurelia. As a child, a *daughter* no less, her chances of prevailing were non-existent, yet she refused to acknowledge the fact and this carried her a long way.

Most of Aurelia's battles were minor: the choice of a gown, censorship of her reading matter, whether or not she must accompany her mother's morning calls around the neighbourhood. These she sometimes won, more usually lost. But championing me was the first of several causes over which she would have her way no matter what. On this occasion she achieved her victory with sheer obstinacy, showing an iron will far from palatable in a young lady. I believe she also resorted to a tantrum. However, just as even the most brilliant general can benefit from reinforcements, so was Aurelia's campaign fortified by unexpected allies.

The first of these was Lady Vennaway's visiting troupe of sisters. Although all were horrified by me, some also expressed sympathy for my poor infant self – and relief that Fate had brought me to a family with such ample fortune that I surely would be no trouble to anyone. (It may be that mischief towards Lady Vennaway, the proudest and most beautiful of the sisters, lurked behind these philanthropic sentiments.)

The second was the appearance, just two hours later, of the Reverend Mr Chorley. If he was dismayed by the gaggle of ladies into which he stumbled, he was soon distracted by the news that awaited him. Aurelia, stubbornly absent since my arrival, suddenly reappeared and informed him of her discovery. Her florid description of the poor blue baby was further

embroidered by Gwendoline, the youngest and least circum-
spect of the aunts. The good reverend was also of the opinion
that God had brought me to the Vennaways in order to pre-
serve my life, as well as to bless Lady Vennaway with a priceless
opportunity to do her Christian duty and set an example to the
whole village.

For the Vennaways, reputation was everything. Her ladyship was cornered. General Aurelia prevailed.

Chapter Three

In the waning light of my lantern I take an envelope from the pocket of my black dress. I weigh it in my hands and think back to the reading of Aurelia's will. It feels like a full lifetime ago. In fact it was just yesterday.

The funeral — vile occasion — took place in the morning, then we all retreated to nurse our grief in private. At four o'clock, we gathered in the study: Lord and Lady Vennaway, Aurelia's cousin Maude, myself, Cook and Mr Clay, the village school teacher. In short, her beneficiaries. And Wilberforce Ditherington, her lawyer, of course.

It was a room well befitting the sombre occasion. Indeed the whole house, though splendid, is grim and austere. A new visitor to Hatville might be deceived by the grounds, which are vibrant, lavish and vast. The lush fields and rippling woods, the grand lawns and orchards, the walled gardens massed with herbs and roses are all unchanged these hundred years. Yet the beauty, the abundance, is all on the outside.

The façade of the house is impressive, to be sure. Once

inside, however, the new arrival would be hard pressed to contain a shiver. Two of the wings are veiled in dustsheets, for three Vennaways are too few to fill them all. The furniture in the grand rooms is splendid in its way, but also old-fashioned and bare. The tables bear food and the chairs provide places to perch, yet any further inspiration is lacking; it would occur to no one at Hatville to consider comfort or ornamentation.

From the moment of Aurelia's death I felt my own light die inside me. So the Amy Snow who stood yesterday in the corner of the gloomy study, most despised of all present, could no longer feel the excoriating looks shot her way. Mr Ditherington read to us how Aurelia wished to dispose of her personal fortune and the words blew over me like sand. Sums of money, he intoned, had been distributed to the various philanthropic causes Aurelia supported: the Society for the Education of the Lower Classes; the Surrey Anti-Cholera Movement; the Alliance for the Promotion of Humane Housing for the Destitute and so on. Aurelia's parents gazed out of the window, as ever unenthused and mildly disconcerted by Aurelia's charities. Then Mr Ditherington came to the more personal bequests and the Vennaways paid attention once more.

Mr Clay trembled when he heard the sum she had bequeathed to his little school. It would mean repairs, supplies, extension, his long-held dream come true.

Cousin Maude was delighted to receive all of Aurelia's sumptuous dresses, bonnets and cloaks. Even as an invalid

Aurelia had remained incongruously passionate about the latest fashions and regularly commissioned bespoke gowns from London. She had always been considerably – justifiably – vain.

Cook wept when she heard that Aurelia had left her several items of jewellery, including her gold and ruby heart-shaped locket. Lord and Lady Vennaway looked pained but Cook was not the dangerous one here. She was a family servant of long-standing; it was inevitable that Aurelia should have some affection for the woman. And, being Aurelia, she was bound to be inappropriately generous.

It was I who was the danger, for I had been closer to her than anyone. Despite my shameful beginnings, and their insistence that I was a lowly, utterly dispensable servant, Aurelia had persisted in elevating me to lady's maid, then companion and, in the last months, private nurse. They had tried to evict me with multiple cruelties both petty and great. But Aurelia would not be parted from me and I have a powerful capacity for endurance.

When my name was read, the whole party stiffened. Aurelia's parents bristled, waited to hear what insufferable extravagance she would bestow upon me posthumously. In the event, it was surprisingly inoffensive:

To Amy Snow, true friend and devoted companion through these long years of my illness, I leave ten pounds, a sum that I know she will manage wisely to start a new life wherever she may please. Also, my gold and garnet ring, which I entreat her to wear in memory of me. Also, my recent sketchbook capturing my impressions of this past autumn, made brighter through her friendship, which burned like a good fire to dispel the chill of my impending departure.

I was aware of the sighs of relief all around. There was no need for a scene so soon after Aurelia's death. The ring she had left me was less valuable than Cook's locket – of sentimental value mostly. The money at least removed the necessity for them to decide what to do with me; I knew they would not supplement it with a single penny. The sketchbook, though vastly personal, was more meaningful to me than to them. They could bear to allow it. Ah, how well she knew us all.

Ten pounds. This was the sum of money that Mr Ditherington gravely counted out and pressed into my palm late yesterday afternoon. A ring and a sketchbook. These were the keepsakes I slid onto my finger, tucked into my carpet bag, knowing I would leave Hatville Court for ever the next day. I would have been packed off the moment Aurelia passed if her feelings for me had not been so well known in the neighbourhood. If I had not been at the funeral, people would have talked and the Vennaways could not abide talk. Then of course I was needed at the reading of the will and they could not be seen to turn me out so late. Such tenuous threads of timing and circumstance made possible what happened the next morning. This morning. Today!

I slept fitfully, riven with loneliness and afraid of a future that I could not imagine. But I trusted Aurelia: if she said I could start a new life with ten pounds, then that is what I would do. This uneasy mix of trust and fear bore me through to morning, when I struggled upright in the dusty winter shadows to stand at the window and stare at the horizon, in the hope that it would yield some inspiration.

And so it did, though not in a way I could have anticipated. Mr Clay was pacing in the kitchen garden.

I was astonished. He had of course gone home yesterday after the reading. Why was he back so soon, and amongst the vegetable plots? Surely he could not have business with the Vennaways, a lowly schoolteacher with no breeding?

Then he looked up and saw me and raised a hand, his mouth opening into an 'Ah!', though of course I could not hear it. He made a sequence of gestures expressing an invitation to join him, an imprecation to be secretive and a great, good-mannered deference all at once. I had not known that communication without words could be so fulsome. Hastily I dressed and bundled back my hair, then ran through the silent passages, out into the walled kitchen garden.

'Is there somewhere to speak in private? Away from the house?' he asked at once in a low, urgent voice. Whatever his business, it was clearly too important to waste time on niceties.

So I led him through a gate, along a lane and thence into a small copse. Shrouded by trees and January mist, we would not be observed. The wind whispered secrets in its own incomprehensible language. The trees stood in enigmatic silence, bare and black like the truth of Aurelia's death.

He glanced around and, satisfied that the place would do, whipped off his hat. 'I beg your pardon, Miss Snow, for disturbing you at such a difficult time. Only, you see, I was charged to come.'

'Charged by whom, Mr Clay?'

He looked bewildered by his own words. 'By Miss Vennaway.'

My heart stilled. *How could this be?*

He reached within his overcoat and drew out a parcel. Clutching it, he hesitated. 'After I returned home last night I felt . . . uplifted by the generous bequest she had made me. I sat in my study and wrote an extensive letter to Miss Page telling her of Miss Vennaway's generosity and vision. Miss Page and I are betrothed, you know.'

'I know, Mr Clay, I know.'

'And then, well, I partook of some chops.'

'Chops, Mr Clay?'

'Yes, chops. Simmered with herbs and onions, delicious. I find that good fortune brings on a hearty appetite. And so it was some time before I returned to my study to open the package that Mr Ditherington had entrusted to me. It was quite large, as you may recall, and I expected it to contain a great many legal papers.'

I could not recall the package, distracted as I had been during the reading of the will. But if there were some final word from her, I would give everything I owned for it.

'In fact, it contained very little for me. A banker's draft for the amount stated and a letter containing very kind sentiments for the school's future and my matrimonial happiness. The letter also contained a request. And . . . there was this.' He handed the parcel to me at last.

'Amy Snow' was written on the outside in Aurelia's familiar handwriting, in Aurelia's favourite violet ink. I could hardly believe it. I looked up at Mr Clay's earnest face.

'The request was that I should deliver this to you in person before you left Hatville Court, and let no one else know that I had done so. I could not let her down.'

'She has thought of everything,' I said in a low voice.

'You meant everything to her. I wish you luck, Miss Snow. I hope you will count me as one friend, at least, wherever you may go.'

He bowed and I curtseyed, then we took our leave. He wished me Godspeed and I blessed his endeavours for the school, strongly suspecting that I would never see good Mr Clay again.

I would not linger. I was dressed now and half packed. If I could leave before encountering the Vennaways, it would spare us all one last discomfort. But first I was impatient for some word of further explanation. Hastily I opened the parcel and withdrew an envelope. The envelope contained a sheaf of money that I did not count and a letter, which I read at once. I dared not risk lingering to read it in the house; even in my room I could not rely upon privacy. So I stayed in the copse, in the half-light, reading and shivering and quite unable to believe the words before me.

Then I hurried back inside. I finished packing, buckled my carpet bag and brushed my wayward cloud of dark hair, readying myself for the road.

My heart nearly jumped into my mouth when the bedroom door suddenly burst open. I spun round to see Lord Vennaway stalking towards me, face grey, moustache shivering on his lip.

'You!' he rasped, running a hand through his hair, plunging it into a pocket, withdrawing it in a fist, pocketing it again. 'You are here and you should not be, you should never have been. Who are you, anyway? Taking advantage of my girl's soft heart and innocence. Wheedling your way into her affections. Staying here where you were not welcome. Schemer! Vagabond! Baseborn! *You* should have died, not her. We treasured her, but she was blighted like a rose. And you were poison in her ear. You were unfit company for her. She might have lived if you had let her be but you wouldn't. You *wouldn't*!'

I had never heard him speak so. In fact I rarely heard him speak at all – we avoided each other as much as possible in the usual run of things. His wife was more often my tormentor; I had heard from *her* countless times that the wrong child thrived, that Aurelia had been destined for greatness, that I should have been left to die in the snow. Lord Vennaway, by contrast, was merely a disapproving presence – a raincloud over a picnic. The reality of the man, here in my room, angry, tragic and raving, was deeply alarming. I backed away from him.

'What have you there?' he demanded, pushing past me and seizing my carpet bag.

I gasped in horror. The precious package! I must not lose it before I had even inspected its contents. I must not let Aurelia down at the very outset!

At least the envelope was safe in my skirt. Instinctively my hand went to it and I felt its papery crackle. Lord Vennaway stared at me and for an awful moment I thought he would grab my hand, find the letter and the money. But instead he started hunting through my bag – oh, humiliating invasion though it was. Clothes, books, undergarments (I closed my eyes in mortification) and old letters were tossed through the air to land on bed and floor as he grunted in the passion of his search. The parcel was discovered in a trice.

'What's this?' he demanded, seeing Aurelia's handwriting on the wrapping.

I had to speak. 'A birthday present. From Aurelia.'

'A *birthday* present? You don't have a birthday. You have no birth worth marking.' His eyes locked onto mine.

I would not be undone. I had heard worse.

'We used to pretend a birthday for me. In January. The day I was found. It was a few days before she . . . she . . .' My eyes filled with tears. For the love of God I could not say *died*. 'I kept it,' I struggled on, 'to have something from her after . . . after . . .'

Aghast I watched him turn it over as though to open it.

'No!' I could not help myself. I reached out to seize it and he pushed me hard away from him.

He tore the paper and I watched, wretched with helplessness. Some kind of gauzy green fabric spilled out, soft and feminine, perhaps with embroidery, I could not tell in the shock of it all. He cast it away too. The wrapping landed on the bed, the green gauze slithered to the floor.

'Get out!' he hissed. 'Leave my house and never return. We have tolerated your unsavoury presence too long. Now Aurelia is gone and any affection for you is dead with her. Know that if you ever set foot on this property again we will call the constable and make sure you are removed for good.'

Shaking, I gathered my possessions. No careful packing this time; I just bundled them in anyhow. The green fabric and torn wrapping I stuffed in first, then everything else on top, while he watched me fumble and drop things. My only thought was to escape with Aurelia's bequest undiscovered. I packed so badly the bag scarcely closed; my old grey dress spilled from the top.

There were no farewells. Not even Cook came to see me off, though I imagine she was forbidden to. The door was slammed behind me and I was on that long, straight road while my hair still crackled from the brushing. But the money and letter were undetected and the parcel was still in my possession. That was all that mattered.

Chapter Four

The Barley Room in the Rose and Crown is a quarter the size of my room at Hatville and contains twice the amount of furniture. It smells of polish and soot. It feels lonely and unfamiliar but it offers blessed privacy; at last I can investigate Aurelia's gift thoroughly.

The green fabric is silk, embroidered with tiny sprays of *Myosotis* — forget-me-not. It is a light stole such as fine ladies wear to summer balls to veil ivory shoulders. When I bury my nose in the silky folds, I fancy I can smell jasmine and moonlight. It is not the season for such a pretty thing, nor am I the girl to wear it.

I count the money and discover it is a hundred pounds. I gaze at it in bewilderment, then hide it, for want of a better place, in my wash bag. It is not yet safe for me to have it.

I read the letter again by lamplight, hours after my first reading in the greyish sigh of early morning. Now the page is lit by the lantern's deep golden glow.

My treasured Amy,

If you are reading this letter, then Mr Clay has carried out my request, as I feel sure he will, and I am gone, as I know I must. Dear heart, I know you must be in great pain now. We have been lucky, haven't we, in our time together? I do not know many who can boast the depth of affection and great camaraderie that we have shared. I may have been born an only child, but I have a sister nonetheless.

Enough of this, for you know my sentiments well enough and there is much that I must tell you. Close as we were and are, dearest, there are secrets I have kept from you. Not through lack of trust, I hope you know. You will understand when you learn them, as I always meant that you should. But they are not secrets I can simply set out in a letter – at least, not this one. I wish with all my heart that I could tell you in person, our heads bent together in the firelight as we have sat so often. Prepare yourself, dear Amy, for much that you do not know.

Do you remember, dear, when you were little, how I used to delight in creating treasure hunts for you? I would labour away at clues and secret locations after you had gone to bed, creep out to plant them and then enjoy every moment of watching you run about the place to find the treasure! (Usually nothing more than an old doll or a lace hanky, but we both know why that was, don't we? And once, some handmade chocolates that I brought you from London – at least you could eat that gift before they took it! Oh, very well then, we both ate it.)

What have these old memories to do with here and now, you must wonder. Just this: this is the start of my last treasure hunt for you. Think of my letters (for there will be several) as the clues – each will lead on to the next. I have planned for my story to unfold just a little at a time, with every letter taking you further from Hatville, further from the ignominy of your treatment there: safer and stronger and freer. By the fourth or fifth letter, the trail will long have run out for anyone else. No one knows me as well as you, dear.

So forgive me if there are no answers here. Forgive me, too, if the tone of this letter is all wrong. Perhaps these are not the perfect first words to send to someone from beyond the grave. But you see, as I write this, I am still here, seated at my desk in the room you know so well. I said goodnight to you just five minutes ago and I will see your sweet smile tomorrow. We plan to sit in the rose garden after breakfast. It is hard to write as a dead woman when life is still so sweet.

Yet my death approaches. When it comes, you will be friendless, for we both know the unfortunate – nay, cruel – attitude my parents hold towards you. Our friendship is precious and I hope that you will never regret it, but it kept you a prisoner also, tied to this house and dependent on me. Now you can fly free, little bird! And I will help you, for you have helped me, more than you will ever know.

So. You are grieving, you are alone. But you do not want for means. I enclose a sum of money for you. There will be more, but this will do for now. Ten pounds indeed! As if I would ever leave you such a negligible amount! That they could even believe it of me is enraging, and yet also highly convenient. The green stole is a gift. It will become you, Amy, though I doubt you will believe me.

Your first instruction in this treasure hunt? To journey to London, my dear. That is your first destination. You have money, you can travel in comfort, enjoy the journey if you can. Marvel at seeing a part of our kingdom so different from Enderby! When you get there, find a bookshop called Entwhistle's. Go to the natural history section. (A lady browsing amongst the works of Mr Beckwith . . . Oh, the scandal! Be sure your fragile brain does not explode, dear!) Cast your thoughts around the book we discussed at length that summer's evening after Mr Howden came to dine. Consider the variables and you will find a letter from me to you. How have I achieved this? Ah, but I am a magician, my little bird.

To end, dear Amy, take heart. I do not expect you to recover from my loss overnight, nor forget me, nor replace me (for I am one of a kind, am I not?). But I do expect you to live. And live well. For the life you have known hitherto, our friendship notwithstanding, is not life as it can and should be.

Follow my trail, I beg you. Not only because it will take you further than you can ever imagine but because I have unfinished business which only you can now conclude. Our games and adventures are not at an end yet. Ha! It will take much more than death to silence <u>me</u>!

With greatest love,
AV

Chapter Five

⸺⟡⸺

She was always irrepressible. Even when the iron fist of her diagnosis fell, crushing the hopes of Hatville Court beneath its grievous blow, she laughed. She actually laughed! And my life changed for ever.

Until then, I had lived a strange sort of existence, all piecemeal and patchwork, which is hardly surprising considering how I began. The bank of snow was replaced by the potato bucket, and the potato bucket by a crib when Lady Vennaway bowed under the all-seeing eye of Society and decreed that I could stay. Her provisos were that she should never see me, never be troubled on any matter concerning my upbringing and that I should be employed as a servant as soon as I was old enough to be of any use to anyone.

The crib was donated by Marcus, who managed the estate. His wife had borne him seven children in quick succession and then informed him that if he ever came near her again in the amorous way he would lose a limb and be forced to seek new employment. The crib was positioned in the corner of the kitchen and that was where I passed my first year.

Cook was the person to whom the largest part of my care fell. She was big-hearted, capable, and almost always there. But she was busy, and when she needed to, she would pass the responsibility to one of the maids (a revolving cast of characters, due to the horrors of working for Lady Vennaway) or to Robin, the undergardener, then only eight years old but with extensive experience of small sisters. He was a gentle soul, responsible beyond his years, the kind of person who inspired a sense that all would be well.

I was fed in my first months by a wet nurse named Lucy and my sanitary needs, when Cook was up to her elbows in dough, fell to whoever was in the kitchen at the time. Stopping in for a snack, therefore, could be hazardous.

I grew, as babies do, into a person too big to lodge sensibly in a kitchen. When I began to crawl, I was a veritable hazard in a world full of cleavers, flames, glass jars and bottles. So the diaspora of my carers expanded across the Hatville estate.

Robin would plant me in a wheelbarrow when the ground was wet, and take me with him while he tended the lavender, gathered apples and mended walls.

Cook also called upon Benjamin, the lowliest of the grooms. Too insignificant to exercise Lord Vennaway's famous horses, he was confined to stable duties – mucking out, cleaning leather, mending hay nets and the like. Thus I could stay in one place all day, under a watchful eye, and all out of the sight of Lady Vennaway, which was the most important criterion that any arrangement for my care must meet. They say I could be content in a pile of hay for hours.

Even Jesketh, the butler, silver-haired and stately, was pressed to take his turn when needs must. When he objected, Cook threatened the withholding of cherry pies. And so, by hook or by crook, I was kept alive.

Then, of course, there was Aurelia. It was she who named me: Snow, for obvious reasons, and Amy, after her favourite doll. This was a very great compliment indeed, for this first Amy came from Paris and wore a midnight-blue satin gown. She had blue eyes, black hair and was altogether the prettiest thing Aurelia had ever seen. She was a hard precedent to follow and I believe no mortal child could live up to such standards of loveliness.

My first proper memory is of Aurelia. I think I was around two years old, so she would have been ten. I was grubbing about in the stables when she came in in a flurry of skirts to ride her pony. The memory doesn't include the pony's colour or name (though I've been told since that she was Lucky, a dapple grey) and I cannot even remember the colour of Aurelia's riding habit (deepest green with scarlet trim, according to legend). But I do remember the whisk and the swirl of her: the flounce of her entry into the stables; the stamp of buttoned boots on cobbled floor; the rising of alarmed wisps of straw; and the sweep of her ascent into the saddle. Then the turn and hurtle of Lucky and her disappearance into the light.

As I grew, I developed from a pinched, blue baby to a pinched, pale child, undersized and odd-looking, so I was told, with a great mass of sooty black hair and hazel-yellow eyes too big in my narrow face. Once I was, in Lady Vennaway's words, 'old enough to be of any use to anyone', I was immediately seized upon to be of use to everyone.

Robin taught me to distinguish weeds from plants, and I was taught to hold a currycomb and groom a horse as soon as I could stand upright. Cook showed me how to sort through apples, potatoes and other wholesome produce to check for rot.

My landscape was mostly of legs: kitchen-table legs (and the kingdom of crumbs and onions between); brown-trousered legs hard at work; smart, black-trousered legs standing guard over the Vennaway domain; horses' legs; legs up ladders; and legs hidden by skirts in a constant whirl of activity.

I have only dim recollections of this period but they are mostly pleasant. I remember it in shifting blocks of smell, sound and colour. The kitchen was onions and syrup, clanging and shouting, black oven and red fire. The gardens were earth and apples, the soft, rhythmic chuff of spade in dirt, rainbow and raindrop. The stables were hay and horse, whinny and wind, gold and brown and dust and gleaming.

From as early as I can remember, Aurelia would appear almost daily and play with me or take me for walks. Although I spent a great deal of time in the gardens anyway, they appeared so different when she held my grubby little hand in her elegantly gloved one and pointed out her favourite flowers and birds. She knew just as much about the plants and creatures as Robin did, but it was a different kind of knowledge. She knew the Latin names for things and where they originated from; Robin knew what they liked and how to make them thrive.

I adored her. She was beautiful, kind and radiant and treated me as her own special pet.

My favourite times were when she would read me to sleep. My bed was by this time in the scullery. No one else slept there; the servants were housed far away, high in the attics. But I was reckoned to be too little to cope with all those stairs, and the working day was such that I was only ever alone for a very few hours each night. Sometimes Aurelia would slip down at bedtime, pull up a chair and lean close. I would lay my head on her arm and listen to her voice: melodious, merry and somehow different from all the other voices I knew. Whether there was drumming rain outside or whether a lilac summer dusk hummed and twittered as a fine day faded, those times felt magical and blessed.

Chapter Six

On my first night away from Hatville Court, in the narrow bed in the Rose and Crown, I sleep poorly. It does not surprise me. Since Aurelia died my heart is like a wild animal. It sleeps with one eye open, with a new wariness I feel will never go away. I wake early.

A series of realizations crowd in upon me like guests at a ball, so swift and swooping they leave me breathless. Emotions accompany them like chaperones. No Aurelia – grief like the tightest, meanest of corsets. No Hatville Court – an equal blend of fear and relief. Today, apparently, I am to go to London! A lurch of trepidation. And the letter. *Letters!* Wild hope and joy. There is more of Aurelia to come, to keep me moving forward through these dark days.

I wash and dress. I have no appetite but for the first time in days I am minded to look after myself, so I will eat. I have business to carry out, Aurelia's business. How clever she was! She knew that if any one thing on earth could compel me onwards, it would be my sense of devotion to her. She could be dead a thousand years and I would still want to please her.

I read her letter once more, then bury it deep in my skirt pocket again. I will carry it with me at all times.

To my relief, the landlord is at large in the hall; I did not want to seek him out. Even without the torrent of emotion that threatens each minute to topple me I would find this hard. I have a retiring disposition, I suppose. My life has ever been Hatville; I have rarely left it. And Aurelia was right: it *was* a prison. But I never thought of it like that, not while she was in it. We were like two birds, keeping each other company in a very fine cage.

Now she is forcing me to see the wider world, but in this moment I do not feel I can thank her for it. I don't expect to find a warm welcome outside Hatville. I am accustomed to feeling I am an inconvenience, yet I know that to carry out Aurelia's wishes I will have to depend on others for help and information though not, thank God, for money. So I am inordinately grateful when Mr Carlton enquires whether he can help me with anything.

'Thank you, Mr Carlton, you are very kind. I wonder, have you any idea of the times the trains will run today? I shall walk to the station and then . . . I wondered . . .' I run out of words. I have never taken a journey before. I hardly know how to shape the questions I need to ask. And I don't want to leave this shabby inn before I have to; it represents my very last link with the life I have always known.

'Certainly, Miss Snow, certainly. If you'll be so good as to accompany me to my office, we can find out everything you need to know.'

At the door he stops and twinkles at me. 'Never fear, Miss Snow, we shall consult Mr Bradshaw.' I look around for a benevolent gentleman with white whiskers and a wise expression. The room is, however, quite empty aside from a dense crowding of bookshelves and a very large, untidy desk. It is laden with papers and quills, and ornamented with three long spikes on which tufts of bills are speared. Empty stools stand about.

'Now then,' he beams, taking down a thick pamphlet with pretensions to being a book. Tracks in the thick dust on the shelf betray that this volume is frequently used. 'This is the most marvellous publication that ever was, Miss Snow. Do you know Mr Bradshaw?'

'I fear not.'

'He is the author of this splendid compendium. A collection of all the timetables of all the trains run by all the train companies across the land. Do you know how many rail journeys that is, Miss Snow?'

'I'm afraid I cannot guess, Mr Carlton.'

'No more can I! No more can anyone, excepting I suppose Mr Bradshaw himself. Well now, in a word, the answer is *many*! *Look*, Miss Snow, at all these trains!' He riffles the pages of the book at me in helpless wonder. There do seem to be a very great many trains.

'Just think,' he continues, 'until only a very few years ago stagecoaches still ran in our part of Surrey. Progress, Miss Snow, progress!' He pores over his oracle, licking his thumbs. On each page I see a dense thicket of black print, all columns and figures and lines. If this represents my future, I am more daunted than ever.

'Ha!' he triumphs, when he comes to the right page. 'Allow me, Miss Snow?'

'Gladly, sir.'

'Up or down?'

'I beg your pardon?'

'Are you wanting trains going up or trains going down, Miss Snow?'

I hesitate. I had been under the impression that they all run flat along the ground but I think perhaps nothing can surprise me any more.

'North or south, Miss Snow? Up towards London or down towards Brighton?'

'Oh, I see! Thank you, Mr Carlton. Well now . . . ' I try to phrase my response in such a way that it sounds as though I am just thinking through my plans, that I am going to London because it is the most obvious place to go and not because I have a predetermined destination. I must remember that to outside eyes I am yet aimless and unfixed, with only ten pounds to my name. How careful I will have to be in all I say and do.

Finally we establish that I will not need to leave the Rose

and Crown for almost an hour. Mr Carlton insists on sending a boy to carry my bag and put me on the train. I almost refuse, so loath am I to be any trouble to anyone, but Mr Carlton will not hear of a young lady managing a station alone.

'Not the thing at all,' he frets. 'The railway is a wonderful thing but there is every sort of a person in a station, Miss Snow. And I believe you have never taken a train before? Do you know the protocol?'

I have not and I do not. Mr Carlton describes to me the quirks of buying a ticket from the house adjoining the station and what must be done if the owner is not home, the importance of choosing the right carriage and the optimum seat, how to address fellow passengers and where to stow my ticket for safekeeping.

'For ladies, I always recommend the left glove, Miss Snow. The left glove cannot be bettered for this purpose. Tickets seem to have a great propensity towards escaping, you know, and that is a very great inconvenience indeed, for the inspectors simply will not believe that you have purchased your ticket and lost it. They *will* insist or imply that you are trying to defraud the railway company and that is an insult not to be borne, Miss Snow . . . hence, the left glove.'

'The left glove,' I murmur, head spinning. 'Thank you so much, Mr Carlton, I don't know what I would do without your invaluable advice. Who would ever have thought there could be so much to think about?'

'Indeed, indeed. 'Tis not like the old days. So many of my customers are uncomfortable with the changes that I have taken it upon myself to be as informative as possible to ease the path of progress. I have been pondering the idea of writing a book: *Hints and Advice for the Inexperienced Traveller*. Do you think such a project would find favour with the public?'

'I should think it invaluable, Mr Carlton. Do write it!'

'Thank you, Miss Snow. I think I shall. Disseminating knowledge is the human duty, sharing it about so that all can benefit.'

'Why, that is exactly what Miss Vennaway used to say!' I smile, then fall quiet.

Mr Carlton nods. 'I have heard that she was a remarkable young lady. My very sincerest condolences, Miss Snow.'

Chapter Seven

When I was six years old, and Aurelia fourteen, a queen came to the throne. I remember Aurelia beaming, her hair flying as she spun me around and around in the kitchen garden, her dress a rainbow. It was summer, and I swear the air was full of butterflies.

'When you were born, our ruler was a king,' she told me breathlessly as we tumbled to the ground, 'but now a woman heads our nation – a *young* woman, only four years older than I! Oh, Amy, it makes me feel as though anything is possible. They say she stepped into her new responsibility with as much equanimity as if she were stepping into a parlour for crumpets. If she is too young and foolish and *feminine* to be equal to the task, clearly *she* is unaware of it!'

I remember the sense of optimism that infected the world but I was too young to understand the implications of a dawning age. To me the queen seemed imaginary, like the princess who kissed a frog or the young woman who cast her hair from a tower in the storybooks. Aurelia, however, fancied a real sense of connection between herself and the monarch. They were both only children. They were both in possession of more ideas than rightly belonged in a pretty bonneted head. They had both sworn they would marry only for love. The imagined Victoria, proprietorially discussed by Aurelia and me, came to seem like a third, absentee member of our happy little club. We often planned what we would ask her if she came for tea.

It was as I grew a little older that my troubles began, or at least that they came to the surface, as they were always bound to do. By seven I was of an age where, had my circumstances been different, I might have been plucked from a workhouse to go into service. I would have been chosen for a particular purpose and trained to meet it.

As it was, no requirement brought me to Hatville; I was simply there. Thus the selection of a line of work for me was somewhat arbitrary. Just as well my preferences were not considered, for girls could not work in the stables or grounds. Given Lady Vennaway's strictures that I should stay out of sight, the kitchen was the obvious choice, but Cook and Rosy and Dora were already there so unless the family was entertaining I only got under everyone's feet. The housemaids resented me for having such a light workload. I was happy to do more but Cook would not risk me encountering Lady Vennaway, an event she feared on her own account as much as on mine. I was often puzzled as to what I was about, and a frown became my habitual expression.

So whenever Aurelia appeared, bored and lonely as she so often was, Cook was all too happy to have me taken off her hands. It solved the problem at first. But that I was neither fish nor fowl became increasingly apparent to all.

The difficulty was I was at home at Hatville. Just as Aurelia took for granted her large house with its spare Regency trappings and her role as the first young lady of the neighbourhood, visiting the farm workers once a week, dispensing food and a few coins when a new baby was born, so I took for granted my bed in the scullery, the kitchen's crowded warmth, my free roaming rights. When I learned that Hatville contained areas as yet unknown to me, bedrooms and a ballroom and a library, I naturally wanted to explore them. Cook and I were making cherry pies together when she tried to explain that they were not mine to explore, that it was not my home.

I was dumbfounded. 'Of course it is my home. I've lived here always, with everyone I know!'

'But Hatville *belongs* to other people. It is *their* home and you are their servant.'

'But . . . who *are* they?' I wanted to know.

'Lord and Lady Vennaway are master and mistress here. You've to work hard for them, Amy, same as me and everyone else.'

I wondered why I'd never seen this master and mistress.

'Because they're very grand and very busy. Why, Hatville is so large that your paths need never cross.'

'But have *you* seen them, Cookie?'

'Yes.'

'And Robin?'

'Yes, Robin too.'

'And Marcus and Benjamin and Jesketh?'

'Why *yes*, Amy. Now mind what you're doing.'

Cook was puffing as she kneaded the huge mound of dough. I huffed through my heavy fringe with equal concentration as I removed the stones from the cherries. I was sceptical. Two people whose existence meant my home was not my home . . . and everyone had seen them except me? It hardly seemed likely.

'Cookie . . . *how* then has everyone seen them, if the house is so large and they are so busy?'

'Because Master and Mistress need to meet their servants, to give them instructions and so forth.'

'Well then, why have they never given instructions to *me*?'

'*Amy!* Stop asking questions and *stop* eating those cherries!'

Poor Cook. My precarious position would have been difficult to explain to anyone, let alone a curious child.

Later, while the pies turned gold and fragrant and we were clearing up, it arose that Aurelia was the daughter of these Other People. Hatville Court was *her* home too, where it was not mine!

I laughed in disbelief. Aurelia and I saw each other every day. She told me stories and had me ride in her arms on Lucky.

46

She taught me to play cards and race twigs on the stream and never gave me any instructions at all!

'How can her parents be my master and mistress when Aurelia is my friend?' I asked in a small voice.

'Because,' explained Cook, perspiring, 'she's not your friend. She is the young mistress. You must never forget that.'

'But . . .' I began, then seeing Cook's expression, fell silent.

I understand better now the invidious position Cook was in. Aurelia's treatment of me set me apart, suggested a status and favour that could not be sustained, and was directly at odds with her ladyship's wishes. Yet what could Cook do? It wasn't a servant's prerogative to lecture the young lady of the house. She did try to explain, but Aurelia would have none of it. She enjoyed playing with me, she had no one else, and besides, she had found me.

At the time it all seemed fantastical nonsense to me. I remember puzzling over it for three or four days that summer, then deciding to worry about it no longer.

Then one day, for the first time in living memory, Lady Vennaway appeared in the kitchen. Usually, her bell would summon Cook or Dora. One or the other would jump, untie her apron, dust herself down and run from the room even if a broth was just coming to the boil or a roast was halfway out of the oven. I was sitting under the table, taking the heads off strawberries when she came. I only became aware that something had changed because the chatter suddenly stopped and even the bubbling pots hushed down to a simmer. I saw skirts crumple in curtseys.

A crystal-clear voice, like and yet unlike Aurelia's, said, 'Where is the child?'

'Here, m'lady.'

Cook sounded subdued. Her red hand flapped in front of my face, beckoning me from under the table. I scrambled out, deeply curious to meet this fabled mistress, owner of Hatville, ringer of bells, in whose existence (like God's and Samuel Pickwick's) I had hitherto believed only tentatively.

I stood before her and stared. She looked like the ice queen depicted in one of Aurelia's books, unbearably haughty and painfully beautiful, with a flowing gown and loose auburn hair. She was so fierce and radiant she made me want to hide my face.

It is strange to remember, now, that my very first instinct was that I wanted to please her. This is what hurts the most – for it was immediately clear that I did not. She looked down on me from her great height and I saw from her face that the sight of me made her sick.

I still clutched a knife in one hand and a strawberry in the other so I dropped them, in case it was they that offended. It was not.

'What is the matter with her?'

'Sorry, ma'am, I believe she be nervous,' muttered Cook,

pushing me out of the way so that she could pick up the things I'd dropped. She had never handled me so roughly and I felt wounded.

'Curtsey, child,' she ordered, and I bobbed, and wondered.

'I will see her alone. Have her follow me.' The mistress turned and left the room.

I felt the kitchen sag with relief but Cook grabbed me by both arms and stared into my face. 'Oh dear,' she muttered, 'oh dear, dear, dear.'

She pulled my hands out to examine them and she didn't seem to like those either. They were stained with pink juice and their usual coating of black grime. She spat into her own palm and started rubbing at them roughly.

'No time, Cookie, no time,' whispered Dora.

Sure enough a furious voice came from the passage: 'Well, is she coming or *not*?'

'Go!' Cook was tugging at my apron ties and shoving me out into the passage all at the same time. 'Be respectful. Be good!' And I ran after the lady of the house.

I chased her down a long corridor with a high ceiling. I could not help but marvel as I ran, for I had not been there before. Its wooden-panelled walls bore dark portraits of pale-faced men in high collars and a good deal of lace. Some had horses, some had small children and wives, some had brown and white dogs of all shapes, sizes and arrangements of hair.

Unfortunately as I ran and twisted and stared and ran, my

apron ties, half freed by Cook, came loose altogether. The apron slid off my small frame, tangled up my feet and I fell – *smack!* – on my face.

My cheek and hands stung and my head rang. Lady Vennaway turned and glanced at me contemptuously.

'Oafish child.'

Then she resumed walking and I resumed scurrying, looking where I was going this time and clutching my apron in both hands.

In a cold study with an empty mantelpiece and a bare desk, she closed the door behind us. She sat on a spindle-legged chair, stood me before her and looked at me.

Set out in words, it might seem that worse fates could befall a child. But when the looker was Lady Vennaway and the looked-at was me, it was a dreadful experience.

Like her daughter, she had the most expressive face, with large eyes and delicate bones that conveyed every thought and feeling. But whereas Aurelia's feelings were always frank and warm, her ladyship's were altogether different.

In that gaze my innocence shattered. Her blue eyes bored into mine, and I watched shadows I could not name scudding across them like clouds. Her exquisite upper lip curled, though otherwise the lovely face was still and impassive. You might have thought her impervious to me, but for those eyes and that lip.

Then she spat into my face.

It was so sudden, so shocking, that I stumbled backwards. Her spittle hit me hard in the eye and ran down my face. I wiped it away at once, then dragged my hand down my dress. I did not understand, yet I felt humiliated in a way that was all new to me. I wanted to wash my eye out, not only because it smarted but because I could not bear the thought of this woman's venom somehow finding its way into my eye socket and seeping down into my soul.

Then she stood, dragged me to the door and slammed it behind me.

I stood shaking in the corridor, fairly sure I'd been dismissed but too confused to know whether I could leave or stay. No one had ever treated me thus. Her ladyship did not emerge, however, and in time I dragged myself off.

I found myself to be quite lost. We had turned a corner or two after I fell and I could not retrace my steps. All the passages here, all the doorways, looked the same. I soon found myself at the foot of a grand staircase we had not passed, a broad and lofty spiral, curved and cream like the shell of a monstrous snail. Above were galleries and soaring walls – all silent, cream expanses. I dared not climb it but feared to retrace my steps and perhaps meet the mistress again.

I had hoped that her inspection of me might mean that I was to become a proper servant who did not have to stay hidden but, little as I knew about it, I did not think staring and spitting could be the usual way these interviews were conducted.

Anger and curiosity propelled me in another direction. Through an open door I glimpsed an enormous chamber and was instantly lost in wonder. The walls were painted icy blue and a chandelier as big as a host of angels swooped and sparkled from the ceiling. Long, sage-green curtains swept from tall windows to the ground and a gleaming wooden floor reflected the light. I had somehow strayed into a strange, wintry world.

'Amy Snow!' thundered a voice, and I flinched. 'What on *earth* are you doing here?'

It was Jesketh, furious but familiar. I had never been so glad to see him.

Chapter Eight

I spend my last hour at the Rose and Crown neatly repacking my bag, still all a-tumble after my hasty flight from Hatville. My clothes are creasing by the minute. I have nothing of any loveliness, yet I shall try not to look worse than I must.

It is a reflective occupation. It unnerves me to see pieces of my old world here where I am all at sea.

I pull everything out and put them back in neatly. I pack the heaviest things first: my only other footwear, a pair of flat grey pumps for indoors or the summer, and my books. I have brought five. It was a great heartbreak to choose so few but I knew I had a long way to walk and no one to carry them but me. I have brought my Bible, the illustrated book of fairy tales that Aurelia used to read to me when I was small, *Ivanhoe* by Sir Walter Scott and of course two works by Mr Dickens. The very sight of them evokes memories of Aurelia, so helpless with laughter she was unable to read, clutching my arm.

Next goes in the sketchbook that Aurelia bequeathed me. I cannot look at that either.

Then my small toilette, containing hairbrush, hand-mirror, linen washcloth and a small pot of Cook's homemade camphorated dentifrice . . . and one hundred pounds.

Next my heavier garments: a heavy wool dress, identical to the one I am wearing, only made up in grey instead of black. A spare woollen shawl. Dark, inoffensive colours. Then my brown summer dress. Aurelia's green stole, now folded tidily. And finally, a packet of old letters, tied together with gold ribbon and all addressed to Amy Snow.

These are from Aurelia, from the time she went away from Hatville for a while. It is not a time I care to remember and the letters were a mixed blessing when they came, yet I have brought them with me because I could not bear to leave them behind.

It is not much to show for seventeen years on this earth, I consider, as I press the clasp shut. And somewhere in there, I fancy, folded up tight amongst the shoes and dresses shabby from overuse, are my dreams, equally tatty from neglect.

Aurelia always had an abundance of dreams and spoke of them often. They always included me. She longed to come into her fortune and leave Hatville for ever, to travel, to fall in love a great many times – to change the world. My fate was bound up in hers – she had saved my life, after all – so she always assumed I would go wherever she went and for the first years of my life I held the same assumption. But in the deepest corners of my heart tarried other wishes.

I did not want to be always on the road, as Aurelia did,

sweeping up and down the kingdom like the queen before her. I wanted a home, but not a home like Hatville with its iron bars of heritage and pride. Sometimes, in quiet, private moments, lying in my scullery bed or dreaming in the stables, I saw a cottage, small and square, in the centre of a green lawn kept from rampancy by a greedy pony. A laughing husband who would keep me safe from insult. Children who would get into scrapes and make me enthusiastic gifts from paper and paste; children to whom I would give love and security – all the things I had never had. But I never told Aurelia, for they would seem very poor dreams indeed compared with changing the world. Besides, who would ever want me? Never given voice, my dreams dwindled.

Those dreams seem very simple to me now, a crude, crayon-drawn picture by a wistful child. But the beauty of impossible dreams is that they are impossible – the hows and whens don't really matter. I suppose the true longing was not after all the outline of the image but the feelings beneath its surface. I wanted peace, a sense of belonging and love.

I startle when Tom, Mr Carlton's boy, comes to escort me to the station. I have not thought of that cottage, that husband, those children for many years. And peace and security seem more remote than ever.

It is a very small branch at Ladywell, I am told, yet to me it is overwhelming. To see finally the railway tracks of which I have heard so much but only seen illustrated! The black, greedy arms that snake across our country, dividing it up into slices. The newspapermen tell us that they link here with there and A with B until distance is annihilated altogether and anyone can go anywhere, any time they want!

There is no station building but a platform open to the elements; a bitter wind blows straight through. It hums with people already, although we are in good time.

Tom takes the coin I proffer and purchases my ticket for me. Second class. I cannot be seen to travel first class so close to Enderby, yet I cannot find the courage for third. I stow it, naturally, in my left glove.

He leads me onto the platform and positions me in a very particular spot.

'You'll be next to a door here, miss. Be able to jump straight on. I'll wait and help you with your bag, o'course. Now, have you looked around and decided which passengers might be the conversational types?'

I can't say that I have, but Tom points out an energetic-looking family as examples of the sort of traveller to whom I might confidently address any enquiries, and two men in caps and dark jackets, as being 'ones for avoidin''.

I am too scared not to take every last piece of advice that comes my way, yet I find it hard to concentrate. I am leaving Ladywell. I am leaving Ladywell. I am leaving Ladywell. I have only ever been here two or three times before yet it feels familiar compared with whatever lies ahead.

The train, when it comes, is a great, black, blowing monster and I am in equal parts thrilled and terrified to see it. The doors are flung open with a racket as though devils are shaking the iron gates of Hell; great towers of steam fill the air.

I am a traveller in the Railway Age. I am a young woman of the world. I have important business to conduct. But why, oh, *why* is Aurelia not here to share this adventure with me?

Chapter Nine

Before my arrival, Aurelia was exceptionally lonely. As she told me when we were yet very young, her mother kept losing all her babies so there was no one for her to play with. And that was why, she believed, God had sent her to find me, knowing she would not be so careless as her mother. I was exceedingly glad that He had.

Although Aurelia had cousins aplenty she found no kindred spirit amongst them. To start with, I was her pet, like the broken birds and trapped animals she kept rescuing and housing in unlikely constructions — a field mouse in a dolls' house, a snake in a bath tub. Robin always abetted these missions of mercy. He showed her how to set a bird's wing, how to make a simple salve of dock leaves. But he was a quiet boy, and the animals had still less to say, and Aurelia had a great many thoughts tumbling inside her.

She had always wanted someone with whom she could share her ideas, someone to help her understand the things that made her laugh and the things that made her want to scream. At six, seven, eight years of age, I was still no equal for her but I was the next best thing: a willing pupil.

I was not stupid myself, it transpired, nor lacking in curiosity. She taught me to read and write and count, to draw and ride. I was not the only servant at Hatville who could do any of these things, but it did not make me popular.

Aurelia did have a grown-up friend, of whom I sometimes felt jealous. Mrs Bolton was a slender woman of around thirty, with a world-weary air, a selection of rakish bonnets and a jaw squarer than Robin's. She always dressed in peacock colours: navy or dark green, with flashes of gold and amber. She did not suffer fools, Aurelia always said admiringly, which made me worry that she thought *me* a fool – Mrs Bolton was certainly scant in the attention she offered me. She and Aurelia held intense discussions about The State of the World, and The Lot of Women, which made me feel every bit as young and small as I really was. But I never seriously doubted Aurelia's affection for me and I was comforted that Lord and Lady Vennaway didn't approve of bold Mrs Bolton either.

A long while had passed (it seemed to me) since my first encounter with Lady Vennaway. The memory of that day did not come back to me often, but it was there, like an invisible fence. Aurelia and I had the run of the grounds, so long as we avoided the croquet lawn, the terrace, the rose garden – anywhere we might encounter civilized folk. Robin always warned us if we strayed too close and we would dash away like elves to the farthest reaches of the grounds. Nor would Cook allow me to accompany Aurelia when she walked into Enderby to do what she called her 'Lady Bountifuls'. From her stories of the cramped homes of many of the villagers I knew I had much to be thankful for, yet it is the nature of bright, curious children to forget the fact.

It was inevitable that the time would come when Aurelia would want to share her indoor kingdom with me. And inevitable too that when she did we would be caught. Once, learning to play the piano, I was hauled from the stool mid-scale by Mrs Last, the then housekeeper. I was dragged back to the kitchen and pushed through the door with a wallop.

On another occasion, Aurelia had me trying on one of her gowns. We had always been dressed differently: Aurelia in lustrous fabrics with sashes and ribbons, and frilly white bloomers peeping out beneath full skirts, I in the plainest of work garments, flat shoes and a simple white cap. How she envied me.

It was one of the maids, Peggy, who spotted us this time.

My grey serge was in a puddle around my feet, the blue satin was halfway over my head. I was shivering in my white cotton shift in between when the door banged open.

Peggy had been most eager to share intelligence of my whereabouts: Lady Vennaway had come. Her shriek rings in my ears to this day. You would have thought me a rat upon her dinner table.

I was blinded by petticoats and the dress was snatched from me with such force that I heard the satin rip. This time Lady Vennaway herself manhandled me to the kitchen before I could properly fasten my dress, her fingers digging into my flesh.

She threw me, actually *threw* me, inside. I staggered against the stove and burned my arm, though glancingly. I had two far greater concerns, however.

Amidst all the confusion, I had heard one thing clearly; Lady Vennaway had absolutely, in the clearest possible language and with a host of accompanying threats, forbidden Aurelia to see me again. And now I watched Cook's ever-ruddy face drain of colour as Lady Vennaway gave her such a castigation as I had never heard.

That night I cried myself to sleep for only the third time in my life. The first time I had eaten too many strawberry tarts and my stomach pains were fierce. The second had been over the travails of Oliver Twist.

This was of an altogether different order. My only friendship had been threatened – ended, I believed. And because of me, however unwitting, Cook was in a deal of trouble.

She had always done her best for me and now she had been humiliated in front of the kitchen maids, who stood gawping at the drama. Her place was in jeopardy, Lady Vennaway raged. I did not know exactly where Jeopardy was but I knew it to be highly undesirable, like Bedlam or Prison. I did not want Cook to be sent away to Jeopardy because of me.

I thought for a long time that night. I had never thought so much before. I had merely taken the days as they came and accepted the circumstances of my life as they appeared before me. I had seen the strictures regarding where I could and could not go as arbitrary rules from the adult world. Adults liked rules, I knew, and I would not begrudge them their foolish pleasures. My first meeting with the mistress had been deeply shocking and horrible to think about – so I had ceased thinking about it and the problem had been solved.

But now I understood that what Cook had been telling me all along was true: the world was such that Aurelia and I could not be friends, and if we did not take care, people would suffer.

Long after I had gone to bed, Cook came in to see me. She sat on the foot of my little bed and it tipped a little southwards.

'Is everything cleared away now?' I asked, for there had been a dinner, with eight courses and many wines.

'Yes, everything's done.'

'Did you finish the batter?' I asked, for fresh cakes were required tomorrow.

'All ready to bake in the morning. The reverend's coming so I'm doing a lemon pudding as well as the fig and raisin.'

I knew how nicely the kitchen would smell next morning.

'Do you understand, now?' she asked me and I knew she was not referring to the cake.

'I do,' I sniffed. 'I'm sorry, Cookie. I did not mean for you to be turned upon. You kept telling us and we would not listen.'

She nodded and passed a rough hand over my hair.

Encouraged, I continued. 'Lady Vennaway is a horrible, horrible woman, is she not, Cookie?'

Cook hesitated. 'Everyone has their own story, even those we find the hardest. Best to accept things the way they are and count your blessings. After all, Amy, you're luckier than many and shorter than most.' It was a jest often voiced amongst my companions, on account of my small size.

I nodded and smiled but as I did so I knew it would be hard. That afternoon, buried beneath the shock, I had felt anger, like a little hard seed waiting to sprout.

'I don't want you go to that horrible place,' I told Cook as she got to her feet and my bed rocked back to the horizontal.

She paused, puzzled. 'What place?'

'Jeopardy. Mistress said your place was there but it *isn't*, it's here with us!'

Cook was too weary to correct my misapprehension but she told me what I needed to hear. 'A fine cook is a hard thing to find. One who can cope with a house like Hatville rarer still. As for one who can tolerate her ladyship, well, there's probably only one such in all of England. So don't you worry now, I'm going nowhere, except up four flights of stairs to my bed. Mistress knows which side her bread is buttered.'

I was unsure why the mistress should concern herself with buttering bread at all when she could have cakes baked fresh to her command, but I promised myself that I would mind Cook better henceforth. She was all I had now. After the dreadful things that Lady Vennaway had said to her daughter, I knew that I would never see Aurelia again. The thought was almost too terrible to bear.

Then morning came, and with it the warm, sweet fragrance of baking. And Aurelia, radiant in the doorway.

'Come on, Amy, it's a beautiful day! There is dew on the cobwebs and rainbows in the dew and the world is altogether as it should be. Let's go outside!'

Chapter Ten

What a wonder to see the countryside of Surrey through the window of a train! What an experience to be carried, jolting and swaying, past fields and streams and woods and cottages. What a marvel to see it fly past so swiftly!

What is there that is not remarkable about the railway? From its rapid growth to its staggering speeds – *thirty miles per hour*, I am told, in some places! – to its pounding and steaming and gleaming . . . all quite, quite extraordinary. Yet the *most* remarkable feature of the railway, to my mind, must surely be its passengers.

I share a carriage with a couple in their middle years, Mr and Mrs Begley. They introduce themselves as they squeeze in with a goodly number of cases between them and sit just opposite me. I believe Tom would have approved them as conversational partners for me, but in truth I have no choice in the matter – Mrs Begley has not drawn breath since Ladywell.

'Oh, my Lord!' she exclaims, fanning herself with a limp hand. 'What a trial, what an exertion, this railway nonsense.

Look at me, I am shaking!' She holds out a hand, mere inches from my chin, which I inspect with interest. It *is* shaking.

'Miss Snow,' interjects her husband, 'Charlotte, the railway is a marvellous system! Look how comfortable we sit! Providing we bring our travelling cushions with us, of course. Look how neatly stacked our luggage! Unless it is shaken loose. Look at the proliferation of stations and routes and destinations! Why, with such a system as this, any mischance must perforce serve only as a pleasant diversion!'

'Not at *all*, William! When you think of the accidents, the explosions, the overturnings of which one reads *every* day in the papers! Terrifying, Miss Snow, quite terrifying.'

My companions keep up their heated conversation all the way to the very outskirts of London. It is clear that debate is an expression of affection between them and I welcome the distraction from my thoughts. Fond memories of Aurelia are with me at every moment but so, I am shocked to realize, are old resentments, long-buried.

It is the sight of those old letters this morning that has drawn them from the recesses of my mind. I had been pleased to forget our earlier, temporary separation, long before Aurelia's passing, when I believed myself forgotten by her. Then, I blamed Mrs Bolton for taking her away from me. I was wrong to do so, for Aurelia was most determined to go. Then, as now, she asked me to trust her – yet I had to endure at Hatville without her for far too long. I think it was too much to ask of one so young. Together with my fear about arriving alone in the great city of London, such ruminations on the past are far from comforting. Perhaps this is too much to ask of me, too.

As we pass through the pleasant village of Dulwich, Mrs Begley tells me their plans. They are to stay with their married son in Pentonville. His wife is expecting their first child. He works as a senior clerk in a large bank and likes it so very well that he cannot think why everyone is not a bank clerk.

I think of all I have read of murders and pickpockets and tricksters. I remember from gloomy newspaper reports that Seven Dials is a dire place, the Old Kent Road too. The other blackened names elude me; I feel ill prepared indeed for London.

As the city hails into view, grey and heaving like an ocean of stone, Mrs Begley falls briefly silent and I seize my opportunity to ask these fonts of knowledge for some counsel.

'Miss *Snow*! Am I to understand you? Pray, correct me! Do you mean us to believe that you have nowhere to stay . . . that you are *alone*? Oh, Miss Snow! This is ill-considered, I fear. Oh, whatever can be done?'

'Now, now, Charlotte, mere practicalities – creases to be steamed out! Do not look so alarmed, Miss Snow. All shall be well. When we alight, Mrs Begley and I will see you into a cab. I'm afraid the Bricklayers' Arms is not positioned in the most salubrious of neighbourhoods.'

'Indeed *no*! The Old Kent Road! Gracious heavens,

whatever were the railwaymen thinking of, building a passenger terminus in such a perilous quarter. *Perilous!*'

We are quiet for a moment before I dare to venture another question. 'Do you think you could possibly suggest somewhere I might stay? And I shall be very grateful for your assistance in finding a cab. Only . . . where should I go in it? A good area, a respectable place.'

'Do you have sufficient funds, my dear, to pay for somewhere tasteful? For London is *shockingly* dear, you know.'

'*Charlotte!*' Mr Begley looks scandalized.

'Well, William! I am only looking out for the girl. I do not want to *ruin* her, you know!'

'Even so . . . one cannot simply . . . *enquire!*'

Fearing to be the cause of another dispute, I interject. 'I am quite happy to pay for a good place. It is only for two nights, then I shall be joining friends . . .' I tell the lie both to lessen their alarm on my behalf and because I badly wish it were true.

Mrs Begley casts a lofty look at her spouse. 'In that case I have no hesitation in recommending Mrs Woodrow's establishment, a boarding house for ladies situated close to St James's Park, in Jessop Walk. Can you remember that, dear, Jessop Walk? Number seven. No! Number six! No! Number eleven, is it, William? On the right, in any case, as you look towards the campanile. The right or the left at any rate . . .'

Chapter Eleven

━━━⟨∾⟩━━━

If Aurelia had been a man, she would have been considered a humanitarian visionary. She might have stood for Parliament and passed new bills *if* she had worn breeches and whiskers. Her parents would have described her as energetic. Instead, she had tumbling chestnut curls, navy-blue eyes, a narrow waist and a ready laugh – and they despaired of her.

When the talk in the drawing room was all gossip, Aurelia took the controversial view that the subjects were real people with their own sensibilities who should be protected. I remember one local scandal that kept her mother, aunts and cousins thrilled and appalled for weeks. Our neighbour Mr Templeton, respectable master of a modest but prosperous home, had fathered a child on his housemaid. It was a far from uncommon story, of course. Yet in each and every instance, it seems, the done thing is to behave as though nothing so terrible has ever taken place on our green planet hitherto.

While everyone else reported nuggets of information (the maid was uncommonly pretty with strawberry-blonde curls;

Mrs Pagett in the village had never liked the way Mr Templeton looked at her) or passed judgements (he was a disgrace to the neighbourhood, a beast in breeches; she was a young hussy and the housekeeper was lax not to have kept an eye on her), Aurelia asked questions.

What would happen to the young girl now, with no employment and a blackened name? Was she not very young to have her entire life damned before her? And Mrs Templeton? Was she upset or angry, maudlin or vengeful? What had made Mr Templeton do it (aside from the obvious, of course)? Had he not always been a decent and reasonable man? Other pretty girls must have crossed his path before this, so why now? Could anything be done to help?

Questions like these were part of the reason that Aurelia, though adored, was considered within the family to be lacking in intelligence. Consequently, Mr Henley was commissioned by Aurelia's parents to guide her.

He was a very strict lady's tutor with the reputation of favouring results over method. I venture to guess that Mr Henley, as a man of learning, could not have thought Aurelia stupid, but he was hired to turn her into a very particular being, and in this he was challenged daily. He strove to succeed where a succession of hand-wringing nursemaids and governesses had failed. The subjects that interested young Aurelia – philosophy, literature, economics and politics – were certainly not within his remit. She was to be a wife one day, after all, and not just any wife! He was hired to teach her Latin and music, a little of geography and history and, above all, decorum. Decorum did not come easily to Aurelia. However, his determination became the unexpected cause of another change in our friendship.

When he was newly in post and did not yet know the rules concerning me, he found me in the schoolroom one day and let me stay to share the lesson. And if he was a little condescending to me, well, I was only eight.

Thus he came to notice what several others remarked upon over the years: I calmed her down. With me present, Aurelia grew more settled, attentive and, he liked to think, receptive to instruction. If the truth was simply that she hoped to be dismissed from her lessons earlier so we could escape to our own entertainments, she certainly didn't disabuse him. So Mr Henley, of all the improbable figures, was the next to argue the case for our continued association.

He earnestly explained to his employers that for a restless spirit such as Aurelia's a companion with a steadier disposition and a more pedestrian mind was a beneficial thing. Further, that in the absence of brothers and sisters, placid company could soothe and sweeten the path of correction. He very strongly advised that I be allowed to share her lessons.

Lord Vennaway was too lofty altogether to care either way. 'Why ever not allow it?' he demanded of his wife, bored. Lady Vennaway's more heated emotions had no place amongst these bastions of male rationality. Her womanly feelings must bow to sense and expediency; it was what they were trying to teach Aurelia, after all.

Thus it happened that I was with Aurelia more than her mother could ever have wished and my role in the household subtly changed: I heard myself referred to as Aurelia's companion more than once – though never in earshot of Lady Vennaway. I was now privileged to see Aurelia living in her own world, instead of only in our happy, separate little bubble. And I came to see her in a new light. I realized that whilst to me she was the friend of my childhood (older to be sure, but free and careless even so), other people thought of her as a young lady, with a clear duty before her.

Aurelia was sixteen when Mr Henley arrived, and by then her parents had been discussing her marital prospects for over a year. Aurelia refused even to acknowledge their plans, as though by ignoring them she could will them out of existence. I did not like to admit that Aurelia had a blind spot. I was dependent on her after all, and I wanted to believe her all-powerful. But, watchful little soul that I was, I started to see that reality as Aurelia determined upon it and reality as everyone else saw it were not always the same.

Shortly after Mr Henley joined us, her parents started entertaining suitors at Hatville Court, and shipping Aurelia off to balls with her aunts and cousins as chaperones (Lady Vennaway would not go herself, being wary of anything that might be considered an amusement). At first Aurelia enjoyed the novelty of dressing up and dancing and being admired. She laughed outright at the men who came to dinner. Just as I looked up to Aurelia, and learned from her, she in her turn adopted airs she copied from Mrs Bolton. She behaved as if she was blithely unaffected by it all. I was taken in at first.

But time passed and Lord and Lady Vennaway became more explicit about their plans. They forbade Aurelia to change the subject or flounce from the room when the subject of marriage arose. Arguments grew more frequent. And Aurelia was afraid. She was loath to admit it but I often saw her staring around her wild-eyed, like a horse bridled with curb chain and martingale too tight.

I do not doubt that they loved her – no one ever could who saw the way they looked at her. But they were people for whom love was a complicated affair, very closely bound up with, and easily confused with, matters of proprietorship, duty and control. Being who they were, the public eye upon them as it was, the honour of their family *so* great . . . well – there were *expectations*. They wanted her well mannered, modestly dressed, reserved and blushing, an immaculate prize for some wealthy noble with fine whiskers who could match or better the Vennaways' fortune and prestige.

They foresaw a future of stately grandeur for her – producing heirs, gracing society, decorating her husband's arm. Aurelia, however, had read too much and lived too little. Inspired by the vast libraries of Hatville, and with no wise guide to understand or check her, every wild daydream seemed possible to her. She wanted a life of travel and intrigue, romances of her own choosing (she was determined there should be several) and to use her fortune and privilege to do philanthropic works. She wanted to be a new kind of role model for rich young ladies. ('Subversive and scandalous!' spat her father.) She wanted her name in the history books, never mind that no history book we had ever read recognized the opinions of women.

'Then I shall be the first,' she resolved, tossing her lovely head. 'Everything must happen for the first time at some point, otherwise nothing would *ever* have changed and we should still be burning whole villages to the ground.'

'Some things are not *meant* to change!' thundered Lord Vennaway.

'*Some* things are long overdue for change,' blazed Aurelia.

I could almost pity the Vennaways senior. The proudest, most conservative family in the county – no heir, only one daughter. That daughter everything they could wish in terms of beauty, grace and a loving heart. That daughter also harbouring dreams of . . . social reform. Keeping far-from-suitable company (myself, Mr Clay and Mrs Bolton, the nearest thing Surrey had to a bluestocking). It was an unsavoury business.

Of the many suitors that they had auditioned over the years, two were now leading the field, and they were growing impatient. Lord Kenworthy and Lord Dunthorne were very different men, yet each as deeply unpleasant as the other. Giles Kenworthy was some twenty years Aurelia's senior, cold and rigid, with dry skin and a face that could not smile. The first time I saw him I was peeping out of a forbidden library and he was sweeping along the hall as though riding down a fox. I was thankful that he did not catch sight of me. He had eyes that made me want to run away.

Bailor Dunthorne was young and debauched, drenched with an oily charm. He was handsome and flashy and vigorous. Vigorous enough to beat a horse bloody – we saw it. Handsome enough that an inconceivable number of young women had succumbed to his dubious charms and received scant rewards for their favour – Mrs Bolton told us (or at least she told Aurelia, and I was there). He had a habit of paying impromptu visits, happening upon us when we least expected him. Ever his adversary's opposite, he condescended to ruffle my hair and bend to my height, sweeping his dark eyes over my face whenever he saw me. It made me shudder.

Both gentlemen were of exquisite lineage and impressive fortune. The Vennaways had decided that either would do. When Aurelia turned eighteen, it was time for her to choose; they had indulged her sensibilities long enough. But Aurelia would not cooperate. She would come into her fortune in three short years, she argued; she had no need of a husband. She often pointed to the young queen as role model and exemplar. '*Victoria* refused to marry unless for love. Victoria seriously considered remaining unmarried, like Queen Elizabeth before her. Victoria only married her Albert because they have a *true understanding.*'

'*Her Majesty*,' roared her father, 'is queen of our nation and in a somewhat different position from *you*! Your responsibility, Aurelia, is not to govern the country and your duty is not to the people. It is to family. It is to marry and continue the Vennaway line. I have not been granted a son and I will *not* have my daughter fail me as well. *Her Majesty* is not my concern. You seem to think you have a choice in this, Aurelia. I assure you that you do not.'

Two equally strong sets of ambitions duelled, but of course her parents held all the power. They were bound to prevail, and Aurelia was so lovely that men would overlook her unusual convictions in their lust to possess her.

So the Vennaways reassured themselves: yes, she lacked judgement, tractability and deference, but she more than compensated for this with beauty, breeding and thirty thousand pounds a year.

As for me, I was ten years old and could see no way for the impasse to be resolved. And what kind of man would nurture and support her pioneering temperament, her passionate heart? More likely by far that she would be oppressed and raged at until her spirit was battered. Lord Kenworthy, for example, would think it a fine thing to procure a woman like Aurelia. He would then steadfastly prune away any of her traits that did not meet with his approval (and that was a thing very rarely earned indeed) as though she were a recalcitrant sapling. She confided her fears in me, for she had no one else. He would, she fretted, foist baby after baby upon her until her body and spirits were worn and she would start to be some other person.

Young as I was, I worried sorely for her, and I confess to no small concern on my own account as well. I could tell from the way Lord Kenworthy looked at me that I would not fare well in *his* household – if I were permitted to go there at all. I would doubtless be slickly welcomed to the Dunthorne home and that could be worse. It was impossible to think of a way out.

And then nature took care of it.

She collapsed in the orchard one day during a picnic; the Vennaway cousins were visiting. I had been put to work, as was usual when pleasant times were to be had. I was helping Robin gather plums and their shrieks of laughter – Aurelia's loudest of all – reached me through the trees. I didn't notice when they fell quiet; I was crouched in the grass, tying my apron into a bundle because my basket was full, the material slithering about unobligingly.

What I noticed was Robin dropping an armful of plums. They thudded one after another to the ground and bounced; it was unlike him to be so careless with the precious harvest. I looked up and saw his face white as ash, then he leapt from his ladder without a word and ran on long legs towards the party. I stood slowly, a bad feeling scurrying up and down my spine like a spider. Unable to move, I watched as Robin carried her lifeless-looking body back to the house, her cousins clustered nervously around. The sight of her dangling arm in particular has stayed with me always – a chilling premonition of the future.

Dr Jacobs was summoned. After a long, grave examination he told us that Aurelia's vibrant beauty and high spirits were a cruel disguise on the part of Fate. Her heart, expansive and courageous as it was, was weak, diseased and would not carry her through her twenties.

Aurelia greeted the news as though it were the cleverest device she had yet dreamed up to thwart her parents' matrimonial plans for her. What a merry to-do! For no one would have her now. No one wanted a wife who would die in a few short years, necessitating the tiresome search for another. Of course, they might have undergone the inconvenience in order to inherit her fortune but, warned Dr Jacobs, there was a very real possibility that childbirth could bring on an even earlier demise. He strongly advised against marriage and all its consequent activities. Without the possibility of an heir, the Vennaways had no reason to marry her off. Better keep the fortune in the family. Aurelia nodded complacently. Better it go to Cousin Maude than to a *stranger*.

So Aurelia had her way after all – at a cost. There would be no illustrious wedding. There would be no precious Vennaway heir. But neither would there be travel, passion or reform.

Or so I believed.

Chapter Twelve

Thoughts of that time settle heavy upon me as the train slows and halts. The days following her diagnosis are echoed now in the dark days that follow her death. Now as then my brain resists it – death and Aurelia are two phenomena that do not sit easily together. I half expect to find her here, waiting for me.

London is a series of vivid, fleeting tableaux, a pack of cards that won't stop shuffling. The throng at Bricklayers' Arms further reveals Ladywell for the sleepy backwater it is. I see hawkers, hollerers, scantily dressed women and barefoot children. As though the experience has set me outside myself, I see my own person: a girl of seventeen who feels a hundred years older, dressed all in black and shrinking from the chaos.

The faces of Mr and Mrs Begley beam like tangerines as they spy their son in the crowd. He cordially greets them with news that the young Mrs Begley is at home in Pentonville, supervising a welcome luncheon. I feel I would give them my whole hundred pounds if I could go with them.

But I am in the way of their happy reunion. I fear I have

been forgotten, then experience a nauseating relief at suddenly being remembered and bundled into a cab with shouted good wishes and hasty, duty-done farewells.

The cab sets off at a great rate through a sea of traffic. I am flung forwards, flung backwards. Flung from side to side. My carpet bag flying about the interior like a bluebottle. An omnibus hurtling towards us, missing us by an inch. Horses whinnying in alarm. A rain of curses from my driver. A world so different from Hatville, where all was grace and state and order.

At last, a cry from my driver: 'Jessop!' The cab draws up in a quiet street with terraced white houses stained grey with the pall of the day. I tumble out, unconvinced that my bones retain their original configuration.

After trying at number six – Mrs Begley was sure it was number six – I am directed instead to number eighteen. In Jessop Walk, a moat-like ditch separates street from houses. At each property a little walkway bridges the divide and high spiked gates protect against villains. Despite these precautions, the houses are narrow and the inhabitants could quite easily peer over a garden wall into the lives of their neighbours. At Hatville, if we wanted to see a neighbour, we had to walk some miles.

I am reassured that Mrs Woodrow is a scholarly looking woman with spectacles and grey woollen mittens. She is not fat, slatternly, drunk nor inquisitive (I had not been aware how much the novels of Mr Dickens would shape my expectations of landladies). I pay for two nights' lodging in advance and she agrees that I can extend my stay if I need to.

'Assuming, that is, a crowd of wealthy and important guests don't all descend at once,' she adds drily. 'It is January,' she continues, seeing that I take her seriously. 'No one ever visits London in January.'

Looking out of my small window I can quite see why. A light rain has begun falling, adding its own lustre to the day. The sky sags over the hodgepodge of cramped gardens, washing lines, vegetable plots, outhouses, roofs, windows and walls that fit within my view of roughly two feet squared. Home . . . if such it ever was . . . is a long way away.

My room has bare floorboards and a narrow bed covered in a plain coverlet. The walls are brown and there is but one small painting in an ugly frame, a sentimental shepherdess simpering at a rosy-cheeked swain. There is a washstand, one chair and a small table bearing a glass jar of snowdrops.

The sight of them leaves me awash with memories: the road between Hatville and Enderby; countless hidden corners of the estate; dark lush leaves and drifts of little white flowers; fresh air and the promise of spring with Aurelia . . .

I wonder if this is what she imagined for me.

Chapter Thirteen

The household was devastated by Aurelia's diagnosis. I caught Lord Vennaway reduced to tears, and turned away out of respect. Lady Vennaway took to her bed, then got out of it almost at once when she realized that a decline was an ill use of precious time with Aurelia. Lord Kenworthy disappeared like a shot cannon, soon to become engaged to a wealthy young lady from Kent, so we heard. Every cloud has its silver lining.

I could not catch my breath from the shock of it. *Aurelia!* She was far too bright a flame to be prematurely extinguished. If this sad destiny had been anyone else's, I might have been able to conceive of it: Lady Vennaway was too brittle to sit comfortably in this life, Cook was eternally tired, Rosy was always coughing and scratching. As for Marcus, he was forever falling off walls and dropping hammers on his toes and getting trapped under logs. But Aurelia? Goddesses don't have weak hearts.

She remained in good spirits. In fact, she was so little changed in that first year that it was easy to suppose Dr Jacobs mistaken. She insisted, though, that I must cease my ambiguous role in the household and become her full-time companion.

'It is time to stop this nonsense now,' she told her parents soberly one day. 'I know you disapprove of Amy and I will stop trying to talk you out of it if you will accept my decision and allow her to carry out her duties in peace. I do not know what lies ahead of me or how long I have. Amy calms me and I trust her absolutely. Whatever befalls me now, I want her by my side.'

Of course, she said it when the Reverend Mr Chorley and Dr Jacobs were present; she never hesitated to air her private business before the pillars of the community if it served her interests. Dr Jacobs expressed his medical opinion that I was a beneficial tonic for Aurelia. Mr Chorley urged compassion and said I was a gift from God. I loved him for that.

And so I bedded down in the scullery no more but was moved into the room next door to Aurelia's. We continued to take lessons together, though these were now a desultory affair. Mr Henley was no longer grooming her for marriage, but Lord Vennaway had become so distracted with grief that he neglected to dismiss him.

Aurelia continued to walk the two miles into Enderby each week to visit the villagers, as well as to discuss the plight of the unfortunate with Mr Chorley, Mr Clay and Mrs Bolton, but now I went with her. Everyone, irrespective of fortune or status, was appalled at the ill fate that had befallen Aurelia. She forbade anyone to talk of it, but everyone did.

Lady Vennaway's persecution of me eased, save for her insistence that I dress like a governess, provoking another battle. Aurelia chafed at the unkindness that it represented and swore that seeing me so drab would hasten her demise. Lady Vennaway would not hear of a lowly companion wearing beautiful clothes. Aurelia argued that to look upon beautiful things raised her spirits. Lady Vennaway retorted that Aurelia's spirits seemed unnaturally high to *her* and that if she didn't like it she could send me back to the scullery. I did not care so I told Aurelia that she could yield with honour. There were greater things to concern us, after all.

The second year brought the first signs of her ill health, unwelcome and inevitable as the shortening days and withering leaves of autumn. She began to complain of fatigue, a word that was never in her vocabulary before. 'It is not that I am *tired*,' she told me, 'it is not the feeling one has after a busy day or the longing to melt into sleep. It is like a weight upon me and I cannot wrestle it.'

We still walked into Enderby, but only on a good day. Sometimes now we took the carriage and sometimes we stayed at home. Aurelia grew frightened. What would her condition impose upon her in the time that remained? She didn't mind death, but she didn't want to be changed before it came.

In December 1843 we celebrated Aurelia's twenty-first birth-day. Her parents wanted no ritual at all to mark her passage into an adulthood that would be all too fleeting. Aurelia wanted a ball. They compromised with a dinner for selected family members, prepared by Cook, aided by me. And Aurelia came into her fortune.

Chapter Fourteen

I eat a little of the cold collation Mrs Woodrow has brought me. There is a cut of ham, some bread and butter, an orange and a mug of ale. I am not fond of ale, but I take a swallow, then leave the rest untouched for later. I head downstairs and ask Mrs Woodrow if she knows the whereabouts of Entwhistle's Bookshop. She does not.

So I step into the cold, damp afternoon and commence to wander the streets. The size of the city becomes apparent as I walk, street after street after street, never passing a shop of any kind, let alone a bookshop.

The absence of a chaperone makes me painfully self-conscious. If Aurelia had ever paced the streets of London alone, Lady Vennaway would have died from shame. I am, in addition, all too aware of my shabby appearance. At Hatville, everyone understood that I was lowly, but here, out of context, I look as unimportant and lacking in connections – and therefore as vulnerable – as I truly am.

These reflections chase me back to Jessop Walk. My first

explorations have been discouraging but I am glad I have been cautious when I see that night falls sooner and swifter here than it does in the country. Gaslights, something I have never seen before, flare eerily in the murk and usher me on.

Alone in the chilly, charmless room that is mine for the next two days, I swallow the remains of my luncheon and stare at the wall. I don't know what to do. So I take up the pages I began in the Rose and Crown last night. I wish I could stop myself journeying back in time each time my quill touches the page. I wish that my present had more to recommend it. Yet I find myself thinking of my origins, something I have not done for many years. This is a certain route to drawing yet another blank. *Who am I?*

I used to wonder about my parents all the time. So did Aurelia. From my earliest youth, one of our favourite fascinations was speculating about my birth. It was too great a mystery not to! A baby left in the snow with no clothes and no clue . . . For a fanciful sprite like Aurelia and a solemn little girl like me, who longed to be *something*, it was fertile ground.

At first we assumed I was a princess, stolen away by wicked usurpers, bent on the downfall of my kingdom. But we found two flaws in this theory. One was that none of the periodicals Aurelia avidly read had reported a missing princess baby in their Foreign News columns. The other was that if I were ever found, my duty would be to go and rule my country. Aurelia would be alone again and it sounded tedious to me.

Our next hypothesis was that I was a gypsy. This had more to recommend it, as some travelling gypsies had passed through Enderby the previous year. Gypsies, we understood, were extremely feckless and disorganized. They might well have lost a baby. But gypsies could not have travelled across the Hatville estate, fenced and fortified as it was, so how did I come to be there? I did have very long black hair like the gypsies, but my skin was pale and my eyes too light. We discarded this idea also.

Aurelia proffered the idea that I was Lord Vennaway's 'love child', a term she heard liberally sprinkled about Hatville's drawing room. I was too young to understand fully what that meant, and I'm not convinced she did either. We liked the possibility because it would make me Aurelia's sister and it would certainly explain Lady Vennaway's attitude towards me.

Now that I am older I have come to accept that, despite Lady Vennaway's attitude, I am not likely to be Lord Vennaway's illegitimate daughter. Physically, I look even less like a Vennaway than I do a gypsy or a princess. Also, I believe if Lord Vennaway were to take his affections elsewhere than to his wife, he is hardly the sort of man to do so with the sort of woman who would leave a baby on his estate. No, he would have very discreet, tasteful affairs indeed. Besides, it never *felt* true. When Lord Vennaway beheld me, I saw indifference, disdain and mild irritation. I never saw love, I never saw curiosity and I never saw guilt.

It was hard for me to admit how much pain it caused me, not knowing who I was. I would have given anything for even a shred of information about my parents. A name, the shape of a nose, a favourite song . . . anything. I would have snatched at such details and kept them locked safe in my heart. But I could not put it into words.

Even so, as Aurelia matured, she came to understand that my beginnings were no romantic fairy tale. In time she conducted a thorough enquiry, much to her mother's horror. This was one battle won by Aurelia, however, for her mother could not prohibit conversation. Aurelia herself questioned every family in Enderby, entreating them to mine their memories, dredge up any clues.

It all came to nothing. If anyone in Enderby had borne me, or knew who had, they kept silent.

Most likely my mother was some poor unfortunate passing through in disgrace and seeking a fresh start. Most likely she blamed me for her circumstances, or was simply too weak to carry me any longer. I may never know.

Would I wish to? Now? Surely, if God had meant us to know everything, He would not have made the world so very mysterious. I have grown accustomed to the blank spaces around the shapes of my life. I have grown accustomed to living with questions.

Chapter Fifteen

The upheaval and rearrangement of life as I knew it began on a dull January day. It seems that all events of note in my small life have occurred in January – my birth (and subsequent arrival at Hatville), the death of Aurelia (and soon enough, my departure) and this. I believe I must avoid January in future. Is there some way I can will myself into a fairy-tale slumber for the duration of all future Januarys and emerge, unscathed, each February? But I digress. I was never so whimsical when Aurelia was alive. Her flights of fancy were wild enough for us both and I was the steadying influence.

I do not feel steady now.

Aurelia was twenty-one and I was thirteen. This is how I always remember life, measured in the years, too few, of her bright-burning existence, with me – eight years younger, smaller and plainer – trailing behind like an obedient comet. The clouds that day had knitted together into one solid entity, so closely woven and absolute it seemed no sun would ever emerge again.

Aurelia had summoned her parents to the parlour and the four of us were gathered together, an extremely rare circumstance. The French mantel clock, with its design of leaping fishes wrought in blue and ormolu, told me it was late afternoon. The weather offered no such clue; it had been dusk all day. Lord Vennaway grudgingly lit the candelabra.

'Mamma, Father, Amy dearest, I have some exciting news,' Aurelia began in that bright, soothing tone that foretold no good, not on any occasion. 'I have been favoured with an invitation. 'Tis a wonderful opportunity, though it means I shall be leaving you for a while and going away.'

Her words dropped into silence dense as cloud.

'Don't be ridiculous, Aurelia.'

'Indeed it is no jest, Father. Mrs Bolton goes to London in March for the opening of a marvellous new library. Is that not splendid, Father? Then she goes to Twickenham to spend some weeks with her cousin who has newly given birth to a baby girl. Imagine that, Father! I shall see places I have never seen, have splendid experiences and be exposed to some of the finest minds in our country today, for Mrs Bolton plans entertainments, lectures and soirées. She is incomparably well connected in progressive circles. This is very important to me, Father, Mamma, given my situation and the limited time left to me to enjoy such things.'

I pleated my dress in my lap. That Aurelia would mention her condition so early – before an argument had even properly begun – showed me how intensely she wanted this. It also revealed that she was uncertain of prevailing.

'Preposterous notion.' Lord Vennaway took a draft of his porter, coughed heftily and set it away from him. Lady Vennaway had turned grey as the day. 'Mrs Bolton,' spat Lord Vennaway when he recovered his breath, 'is a dreadful woman. We should never have permitted your friendship with her – this is our lesson for yielding to your headstrong inclinations. What can you be thinking, Aurelia? As if we should allow you to career around the countryside in your condition and in such disreputable company. Absolutely not. No.'

'Father!' said Aurelia. '*Yes!*'

'*Naturally* no! Now. Lord and Lady Drummond arrive for dinner at eight and I do not want this unsavoury proposition hanging over our evening. This is the end of it, Aurelia, I will not be swayed. We allow you too much liberty, indeed we do, but if you believe you can talk us round in this you delude yourself. Tell Mrs Bolton you may *not* join her, and pray loosen your friendship henceforth. How could she suggest such a thing, delicate as you are? *No.*'

It sounded final to me. Lord Vennaway was a formidable man. Let me state that clearly lest he somehow appear a blustering father helpless before the charms of a beloved daughter. In politics he was feared. In his select social circle his approval was avidly sought. As a young girl who had not found favour, I could personally vouch for the face of his displeasure. I felt certain that Aurelia would not triumph on this occasion and for once I hoped she would not.

The clock ticked, the grey outside deepened. I breathed more easily. Then:

'Father, I very much fear that I cannot accept your decision.' Aurelia's voice was low. 'I am soon to die and I will do this. There is no longer any concern that I will wreck my marriage prospects, and it is hardly as though travel and self-improvement are disreputable pastimes. And I *do* consider my health. Later in the year Mrs Bolton plans to travel on the Continent but I do not propose to join her there, though I should love to see Italy and Switzerland more than anything. I do not think three months in the south of England can be considered too imprudent. I realize it will upset you and perhaps cause a rift between us. I do not wish for either of those things, yet I intend to go.'

'*Aurelia!*' Lady Vennaway's voice was pained.

'Leave the room.' Lord Vennaway did not look at me or use my name, by which I knew he was speaking to me. I gladly complied. I could not bear to listen.

Aurelia was forbidden the dinner with the Drummonds. She professed not to care a fig but I knew otherwise. Lord Drummond was handsome and winning, his wife was elegant and lively and they were close to those who were close to the young queen and her Albert. When she stormed upstairs to join me in our sitting room, she was without her usual flounce and fury; she looked shaken and scared. Things had been said that could not be taken back.

For once her parents' wishes and mine aligned. We none of us knew how long Aurelia had left and we were jealous to spare or share her.

Chapter Sixteen

My first full day in London. I am dressed early and ready to go out when there is a knock at my door. I startle. I am unused to my privacy being respected so.

In the event it is merely Mrs Woodrow telling me that there is breakfast downstairs if I want some.

I follow her to a small dining room with an enormous table squeezed into it, though no one is there to eat at it but me. There are kippers and porridge and chops and kedgeree and I have an appetite for the first time in a week.

'Did you find the bookseller you sought yesterday, Miss Snow?' asks Mrs Woodrow when she has ensured I have everything I need. I tell her I have nothing happy to report but that I hope today will yield a better result.

'Is it *very* important that you find him?'

I reply that it is absolutely essential and feel glad that she does not question the matter further; I am aware that it must sound very curious.

'Do go to Regent Street,' she entreats. 'I am certain that any bookseller of repute must be found there.'

What a difference a mood can make! London looks all different this morning: still grey, still vast and bitterly cold, yet I have a destination and a plan, and every hope that I will return to Jessop Walk this evening with the second letter in my hands – and learn what awaits me next on this treasure trail.

In my optimism, I choose to walk instead of catching another cab, and despite my heartache, I take some pleasure in seeing St James's Park, the palace and the famous library – sights I have read and heard about – here before me! It seems not impossible that the queen will come stepping through the fog towards me. Even the mists seem different this morning, confiding and conspiratorial rather than obstructive and sinister.

Mrs Woodrow gave me strict directions: 'Do not stray south towards Devil's Acre, Miss Snow – do *not* find yourself there, nor east towards the Strand – crawling slum.'

I am fairly confident of the way. For a short time I lay aside the urgency of my quest, indulge myself by following another of Aurelia's instructions: 'Marvel at seeing a part of our kingdom so different from Enderby!'

I am charmed when I see street stalls selling roasted potatoes and hot chestnuts. Enticing aromas fill the air and I have money in my pocket, for the first time in my life. I allow myself one hot, comforting treat and then the other, despite my hearty breakfast, for walking has made me hungry again and the cold is seeping through my clothes. I have never liked the cold.

I polish off my last potato and sink the chestnuts in my pocket, licking my fingers and reflecting what great freedom there is here compared with Hatville. I no longer feel the need for a chaperone and I no longer feel out of place in my shabby garb. Then, suddenly, my stomach lurches. If I do not feel out of place, then I have strayed.

I look around and realize that there are children huddled in doorways, holding out thin hands. Only a few, but no one is moving them along; they belong there. Young girls are selling snowdrops from straw baskets and there is a great din of cheery traders hollering out their prices and bragging about their wares. It does not feel so very threatening, but none of this was in Mrs Woodrow's description of my route. I hasten back to the chestnut stand.

'Back again, love?' The vendor is a handsome young man who winks at me, making me blush. 'Can't 'ave polished 'em off already, skinny little fing like you? Or 'ave you come back to see me? I'm workin' 'til seven but if you come back then, I'll take you out, darlin'.'

I am tongue-tied. The endless rules of etiquette taught with all seriousness to Aurelia, then passed on with great derision to me, have not prepared me for being addressed so familiarly on a street corner by a complete stranger. Despite my best efforts to look away, I catch his sparkling eyes . . . and I cannot help but wonder if this way is better. Were Lord Kenworthy's formal, strategic advances to Aurelia more to be desired?

Rightly or wrongly the young man does not scare me, so I ask him where I am and how I might reach Regent Street. He puts me right with directions so detailed I feel a suspicion that he is trying to detain me. I am trying to listen carefully when he interrupts himself with a loud roar, which makes me startle nearly out of my boots.

'Oi! Bugger off, you little fief!' he bellows, starting out from behind the stall. I jump back in shock and catch sight of a small figure darting away into the throng.

'Bloody little pickpocket, 'scuse the language, miss. 'Ave you got everyfing?'

Shaken, I check my pockets. Some coins have vanished, and my chestnuts. I had not so much as felt my cloak twitch. However, the rest of the money I brought with me is in another pocket and the letter is still safe in my skirt, so I know at once that I have been fortunate. Imagine if the letter had vanished! I am limp with horror at the thought.

'*Thank you*, sir,' I say fervently and he guffaws.

'I ain't no "sir", miss, but if you get tired of mixing with the toffs up on Regent Street, come back later and talk to me again. Tommy's me name.'

'Thank you, Tommy.' I buy another bag of chestnuts – my

money and I are parting company more speedily than I anticipated – and I hurry back to my route.

After a while I recognize a landmark or two – an Anglican church and a small private garden – and I see where I went wrong. It was so easy to stray! One moment dutiful Amy Snow, following instructions as ever, the next a roving street urchin being propositioned by a hot chestnut vendor! *Who am I?* It is hard to know the answer in these endless, flowing streets and mists. My legs are trembling.

My earlier high spirits have fled and I am sorely tempted to return to Jessop Walk, to curl up in safety and escape into a book. I am not cut out for adventures. And yet I remember Tommy's grey eyes, lively and clear and . . . interested. I frown. No man has ever looked at me that way before. This requires some understanding. What did he see then, as I stood before him?

I remember myself as a stubborn little child – pensive and quiet, yes, but with a strong will and a dash of temper. I no longer recognize that determined little person in the woman I am now. It seems that somewhere along the way I began to believe everything Lady Vennaway said about me. From knowing myself despised by these grand people, I came to feel myself worthy of disdain. I came to believe, I suddenly see with horrible clarity, that no one would ever want me for a wife. And with so much dreadful attention lavished on *Aurelia*'s marriage, *Aurelia*'s beauty, *Aurelia*'s suitors, perhaps I started to feel I was better off alone. But that was not my heart's truth, I understand now, and hot tears spring to my eyes – the first in a long while that have not been about Aurelia.

Again a picture flits into my mind: the cottage and garden, the pony, the smiling husband. It is the second time in two days for them to troop into my thoughts, after being so long put aside. Submitting to Aurelia's grander designs was not the only reason I let my dreams fade. I gave up on them, I realize, and I didn't even know I had done it.

Tommy was a flirt, I conclude with a watery little smile. An invitation to stroll about Haymarket is not an offer of marriage. But perhaps it is what normal girls experience. The thought fortifies me enough to propel me on my way again. The chestnuts are all devoured before I reach Piccadilly, leaving me with a burned mouth and a lesson learned. London is like a river current, it demands to be taken seriously.

Regent Street is like nothing I could ever have imagined. Glittering windows display a panoply of jewellery, birds, quills, statuary and other items I simply cannot recognize or name. The Pantheon in Picadilly is like something Aurelia might have dreamed up in one of her stories: a great glass arcade with fountains, statues and galleries, where finely dressed ladies and gentlemen stroll and preen.

I begin at once, enquiring in shops that might have any connection, however tenuous, to the world of books. Poorly dressed as I am, I meet a range of receptions from faintly condescending to a flat refusal to communicate with me. I welcome their disdain as evidence that I am where I intended to be and, therefore, relatively safe. Besides, I am used to it.

I pace from store to store but my search reveals nothing. No one has heard of a bookseller called Entwhistle. After exhausting Regent Street and Oxford Street both, I contemplate the size of London and the dismaying fact that Entwhistle's could be anywhere within it. It will be like searching for a needle in a haystack, a pea under a thousand mattresses. In fact, it will be exactly like searching for one of Aurelia's elaborate clues on the Hatville estate.

Do you remember, dear, when you were little, how I used to delight in creating treasure hunts for you . . .?

How could I forget? They are amongst my happiest recollections. There is such magic for a child in knowing that secrets are hidden all about! (For a weary adult with no assured future it is less enchanting.)

Her clues might be riddles or verses, or even sketches of the location in question. We could spend a whole day on such an adventure – me screwing up my forehead, huffing through my heavy black fringe as I tried to unlock the mystery, Aurelia stifling laughter as she watched me draw a wrong conclusion and race off to a dead end. Sometimes she was too clever for me and I would find myself defeated, but she was always there to explain the puzzle. She is not here to help me now; I pray she has not overestimated me.

By three o'clock in the afternoon the crowds have more than doubled. I am eyed askance and swept past and jostled. I start walking further afield, this time keeping a watchful eye on my surroundings. There are fewer people to ask here but their answers are the same.

I am about to draw today's hunt to a close when, in desperation, I enquire at a cobbler's.

'Not the foggiest, miss,' I am told, 'but try old Manning, you know him? Second left off Parsley Street, that's by the inn with the contented swine on the sign. He's a stationer, and he knows everything, to boot. Boot! Ha!' The cobbler raises the boot he's holding and waves it around.

'*Definitely* my last enquiry today,' I promise myself. I am tired and footsore beyond imagining. Darkness is a whisper away.

'Entwhistle? Never heard of him,' says Mr Manning, predictably, scratching a tufty head. 'Entwhistle, you say? No, no idea.'

'Thank you anyway.' I find it impossible to smile.

'Stay, though, I have a directory here somewhere – all the booksellers in London. If you can wait, I shall look it up for you.'

The street outside is awash with shadows, but there is only

one possible answer. A directory! This will save me weeks of searching! In a moment I will have an address, or at any rate one of the long, colourful, circumlocutory descriptions that I have learned today pass for addresses here in London. I may yet find the letter today!

'No, I'm sorry, miss, no such name.' Mr Manning folds up his directory.

'I beg your pardon?' Sheer disbelief floors me. Of all the outcomes I had been imagining, this was not one of them.

'No Entwhistle. Not that it surprises me; it's rare I don't know of a fellow dealing in books.'

'You must be mistaken. Please look again!'

Mr Manning looks irritated but humours me and shows me the relevant listings, even pronouncing them aloud with painstaking clarity as if he doubts I can read.

Sure enough, the list jumps straight from 'Durrant' to 'Everley' and there is nothing in between. I turn over the document, looking for a postscript or an addendum. There is nothing. I clutch it and read every single name on it, one by one, using a finger, in case it has been listed out of place. Mr Manning watches me curiously. No Entwhistle.

'Was there something particular you wanted? A specialist item perhaps? I could order it for you.'

'No, sir, there is nothing you can do. Thank you for looking.'

What a difference a mood can make. I return to my lodgings

with the heaviest of hearts, utterly baffled. I barely notice the jouncing of the cab, the dingy streets.

I feel nothing but dread. For if there is no Entwhistle's, there can be no letter. And if there is no letter, then the trail is dead.

Chapter Seventeen

The argument raged for weeks. Proud Mrs Bolton came to the house in her peacock colours, with entreaties, references, credentials. Correspondence flew between Hatville and other interested parties, namely Mrs Bolton's connections, objects of the proposed visit. Dr Jacobs was consulted. He gave the plan his blessing. A London consultant was summoned. He did not. Aurelia did not much credit his opinion, merely wondered how much it had cost her father.

While the future of this, her latest and wildest project, hung in the balance, Aurelia haunted the halls, white-faced and tense. The days became an exhausting sequence of dramas: private conversations between Aurelia and her parents behind tightly closed doors, doors slamming, footsteps storming and fits of angry weeping. I was a helpless, baffled onlooker. When I asked Aurelia what had been said, she would just look at me with desperate eyes and thin lips and shake her head. This was the same Aurelia who had told me every last thing she heard about Lord Kenworthy, about Lord Dunthorne, every scrap and scandal. She had never spared my girlish sensibilities before. In the eighteen months since her diagnosis I had grown used to our new closeness and now I felt horribly excluded.

I felt cross with her then, I did. I understood that she did not like to be thwarted, of course, but it was only a holiday! I told myself, in secret, dark moments I could not admit to anyone, that she was being hysterical. But one day I slipped into the library and found Aurelia seated in a wing-back chair by the window. She did not hear me – I had perfected the art of moving as unobtrusively as possible in order to cause the least offence. Her book had fallen to the ground – her face was buried in her hands. I knew then that her despair was real and I did not know what I could say, so I left her alone.

I could not understand. I was but thirteen. Her companionship was the greatest joy of my life and I wanted to hoard every precious moment remaining to us. Why did she not feel the same?

I did not like myself for leaving her in the library that day. It was the first time that I felt useless to her. I did not know how to talk to her any more. I missed her even while I still saw her at Hatville every day. At first I would cry myself to sleep but I couldn't bear that, it felt too tragic – as if she had already gone, as if she had already died. I dared not let myself think ahead to *that*.

I was not to accompany her on her journey either. I was too young for the plans that had been laid. It would be tiresome for me. By going alone, she promised, she could return in the highest of spirits to share the highlights with me – she would entertain me for hours.

I did not want to endure three months at Hatville without her, not for any entertainment.

Yet she went. I knew that she would. Once an idea possessed her to that degree, she never, ever gave up on it.

The night before she left, we sat talking in front of her fire. I sat in a large chair with my knees drawn up to my chin and my arms hugging them close. I could hardly believe that after tomorrow morning I would not see her for three whole months. It seemed an intolerably long time to me then.

'I will miss you so much,' she murmured, to my infinite relief. 'You know I will, don't you, little bird?'

Oh, there was so much I wanted to say to that! *Would* she really miss me? Would she still love me best? I craved reassurance but the preceding weeks seemed to have robbed me of the habit of easy speech. I did not answer at first and when I spoke it felt inadequate.

'But you don't *have* to go,' I argued, knowing it was too late. Mrs Bolton was to collect her early the next morning. Her trunks were packed – and mine were not. 'And you don't have to leave me behind. What if . . .'

'What if . . . ?' she prompted gently, knowing what I was about to say.

'What if you *die*? What if you go away and I never see you again? Is it *so* important to you? So very important you would risk us never sitting together again?' My voice had risen and grown tearful, so I hugged my knees much tighter.

'Oh, little bird, never think that! Nothing would be worth that. But there *is* no such risk. I don't claim to know when I shall die, but I promise you the time is not near. I should feel it if it were and I should not go. I have to go.'

'But . . . *why*?'

She sighed and we both stared at the flames. I thought she would not answer me. When she finally turned to me, it was with the saddest expression. I had never seen her like this before. I was accustomed to compassion, obstinacy, a crusading spirit, but never this naked, defeated grief.

'Amy, I have never had control over my life. I have marched all over this small corner of the world as though I did, but it was pretence. Advantages I have, advantages aplenty, but control, no. I am not my own person.'

I rested my chin on my knees and gazed at her, listening. She hesitated again with a faraway look in her dark-blue eyes. She looked as if she were sorting through a great many things she would like to say in order to pick the ones she would, or could.

But when she spoke again, in a soft, considered voice, it was only to say things I had heard many times before.

'There are walls all around us, holding us in. At every

moment one circumstance dictates the next. A neighbour pays a call and we politely receive them or politely pretend to be from home. One person decides to hold a dinner and someone else cooks it. Someone else cannot afford to eat, so they die. And no one questions it, at least, no one in *my* family. I have always known this, Amy, I have always seen it. But I have been able to go on with my life nonetheless. But lately, perhaps since we learned about my heart, I don't know, I cannot stop seeing it – I cannot turn off this awareness. It grows unbearable of late. The *stupidity* of it all, Amy, the conventions, the things we must do and the things we must not. The things that are respected and revered, like an advantageous marriage, when all it amounts to is selling a woman for money, like a horse! And the things that are frowned upon, when they are good and true things . . . it's all so nonsensical. And there in the middle of it all am I and what good does seeing all this actually *do*? I can win small wars. I can take food to the villagers, support the dear reverend's charitable projects, I can be kind to someone who has been disgraced, whether or not it scandalizes my mother. But these things do not change anyone's lives, not permanently.'

I nodded and did not trust myself to speak. I could not understand why she was talking to me as though I were a stranger who did not already know her every thought. I did not want social commentary, I wanted her to tell me that she loved me and could not be parted from me.

'Until now, dear, my greatest victory is you! I have kept you safe, here with me, I have educated you and given you a chance at a better life after I am gone. And that you are my greatest friend is the very happiest of outcomes. But even that is poisoned, Amy, for what has been the cost to you? I find myself questioning everything, of late. I am grateful every day that you are here with me. But I am not sure that I have done you such a very great favour. I have made you . . . a misfit! I should set you free, only it would break my heart to come back to find you gone.'

I was appalled. This had never occurred to me. Now, as well as worrying that I might be neglected, forgotten, I needed to worry that she would cast me out through some misguided notion that it would be better for me. 'Aurelia, how can you say that? You've done everything for me! I would never leave you. Not ever!'

She raked her nails over her scalp until her hair stood up. Her cheeks burned and tears glowed in her eyes. 'During my life I have fought passionately – over bonnets. I have stood my ground to defend my rights – to wear feathers. Everyone knows where I stand – with regard to ribbons. The concerns of a spoiled child.'

'Aurelia! No! You have fought for a great deal more than that! You *know* you have!'

'But to what avail? And in what sphere? With my *parents*? I have hated them for how they treat you Amy, *hated* them. One should not hate one's parents. And now . . .' She took a deep breath. 'Sometimes, Amy, the people you love are, are . . . well, sometimes they are *bad*!'

I knew better than anyone that Aurelia's parents were not good. But I did not understand the depth of her anguish – why so extreme, and why now? Nonetheless, I scrambled from my seat and held her while she cried.

At last she grew calm again and rested her head on mine. 'I wish to die having done *something* remarkable. Perhaps a journey is not the noblest of causes, perhaps I am being selfish again. But it is the best I can do now. One day, Amy, I'm going to die, and far sooner than I would like. There is so much I wanted to do. This will not even amount to a tiny part of it, but it is *something*.

'Three months will not see the end of me. The time will fly past, and I promise to write to you every day. Then I shall return to you to live out the rest of my days, however many they may be. But I *will* have this first, whilst I still can. I am a grown woman of plentiful fortune. To be told, once again, that I *cannot*, is no longer to be borne.'

I swallowed, and squeezed her hand. Although I desperately wanted to, I did not ask the questions I burned to ask. What use was a companion at Hatville with no one to accompany? During her absence what would I do? *What would I be?*

In the end I was left to my own devices entirely. The Vennaways, to my relief and astonishment, were not actively cruel. I learned later that Aurelia had threatened *never* to return unless she was assured that I would be waiting for her, safe and well. Instead they ignored and avoided me.

Aurelia's departure seemed to have roused her father from the stupor that had held him since her diagnosis and he once again attended to his affairs. Mr Henley, the tutor, was released. He secured employment in a school in Edinburgh.

The rest of the household was, as ever, fully occupied with their own ample workloads. No one checked up on me to see whether I was dressing, studying, eating . . . I went several weeks unsure of whether I actually existed. I passed whole days without speaking and felt so wretched, purposeless and alone that I wanted to scream. In fact, I was very silent.

Without Aurelia's animating presence, the house felt like a mausoleum. I could no longer hold at bay my fears about her death. This was, I realized, only a foretaste of the time when she would be gone for ever. How would my heart survive without her? And what would become of me when I was banished from Hatville?

For a short time I prayed constantly for her health. Nothing would change the eventual outcome, I knew. Even so, I pleaded with God that I need not confront it *yet*.

Desperate for company, I sought out anyone I could. On the occasions that Dr Jacobs attended Lady Vennaway, I hovered on the staircase like a silent sprite, hoping to catch him yet too afraid to frame the question I wanted to ask. Despite my shyness, he seemed to understand.

'Never fear, child,' he would say, 'she has time enough yet. Maybe two years, perhaps even longer . . . unless she is very unlucky.' Once, he sat beside me on the top stair and talked to me of valves and ventricles.

I went on like this for a month, maybe more. And then, despite my belief that without Aurelia my life had no meaning, my wild fears quieted. Every night the darkness looked likely to go on for ever, yet every morning it lifted. Every day I grew a day older. Not only was I alive but so was she. When I realized that a month had passed, and that in only two more she would be back, my spirits lifted a little. I was a young woman now, I told myself; the time would pass more rapidly if, instead of feeling sorry for myself, I put myself to some use. So I conscientiously put my fears aside to try to live a little, each day. I walked into the village often, and visited the workers in Aurelia's stead. I took food when Cook would permit it. I called once or twice on Mr Chorley in the vicarage and Mr Clay in the school, though I could not offer Aurelia's sparkling conversation.

At Hatville, I helped Cook with a few small things although, after my long absence from the kitchen, there was less need for me now than ever. So I would take myself off to the gardens and beg Robin to let me do some planting.

Though Robin rarely spoke, his was the presence I found most soothing. The young boy who had wheeled me around in a barrow had grown into a tall, bearded man of one-and-twenty but our friendship remained unchanged. A comfortable resonance existed in our silence – as if his spirits and mine occupied a similar domain.

One evening, as I dusted the dirt off my hands and stood up, he seemed to sense my reluctance to return to the house.

''Tis not the same without her,' he said unexpectedly. 'There's none like her.' I felt a rush of gratitude for his understanding.

In my remaining hours I read, studied and played the piano. I wrote to Aurelia and told her all the news of home, trusting that she would still find interest in such things. And every day I received a letter from her. Whereas at first I only appreciated them because they signalled she was alive, I came to enjoy them for their own sake. Her writing style was just like her: warm, irreverent and funny. By now she was in Twickenham, staying with Mrs Bolton's cousin, a Mrs Constance Wister. Aurelia professed herself enchanted with the effusively furnished home and great proliferation of children.

My dear, you should <u>see</u> Mulberry Lodge! It could not be more different from Hatville if I had scoured the earth for its opposite. Constance delights in all things modern and has filled her home with statuary and wallpapers (sometimes in quite astonishing colours!) and furniture that is jewelled and studded and striped! She is a lovely, warm-hearted woman, Amy, whom you would like very much. I do so wish you could meet her. Perhaps one day you will. She has a husband every bit as affable as she, two parrots, a splendid dog and approximately three hundred children . . .

And so the days passed. The elements of life were the same, just repositioned, and lacking the centrepiece.

Chapter Eighteen

My second day in London. I have picked up a pestilent head cold. My throat rasps, my eyes sting and my head buzzes like a nest of wasps. I stay curled up in bed, fully dressed, trying to control my shivering.

I have existed in this world without her for a little less than a week. It is an incomprehensible grief, now joined by frustration and dejection. What a merry little trio they make. There is no Entwhistle's! This unwelcome fact will insist on advertising itself though I should dearly love to forget it, even for a moment.

I try to tell myself that all is not lost, but all I want is to hide away, nursing my heartache until I feel stronger. I cannot face another day of tramping London's grimy, winding dead-ends now I know there is no Entwhistle's to be found. I have failed Aurelia at the first hurdle.

If not for the treasure hunt, I might spend my days consulting newspaper notices and writing off for employment. I try to persuade myself I should give up the quest and secure some position as a governess or companion. Of course I will not.

I almost despise myself for my dogged devotion. Did Aurelia not think about the position she has put me in? Did she really believe that travel, secrecy and impossible challenges would be in *my* best interests at this time? Once again I am caught between worlds because of Aurelia's wishes.

I recall that intense, painful conversation, the night before she went away. I was so shocked when she said she had made a misfit of me. But it was true, I consider. Even as I think it I can see her dear lovely face streaked with tears and hear her words: '. . . that you are my greatest friend is the very happiest of outcomes. But even that is poisoned . . . I should set you free . . .'

'But I'm *still* not free, Aurelia,' I croak, then swallow painfully. I feel guilty when I remember how grateful I was to receive that first letter in the kitchen garden at Hatville. What a lifeline it seemed. How quickly that gratitude has been dimmed by misgiving. Of course I did not know then what she had in store for me.

I remember again the strong-minded little girl I used to be. When I was very small, it was a pure joy to do everything Aurelia wanted. But as I grew older, life was always too *complicated* for joy. Did I decide, somewhere along the years, that it would be easier to make Aurelia happy than to be happy myself? If I did, can I really blame Aurelia for doing likewise? And now I am suspended in this impossible quest.

I curse Mr Entwhistle with all my heart. Has he died too? Gone out of business? Whatever was Aurelia thinking, laying my path upon such crumbling foundations? Surely if she knew anything, it should have been that life is precarious, even for the youngest and brightest. Who *is* Mr Entwhistle, for heaven's sake?

Shutting my eyes, I tell myself I have done my best. I have travelled all the way to London. Yesterday I walked and walked and searched and searched and my trail has turned up no continuance. There is no Entwhistle's. What more can I do?

I tell myself I am exhausted, that all will seem better tomorrow, but I do not believe myself. It occurs to me that I am – no, I will not think it. Yet the feeling persists and I mouth the words silently, both to save my throat and because they are so shocking: '*I am angry with Aurelia.*'

I curl into a ball on my side, turning my back on the quest and the letters and Aurelia's great secret. I do not care any more.

I open my eyes and sit up so quickly my head spins. *Of course I care.* There can be no peace for me now until I have learned whatever it is she wanted me to know. I curse Aurelia too, then feel terrible and apologize. She remains maddeningly silent.

Miserable, I climb from my bed and make my way along the hall, swaying. I beg a hot toddy of Mrs Woodrow for my cold. She is sympathetic and brings one to my room. Most people make them with brandy, she tuts, swearing rum is more medicinal.

Sitting up in bed, I sip and read Aurelia's letter for the hundredth time.

> Cast your thoughts around the book we discussed at length that summer's evening after Mr Howden came to dine. Consider the variables . . .

The memory of Mr Howden coaxes a wry smile. A tedious man, insipid and patronizing. He was a sometime guest of the senior Vennaways, one of the several they assessed for suitability as a future husband for Aurelia over the years. I only ever saw him once – in those days I was still not permitted to dine with Aurelia.

Heavens, I think, if Aurelia depends on such distant memories, the thread is a fragile one indeed.

He was a gentleman, which meant of course that he had no useful employment whatsoever, but still insisted on referring to himself as a 'man of science'. Aurelia told him that she would very much like to study science – an effective and frequently employed way to put off men she found unattractive. Mr Howden, apparently, took it as evidence of her willingness to try to please. Ha!

So he gave her an impromptu tutorial there at the table while his host and hostess looked on with bated breath, hoping that here at last was a man willing to humour their strange daughter. Ha!

Once their dinner was over, Aurelia came straight to the kitchen and re-enacted, at great length, the whole of his discourse. His favourite phrase, 'consider the variables', was liberally peppered throughout. By the time she finished I was doubled over with giggles, of no further use to Cook, who shooed us from the kitchen into the hall just as Mr Howden was leaving. Jesketh, ushering him out, gave an unholy frown when he saw me. Mr Howden appeared not to notice me whatsoever, but he seized Aurelia's hands and bowed low.

I gleefully took in the thin red nose, the flattened brown hair and the nervous tremble that Aurelia had described only moments earlier. The thought of flowing-haired, cupid-lipped Aurelia with such a fool was ridiculous.

Mr Howden, however, seemed to think he and Aurelia had a fine understanding. 'Remember, my dear, consider the variables,' he whispered loudly as Jesketh pushed him through the door, then he *winked* at Aurelia!

We could not contain ourselves. We burst into fresh laughter and, I'm ashamed to say, ran away from poor Jesketh, who was attempting to propel me back to the kitchen. Instead, we ran to Aurelia's room (by this time I had grown accustomed to being discovered there and swept out like a stray cat), and together read the last, longed-for chapter of *The Old Curiosity Shop* and cried.

The gist of Mr Howden's treaty, as I remember it, was that in science, everything was very logical and very linear. Causes could be traced backwards and effects could be predicted forwards and the only thing that made the discipline appear so tangled and confusing to the uneducated mind was the mass of variables that were at work in any given experiment. To explain this simple argument, he had elaborated many times over, using very short words, in considerate deference to Aurelia's ill-equipped, feminine brain.

I considered the variables now as best I could through my own ill-equipped, congested brain. I had assumed that because Aurelia told me to find a bookshop called Entwhistle's I would find one. Perhaps this was a premature assumption. Perhaps all assumptions are premature when it comes to Aurelia.

If it is not called Entwhistle's, then what might it be called? Was I to work my way through the entirety of Mr Manning's directory, visiting bookshop after bookshop and scouring each in turn, floor to ceiling, for a hidden letter? Or perhaps Entwhistle's was not a bookshop at all! I could imagine my enquiries now:

'Where might I find Entwhistle's, if you please?'

'What is Entwhistle's?'

'I do not know.'

'A shop, a solicitor, a bank, perhaps?'

'I do not know.'

'A tavern, a tailor, a hot chestnut vendor?'

'I have not the slightest idea.'

Impossible! Utterly impossible.

What of the other variables . . . the city? Is there a bookshop called Entwhistle's somewhere else? The prospect of expanding my search to the entire British Isles does not cheer me. What if the clue is a trick? Is there some secret code embedded in her words? Years ago, whenever she wrote my clues in code, she would always draw a little shovel in the corner of the page, to symbolize that I would need to dig deep. There is no shovel on this letter.

It is not in code, it's just maddening. I shall be stuck here in Jessop Walk until my small fortune is spent and my sanity gone.

I screw the paper into a ball and hurl it across the room. It bounces off the wall to rest beneath the smug shepherdess. My poor, buzzing brain is quite exhausted by these fruitless cycles of anger and remorse and renewed dedication. I should quite like to stay angry and have done with it. If only loving someone were that simple.

I hobble from bed once more to beg myself a second rum toddy.

Chapter Nineteen

Aurelia stayed true to her promise and sent me regular letters, which I devoured at once and re-read often. They contained little souvenirs and sketches – trifles to bring her travels alive for me, nothing so valuable as to provoke the risk of confiscation.

June. The horse chestnut trees were thick and spreading and the smooth lawns hummed with bees. Those were days of blue and gold and blazing flowers; days in which I believed that my ordeal was nearing an end. Beside myself with happiness, I counted down the final days of Aurelia's journey and planned her welcome home.

Letters came, to me and to her parents respectively, explaining that she was extending her trip.

London and Twickenham had been delightful, but now she had been invited to Derby! Derby was a fascinating town by all accounts – she simply must accept and see the famed countryside while she was there. She would return in August, not in June as planned. Disappointment struck me like lightning.

I felt disorientated. I wanted to trust that this delay would be a singular occurrence, but I did not.

She warned me that Derby would mean a break in our correspondence:

The journey will be a long one, little dove, and there is a great deal to prepare: shopping and packing, endless goodbyes, etc. So it will likely be a few days before I can put nib to paper to write to you (or, indeed, draw a breath!). Please do not be alarmed at this delay. I look forward to embracing you and hearing every detail of your summer when I come home in August.

When the anxiously awaited letter came, three weeks later, it was full of apologies and exclamation marks. Already it did not sound like Aurelia. Flamboyant she had always been, and vain and excitable. But now all she seemed to write about was the social whirl of Derby – of balls and walking parties and handsome young men. In short, she sounded like the daughter the Vennaways had always longed for.

Amy dearest, Meyrick Flintham told me that I was the greatest beauty in the kingdom! (His is an educated opinion. If the rumours are to be believed, he has made conquests of half of them.) Of course, I am not to be won with a few pretty words. I merely tossed my head and spun off on the arm of David Gresham, who has forty thousand a year.

I continued my new existence with an ever-waning spirit. Her letters grew fewer and farther between.

August. Endless scorching sun and the stream dried up to a snake-skin of stony earth. Only two events of note.

The first was the kitchen maid Dora's wedding. Lord and Lady Vennaway did not attend. The rest of us crowded into the little church to perspire our way through the vows. The hymns met no competition from the birds outside – likely holding feeble wings to their little feathered brows and languishing in shady nests.

Thus Dora left us for ever. She was sharp-tongued and impatient but her husband gazed at her with an adoration and pride that were evident to all. I confess to a moment of envy, wondering what it was about her that had brought about this circumstance while I had no one – *no one* – of my own.

The second event was another postponement from Aurelia. From Derby she wrote of an opportunity to see the industrial North, the wonder of factories and cotton mills – progress made manifest in bricks and iron! We should expect her in time for Christmas. I could not help myself. That letter went straight on the fire.

September. Mist swirled over the lawns in the mornings and I recalled Aurelia teaching me to dance in the ballroom when

I was small. I had no one to laugh with me now and, despite my anger, I missed her. Rain began to spot the windows.

In Dora's absence, Cook began depending upon me as an unofficial, unpaid kitchen maid. She thought it best to hide the fact from her employer – Lady Vennaway was in favour of nothing that might help me feel more at home. We had several nerve-jangling almost-encounters that resulted in me being bundled out of the side door or, on one memorable occasion, being tucked into the pantry alongside the jugs of milk.

It was not a comfortable experience (I refer to working in the kitchen, not hiding in the pantry). My close friendship with the young mistress, my spacious bedroom next to hers and my education made the other indoor staff, as ever, suspicious of me. Aside from Cook, Jesketh and Rosy, there was no one who had worked inside the house when I was a child and knew how my life had unfolded. But at least there were people around me every day and I slept better for having regular occupation.

Aurelia's letters were irregular and few. Worse, they somehow always missed the mark.

Amy, I knew you would manage <u>perfectly</u> well without me, you see! How busy you all sound there. Marvellous. You are good to keep writing to me so devotedly. As for me, the whirl continues, my dear! This afternoon I shall go riding with a young Italian count with an enormous moustache . . .

Perhaps my yearning for her friendship – my *raison d'etre* – made it impossible for any letter now to satisfy. It had become clear that she no longer longed for my letters as I did for hers. Her words were distracted; I could not imagine her watching for the post, snatching up an envelope and poring over the contents.

Sometimes she asked after someone in Enderby when I had just, two weeks earlier, told her all about them. It was apparent she had not read my words properly. Local news was exceeding small, and I felt duller than ever; my letters must have seemed so dreary.

She did exhort me to keep up my studies; she set me targets, recommended books or poems we might discuss on her return. But during those months it was hard to believe she would *ever* return. She had hurt me and it was my small rebellion to cast aside the interests we had always shared.

I did, however, learn to make soups, roast game and roll a tolerable pastry.

Christmas: rain and sleet. No gifts, no friends and no idea of when Aurelia might come home. Cold nights shivering with moonlight and bitter questions. *How* could she discard me like this, and with so little reassurance? Her treatment was especially painful given that I had famously been abandoned once before. I remembered her words, the last time we had talked: 'Sometimes, the people you love are *bad*.'

My long-cherished image of Aurelia as the bright angel who had saved me from the snow and who would always love me shivered and faded like a rainbow. I had earnestly tried to understand her need to escape for a time. I had worked conscientiously to accept that different things mattered to us. But I found myself wondering if she had ever given half so much thought to understanding me.

January dragged round. Aurelia was in Bath, where, apparently, she was deeply fascinated by a certain Frederic Meredith. It was months since there had been talk of her return.

Chapter Twenty

Rain. Pounding, drumming rain batters the city mercilessly as if trying to rinse the answer from my head.

I enjoyed an unexpectedly pleasant sleep after three toddies and it is now my third day in London. Inspiration for how to continue my quest is still entirely lacking. The frustration at being trapped inside, spending my money and achieving nothing, is gargantuan.

My cold is somewhat better today, whether from the rest or Mrs Woodrow's medicinal rum I cannot say. As a result I am pacing up and down, worrying away at the problem. I consider the possibility of solving Aurelia's mystery from an entirely different angle. If I admit defeat and abandon Entwhistle's, surely there are other ways? There may be others in whom she confided. Frederic Meredith perhaps?

Back in those dark wintry days of my adolescence, the name Frederic Meredith came to fill me with dread. Aurelia stopped mentioning other men around the time she met him. She wrote of him in the most glowing terms; they filled me with disgust.

'His fine, gentlemanly features', 'his commanding figure', 'his quick intelligence and keen sensibilities' all made me wish that Frederic Meredith might be dispatched with all possible haste. She described such a paragon of manhood that he might have stepped straight from the pages of a novel. I wished she might rediscover her own once-keen sensibilities and remember the foundling child she had promised to keep always at her side.

I have long presumed a love affair between them, although she dismissed it afterwards and seemed surprisingly uninterested in discussing him, given that she had written of little else for months. I wondered if perhaps he had let her down, unimaginable though that was. Either way, *I* harboured no wish to hear more of him.

Now I wonder if an affair *is* the secret, though why she would go to quite such pains to disguise the fact now that she is gone I cannot imagine. But if it *is* so, why not go straight to the heart of the matter? I could go to Bath, make enquiries, find Mr Meredith and . . . my wild plans falter. What if I am wrong? What if the secret must be kept from him too?

For the first time in the four days since I received Aurelia's first letter I have leisure to ponder what the great secret might be. I confess I am wild with curiosity. Did she leave a sum of money to a charity of which her parents would not approve, one of Mr Dickens's reform houses for ladies of easy virtue perhaps? Might she have disgraced herself in polite society, offended some leading lights, spoken indiscreetly of her family . . . These are all weak and utterly implausible explanations.

I think of Mrs Bolton. She visited Aurelia once or twice after their great journey together, then went travelling in Europe as intended and never came back. Her modest house in Enderby was closed up. From time to time Aurelia received a letter from France or Italy or Portugal, but if they contained any exciting news she never told me.

'Mrs Bolton asks after you, dear,' she would say fondly, looking up from the page. Or, 'Mrs Bolton requests me to pass on her warmest wishes to you.'

Mrs Bolton and I enjoyed a more cordial acquaintance from separate continents than ever we did when we lived in the same village.

What if Mrs Bolton is also to be kept in the dark? Aurelia's fervent, some might say excessive, insistence on silence ties my hands and hobbles my steps. The only way I can be sure of *not* betraying her is to follow her instructions to the letter. Letter by letter. But there is no Entwhistle's . . . Lord, what a wretched state of affairs.

I lie on my bed and try to read a bit of *The Pickwick Papers* but I cannot concentrate. I keep fretting at the puzzle, I keep sinking back into the past.

'*So* much secrecy, Aurelia?' I demand aloud, 'Need there really be *quite* so much difficulty?'

After all, whatever she has done, they cannot harm her now. And surely they would not pursue *me* now, simply for the joy of thwarting me?

Yet a memory surfaces. I was seven or eight perhaps. Aurelia was gone for the day, visiting cousins. When she returned, they would come too, with assorted aunts, uncles and infants in tow. There was a great deal to be done to prepare the house.

One of the housemaids was sick and Cook made the grave misjudgement of letting me help in her place. We thought Lady Vennaway was taking morning calls, as was usual on a Wednesday, so Mrs Last set me to dusting and polishing the dining room. But the mistress had no callers that day, and took it upon herself to prowl the rooms checking for shoddy work.

I had worked hard and felt proud of the result. The furniture gleamed and the mirrors sparkled.

Oh, the mirrors. Thinking myself alone, I had taken the rare opportunity to look at myself. There was of course no such thing in the kitchen or scullery or stables, and my appearance was often commented upon, so I was naturally curious.

Dora had told me I was very plain indeed, a nasty-looking little thing. Rosy told her not to be unkind, it wasn't my fault. I had asked Cook if this were true and she flapped a hand in exasperation and told me to stir the preserves. Then I asked Jesketh and he said handsome is as handsome does. Robin said

I'd do. Aurelia said I was adorable. Everyone commented on my small size.

So Lady Vennaway caught me in a private and highly uncharacteristic moment of self-appraisal. This is what I saw:

A face shaped like a teardrop with pale skin and curtains of dusky hair. A thick fringe hanging into my eyes, parting a little in the centre to reveal a small frown between my eyebrows, though I was not aware of frowning. A wide mouth. Big eyes in a strange shade.

I sighed. I was very small, yes. My hair was too sooty, too heavy. My smile was too rare, and then too wide and lopsided when it came. I experimented now; the result was a grimace. Fit to scare the chickens, as Dora used to say.

I heard a shriek and the mistress appeared in the glass beside me like the wicked queen in the story books. The unguarded intimacy with myself made me jump all the more. Of course, her lovely mouth opened and the horrible words came pouring out and I was suddenly sick of it all.

'I've done my work!' I cried in fury, stamping my foot. 'I've made it beautiful. I did it to help! Dolly's in bed and if it weren't for me there would be dust in your sausages.'

As if in a dream, I watched her long arm reach out and grab my hair, all of it, in one thick tress. By this rope she dragged me – to the kitchen, naturally, where Cook was dressing a pheasant. She looked up in shock as Lady Vennaway picked up a cleaver from the table.

With the deftest of movements, the mistress twisted my hair swiftly into a coil and sliced it all off at the neck. It took one clean cut.

'Vanity is a sin,' she shrieked, 'and particularly laughable in *you*.' Then she left.

Alone, Cook and I looked at each other. I could not explain. My hair lay on the floor, lengths and lengths of it, it seemed. I picked it up. There seemed to be even more of it than when it had been attached. I could feel the new short ends flying up around my face.

'The dining room is clean,' I said at last and took my hair out to throw on the rubbish heap.

I subsequently learned from novels and periodicals that every third orphan has her hair severed at some point. However, this in no way diminished the feeling of invasion and personal grief that I felt at the time. Nonetheless, in the longer term Lady Vennaway unwittingly did me a favour. Long, my hair refused to sit in any style and resisted every attempt at constraint. Short, it curled comfortably around the edges of a cap and saved me hours of brushing each week. Long, it had been good for nothing except tormenting Aurelia.

I smile as I remember Aurelia pretending fury every time we compared the length of our hair. No matter how she brushed or treated hers, mine was always longer. Even though my dull, sooty lengths were clearly no match for her bright, silky waves, she made a great display of being envious.

She devised a game whereby we would lean over the fence beside the stream and dangle our heads over the water, to see whose hair could touch its surface. It was an absurdity, of course, because it was not a measure of hair length at all – Aurelia always won simply because she was taller. But it made us laugh every time.

Inevitably, the first time, I fell in. I was so determined my hair should touch the stream that I tilted right over, feet in the air. I lost my grip and in I went. I was unharmed but wet, muddy and fearful of Dora's ridicule.

After my hair was cut off, we went back to racing twigs instead.

Now, in London, I sit and think that perhaps I am not safe from the Vennaways after all. Perhaps a woman who could treat a child the way she treated me is a woman ever to be feared. Perhaps it is just as well that I am far away, a small, anonymous figure in a great, teeming city. It must be the best place in the world to get lost.

Something about my reminiscing has unsettled me; I feel restless. I want to walk in the hammering rain and breathe the cold, wet air. What is it that tugs at my thoughts? It is not the cutting of my hair.

Something else.

Aurelia and I playing at the stream. Missing her. Racing twigs. Dangling over the fence. Shrieks of laughter filling the air. Missing her. Falling in and the smell of mud. Aurelia in tears of mirth at the sight of my sorry, blackened figure. Missing her. Aurelia cheering me up by telling me a new story as we trudged back to the house. It was about two rabbits called Entwhistle and Crumm who opened a tailor's shop in Hampstead. I adored that story, which ran to several instalments over a number of days.

Entwhistle wore a red waistcoat and Crumm wore a blue . . .

And all of a sudden it hits me like a blow to the head. The tide of memory has carried me, as surely as a twig on a current, to my answer.

Chapter Twenty-one

In the event, a full twelve months had passed before we saw Aurelia again. It was the following March before she returned to us, with spring winds in her hair and daffodils waving a greeting.

I was in the schoolroom – I cannot now recall why – lost in the sort of sad trance that had become my accustomed state of mind. Roused by a rattle of carriage wheels, I glanced through the window without much interest, presuming it to be one of Lady Vennaway's callers. But something about the scene made my heart catch.

The carriage cut a fair dash along the gravel; stones flew up about it like droplets in a fountain and caught the pale sunshine. It rounded the chase at speed, leaning daringly to one side. Even the horses seemed to canter with a rakish air, as if their only pleasure was in showing off their strong legs and tall feathers, and pulling a carriage mattered not a whit. Thus I had a strong suspicion about who was inside it, even before it came close enough for me to recognize Mrs Bolton's navy and silver phaeton.

I ran.

When Aurelia emerged from the carriage, Lady Vennaway caught her in the longest, tightest embrace I have ever seen. She wept and wept, and kissed her and wept, then refused to speak to her for a month. Lord Vennaway was his usual self, forbidding and taciturn, yet there was no mistaking the emotion in his gaze when he enfolded her, briefly, in his arms.

I felt a rush of love, immense joy and relief. Fear, of course, that I had lost the girl I had known so well. She looked impossibly glamorous and foreign to my sheltered eyes. Although one-and-twenty when she left, to me she had still been my girlhood friend. She returned undeniably a woman, composed and set apart – from all of us. I recognized none of the clothes she wore, nor the stylish parasol, nor the outlandish emerald-green gloves.

I quaked; what could a poor, stay-at-home child have to say that might interest such a creature as this? Sufficient and more, it transpired. Her poised, distant face broke into its familiar bright smile the moment she saw me. With a joyous laugh, she picked me up and whirled me round in the old way, then set me down for inspection.

Aurelia was equally struck by the change in me – a change I had not until then considered. I was past fourteen when she returned, a young woman myself. That long, lonely year had taken its toll. Little wonder I looked different – taller, thinner, older. I had grown up, and lost my childhood innocence. I no longer thought Aurelia perfect but, I discovered in a rush of joy, I loved her no less for that.

The weeks that followed were glorious! Our friendship was restored – her affection so tangible, so evident in her face and voice that I started to wonder why I had ever doubted it. Days of walking, talking, laughing with Aurelia, hanging onto every word she said. At last she sat before me again, and I told her fully and honestly my own small happenings, my fears and concerns. I had never spoken to her thus before, and my new candour seemed to bring us closer than ever. We talked at such length and in such depth that it never occurred to me to doubt that she was telling me everything.

And so began the final phase of my life with Aurelia: once again constant companions, both of us tempered in different ways by her absence.

Aurelia seemed to have found whatever it was that she had been seeking and appeared more settled at Hatville than ever before. I expected she would reminisce about the friends and places she had fought so hard to visit, but after the first excited flourish of stories, they drifted away like a dream.

Once or twice a letter arrived for her, addressed in unfamiliar handwriting. These, she spirited away and I never learned who had sent them. I assumed a continued correspondence with Frederic Meredith, but when I told her I'd been afraid she would marry him and forget me, she laughed heartily until coughing took over.

Her health deteriorated rapidly after just a month at home. Where previously it had been hard to believe that Aurelia was ill, now it was impossible to forget the fact. Once so robust and lively, she grew weak and pale. She had staved off her decline for a long while, but when it came it was dramatic.

A wheeled chair was brought to Hatville and if she wished to see the rose garden or the stream, I would push her there. On a good day she could walk slowly, leaning hard on a cane. On a bad day – and they were frequent – she could not get out of bed. The Vennaways could not have married her off now if they'd still wanted to. It seemed that she had returned just in time to say goodbye, yet she clung onto life tenaciously and weeks turned into months, which turned into improbable years. In her refusal to succumb to probability, at least, she was quite unchanged.

Despite the heartbreak of watching her struggle, I was not unhappy. Strangely, it was the most peaceful time I can remember.

One sad change at Hatville was the departure of Robin, who had been offered a position as head gardener at the estate of an eminent Gloucestershire family. I admit I was shocked to see him go. It was not that I had underestimated his skill, it was simply that I had never considered it. He was so modest and quiet that I would never have noticed his talent with agapanthus, nor realized that Hatville was famed for its fruit yields, if his new appointment had not brought the matter to our attention.

'He has a way with living things,' Aurelia said quietly. I could understand her sadness. Plants burst to life beneath his fingers, but she was fading away.

Since her return, there was a new, more reflective quality about her. We spent less time playing and laughing, and more time strolling, when she was able, pondering the ways our pasts had shaped us. We sang and read aloud less but talked more deeply and sat in silence more. She was now less sparkle than gleam, less fire than deep, silent, shining water.

As for me, I had managed to endure the year apart armed with nothing but faith and my own strength. This knowledge gave me something I had not possessed before. I could not put a name to it but I felt it living within me nonetheless.

We both knew these days were gifts, given to us to enjoy to the best of our abilities and to use as wisely as we might.

We were granted nearly three beautiful years.

Chapter Twenty-two

Mr Manning the stationer's face falls when he looks up and sees my dripping figure framed in his doorway. Professional courtesy visibly wrestles with dismay.

'You are back,' he observes.

'Good day, Mr Manning, I hope you are well. I wonder if I could possibly trouble you for one final glance at your directory?'

'I doubt any new names have appeared on it overnight, miss. We do not have brownies here who scribe away by moonlight.'

'I am certain you do not, sir, but I wish to look for something else if it's not too much trouble.'

He shrugs and stretches his neck in one direction and then the other before handing the directory to me.

'Gloomy day,' he mutters.

'Extremely gloomy,' I agree, unable to stop smiling. I leaf eagerly to the letter C. And there it is.

Crumm & Co. Waistcoat Lane. Next to the crooked courtyard behind St Angelus. Holborn.

The address erases any trace of doubt. Waistcoat Lane! No wonder Aurelia thought of our childhood story. I offer up a swift prayer that her future clues will not require quite such a lengthy and tangled trawl through my past.

I read the directions again and dash from the shop, throwing thanks over my shoulder as I go. My cab is waiting and there is a furious hurtle to Holborn, during which all my resentment towards Aurelia's quest is forgotten. I can hardly breathe for anticipation.

'Want me to wait again, miss?' asks the driver when we pull to a splashing halt outside St Angelus.

I pay and send him away. After the delays and stagnation of the last days I shall not be leaving Mr Crumm's establishment until I find the letter. If I am locked in overnight, so be it.

Holborn is deserted. Indeed, all of London is subdued on such a drudge of a day. My skirts drag with the weight of the water. The hammering torrents may very well have dented my bonnet. I do not care. Soon I will hear more from Aurelia.

There is the courtyard, crooked to be sure, shaped like a crumpled handkerchief. Beside it a narrow lane – I half expect to see two sartorial bunnies bounding ahead to show me the way. And here is the shop, painted burgundy, with a bulging mullioned window and the words Crumm & Co neatly painted in gold, above.

As I pause on the threshold, quivering with anticipation, the door flies open with a friendly jingling of bells and a tall gentleman in a vast overcoat nearly trips over me.

'Pardon me, miss,' he says in mannerly tones, and holds the door for me before going on his way.

A pleasantly lit interior greets me, thanks to candles and gas lamps both. It is welcome brightness on such a dark day.

'Good day, madam.' A contented-looking man of perhaps sixty looks up from a ledger and smiles. 'May I assist you with anything?'

'Good day, sir. I shall look around, thank you.'

'Indeed, indeed.'

Go to the natural history section . . . Cast your thoughts around the book we discussed at length . . .

I step a little further into the shop. I decide I will most certainly *not* go to the natural history section. Now that I understand the tone of Aurelia's clue, I believe this is another device to confound anyone but me. For although Mr Howden had talked of a great many books that night, desirous to show off his erudition, the book that *we* – Aurelia and I – shared was, of course, *The Old Curiosity Shop*.

'In fact, sir, excuse me, could you direct me to the works of Mr Dickens?'

He emerges from behind his desk and shows me the relevant

shelves. Then he appears to startle and look at me more closely, though he collects himself quickly.

'Why! I wonder . . .' he exclaims, then stops. 'I wonder if there is anything else I might help you with, Miss . . . ?'

'Nothing else, thank you.'

But he is looking at me so carefully. Perhaps it is just the sight I present, bedraggled and pale, oozing rainwater. Perhaps it is the fact that I am in mourning – or unchaperoned. Whatever the reason, he has a pleasing, low voice and the sort of presence that prohibits offence.

'I wonder, miss, if you have noticed our collection of early numbers over there? We are not a library, but I am a great devotee of the contemporary writers so I keep a copy of everything by Mr Dickens and two or three others. Periodicals and bound books alike are stored in this glass case. They are not for sale but I shall leave the key in the door in case you wish to peruse.'

He returns to his desk and leaves me in peace. I frown – more than usual. There was something odd about the whole interaction.

I find *The Old Curiosity Shop* on the bookshelves. I remove my wet gloves and rapidly feel around it – tops and undersides of the shelf. I know the letter will not be in a book, for the books are there to be sold. Nothing.

I feel behind the shelf, to see if it slides forward, to see if anything could be hidden there. Nothing.

I am already half certain of the outcome when I move to the glass case. I glance at Mr Crumm but he remains engrossed in his ledger. I unlock the case and find the long line of editions of *Master Humphrey's Clock*, the magazine I remember so well from childhood. Here are the copies containing the closing chapters of Little Nell's sad story and here is the very last, on the end of a shelf, against the wall.

I carefully remove the magazine, turn it over in my hands; nothing slides out. I riffle gently through the pages and find a place where two or three are stuck together lightly, perhaps a little binder's glue gone astray. Or perhaps not.

I slide a finger between the pages and it falls open exactly where I expected – the tragedy of a heroine who dies too young.

Between the pages lies a plain white envelope inscribed with just two initials: 'AS'.

Chapter Twenty-three

Hands shaking, I unfasten my cloak, sink the letter into my dress pocket beside its predecessor and wrap myself up again. I restore the magazine, lock the cabinet and pause a moment to marvel. Here, in this city so far from Hatville, in an out-of-the-way alley, in a neighbourhood I never before visited in my life, waits a letter to me from my friend. I feel as though I have strayed into a novel myself.

I am in a fever to read the letter, yet I do not want to do so in a public place. Nor do I wish to return to the room where I have been so recently confined. Also, I wonder if there might be further answers in this shop that Aurelia's letter cannot supply. Did this gentleman know her? He seems to know *me*.

I drift back to the books for sale and decide to purchase *Oliver Twist*. It was hard to leave Oliver behind at Hatville. The bookseller inspects my choice with interest.

'A fine novel. Strange to say, I had imagined you would choose something else . . . *The Old Curiosity Shop* perhaps?'

I have not imagined it. He knows something. 'That is my favourite, sir, but I already have it.'

'I see. Then have you found *everything* you need today?'

'I have indeed. Thank you, Mr Crumm, is it?'

'Albert Crumm at your service, Miss . . . ?'

'I am Amy Snow.'

'Of course you are, my dear, of course you are. Oh!' He emerges from behind his desk again and clasps my hand in a hearty shake. 'I am so very glad to meet you at last, although . . . I suppose this means that Miss Vennaway is no longer with us.'

'I am sorry to tell you that she died, sir, but a week since. She was a friend of yours?'

'I am honoured to have made her most cordial acquaintance, yes. And through her, I feel I know a little of you, Miss Snow, if that is not a presumption. My sincerest condolences.'

'Thank you. Can you tell me, Mr Crumm – I find myself in a wonder – how she has managed this . . . this . . . ?'

'Miss Snow, do you agree that this is no conversation for business hours? I realize I am a stranger, but would it be very awkward if I were to invite you to dine at my home this evening? My daughter Kate will be there, and her young sprig of a son, Henry. We should be very glad to have you.'

I am sure some etiquette prohibits it, but loneliness compels more powerfully than convention. I can hardly contain myself for happiness, and fear I might cry in front of this most sympathetic of gentlemen.

'I should be delighted, Mr Crumm. I have no friends in the city, and to meet someone who knew Aurelia . . . well, I cannot thank you enough.'

He will close the shop in an hour, he tells me, and asks if I would care to wait in his office. 'Perhaps you might pass the time reading your new acquisition.' He smiles. 'I am sure you are impatient to do so.'

I am lost for words as he drags an armchair over to a lack-lustre fire, which he stokes briskly to a blaze. He takes my bonnet and cloak and asks me to watch the shop for a moment so that he can run next door and buy coffee for us both. Within moments all my needs are catered for; I have my letter and solitude to read it. I am drying out by a fire so hot it makes me shiver and I have a steaming drink to sip. I have the prospect of company this evening and, yes, privacy to weep a little as the tensions and discomfort of the last few days fall away.

I draw the letter from my pocket. It is smooth and clean compared with the first letter, now so considerably perused and toted about (not to mention entirely crumpled). I shift the chair back a little – with my luck, all I need is to drop the precious pages in the fire!

Yet I hesitate, and think with dread how close I came to giving up, losing the trail. What if this letter, too, is impossibly cryptic? What if I am to remain in London or go somewhere even worse? What if I am to go *abroad*? I swallow, and slip my finger under the flap. Knowing Aurelia as I do, or rather, realizing I do not know her half so well as I thought I did, I suspect history is about to rewrite itself, in flowing violet ink.

My treasured Amy,

You have done it! You have followed the trail and found your way to the next instruction. Congratulations, my little bird, you are quite as clever as I!

Did it take you long to find your way, dearest? How utterly, utterly frustrating that after plotting my most ingenious trail ever I can never discuss it with you, never hear what your adventures have been. I could cry, my dear, for rage at all that I will miss.

I am sorry if this first challenge has been difficult for you, Amy. London is not the easiest place and I know that you have not been situated to enjoy it, alone as you are. But it was essential that the hardest part came first. <u>Surely</u> no one else could have found this letter?

You are to go to the country next, little dove, and not so very far, merely to Twickenham, as I did before you. You will stay with my friends there. Dear people! Hush now. I know what you are thinking:

'But I do not know them! What if it is inconvenient? How can I appear on their doorstep and invite myself in, a total stranger?'

I lay down the paper and look around the room. That is exactly what I was thinking.

Be reassured, small sister, there is NOTHING about which you need fret. The idea that you should stay in their home was all theirs, not my suggestion at all. The instant you say your name you will be welcomed to the bosom, dearest, I promise.

I see I am nearly at the foot of the page and it seems an apposite moment to pause and ask you one very important favour, dearest. It may even be the <u>most</u> important thing you do for me in this whole adventure. Before you turn the page, promise you will do this one small thing for me . . .

'I promise, Aurelia,' I sigh. Of course she knew I would. I turn the page and am surprised to read:

Burn your clothes, dearest, I beseech you. No, I do not draw inspiration from the native peoples of hot climes. (Would that I were there! Any clime warmer than Surrey in February would suffice!) I do not suggest you go naked. The world, my dear, is not ready for that. But you know it has long affronted my affection for you to see you clad as you are. Your appearance will not be your priority because of your unnatural lack of vanity. You will say you are in mourning and let that be your excuse to wander the world in hideous blacks and greys indefinitely if I do not take decisive action!

Soon you will be indulged as I could not indulge you when we were together. Think how overjoyed I shall be when I squint down at you from my celestial chaise longue, where I am certainly consuming candied peel at a fair old rate, sipping champagne and reading the works of Mr Dickens (I am also attended by three or four extremely handsome swains, do not doubt it).

I do not.

There is another reason I hasten to address your sartorial identity. My dear, dressed as you are, you scream to the world, 'Unfortunate!' You are the poor relation, the humblest of companions, the merely tolerated. And so it was at Hatville. But no more. You would attract the wrong sort of attention dressed thus in the wider world. You must leave that identity behind.

So, once you reach Twickenham, you will be suitably furnished − <u>no</u> effort will be required of your good self. Please do not hang onto those old rags 'just in case'. I assure you earnestly there will never be <u>any</u> case in which you will need to dress thus ever again.

Finally, Amy, I don't know what I had imagined in my fantastic conjurings for my time in London but we were not so very wild after all. Mrs Bolton and I dined, we went to the theatre, we visited Mudie's and the London Library and the British Museum. In short, nothing that would not have shone the brighter for sharing it with you. I wish I had not left you behind.

I suppose I had nurtured a fond hope that I would do something shocking, you see − I was not thinking straight when I left. My parents . . .

But no, I cannot tell you at this delicate stage. 'Tis yet too soon. What if someone else should read this, not you? I cannot see how, but what if I have overlooked something? I must keep my secrets a little longer yet.

Forgive me, small sister, if I close here and leave you none the wiser. My comfort cannot be in unburdening myself just yet. My comfort must come instead from knowing that you will soon be safe in Twickenham. It makes me happy to imagine you there.

Do you miss me still? Selfish to the last, I hope so, and yet I hope that is not the whole of it for you. I want you to relish Twickenham, Amy. Be happy! Find hope!

With greatest love from your devoted
AV

I read the letter three times through, then sit quietly for a long while, staring into the crackling flames.

Chapter Twenty-four

Albert Crumm's house is but a short walk from the shop. The rain having eased to an uncommitted drizzle, we are glad of the fresh air.

His daughter Kate is as cheerful and altogether welcoming as I could have imagined. However, she has contracted the cold which I have also suffered so, after making my acquaintance, she begs to be excused and takes herself to bed with a weak broth. It offers the chance to talk alone with Albert before dinner. Henry the Sprig, he tells me, will be home for dinner as surely as a dog.

We settle in a dark drawing room. Central London accommodations, he apologizes, are not overly spacious and the house is old and sparing on windows. Albert rings for another coffee; he is a great addict, he confides cheerfully. I choose hot milk with nutmeg; I have trouble enough sleeping as it is.

'Please tell me about Aurelia,' I beg. 'I miss her so much and this trail of letters mystifies me entirely. When did you meet her? How well did you know her? Above all, when and how did she arrange for a letter to be hidden in your shop?'

'So much to tell you,' Albert nods, ordering his thoughts. 'But I must only talk until Henry comes. He's a very good boy but Miss Vennaway impressed upon me the need for absolute secrecy.'

'She has said the same to me. It is a relief to talk freely even for five minutes. I am ill-practised at concealment and I feel I am doing a very poor job of it.'

'You need an official story, Miss Snow. It would make your life easier. Now let me see. I first met Miss Vennaway in 1844, so that would be . . .'

'Almost four years ago . . .'

'Just so. We met at the theatre. Drury Lane. Terrible play, beautiful actress. I was with an acquaintance who just happened to be an acquaintance of Miss Vennaway's friend Mrs Bolton. We were introduced, and were of one mind about the play. The following week, another play – exquisitely crafted, appallingly acted. We exchanged words again. They invited me to join their party for a post-theatre supper. Your friend was a great lover of literature, of course, so we had much to talk about.

'Over the following month we met several times at various functions and struck up a friendship, new and fresh to be sure but like-minded and very warm. She honoured me with several confidences. I learned of her heart condition, of your unenviable position in her home and of the difficult relationship with her parents. She missed her dearest friend – you – sorely, and for that reason considered returning home early.'

'She did?'

'Indeed. But she dreaded seeing Lord and Lady V again. Miss Vennaway explained that they were excessive proud and cold. She told me too that she had been bullied, that was the word she used, into an unloving engagement prior to her departure. She said she could not return until she could forgive them. She left London in the April, I believe, and I have never seen her since.'

I frown. 'Did you say, sir, that she was *engaged* before her departure? They did place an enormous amount of pressure on her to marry and marry well, 'tis true, but no engagement was ever finalized. And when her weak heart was discovered, that was all over.'

'Do I have it wrong? No, I am quite, quite sure that is what she said.

'Then, perhaps three years ago, I received a letter from Aurelia, asking me if I would grant her the greatest of favours – she did not specify what – and promise absolute confidentiality. I wrote back at once and said yes. She was an extraordinary young woman and her story, naturally, affected me very much.

'She replied with effusive thanks – it was clear that this was, indeed, a matter of life and death for her – and enclosed the envelope you found this afternoon. She gave me minute instructions as to its placement and told me that you, Miss Snow, would be directed to it after her time. She said it was absolutely imperative that the letter never fall into the wrong hands and most especially that her parents never learn of its existence. I have been looking out for you ever since.'

The mention of an engagement still puzzles me but I can think about that later.

'Thank you, Mr Crumm, for your kindness and for all you have done. I still do not know Aurelia's reasons, but I know this meant everything to her, and so it does to me. I am so glad that we have met.'

'I too, my dear, I too. Ah, I hear the door. Is that young Henry?' he hollers suddenly.

'Aye, Grandpa. I'm hungry fit to eat the carpet!' comes a muffled voice from the hall.

I turn to meet young Henry, the sprig, the very good boy. I am expecting a slight and cheery lad of fourteen or so in a school cap. Imagine my surprise then when the doorframe is filled by a tall gentleman of well above six feet in height, with tumbling dark hair, matching eyes and a mischievous grin. Young Henry is quite grown up! Young Henry is . . . well, he is handsome. And due to his mother's indisposition, it will be just the three of us this evening. I feel a blush rising in my cheeks; this will be an unaccustomed dinner indeed for me.

'Henry, my lad!' Albert springs up to embrace him with a casual but loving ruffle, such as one might give a spaniel.

'Old one!' Henry cuffs him gently and slings an arm around his shoulder. 'Now where's my dinner? Give it to me at once!'

'You shan't have it! No dinner for sprigs tonight!'

'Then I shall go elsewhere immediately . . . Oh, hello! No I shan't. Who's this?'

'That'll teach you to bring some manners through the door with you. Henry, this is Miss Snow. She came to the shop today.'

'Grandpa, must I forever be telling you? You can't keep dragging the customers home! If they don't want to buy anything, that's their prerogative. You can't keep them imprisoned here until they relent and buy a Wilkie Collins! Miss Snow, forgive the old one; he is out of his mind, d'you see? I'll have you released upon a trice.'

I would love to respond to his jesting in kind, but in truth I cannot respond at all. I fear my admiration must be written all over my face and embarrassment robs me of the power of speech. I cannot look at him.

'I saw you this afternoon, did I not?' he continues. 'You were going into my grandfather's shop and I nearly mowed you down. I apologize again.'

I had not recognized him as the gentleman in the bookshop doorway. All I had seen then was a hat and a coat. I risk another quick glance at him, hoping he is less handsome at a second look. He is far handsomer. His smile could make my heart burst into flower – if it were not so dismayed. I have never entertained such surprising feelings towards Robin or Benjamin or any of the young villagers in Enderby. Given my own patent undesirability, I had flattered myself I was impervious to attraction. It seems that I am not.

'Idiot child!' Albert intervenes, and just as well, for I still cannot speak. 'I'm trying to tell you. We had a mutual friend who has passed away. I invited Miss Snow to dinner so that we might remember our friend together and grow better acquainted.'

At once the laughing face grows serious. I see compassion in his eyes. He comes over to shake hands. Mine feels very small and icy in his. 'Oh, Miss Snow, I am very sorry indeed for your loss. Welcome, and I am glad to meet you, though I wish the circumstances were otherwise. I see now it must be a recent loss.' He nods at my mourning black.

I find my voice at last. 'Thank you, Mr Crumm, you are most kind. Yes, it is recent, but it was long awaited and so not too . . . well, yes.' I was about to say 'not too great a shock' but it isn't true. The world without Aurelia is as astonishing to me as it ever was.

'How terrible. Then I am even more pleased that you are here, for perhaps we can offer some solace and companionship. I'm sorry for you too, Grandpa. Was it someone I knew?'

'No, Henry, and I had not seen her in a long while. Miss

Snow brought me the news. But do not worry about me. Now, Miss Snow, youngster, shall we eat at last?'

'I should say so!' cries Henry, flinging off his overcoat. 'And Miss Snow, I am not Mr Crumm. I am Mr Mead, but that sounds like my father, so please call me Henry. As you can see, we're hardly *formal* in this house!'

Of course. Kate is Albert's daughter and Henry is her son. I had been imagining a Henry Crumm, a crumb of a boy, but Henry Mead is . . . a different proposition altogether.

'How silly of me! Of course, I met your mother earlier. Then you must call me Amy.'

'Amy. A privilege. Where is my mother, anyway?'

'She's got a cold, Henry,' says Albert, leading us down a dusty corridor to the dining room. 'I lured Miss Snow here with the promise of sensible feminine company and now she's stuck with only the two of us!'

Henry pulls a comic face – a mixture of sympathy and alarm – which makes me laugh aloud, much to my own surprise. I cannot remember the last time I laughed. He looks at me a little strangely when I do; my laughter must be rusty as a hinge on a gate.

He bounds up the stairs to see his mother, while Albert and I take our seats.

'While he is gone, Miss Snow, naturally I do not ask that you tell me anything of Miss Vennaway's letter, except this: does she wish me to help you in any further way?'

'No, Mr Crumm. Your part in her plan is complete.'

'Very well, then let me offer on my own account to help you, should you need it. If you remain in London and need somewhere to stay, my youngest daughter, Annie, lives with me still, though she is gadding about somewhere tonight. I have many rooms spare, from all the fledglings who have left the nest, and I would mark it a very great honour to assist you.'

'Oh, Mr Crumm, thank you. I should like nothing more, for since Aurelia died . . . well, you and your family are like balm to a wound. But Aurelia instructs me to go to . . . to move on . . . and I am afraid I must do so without delay.'

Despite the fact that I feel desperately shy at first, I proceed to enjoy one of the most pleasant evenings of my life. I feel giddy from relief that I have not, after all, failed in my quest at the first hurdle – and from the excellent wine that flows most generously.

Albert Crumm and his grandson are the most congenial of company – witty, warm and sensitive. Henry shows a courteous interest in their unusual guest, though he is a fine young gentleman of the world and I am but a small person who has lived a small life in a small village. He is studying to be a doctor, he tells me, but finds the curriculum unrelenting and insufferably dull. He is relieving the boredom by visiting his grandfather for two weeks. The break, apparently, is approved by his tutors. Like Henry, they hope that he will return to his studies refreshed and adjusted to the rigours of medicine.

'Sprig,' sniffs his grandfather, pretending to disapprove but clearly proud and adoring. 'He's not stupid, you see, Miss Snow, far from it, he just lacks application. Young and foolish, you see, young and foolish.'

'Although I would not want to you think me so *very* foolish, Miss Snow,' sighs Henry, resting his elbow on the table and sinking his chin into his hand. I find myself adopting the same posture as I listen intently. From being unable to look at him, I now find I have the opposite problem and cannot tear my eyes from his face. 'It is simply that I am not cut out for books, at least, not those that are lavishly illustrated with detailed sections of corpses. But do you also think me profligate and flighty?'

I take a sip of my wine, savouring both the taste and the fact that Henry has asked my opinion. He watches me attentively as he waits for my answer. 'I think the study of medicine a very admirable endeavour, but I understand the training is something of an endurance challenge. I do not wonder that you should find it restrictive. But I am sure you will find your way, one way or another.'

'Thank you, Amy.' He looks thoughtful then, as though my comments really matter. I wish I could say more. I wish I could prolong this conversation for ever.

He reminds me of Aurelia – bright in personality and

appearance, able and energetic in his mental abilities, and restless and idealistic to boot. I hope that as a man he will find the world easier to navigate than Aurelia did.

All too soon the clock chimes midnight and I am dismayed. I had no idea so many hours could pass so swiftly with relative strangers. I am eager to follow Aurelia's trail, of course, and indeed I have no choice, but it is hard to be winkled from the company of cheerful friends so newly discovered.

Both Henry and Albert insist on escorting me back to Jessop Walk in Albert's carriage. I think they feel that the presence of two gentlemen is more seemly than one, and Kate is still in bed. Occasionally, her sneezes have drifted down to us like dandelion seeds. I am touched and appalled when she staggers to the stairs to call farewell to me. I return the courtesy by prescribing a rum toddy.

The gentlemen rattle me home, except that of course it is not home at all. The dusty, poky house in Holborn felt more welcoming to me than Hatville ever was, and Jessop Walk is lacklustre and lonely in comparison to both.

I tiptoe through the silent house to my room. This evening's laughter and warmth have made me lonelier than ever and I sit on my bed, still wearing my cloak and boots. I feel I need some time for this experience to sink in. For the very first time I have had a taste of belonging. It is the feeling that accompanies that old dream of mine, the one with the cottage and the pony . . .

I cast my mind back over the last few days. My landlady here, the Begleys on the train, Mr Carlton in the Rose and Crown, they have all been helpful and courteous. And I have been thankful in the extreme for it! But with them all, I was still Amy Snow of Hatville, stiff, awkward and nervous of giving offence. With Albert and Henry . . . I felt something different altogether. I felt *comfortable*! I talked with them – I *laughed*!

With all my heart I wish I could accept Albert's invitation, meet his daughter Annie, lodge in their home. But the decision to stop and rest is not mine to make. I have to keep moving on. I cannot abandon my quest every time I have a congenial encounter.

I sleep fitfully and wake to a sparkling morning. The rain has stopped and I am bound for the country. It is the first day of February.

PART TWO

Chapter Twenty-five

At long last, something is easy. I need go to no exhausting lengths to discover the address of the family I must visit, nor must I mine my memories, sifting through long-forgotten moments as though searching for weevils in flour. I know more about them than anyone else Aurelia encountered on her travels. They are the Wisters of Twickenham; to be precise, of Mulberry Lodge, Orleans Lane, Twickenham Meadows, Middlesex. I used to fancy the address exotic when I saw it inscribed at the top of Aurelia's letters.

Apparently there are any number of ways to reach Twickenham: by omnibus, by stagecoach, or by boat. Or one could go by train to Richmond and then walk. So I learn from the informative Mrs Woodrow, who is happy to discuss the merits and drawbacks of each journey.

Thus, after a brisk walk through rain-washed streets, I am seated inside a gleaming mail coach at St Paul's, peeping through the window at the great cathedral. The vast façade of

Portland stone is blackened and smoky. As the early morning freshness falls away, it seems to fume and brood.

The coach reminds me of one of Lord Vennaway's horses; it is so sleek and well kempt, tacked out in shining brass and leather. It has a name, *Meteor*, which actually *was* the name of one of Lord Vennaway's horses. Although that first Meteor was not maroon and black, nor did he have scarlet wheels, nevertheless the one reminds me of the other; something about pride, the promise of speed and impatience to be off.

I paid without hesitation for a seat inside. The thought of swinging myself up onto the roof and rocking along all the way to the country, exposed to the elements, requires a sense of adventure as yet dormant in me. Anyway, I no longer have to pretend I am eking out a small sum of money; no one here will recognize me.

Nevertheless, I look all around me before allowing a tall gentleman with very blond hair and very blue eyes to help me climb inside. I hardly expect to see a predatory Vennaway at this stage – yet still I feel an irrational, sharp instinct to check for danger.

There are six of us squashed inside, including a governess with two young charges, both girls, one several years older than the other. I make the inevitable comparison and feel it all over again, the loss of her. Then there is an extremely rotund gentleman with a red face. His belly is so high and straining, so buoyant and round, that it threatens to take him over altogether. I cannot help but think that a gentle walk might serve him better than a jolting, jerking stagecoach. In fact, a good deal of gentle walking, every day.

The last passenger in is the golden-haired gentleman who helped me board, as finely dressed a person as ever I saw at Hatville. He wears a shining, powder-blue cravat to match his eyes. He makes me feel the way I felt at Hatville, shabby and unprotected. However, he is extremely solicitous to all and offers assistance to myself and to the governess as abundantly as the sun dispensing sunbeams.

'Allow me to offer my services should you require any aid,' he says to me when we are settled. He is seated opposite me and I do not know where to put myself for the nearness of him. 'I understand the delicate position of a lady travelling alone, though circumstances sometimes dictate, do they not?'

I somehow succeed in both nodding and shaking my head at the same time, eager only to convey gratitude for his concern and agreement with anything he says. No fine gentleman at Hatville ever spoke to me with such delicacy – or, indeed, at all – save for Bailor Dunthorne, and *that* is not a memory worth cherishing!

Now he inclines his golden head to the governess. 'And you, madam, not alone but charged with a great responsibility, I see. Likewise if you should need anything, I am at your command.'

'I am unlikely to need anything at all, sir. I only go to

Hammersmith.' Her tone conveys an unmistakable message: *Do not pity me, do not speculate about me; I can manage perfectly well.* I should like to be able to emulate it.

'Of course. Merely a stone's throw and a pleasure to travel with such a precious cargo, I am certain.'

She relents a little. 'Thank you, sir. They are dear girls.' Then she turns her attention to the window. The precious cargo is certainly well trained, I observe. They do not move, speak or make faces at each other. They stop reminding me of Aurelia and myself around Westminster.

With a cry and a crack of whip we are snatched into motion! From the very first instant, I can *feel* the whole process: horses leaning into harness, harness pulling on shaft, shaft yanking at carriage. I can feel the wheels spinning us across the city along routes laid down long, long ago – routes soon to fall into disuse, they say, now the trains are come.

The shining gentleman and the portly gentleman make gentlemanly conversation. 'Sebastian Welbeck,' says the latter, reaching a chubby hand around his own girth. 'And you are Mr . . . ?'

'Garland,' supplies the other, leaning forward easily to shake hands. When he introduces himself, Mr Welbeck turns even redder.

'Quentin Garland of Chiswick?' he splutters. 'Honoured to make your acquaintance, sir, entirely honoured. Financier, entrepreneur, leading light of society, is there anything to which your talents do not run?' He proceeds to grill Mr Garland as thoroughly as a fish for his views about the railway.

I am unsurprised that he is a man of towering accomplishment. I marvel that within two days I have met two men, each blessed with a surplus of looks and manners and yet so different. Henry was easy and frank and merry. Mr Garland is polished, polite and poised. Henry was all rumpled curls and sprawling limbs. Mr Garland looks as though no breeze would dare ruffle him, no act of God could disarrange him. Henry is still trying to find his way in the world, beset with the uncertainties and disappointments of mortal men. Mr Garland is set fast in his life, successful and self-contained. Henry warmed my heart. Mr Garland dazzles me. In fact, he chills me a little. Both are very pleasing to look at.

At Hammersmith we lose the governess and her girls. Three old men take their place, nod curtly and resume a fiery debate about curry powder. Because Mr Welbeck is so large, they all three crowd in beside me.

'Are you quite comfortable there, Miss Snow? Would you like to exchange seats?' Mr Garland enquires in a low voice. His discretion is wasted – the debate rages, intense and flavourful. The horsehair seats are lumpy, and prove scant protection from the vigorous reverberations of the road.

'I am quite well, I thank you, sir,' I reply and my voice comes out in a whisper. I am annoyed with myself for being such a mouse. But he is the sort of person I used to see at

Hatville, whisking past and bent upon seeing Aurelia, and he is but a few feet away. His legs are so long that, even folded elegantly as they are, they reach into my half of the carriage. For once I am glad that mine are so very short and I curl them as close as possible to my seat.

Looking concerned, he leans towards me. I shrink back. 'And do you have a great way to go?'

I hesitate. 'Not so very far, sir, thank you.'

Mr Welbeck looks annoyed at having lost the great man's attention, which he wins back with a detailed supposition about stocks and shares that I cannot follow at all. As we travel and conversations roll around me, I find myself glancing at Mr Garland from time to time. It cannot be the thing, I am sure, but he does rather lend himself to contemplation. He is a man of around thirty, neither young and foolish nor old and stale. I find myself fascinated by the perfect features, the exquisite dove-grey costume and his top hat, the tallest I have ever seen. How does a human being achieve such easy perfection? Mortified lest he should notice me looking, I apply myself to the view.

My thoughts stray to yesterday, to the indigo sky above London and the hammering rain. The discovery of the letter and dinner with Henry and Albert. Is it possible to miss people one has met only once? It seems that it is.

We roll through Richmond. I see gracious buildings, green flashes of river and a beautiful bridge spanning the Thames. I see a world of willows and floating islands. London has been left most decidedly behind.

'A fine view, is it not?' remarks Mr Garland, smiling at me. I think he has noticed the wonder in my eyes.

We rattle to a halt at the bridge, pay the toll and rattle off again into Twickenham. We pass through meadows and market gardens, all glimpsed in snatches and patches, pinned awkwardly as I am by the curry-loving gentlemen.

'Twiiiick'*num*!' cries our driver, drawing us to a dramatic, whinnying stop. 'The George, King Street, ladies and gents.'

I start to my feet, self-conscious in front of so many male companions, but they are all indifferent, saving Mr Garland. He is out before me and the door swings wide. He is helping me disembark; my bag is in my hand.

'Miss Snow, is there anyone to meet you? May I escort you anywhere?' He offers me his arm. I do not know what to do with it! I solve the conundrum inelegantly, by holding out my hand for him to shake. My shabby gloves and his perfect ones meet briefly.

'Not at all, sir, though you are very kind, and I thank you. I have but a short way to go from here. It is a beautiful day and I love to walk, I assure you.'

He hesitates, then sweeps me a bow of consummate elegance, looking directly into my eyes. I blush, and curtsey. Bidding me good day, he crosses the street to the King's Head, which he doffs his hat to enter, and I heave a sigh of relief at being returned to my customary solitude. I could not fault his manners nor the consideration he showed me, and yet . . . I can let out a breath now that he is gone.

Alone in the bustle of King Street, I acknowledge to myself that, once again, I do not know where I am or which way to go.

Chapter Twenty-six

I do not hurry, for no one is expecting me. I ask the coach driver for directions to Twickenham Meadows, then ask a young girl driving pigs where I might find Orleans Lane. Soon I stand before the gates of the Wister home, Mulberry Lodge. I have spoken to more strangers in the last few days than in all my life before.

The house stands quite alone, serene and self-possessed. It is square and white, arranged around a dark-blue door. Tangled, leafless vines clamber all about it like cheerful children. I slip through the gates and approach the house, which grows prettier the nearer I draw. There are spreading lawns and cedar trees.

A dog emerges from some bushes and lollops to greet me. He is a shambling, hairy hound in a sandy shade. I cannot recognize the breed; like me he is neither one thing nor the other. He bounds about, barking, and I can't help but smile. I have often thought dogs to be the most sensible creatures – no calling cards or conventions, merely food, sleep and romping. There were no dogs at Hatville.

'Hello, Caversham. It *is* Caversham, isn't it?' I kneel down to stroke his back. Hair springs up at every angle. Delighted that his fame precedes him, he yowls in joy and rolls over, presenting an equally hairy underside.

The front door opens. 'Caversham? *Cav!* Whatever's the — Oh! Hello!' It is a young woman, smiling and drawing a shawl close around her. She comes out onto the steps in nothing but her indoor slippers.

'Please don't catch cold,' I call, getting to my feet. Caversham sticks his head in my skirts and follows me. 'Miss Wister, I apologize for calling unannounced. But I should very much like to speak with you.'

'By all means, my dear,' she beckons me in, 'only let me close the door on this vile affair that passes for a climate. There. What is your name? Is it me you have come to see, or my father perhaps?'

'Well, it is both of you. All of you, in fact. Miss Wister, I am Amy Snow.'

A tremulous second passes, during which I fear the name means nothing to her, then understanding dawns in a great bound.

'Oh my! Amy Snow. Why, *welcome*, my dear, come in, come in! We have been expecting you for the longest time. Mama! Papa! Children! 'Tis Amy Snow come to us at last! *Mama!*'

A great many people suddenly thunder out from a great

many different rooms. I can hardly take in my surroundings or their faces, only a vast solicitous fluttering and a great many tight embraces which pull me this way and that but put me back approximately where I was to start with.

My outer garments are removed, my muddy boots are whisked away and a pair of slippers proffered. I am placed with great determination in a chair before a fire and a silver tray bearing a plate of cake and a glass of Madeira is laid in my lap. I am forbidden to speak and urged to eat and drink. I endeavour to comply, though it is a little unnerving to have six or seven, no, *eight* faces watch me as I eat, smiling and nodding the while, as though I demonstrate an inspiring talent. I am welcomed to the bosom indeed.

'Now,' says a motherly woman – Mrs Wister, I assume. 'What would you like to do first, my dear? Would you like to see your room? Would you like a rest? Or would you like to tell us your story? Or shall the girls show you around, so you may feel quite at home?'

I look around me, bewildered, at a room decorated in a deep teal-blue with gold and raspberry accents. I can hardly speak for the difficulty in adjusting from my recent trials to this new and entirely delightful reality.

'Indeed, I hardly know! I did not know until last night, you see, that I was to come here. I do not know how much you know of Aurelia's plans for me, but there was a letter, and she bade me come . . . Only please, if this is any inconvenience at all, pray tell me. I should hate to impose and I can easily take a room in the village if that would be easier for everyone.'

'A room in the . . . ? I should think *not*, Miss Snow. *Easier?* Why, we are so eager to know you we should be tramping back and forth to visit you every five minutes. We should quite wear out our shoes.'

'Of course you must stay with us, Miss Snow,' says another pretty girl, not the one who met me at the door. 'Why, we have all been looking forward to meeting you for the longest time.'

'Miss Snow,' Mr Wister stands up, hands in waistcoat, 'it must be very strange for you, I think. You say you did not know of the arrangement until yesterday? Well, of course, *we* knew of it, for we made it! Therefore we have the advantage of you. Dear Aurelia was a lovely girl but one of life's eccentrics – she has conducted a curious little business here. No doubt she had her reasons. But doubtless you would like to hear it from us, so let me reassure you.

'We made Miss Vennaway promise to send you to us when . . . when the sad time came. We wish you to stay here with us in our home for as long as you would care to – for ever if you like! We are a large brood as you see, and no doubt a little overwhelming, but we're a tame lot, more bounce than bite, just like Caversham over there. I believe you'll be most comfortable here, Miss Snow, if you'll just let us take care of you, feed you up a bit.'

'You do look half starved, dear,' puts in his wife. 'That was well said, Edwin, for I had not thought of it from Miss Snow's point of view. We are strangers to her, after all. Only you see, dear, we have heard so much about you from Aurelia that we feel we know you very well!'

'And I you, from her letters and stories.' I gather my composure at last. The long line of faces begins to make sense to me. 'You are Mrs Wister, of course – Mrs Bolton's cousin.'

'I am indeed, Miss Snow, only you must call me Constance. And may we call you Amy right away? Only, if we stand on ceremony, there are a good many Miss Wisters and Master Wisters, as you see, and it is sure to grow confusing.'

'Aye, and you can't call Papa Mr Wister,' says the oldest boy, Michael, who is fourteen or so and very indignant. 'It sounds ridiculous! I keep urging him to get a peerage, so he may be Lord Wister, which sounds a good deal finer, only he won't oblige me. Mr Wister! And Amy, when I am older, *I* shall be Mr Wister too!'

I can't help but laugh. 'Then I shall certainly call you Michael. Now, let me take the measure of you all.'

I see now that the girl who answered the door is a year or two older than I. 'You are Miss Madeleine,' I hazard and she nods. She is lovely. Her white dress and gold ribbons show off her flaxen hair and creamy complexion to perfection.

'Miss Priscilla.' I greet the second daughter, whom I know

to be my own age. She wears a soft periwinkle gown with pink roses. She has brown hair, brown eyes and dimples that wink like sunlight on water.

'See now, there again!' interjects Michael. 'Miss Priss Wister. They didn't think it through, did they?'

'Perhaps not, Michael. Now who is this? Oliver?'

'No, I'm Hollis.' The next two boys are close in age and very alike with brown hair and brown eyes, Hollis and Oliver. 'Like twins but *not* twins, d'you see?' explains Hollis.

'And this must be . . . well, this must be the *baby*!'

I remember as if it were yesterday, Aurelia declaring that Mrs Bolton's cousin had given birth to a beautiful baby girl. And now that baby is a person of four years old, with a cloud of white-gold curls. Miss Louisa hugs a spaniel puppy that squirms in her arms.

'Clover,' she says softly, lifting the puppy towards me and fixing me with huge blue eyes.

'I am very honoured to meet you, Clover.' I reach forward and stroke the little face; a tiny pink tongue comes out to lick my hand.

I am shy under such intense scrutiny – not just from little Louisa but from all of them. They all look so . . . *happy*! And *easy*.

I imagine how I must look to them: pale and gaunt and shadow-eyed, my black mourning made up in cheap, scratchy fabric. I feel like a goblin in their midst, an unwholesome thing, brooding, secretive and mired in the past. I long to untangle myself from it and be washed clean in the sunlight of this happy, hearty family.

Yet, even newly arrived as I am, I know the time will soon come when I will have to leave.

Chapter Twenty-seven

The Wisters are a prosperous, middle-class family brimming over with good feeling. I am overwhelmed by my new hosts. I realize this after just an hour in their company, over a sumptuous luncheon that appears soon after my cake and Madeira. For one thing, there are too many of them. It makes it hard for me to monitor whether I might be causing offence. I was shy when I dined with Mr Crumm and his grandson but two people is not so great a number that I could not concentrate on them both and assess each comment for danger.

But here! I cannot keep track of the conversation – or conversations, in fact – that flow every which way about me. So many people addressing me at once: asking questions, making jokes, telling stories, rushing from the table to show me shawls and sketches and toy soldiers . . . I am in an anxiety that I will fail to answer someone, or neglect to show sufficient enthusiasm, or that I will simply fall asleep in my soup.

Since my arrival, another member of the family has appeared to swell the ranks: Mrs Larissa Nesbitt, Constance's mother.

Mrs Nesbitt (I cannot bring myself to call this elderly matriarch 'Larissa') looks every inch the sweet, dependent widow. She has white curls under a snowy cap and apples in her cheeks. She appears diffident and frail but, as Aurelia proved, appearances can be deceiving.

Mrs Nesbitt, it transpires, has a great appetite for socializing and is rarely to be found at home. She returns to us during luncheon from a visit with 'dear Jack', by whom, I come to understand, she means Lord John Russell, our Prime Minister.

'I do not know how she does it,' Miss Priscilla mutters to me. 'We think ourselves sociable, but Grandmother knows *everyone*! Even the very grandest folk, who would never *think* of noticing us, become great friends with Grandmother.'

Mrs Nesbitt informs me, in her sweet, winsome way, that it is extremely important for a woman in her position to have her own life and her own circle of friends. She would not, she adds, be averse to marrying again.

Another difficulty is how cheerful they all are. I have little experience with such things and I am hard pressed to know how to speak and act so as not to feel like the spectre at the feast. I do not think even Aurelia was ever *properly* happy – not like this. From its earliest days our friendship was shaped around evading the powers that be, sticking together against the odds. Here, I'm not sure that there *are* any odds.

If I am not offering solace, or deeply engrossed in an analysis of some unsolvable mystery, I am not sure what I have to

offer. Perhaps I can watch and learn their ways before the spot-
light turns on me, so that I may not appear so very curious.
And so, in my earnest, anxious way, I make of these good
people a course of study for myself and quite exhaust myself
long before the evening meal.

Seeing me wilt in their midst, Constance finally calls off the
children and takes me to my room. It has been waiting for me,
she says.

It is airy and pretty, with white muslin curtains trembling
like blossoms in the draught from an ill-fitting window. To
ward off the cold, the fire has been lit and a large copper scuttle
glints with coal.

'Use whatever you need,' she instructs. 'There is the shovel.
You simply must be comfortable. I wanted you to have this
room because Miss Vennaway stayed here so I thought it might
please you. And, in truth, it is the only spare room we have.'

I assure her I am more than content. This is the closest thing
I have ever seen in life to the home I have wished for myself. To
be sure, Mulberry Lodge is far larger than the modest cottage
of my dreams but every bit as welcoming and warm in spirit. It
strikes me as a small miracle to find myself in so homely a place.
It makes me feel as though Aurelia's is not the only path I am
following, that some comforting strand of my own destiny is
woven into my quest after all. I pray that is so.

The care that has gone into making my room a haven more
than compensates for the chill. There are soft pink and green

rugs, a bookcase, a small canopied bed and walls bedecked in rose and ivory stripes. I have never seen papered walls before. A round table and two chairs wait before the window and I can already see myself sitting there in the early morning, looking out over the garden. Paintings decorate the walls. One depicts the house, shrouded in clematis, with Cavendish sitting four-square and military on the top step.

'Did Aurelia paint that?'

'She did. A gift to us when she left, bless the dear girl. And here is your trunk.' She points at a large wooden trunk at the foot of the bed.

'*My* trunk?' She speaks as though I was expecting it but I have never had a trunk in my life, nor the possessions to fill one.

'Why, yes! The trunk Aurelia left for you. It kept her so busy while she was here. The key is in the bookcase drawer. I shall leave you now – you must yearn for peace and quiet. Please rest, and do not emerge until you are good and ready, even if that is tomorrow. Even if that is three days from now! I cannot think what it must be like to be without a home at such a time. Therefore ours must supply the need.'

I thank her wholeheartedly. I do need to rest. This morning I woke in cheerless Jessop Walk and now the afternoon grows dark over Mulberry Lodge.

When Constance has left the room, I look at the trunk. A gift – or gifts – from Aurelia! Waiting here for me all this time!

It is large and made of oak, with brass handles at either end. If Aurelia expects me to take it with me, I do not know how I shall travel. But I shall spare myself the trial of worrying about that for now. Feeling safe for the first time since she died, I draw the curtains on the twilit lawn and the gracious trees and what may be a glimpse of the river beyond. It can wait. Even the trunk can wait. It can all wait.

Chapter Twenty-eight

I wake with a start from a dream of falling. I was plunging
a great way, into an abyss from which I knew I would not
return. Deep snow gentled my descent, but still I sank with my
back toward the depths, arms and legs reaching vainly above.
My black skirts billowed and floated and Aurelia's letters —
there were dozens of them — escaped from my pockets and flew
away like little birds. The snow closed above me and all was
darkness . . .

All is darkness. I am somewhere soft and strange. There is
no reference point by which I can gauge where I am; no chink
of light allows me to make sense of myself. My heart drums. It
is as though the world I know has been snatched away and I've
woken in some other realm.

Gradually memory returns, and with it the knowledge that I
am in bed at Mulberry Lodge. I am safe. And yet I do not know
where to find a candle, a chamber pot, a clock. I do not know in
which direction is the door, the window or the chair with my
dress flung over the back. I have slept in four different rooms in

Amy Snow

just six nights; small wonder I am all at sea. I promise myself
that if it is at all possible I shall stay in this house until I can wake
to sure knowledge of which direction I am facing.

I climb from bed with a shiver. 'Tis an icy night. I tiptoe to
the window, bumping into the table, and draw the curtains.
No moon to aid me, and everything motionless without. It
must be the very middle of night. I can't find candle or taper in
this penumbra so I return to bed.

Now that I am awake, thoughts insist on plaguing me. The
treasure hunt, I reflect, is a mixed blessing. Without it dragging me on, grief might well have swallowed me whole by
now. But at some point, I know, I will need to let go of Aurelia
and forge a life of my own construction. This is not *my* journey; it has been laid out for me by someone else. I am like a
seamstress cutting out a dress to a pattern she did not design,
uncertain of how the finished garment will suit her when she is
done or whether it will even fit. I am still not free.

Yet the prospect of freedom scares me. What should I do
with it? Now that I am here amongst this boisterous, open-
hearted family – three generations under one roof – I feel the
gaping maw of my own family history all anew. *Who am I?* I
wish I knew who my parents were. I wish I knew why they left
me. I wish I knew any tiny scrap of information by which I
might hold onto them: the sound of a laugh, the colour of a
dress . . . I wish, I wish, I wish . . . Yet even as I yearn, a part of
me understands that knowing would not give me what I need.

Aurelia knew all too well her lineage – and spent her whole life resisting it because she swore it did *not* define her.

I drift back into an uneasy sleep and when I wake again, a ragged dawn offers enough light to explore by.

I find candles in the bookcase drawer and light two. I wrap my tatty old shawl around my tatty old nightgown for warmth; it seems almost wrong to wear this miserable garb with its taint of misfortune here in this happy house. Then I settle myself on the floor in front of the trunk.

The key fits snugly and turns easily. It is a new chest, not musty or creaky but smooth and clean; the lid lifts silent and willing. It is full to the brim. A muslin sheet is drawn over the contents and scattered with lavender. The scent rushes up to meet me, heady and evocative of happy summers, but when I lift a sprig, the flowers immediately drop off, dry and brittle. An envelope bearing my name lies on top.

My treasured Amy,

Here I am, waiting for you in the best way I can now. You see, I will never forget you, not so long as I live, and not after that either. You have reached the dear Wisters. They are taking care of you now, and may they do a better job of it than I!

When I found you in the snow, my intentions were all good, I assure you. I believed I could do anything – I <u>wanted</u> to believe it. But I could not make my family accept you. I could not change society to make a good place for you in it.

I want you to know, little bird, that I see all this now and apologize with my whole heart. I know you do not want my apology, I know you do not hold me accountable for the cruelties that have been dealt you. Nevertheless, it is the first step in my unburdening to say that I am sorry and to thank you for your gracious affection despite my many faults. Not the least of these is my selfishness.

Which brings me to the year that I went away and left you – I cringe to think of it, dearest. You were but thirteen.

I was determined to go away, you know that. I had a fever upon me to grab any opportunity that came my way and consequences be damned. But there was another reason for my fervent resolve – one that I have never told you. I shall do so now.

Dearest, you will remember how resolute my parents were that I should marry, how desperately they longed for an heir. The news about my heart put an end to all that, of course. My parents – the whole household, I believe – was frozen with shock.

But time went on, did it not? And I remained, to all intents and purposes, in good health. It was easy for us all to pretend that I did not have that fatal defect, or at least to relax, trusting that I would not pass on for some long while. We all came back to ourselves. The exciting opportunity to go away with Mrs B arose. And my parents began to think (a development that never spelled any good for me).

I looked so well they began to wonder if I might safely bear a child after all. They began to think that it was now more – not less – imperative that I marry. They were going to lose me no matter what – keeping me unwed would not change that sad fact – but if I had a child it would be a living memory of me. Suddenly they wanted a grandson (for of course it would be a boy) more than ever. Not only an heir, an extension of the glory of the Vennaways, but a comfort and boon to them after my demise. They began to insist, once again, that I marry.

I lay down the letter feeling sick. Could this be true? Could they really have been prepared to force their daughter to marry when she was *dying*? Although . . . it was as she said. In those days it *was* hard to believe that she was dying. Her days as a true invalid were yet a way off. She looked as radiant as ever. She caused as much trouble as she ever had. A small, reluctant part of me can understand how the Vennaways would have been able to convince themselves that the risk to her was not so *very great*. I read on:

They summoned me one day, Amy, and told me that they had accepted a proposal of marriage on my behalf. They had even been so good as to set a date in the springtime. You may imagine my horror and confusion. This came so suddenly, and after a time of such comparative peace that I was unprepared. It would take a great many pages to recount to you the conversations that ensued, Amy: arguments, entreaties, orders flung and tears shed. In short, I begged, pleaded, raged, threatened and said the most dreadful things all to no avail. I was to marry Bailor Dunthorne two months thence. I trust you remember <u>him</u>, Amy!

Bailor Dunthorne! How could I forget? An hour spent in his presence was like an hour in a chamber of falling swords. You *might* be lucky. You *might* escape without injury. But it wasn't assured, and the experience was accordingly enjoyable. I shudder, remembering his stocky, cocky frame bending towards me, hands on his knees, his dark face and leering eyes coming closer and closer . . . But he came from an excellent family, a line even longer than the Vennaways. I can see why the Vennaways wanted Aurelia to marry him. As for Bailor, his own father was leaning on him to stop his careering ways and have a son or two. Aurelia always claimed that she was his dream wife, on account of her scant life expectancy.

'Love?' she'd scoffed. 'He doesn't want a wife any more than I want a husband. No, Bailor wants me as a brilliant solution to the tight spot he's in. One placated father, family duty done, one young rake at large once more. I can imagine him now, pleading a broken heart, using me for ever afterwards as an excuse never to remarry, to do whatever he pleased. If any friendship existed between us, it might make a fine arrangement. But I do not like him, Amy, I do not like him.'

No more did I.

So you see, I had an even greater motivation to leave Hatville than you could have imagined, little bird. I had grown accustomed to being misunderstood, contradicted, but I never expected, in the last years of my life, to be forced into this . . . with a man who . . . Oh, Amy, you know what I am saying. Either they did not realize that this was the greatest indignity and cruelty they could visit upon me, or else exerting their will was simply more important to them. I will never know.

Of course, I was still – repeatedly! – forbidden to travel with Mrs B. They wanted me married as soon as possible. In the end, little dove, it came to this: a compromise. I promised that if they would let me go, for just those three short months, I would indeed marry Bailor on my return.

My heart gives a great leap. She *agreed*? I remember those long, intense, whispered conversations, the slamming doors, the sense of stakes far higher than a simple pleasure trip should warrant. Now I understand.

And they agreed! They accepted my terms; I would come back in June with my foolish notions dealt with and tidied away. I would settle down and become a wife; I would begin the serious business of getting a child. Of course I lied. I had no intention of marrying Bailor, in June or ever. I told him as much, in private. When I left Hatville, I had no idea how I was going to insist upon this, but I knew it for fact.

When I went away, Amy, I believed I would never ever be

able to forgive them. But now, close to dying as I am, I need to find a way to understanding, for my own sake as much as theirs. I think they wanted above anything to feel that the possibility of a grandson was not beyond their reach after all. I think they were half mad with the wanting of it. And I can understand that, Amy, truly I can, only that I was to be so entirely disregarded in the getting of one! I do believe that they loved me, in their own strange way. Perhaps every daughter needs to believe that, no matter how many knots she must tie her own mind into to make it so.

I know all too well what she means. How many long hours have I spent weaving scenarios that vindicate my mother, which allow for some hope of love in my past?

Why did I not tell you any of this? Dear little bird, I was ashamed! I felt so humiliated by the whole shabby affair I could not bring myself to tell even my sweetest and best confidante. All I could think of was to gain my freedom and then, away from Hatville, to be able to breathe, to think, and find a way to put right all that had become so difficult and complicated. Little did I know then that further complications awaited me in droves, dear, but that is a story for another time. This letter is quite long enough and I shall delay just a little longer before I tell you the rest.

Have you opened your trunk yet? I am certain you have not. Do so now. Amy, you will find new clothes therein.

Dearest, I want you to set aside all thought of the treasure hunt for the next two months. Perhaps it may seem a great delay to you but you need time to rest and heal after all you have been through. You need to know what safety feels like. I believe this time is the best gift I can give you – better than money or dresses.

I regret that you must move on at all, but in time you will understand. Therefore, there is no clue in this letter. There is nothing for you to do now, except revel in kindness and safety. There is nothing for you to puzzle over, save for how you could have been so dearly devoted to one so scattered and selfish. Do not fear, the next letter will find you in its own time.

Meanwhile, try to be happy. Try to feel yourself a young woman of privilege. The clothes will help.

With greatest love from your devoted
AV

Chapter Twenty-nine

Try on *clothes*? At such a time as *this*? Only Aurelia could think of it.

Bailor Dunthorne. A forced engagement. I had thought I knew everything about her. How much more will I learn before my quest is done?

Nothing at all for the next two months – that is the brief answer to that!

It is not that I do not *want* to stay here, I want that very much. It is not that I cannot benefit from the rest – last night's terrors testify to that. I have not had such nightmares since those dark days after Aurelia collapsed in the orchard. But to wait so long before another clue is in my hands, let alone any proper answers! *Aurelia!*

I am pacing the floor, the sun a pale peace offering upon the floorboards, when there is a quiet tap at my door. It is Miss Madeleine, come to see if I need anything.

I am embarrassed by the state of me – hair in disarray, shabby dishabille – but she appears not to notice. Her eyes go at once to the open trunk and the pages scattered over the rug.

'You've opened it at last,' she says softly. 'There is a letter. I thought there must be. I knew she would not leave you without some last word.'

If you only knew, I think.

'I helped her choose the clothes.'

'Truly?' I am granted a sudden glimpse of Aurelia's time away from me. Shopping for me. Enlisting the help of a friend. Suddenly I feel silly for having been too preoccupied to appreciate this.

'You must be very astonished,' she continues as though reading my mind. 'Everything different and now your clothes are to change also. Shall I leave you alone, Amy, or would you like me to bring up some tea for both of us?'

'Tea would be very pleasant indeed, and your company also. Thank you.'

Madeleine is entirely lovely, I decide. Not in the flashing, flaming manner of Aurelia, but beautiful nonetheless. She is smooth and flaxen and calm. Her limbs are rounded and graceful. Her walk is that of a princess. She may grow plump in later life but she will not look the worse for it. It is her character that illuminates her story-book features and prevents her from being bland. She is as welcome as a new morning.

We take tea at my little table in the window, watching the

sun grow in confidence about the garden. Madeleine seems not at all perturbed by my nightgown. Perhaps it is from having sisters. She tells me tales of Aurelia's visit.

'We all looked up to her, Priss and I, and the boys. She was extraordinarily vivacious and kind. You must miss her dearly.'

'I do.' What a relief to be able to speak of her of my feelings. I unburden myself more than I intend to, then pull myself up short, fearful that I've breached some etiquette, but her face is soft.

'You know, I too had a friend who died very young,' she tells me, her calm features condensing into a frown. It seems there is heartbreak behind her well-favoured exterior and many advantages. It is as Cook once told me: everyone has their story.

'I am so sorry. Is it a recent loss?'

'Not so very recent now. Five years or so ago. Annabelle Sefton was her name. We attended the ladies' academy together and had known each other since childhood. You might think, having so many siblings, that I would not feel the loss of a friend so keenly but I did.'

'I can well imagine. How dreadfully young to die. Younger even than Aurelia.'

'Yes. She was never strong. She had a problem with her lungs. Her parents took her to Italy each winter but she died anyway. She had the sweetest nature and the world for me was a prettier place when I was with her. I am fortunate to have my family, Amy, and we do well for pleasant society besides, but there will never be another Annabelle. What I mean to say is, each person is unique, and loving someone means we love all the small things that make them up. Aurelia cannot be replaced, any more than Annabelle, but you have my true sympathy and friendship, if that is any comfort to you.'

I start to cry. Oh, this is nothing new of course, but in front of someone else, that is new indeed. Madeleine puts her arm around my shoulders until the sobs have passed.

'It comes like this,' she says. 'It grows easier in time, I promise.'

When she leaves, I apply myself to the trunk at last. I know she longs to see me admire the dresses she chose with Aurelia, and I will show her willingly, but I must go through them alone first in case of more secrets.

I fold back the muslin and gasp at the richness of the deep red silk that glows up at me. *Red!* It is an evening gown – lavish and low-cut, with silk roses caught up in the puffed and dipping sleeves. It is an evening gown such as I shall never, ever wear! I cannot stop staring at it, half horrified and half in love. It is a dress for the Aurelias of this world, not the Amy Snows.

I lay it on the bed and reach for the next dress with some trepidation. Another evening gown in a deep, inky purple. Did she imagine my life was to be nothing but balls? There is some fashionable net concoction sewn into the satin contours. I cast it on the bed hurriedly and plunge again, hoping for some more sensible clothing. It comes at last, though not until I have gasped my way through three more evening gowns: a pink, an apricot and a silver. These are another girl's clothes, not mine. And yet they are *lovely*, more lovely than anything I have seen.

Then follows an array of day dresses and I must admit they are perfect. Modest yet stylish, pretty yet simple, in such a dazzlement of colour and texture I want to wear them all at once. Oh, the delight of it! There is not one item that is black, or navy, or brown or grey. I am not to go into half-mourning, I am to explode!

The trunk, like something from one of Aurelia's tales, appears bottomless, yielding up slippers and parasols, shawls and stoles and cloaks. There are corsets with what appear to be hundreds of panels, boned and bristling, instead of the corded four-panel creations to which I am accustomed. There are chemises and garters and stockings. The stockings are all white; some are plain, some spotted, some striped and some with little flowers embroidered thereon. The garters are for the most part functional and inoffensive but *some* . . . ! I am a little shocked.

Interspersed here and there between the layers I find little tulle purses stuffed with money. Hundreds and hundreds of pounds! I do not count it now, but I check each one for notes or riddles or clues. As promised, there are none. Only money and yet more money.

It is hard to understand, properly, that this is all for me. Pretty things were never permitted me, nor had I enough personal beauty to show them to advantage.

Once, Aurelia gave me a comb for my hair, decorated all over with crystals. I must have been seven years old. I was fascinated by how it glittered; it seemed to hold flames captured in faraway places. And every young girl – however plain she may be – if she has long hair, she is proud of it. So I fixed the comb in mine and felt like a princess. Lady Vennaway glimpsed me in the garden that day. She snatched it from my hair, tearing the strands, and threw it in the lake. From then on, Aurelia stopped giving me gifts that we could not read or eat. Filling my chest must have been her delight and her revenge!

But when the whole chest has been emptied and a mountain of brightly coloured clothing shimmers on my bed, I realize what this is. It is a blank page as sure and undeniable as my blank, snowy baby bed. This is a fresh start.

I am looking at the wardrobe and fortune of a grand lady. My head spins with the thought of it. Aurelia, I am no such thing.

'And yet,' her voice argues, as clearly as if she were here beside me, tilting her chin in that way of hers, 'you grew up in a grand house, did you not? Your closest friend was the young Lady Vennaway. You can ride and paint and embroider and play the piano. You can sing a little, though it is best if you do not. You have a fine education. If you are not a lady, then what? I suggest you apply to any servant, milkmaid or tradesman's wife . . . *they* would consider you a lady.'

As ever, it is hard to deny her logic.

Chapter Thirty

The new Amy Snow does not emerge, fully fledged, all at once. And yet, by the time I have been at Mulberry Lodge two weeks I cannot deny a burgeoning transformation inside and out – and all around me. Spring is not yet here, but the song of a solitary, pioneering blackbird when I wake, the smell of something warm and floral on the air in fleeting moments, these signs give me hope. After the past months, hope feels as solid and golden as fact.

Gradually I come to sort the Wister family from one exuber-ant, good-hearted mass into its component members. I feel close to Madeleine immediately and to Priscilla also, though in a different way. She is my age but she feels like a younger sister. She too has a conventional, smooth prettiness made beautiful by character. It is her dimples that convey everything there is to know about Miss Priscilla. If there is mischief afoot, she will find it.

Both sisters are deeply in love, Madeleine with Mr Daniel Renfrew, who apparently grows 'Every kind of fruit known to man, Amy!', and Priscilla with a different gentleman each week. The three of us forge a swift alliance and they do not appear to find me odd or distasteful at all.

I look different, of course. For one thing, I am cleaner than ever I was! All the ladies of Mulberry Lodge take a bath twice a week, a thorough hair washing included, and I am not exempted.

The washing takes place in a tub in front of a blazing parlour fire, and is conducted by Bessy, one of the maids. At Hatville I spent far more time grooming Aurelia than myself, so I feel inhibited at first to receive such delicate attentions. Bessy, however, does not allow for inhibition: delicate is not a word to be associated with her.

While she washes and sloshes, she talks long and openly about her bowel trouble, her womens' pains, her aching back, her swollen glands. She talks with such earnest and ample detail that it seems foolish to pretend such things do not exist, and downright churlish not to respond in kind. My own health is relatively trouble-free, still I rustle up the occasional sinus trouble and feminine twinge to placate her and often find myself wishing I had more to offer. It is refreshing. Odd, but refreshing.

Since Lady Vennaway severed my hair all those years ago, I have continued to cut it regularly. It is no longer short to my chin but hovers about my shoulders. It is very unfashionable but that is a small price to pay for hours saved each week from working away at tedious tangles. Also, I fancy it suits me better so perhaps I am a little vain after all. It curls around my new caps and bonnets in a way that is . . . almost pleasing.

Then there is the way I carry myself now. I had thought at first to betray my promise to Aurelia in one small particular and continue to wear my old corded corsets. The new ones quite intimidated me. But when I did try the new style (aided and abetted by Madeleine and Priscilla), I found I liked it. It is impossible to feel humble in such a thing. Even when I am tired, my reflection shows me looking poised, proud and energetic. It cannot be impossible to have a bad day in such a corset, but it is impossible to *appear* to be having one.

Then there are the clothes themselves. My old drab weeds are gone, not burned but laundered and donated to the local almshouses. At the girls' insistence, and with their attendance, I have tried on each and every item in my chest. Yes, even the scandalous garters, though I took them off again very quickly (then tried them again later, in private). Every gown, even the ones I will never wear, and every shoe. I never liked the colour of my eyes, but set off by the hues Aurelia has chosen, they look striking – cat-like and amber, instead of an indifferent hazel, failing at brown.

I smile more. The little frown is still there; old habits do not fall easily away and there is much to puzzle at in life. But I can smile and puzzle at the same time, it seems. And so this lavishly corseted, beautifully dressed, smiling creature who cannot be me and yet somehow *is* me is the Amy Snow who participates in life at Mulberry Lodge.

And what a life! Edwin Wister is a lawyer and works a good deal in London, in Holborn to be precise. I have been tempted to ask him if he is familiar with Crumm & Co. I often think of Albert and Henry; that first experience of making new friends, when I was so very alone, has left a great impression on me. I cannot deny that I wish – just very occasionally – that I might one day see Mr Henry Mead again. Perhaps I wish it a little more often than that. But secrecy binds me.

We receive a great many visitors and twice a week the ladies conduct their morning calls; I am always invited. In my first few days I preferred to stay home, walking in the gardens or resting in the conservatory. But soon I am tempted to go along, and so I become part of the accepted social circle of polite Twickenham. People accept without question the arrival of Miss Vennaway's young companion; everyone remembers Aurelia. I have a sensation of very crumpled wings unfurling, shaking themselves out despite a few dents and scratches and passing an inspection for fatal damage.

Twickenham is a delight. Meadows and market gardens and mansions that dream away their days. A great variety of personages, from foreign nobility to ladies bent on charitable pursuits to reclusive writers who occasionally emerge, ink-spattered and blinking.

The days roll by, growing tentatively greener, swifter and

more beautiful – like the river. As winter lifts its wearying hold on the land, flashes of blue are seen in the sky, the muted, dreamy powder blue of spring, of the elegant Mr Garland's cravat. The social calendar grows fuller, if that can be imagined. Spring balls are planned and the girls grow excited at the prospect of dancing with beaux glimpsed only in drawing rooms since Christmas. They start to plan picnics and regattas and boating parties to Eel Pie Island, including me quite as if I shall always be amongst them. I yield to the illusion, as though drifting on a gentle summer current. I never forget that I shall not see summer at the river, yet it is sweet to pretend that I shall.

Chapter Thirty-one

With the advent of balls comes the necessity for Madeleine and Priscilla to spend a great deal of time in the shops of Twickenham. It is there, one day, that I see a tall, familiar figure. My breath catches, although I can claim no true acquaintance.

The girls nudge each other as he strides down King Street — he is really very fine. He sweeps all three of us an approving gaze and tips his exceptionally tall hat, then disappears into the King's Head. Inexplicably, I find that I am relieved at escaping the notice of the rather memorable Mr Garland.

But an hour or so later, our paths cross again. We are in a jeweller's shop. Priscilla has great need of a gold chain to display her opal pendant to best effect with her oyster-coloured gown. We are all three poring over a display cabinet when a familiar voice greets Mr Price, the appropriately named owner of the shop.

I cannot help but look up. Sure enough, it is Mr Garland, blue cravat gleaming at his throat, hat brushing the ceiling. He looks like an advertisement for gentlemen's fashions. Mr Garland tips his hat again and smiles, then looks again at me and frowns. Hastily I divert my attention towards a row of gold chains of fascinatingly varied lengths.

'Excuse me.'

My heart thrums unaccountably. For just a brief instant I feel like running away.

'Good afternoon, ladies, I beg your pardon for accosting you like this, only –' he looks directly at me – 'do I know you? You look familiar, and if that sounds like a lamentable excuse to introduce myself, I assure you it's not. My name is Quentin Garland. I should hate to pass over an acquaintance if we have met, Miss . . . ?'

The girls look at me in astonishment. I can tell they know the name. It has been uttered frequently in the drawing rooms of Twickenham since I have been here; he is quite the man of the moment. I have felt foolishly proud to have met the great man, and his gracious address quite sweeps away my urge to run.

'I am Miss Snow, Mr Garland. We met once, briefly. It was on the mail coach from St Paul's to King Street.'

'Why, so we did! Good heavens! I am pleased to find you looking so *exceptionally* well. Twickenham obviously agrees with you.' We shake hands for the second time and this time my gloves are the equal of his own. He has an intent gaze and I can see him registering the change in me, though he is too civil to comment.

I can feel myself blushing. 'Thank you, sir. I think Twickenham must agree with everybody.'

'Indeed. Delightful place. The fields, the river, the . . . yes,
excellent.' He glances around, gesturing vaguely at the won-
ders of Twickenham, then returns his blue gaze to my face. It
is upturned like a daisy, he is so tall. 'And now our paths cross
once again. I confess, I have more than once felt remiss for not
escorting you that day, Miss Snow. King Street is no place to
leave a lady alone. But you obviously found your friends.'

'You were most courteous and helpful, sir. But yes, I found
them. May I introduce Miss Madeleine Wister and her sister
Miss Priscilla Wister?'

'Charmed.'

The girls curtsey, subdued by his illustrious manner, but
Priscilla bubbles up again very quickly.

'I am *plagued* to choose a chain, sir. Do you consider a belcher
chain or an oval link to be more stylish? I do not wish to be
unfashionable; I wish to choose something truly *Victorian*.'

I clasp my hands together to stop them flying up to cover
my face. I cannot imagine a man like Mr Garland, steeped in
the concerns of business and national progress, to have an opinion about ladies' necklaces. Yet he inclines himself to the
cabinet and appears to study the question with consummate
gravity.

'Priscilla, Mr Garland does not want to think about your
necklace!' breathes Madeleine in horror.

But he is not to be rushed. When he turns to us again, we look at him as though awaiting a pronouncement from an oracle.

'The oval link,' he beams, 'will be quite the thing for a beauty as delicate as yours, Miss Priscilla. It is hard to imagine *any* adornment looking ill on one so lovely, yet you are quite right to choose something modern and fresh. Is there a special occasion?'

Priscilla is too overcome to answer.

'There is to be a dance at Lowbridge House in Richmond next Saturday,' Madeleine explains.

'And a finer occasion it will be for your attendance, ladies. Now if you will excuse me, I must take my leave. I am pleased to meet you again, Miss Snow. Good day.'

We are left, all three, gazing after him, like ducklings in a row. The excitement of shopping for a ball was polished to a high shine by the addition of Mr Garland to the experience. With his departure, the gleam is dulled.

Chapter Thirty-two

Despite my absorption in the enchanted kingdom that is Mulberry Lodge, I have not forgotten Aurelia, nor the old days in Hatville, nor the trail of letters. Or perhaps it would be more accurate to say that they will not forget *me*.

For the most part, my manner has grown easier and more confident. I converse readily now and I have not once disgraced myself. But sometimes I find myself scrutinizing an accepting face and mistrusting courtesies. Are they wrong? *Should* I be persecuted? For if not, why did the Vennaways feel so differently? For all those years, *why*? The question pursues me like a sigh.

Mostly, however, I am happy indeed. This at last is my own dream come true: family, good cheer, hearth and home, domestic bliss. Oh, I know it is not *my* family, and not my home. But I like to fancy that by experiencing it here, now I am shaping the possibility somewhere in my future. When Aurelia's quest is finished with me, I shall remember this time, perhaps create my very own Mulberry Lodge somehow, with people of my own.

My favourite refuge is the conservatory, the ultimate demonstration of Constance's taste for the exotic. If I had a home of my own, I would have a conservatory *just* like this. A whole room made of glass! Filled with plants! The conservatory is like a garden within a house. In fact, it is like a jungle in a house.

Tall palm trees sweep the ceiling. There is a hammock as well as several sofas, and a wrought-iron bench painted white. There are orange trees and orchids. The Wisters own two parrots, Solomon and Xerxes, whose spread-winged, long-tailed shapes cast gliding shadows. Their cries make me shiver with delight both at the thought that far-off, tropical places exist and that I am not called upon to visit them.

It is a very wet, very English day when I receive an unimagined visitor. Bessy brings him to me in the conservatory and so I am alone with Quentin Garland for the few moments it takes her to run for reinforcements.

'Good heavens!'

My astonishment bests my manners at first. I cannot imagine what he is doing here and I am horrified to be happened upon so. I am sketching the parrots, with the puppy Clover dozing in my lap and Cavendish spread across my slippers. I spring to my feet, sending dogs scattering.

'Mr Garland! I hope you are well? What an unexpected honour!'

He looks immaculate, despite the rain. He wears his habitual powder-blue cravat but his riding jacket is burgundy with a collar of pale-pink velvet. It would look flamboyant on anyone else, but Mr Garland is not flamboyant. He is elegance personified. I have sometimes wondered if he employs a whole staff simply to dress him. I have fine clothes now but I am still a mortal girl within them. Still I can stumble and bump and still a breeze untidies my hair. Mr Garland, by contrast, could be skating on glass, inside a protective crystal cabinet. Beyond these, admittedly fanciful, suppositions, I have been able to imagine nothing of what Mr Garland's life is actually like. The migration and nesting habits of a rare bird, fleetingly and memorably glimpsed, could not be more alien to me.

'My apologies, Miss Snow.' He bows, deeply. 'I should perhaps have sent a card, only I was passing and the day is so inclement – the prospect of seeing you again and taking shelter for a few moments were together too tempting.'

The prospect of seeing me was tempting? That seems unlikely. It is almost as if he . . . but no – that is too outlandish a thought. 'I am delighted to see you. However did you find me?'

'I had some business with Ashleigh Charlton. He mentioned the Wisters in passing and I remembered meeting your charming friends in town. I told him that I had met their young guest and asked where I might find you.'

Why on earth should he do such a thing? Yet I find I cannot ask. 'A small world,' I murmur.

Madeleine and Priscilla then burst in, to my great relief. The responsibility of entertaining a gentleman alone, even for the accustomed fifteen minutes, feels daunting. We are still standing awkwardly. I had not even offered him a seat! Madeleine rectifies this and we all sit, I rather heavily, like dough being flung onto a table, Mr Garland like butter melting in a pan. Cordial greetings all round. Madeleine offers light refreshment, and Mr Garland declines, while I sit quietly in some bewilderment. *The prospect of seeing me was tempting!* Despite my discomfort, I glow.

'Do you live nearby, Mr Garland?' Madeleine asks with her lovely smile, rescuing the conversation.

'No, I live in Chiswick. My business, however, brings me out here fairly frequently. I often stay with friends – it saves me travelling back and forth all the time. This morning was so pleasing I set out for a ride.' He laughs and shakes his head ruefully. 'When the weather turned, I wished I had thought better of it.'

'Will you attend the ball at Lowbridge while you are here, Mr Garland?' asks Priscilla, fidgeting like a marionette. She has been full to the brim of the ball for days now. 'You helped me choose my chain for it, after all.'

'I remember! And I should like nothing better than to see you wear it. I will attend if I can, although most likely I shall need to be back in town by the end of the week.' He frowns, as though deeply disappointed, although I cannot imagine he suffers from a dearth of invitations to balls.

We go on to talk of inconsequential things, and when he leaves, we all leap up to show him to the door, gently jostling each other in our eagerness to grant him every attention. He vanishes into the rain, whereupon Priscilla squeals and jumps up and down and gloats that even her famously sociable grandmother has not met Mr Garland.

I slump back onto the chaise, frowning. I cannot tell why I am so unsettled by his call when his manners were, as ever, gentlemanly in every particular. I have a sense, rightly or wrongly, that he was verifying an impression. Perhaps he is unused to conducting conversation in a conservatory stuffed to the gills with flora and parrots. Perhaps he disapproved of Bessy's bringing him to me instead of asking him to wait in the drawing room. I saw the gleam in her eye when she announced him; I will hear about this come next bath day.

But I am uneasy, I cannot deny it. I shoot up again, restless, and go to the mirror in the hall to check that it is not I who am surprising in some way. My hair is surprisingly tidy beneath a white cap and I am wearing an apple-green gown. The sleeves are not over full and the skirt is not excessively wide; I am a little reassured. Perhaps I am merely unused to being treated civilly by fine folk.

Or perhaps it is just that he is so gleamingly handsome.

Chapter Thirty-three

The much-anticipated ball is upon us at last. Priscilla almost weeps when I refuse to wear the red dress.

'But Mr Garland may be thinking of courting you! He may be there tonight! He is used to consorting with the most sophisticated of ladies! Oh, Amy, *why* won't you?'

'Priscilla dearest, I am *not* the most sophisticated of ladies! To wear such a dress would take far greater confidence and panache than I possess. And please do not talk of Mr Garland that way! I am absolutely sure his intentions are not what you are imagining.'

I am not being coy. The thought has crossed my mind more than once since the day in the conservatory; it is a persistent nuisance. But it simply *cannot* be, I am quite sure of that. It would be a compliment too far. To be sure, I look very different than I did when we met. I am no longer a shabby, pinched goblin. If I were a generous friend looking at Miss Snow, I would say she was an average-looking girl, with some pleasing features, who is making the best of herself. But *that* is not the sort of girl for Quentin Garland of Chiswick. For heaven's sake!

'Then why did he call on you?'

I cannot answer that. Nevertheless, I veto the red dress absolutely. I feel next to naked in any one of my evening gowns. The red and the purple are the most daring. I look far older than I am and ready for . . . well, they are not modest. The silver is beautiful but it is the colour of a bride, or a princess, or a celestial body fallen to earth, and I am none of those. Shivering in my silk slip, I favour the more subtle apricot muslin. Priscilla pushes me to compromise with the pink tarlatan, and I clamber into it at last.

Madeleine dresses my hair for me, with pink and white roses and a subtle pink ribbon woven through the dark mass. It is not tame, but it is decorated. I have a fine cream shawl with pink embroidery and cream kid slippers with pink roses. I feel like a child playing dress-up, but with no one to seize me and drag me back to the kitchen.

I am self-conscious as we climb into the carriage, together with Constance, Edwin, Mrs Nesbitt and Michael. Michael complains at having to go to a dance while his brothers are building a fort in the dining room. But Edwin says no man should be made to escort five ladies alone and what is the point of having sons if not to share the burden of social obligation?

Despite the soft pink silk and my bare, snowy shoulders, I fear that everyone will somehow see that I was reared in a kitchen, and laugh. Even so, I cannot help but gasp as we cross Richmond Bridge. The shining black depths of the Thames reflect the lights of the tall houses at the water's edge, displaying an elegant world that I marvel to be part of, even for a night.

At Lowbridge Hall, braziers flare in long parallel lines to usher guests to the door. The long drive is an open expanse, busy with carriages coming and going; I have no chance to flee like Cinderella.

As if Priscilla would let me! She grasps my hand as we walk to the door, as we are announced, as we greet our hosts, and as we step into the great swirling ballroom. It is only when Michael and Edwin have found seats for us all that she lets go.

And by then the ball has claimed me. I think I have never seen anything so beautiful. I know that everyone here must have their own history of joys and disappointments, that behind the happy façade any quantity of bitterness or pain might lurk. But for one night these burdens have been laid aside, along with dusty day dresses and sensible shoes. For one night I have stepped into a shimmering illusion. It is not just the spectacle that enchants me but the feeling in the room, such a buoyancy and a brimming as to make me forget all my worries. I long to run onto the floor and spin around, all by myself if necessary.

I do not.

I sit primly, sipping my punch and listening to Mrs Nesbitt's commentary on who is who and what they are about and why ever are they wearing *that*?! She knows everyone, of course.

'There is Mr Gooch, the registrar, and Mr Figg, the beadle. There is Meg Pawley – I met her years ago at Mr Dickens's house in Ailsa Park. She was Meg Fellowes back then, of course.'

I look at Meg Pawley with interest, wishing fervently that *I* could meet Mr Dickens, but Mrs Nesbitt has already told me that he is not currently in Twickenham. The great man's friend is a pretty woman in a lemon-yellow dress, and she is conversing with a statuesque dark-haired matron in a striking gown of jade green, with every ruffle and flounce piped in brilliant snowy white. She looks vaguely familiar; she must be a neighbour of the Wisters, I muse, as Mrs Nesbitt runs on:

'There is her sister Meribelle, never married. Unsurprising. She's a dear girl but has the gift of doing and saying absolutely the wrong thing in *any* situation! What man would take the risk? Now, why on *earth* do you suppose Mr Elms over there has seen fit to wear straw-coloured gloves? And is that *embroidery* on his necktie? Do not catch his eye, dear, for if he asks you to dance you will not want to offend, but those gloves are *not* the thing at all.'

I am fascinated. I do not intend to start judging men by the presence or absence of embroidery on their neckties, but I had no idea that gentlemen might need to dress just as carefully as we do. I have never given much thought to the social challenges of men at all.

I glance at Michael, tugging miserably at his own gloves (exemplary white) and realize that he is being schooled. His hair is carefully groomed with the curls suppressed a great deal – I know not how. I promise myself that I will take him to the river tomorrow, just the two of us. And if he should choose to leap directly from the bank onto Tam Marks the waterman's boat, or take a swig from Tam's father's water flask (which I gravely doubt contains water), I shall say nothing about it.

In any case, he is quickly bored and abandons us for the banquet tables, justifying himself by bringing back thoughtful compilations of fowl, ham and tongue. There are so many guests, and so much food, I cannot help but spare a thought for the kitchen staff, who must have spent the whole day, at least, carving the meats and tying the slices into convenient bundles with ribbons. I am too excited to eat much, but a little jelly or tipsy cake can never be unwelcome.

I offer a fervent thank you to Aurelia for teaching me to dance. Thanks to her erratic yet passionate tutelage, behaving like a lady is so much easier for me than it might have been. I dance with a great many gentlemen, young and slender, old and heavy-set. Despite Priscilla's urging, I do not think of beaux, not least because I know I will not be here long enough to foster any meaningful connections. Then there is my grief, which will be waiting for me in the morning.

Besides, I am not be ready for beaux just yet. If a courtship were ever to unfold, how might I explain my background? I am not confident anyone could love me in *that way*, were they to learn all that is obscure and shameful about me. So I am happy to dance and smile, to say little of myself and be quietly agreeable. As a result I am a great favourite!

There is no sign of Mr Garland, who is surely back in the city now. Once or twice I imagine I glimpse Henry Mead in the crowd, but of course I must be wrong. By now he will be back at his studies, submerged once again in the dreaded medical textbooks.

The highlight of my evening is meeting Mr Renfrew, adored of Miss Madeleine. It is not only because he is a pleasant-looking gentleman with a most agreeable temperament. And it is not only because he is a divine dancer and dressed to perfection in a fashionably tapered coat with a plaited shirtfront. Seeing him dressed so finely made her laugh out loud.

'I am usually covered in mud,' he tells me. 'I believe she thought me incapable of civilized dress.'

'I never said so, Daniel! I mean, Mr Renfrew,' she objects, provoking a sharp glance from her papa.

No, the reason Daniel Renfrew delights me so very much is because as we dance, he confides in me a plan he has been forging for some time. Of course, it is to propose marriage to Madeleine. He has thought of it for some months, he explains, but does not feel he has enough in the way of material comforts to offer a young lady like Miss Wister. But now he has been offered a commission by one of the many dukes who live hereabouts to create a splendid landscape in the gardens of his mansion. The project will be extremely well paid – the opportunity of a lifetime.

'Imagine, Miss Snow! A whole landscape, in a garden!' And he tells me with great enthusiasm of his ideas for a gentle treatment to favour the particularity of the site, which is a little hilly and sweeps down to the river at its far end. He imagines lush lawns and an orchard of cherries and limes, a spiral garden ornamented with obelisks and hedges of hornbeam, and a grapery.

I am fascinated. My early experiences in Robin's wheelbarrow have given me a great appreciation for gardens, though I do not mention this.

Our second dance draws to its conclusion and I promise not to say a word before he formalizes the agreement with the duke.

We are returning to the unsuspecting Wisters when a lady of middle years hails me. I noticed her earlier, in her fine jade-green gown with its brilliant white piping.

Mr Renfrew bows and takes his leave, not realizing that he is leaving me with a stranger. But I am so happy and light, my head such a whirl of cherries and grapes, that I think only with pleasure of making a new acquaintance and smile happily at her.

She is Mrs Ellington, she informs me. A name that, like her face, is somehow familiar to me. At second sight, I am sure I have not met her in Twickenham.

'You were the companion of the young Lady Vennaway, were you not?' she demands, somewhat abruptly.

I agree that I was, my smile faltering and an uneasy feeling creeping over me.

'A young lady dead only a matter of months, I hear.'

I concede the fact.

'Miss Snow, you offend propriety in so many ways I hardly know where to begin,' she challenges, to my astonishment. I take a small, involuntary step away from her and she takes a much larger one towards me, closing the distance between us by some uncomfortable inches.

'Mrs Ellington, do I know you?' I ask, trying hard not to be overcome by her proximity – and hostility. 'Am I to understand that you are acquainted with the Vennaway family?'

'I have that distinction, yes. But I do not wish to reminisce about mutual acquaintances. I wish to challenge your great impropriety. In the first instance, you are not in mourning! You are at a ball! So soon after the loss of someone so infinitely your superior in every way, yet who showed you every indulgence. Now that she can be of no further use to you, you flaunt yourself before society!' She flings her hands up in disgust, as though quite at a loss to fathom my depravity. 'Do you really think that a companion, a *servant*, in point of fact, is a suitable person to mix here tonight? I wager no one else will. Yet you are either ignorant of the gulf between you and us or brazenly indifferent to it. I do not know how you can account for yourself.'

She is as erect and tense as a brass poker. In contrast I feel myself wilting like an old carnation. I look around helplessly. We are stranded halfway between the dance floor and the banquet table. People are all about; some have stopped to listen. Her voice has risen. She is not shouting but she is loud enough that the curious may easily overhear. I notice more than one disapproving face. I think the disapproval is directed at me. I want to reach the safety of my friends.

'I do not intend to account for myself to a stranger, madam,' I say in a low voice, my cheeks burning. 'Good evening.'

I turn to go but she calls after me, this time a little louder, and the ripple of disapproval expands.

'Then you have nothing to say for yourself?' she challenges. 'No way to excuse this flaunting, inexcusable behaviour?'

I pause, reluctantly. I cannot quite bring myself just to walk away. 'Quite the contrary, ma'am,' I respond, still quiet, still extremely polite. 'I have a good deal that I *could* say. However, I have no intention of saying it to one who knows nothing of the friendship between Miss Vennaway and myself, which was both precious and private. Rest assured that I feel only the greatest respect towards her *and* the good people here tonight. Please do enjoy the ball, ma'am.'

Now I begin to walk away on legs that wobble but she takes *another* parry!

'Friendship!' She comes after me, forcing me to attend to her. 'You presume to name it a friendship? How can such a thing exist between the daughter of the finest family in Surrey and one such as yourself, obscure and lacking in fortune or connection? There can be opportunism, there can be ingratiation and there can be an appalling lack of discernment, but there can be no *friendship*. I've heard all about you, Miss Snow! Why, we don't know where you come from! We don't know who your people are! 'Tis a disgrace. *You* are a disgrace.'

And now I am angry. Although my legs still betray me, I turn back to her, holding onto a convenient table for support. I stand up a good deal straighter and I raise my eyebrows. I have faced a worse adversary than this, and when I was a great deal younger. I address her again – and this time *I* am loud. Louder than she. Loud enough that the whole room can hear me – for the music has stopped and all other conversations have fallen silent.

'Mrs Ellington, certainly you labour under a number of misapprehensions, for as you see, I lack neither friends nor fortune. Regarding my origins, you are correct – they are entirely unknown. I was educated with Miss Vennaway and became her companion, nurse and *friend*. We never discovered the identity of my parents and assumed that I was the unwanted product of an illicit union. I grew up in a kitchen, Mrs Ellington. When

I was first brought there, I slept in a potato bucket. I was found in the snow, as a newborn. I was naked. These are the facts to be discovered. Good evening.'

I spin on my heel and walk away. The sheer heady thrill of using the word 'naked' in public and facing down her aspersions with the bald truth quickly ebbs. I fear I have disgraced the Wisters.

But another voice stops me. 'Amy, wait!' Edwin Wister comes racing towards us from the haven where his family are gathered; I see them in a blur, upset as I am. Edwin turns to Mrs Ellington with furious eyes.

'I will thank you, madam, not to address any guest of mine thus again. Miss Snow is under my protection whilst she is in Twickenham. She is an esteemed friend of ours, as was Miss Vennaway before her. *You* disrespect the late Miss Vennaway, ma'am, by treating her protégée thus. This is sorry behaviour.'

He comes after me and takes my arm. 'I am sorry, my dear, I am sorry,' he murmurs as he leads me through the crowd, away from the ghastly Mrs Ellington.

'I too. What I *said*! Only she *would* keep hounding me! I could not have her think I was afraid of her. I did not want her to think I am ashamed. Although I am, a little.'

'Amy!' Michael runs after us.

His father closes his eyes. I am aware that the ballroom is still motionless, watching one Wister after another chase after me.

'Amy, you're a dear girl and we love you!' Michael cries. 'Don't care where you come from! Don't mind what a fat old trout thinks! You're a diamond in *here*!' and he beats his narrow chest firmly with a fist.

Edwin places an arm around Michael and me and guides us out of the ballroom, into the hall, out of the public gaze. Behind us the orchestra strikes up again. I am shaking and find myself leaning against him, though I never thought myself the vaporous sort.

'There, there, my dear,' says Edwin. 'Let us sit and compose ourselves. This was an unfortunate turn to the evening but it will all blow over, never fear. Michael, I understand that you wanted to make a demonstration of our regard for Amy and it was a chivalrous impulse, but please, dear boy, do not say *anything* else. You really were quite shockingly rude. 'Tis not how we have taught you.'

'You ain't taught me to sit back and let a codfish insult my friends either, Papa.'

'Maybe so, but I had already addressed Mrs Ellington and there was no need for you to add your tuppenceworth. I don't criticize your intentions, merely your precise actions. Promise me, Michael, nothing further.'

'Aye, very well, Papa, I promise, only she made my blood boil! Going on and on at poor Amy like that. I wanted to get there and put a stop to it, only I was trapped behind three or four fat fellows who were gawping too much to move. Then you said your bit and I wanted to stand up for Amy too. But I won't call names any more, if you say so.'

'I do say so. Thank you, Michael.'

'But she *is* a codfish, Papa, don't you think so?'

'*Michael!*'

'But she *is*, Papa! You can't say she *ain't*, can you?' Michael refuses to subside until he has forced his father to admit, very privately between us, and in a whisper, that yes, Mrs Ellington is a codfish, and a species of trout furthermore.

Only then does Michael lean his head on my shoulder, a chivalrous young gentleman no longer and a tired boy once again.

Soon the other Wisters cluster around. Constance and the girls reassure me with hugs and kisses. I feel dizzy with relief that I have not scandalized them excessively. Madeleine professes herself delighted with my speech to Mrs Ellington and giggles a little at the interesting detail of the potato bucket.

Even so, we decide there has been enough excitement for one night and that a tactical retreat might be the thing.

We step into the cool April night and I draw my shawl about me. I fancy I hear whispers chasing after me like draughts: 'found in the snow', 'reared in a bucket', 'illicit union'.

While Edwin attends to a slight blockage amongst the waiting carriages, a gentleman tips his hat and bids us goodnight. Constance introduces Mr Charlton. I remember the name; he is the gentleman from whom Mr Garland learned my where-abouts. He shakes hands with us all and presses mine sympathetically. It is a welcome kindness. His own carriage is similarly detained; we make small talk.

'I was glad I could tell our mutual acquaintance where he might find you at last, Miss Snow. He had been most persistent – asked all about for days, I gather. Happy I could help him.'

I am confused. Had not Mr Garland said that he had found me accidentally, thanks to a passing comment? Why ever should he take such a particular interest in me as Mr Charlton describes? And if he did want to see me again, why did he not simply ask me where I was staying when we met in the jewel-ler's that day? I confess I feel a little uncomfortable to think that he would seek me out like that and not be transparent about it. After all that has happened, I do not like to remember that if someone is determined enough I can be found.

Never mind. I fear Priscilla must be disappointed, for I wager he will hear of tonight's events and find *those* interesting, although in no way I could wish.

Chapter Thirty-four

I stay in bed late the morning after the ball. The house is quiet. I bury myself in bedding, trying to blot out thoughts of last night. The initial elation of facing down my foe so boldly is quite vanished and my tender joy at being championed by my friends does not fully heal the wound. Constance bid me not to worry when she wished me good night, but worrying is one of my chief pastimes. My shame is twofold: both at my own behaviour – shouting at a lady at a private ball, brandishing the dubious details of my background like a lance – and at the diatribe I received.

Everything Mrs Ellington said was exactly what I had expected eventually to hear from someone, somewhere, and I realize that my situation is as ambiguous now as ever it was. Despite my clothing, my money and my deceptively refined speech, I will never truly fit, because people always want to know where you come from.

It is as though the past is a swamp full of murky creatures, submerged and treacherous. For days at a time since coming here I have been able to walk on safe tussocks of grass, but last night the beasts surfaced to pull me in. I relive Mrs Ellington's words, her scorn, the look on her face so similar to Lady Vennaway's. Unless I were to create a whole new identity for myself, someone will always look at me that way.

But what kind of a life would that be, to live a lie and look always over my shoulder, fearing to cross paths with someone from the past who could pull it all down in a moment? No. I would never choose thus. I had better find some way to make peace with who I am, for I cannot be anyone else.

I permit myself a brief interlude of fervent self-pity and a crow gives a mournful croak outside the window. I hear voices in the passage and Mrs Nesbitt calling for the carriage. Soon all is quiet again. She has gone off to her salon and will not return for hours.

I have remembered how I know Mrs Ellington. She came to Hatville once or twice when I was a child. If I remember aright, the Ellingtons lived in London but had a country house in Surrey. I curse Hatville and its malevolent shadow.

And how frustrating Aurelia's letter was, with its hints of further complications to come – as if there was not already enough that I had not known! She did not even tell me how she avoided marrying Bailor. When she returned from her travels, our friendship had changed and deepened . . . why could she not tell me then about Bailor?

However, I understand better now her reluctance to return

home. Perhaps even her transformation into the greatest flirt Derby had ever seen. Was she trying to assert her freedom? Was she hoping to find a new suitor – someone of whom her parents would approve but less repellent than Bailor Dunthorne? Did he simply tire of waiting for her to come back? I try to remember if I heard anything of him in those last years but I draw a blank. Aurelia returned to the Hatville bubble and nothing encroached on us there. No news of suitors past, no visitors from her time away. It strikes me now as a little strange. After such a long and lively adventure, so longed-for and so hard-won, for it all just to fade away. Unless something happened that was so terrible she wanted to forget all about it.

My cheerless musings are interrupted by Madeleine knocking at my door. Her beloved Mr Renfrew has appeared to pay us all a call.

'I thought you might be planning to hide away all day,' she smiles, 'but you see, your friends require your presence so you must abandon that project and get dressed at once.'

Dear Madeleine. How thoughtful she is. (And perceptive; I had been planning exactly that.) Nevertheless I climb hastily into a blue Sunday dress and do battle with my hair in order to go and smile and pretend I am not so humiliated I want to cry.

Mr Renfrew does not leave until he has extracted a promise that Madeleine, Priscilla and I will visit him on Wednesday to see his garden as it comes to life in the spring. The roses are yet a while away, but there are bluebells and narcissi and lilies of the valley.

I appreciate the message that his calling so promptly sends to me and anyone else who cares to observe it: Amy Snow is not disgraced, she has friends besides the Wisters. And life goes on, despite scandal.

Chapter Thirty-five

The following day I receive another thoughtful attention from a gentleman: Mr Quentin Garland. It comes in the form not of a visit but of a note. It is brief yet very cordial. Fearful as I am of disgrace, it comes as a welcome surprise and quite washes away any misgivings I had about his recent visit.

My dear Miss Snow,

I trust this humble note finds you well. Pray accept my compliments. And convey, if you would be so good, my kindest wishes to the two Misses Wister of my acquaintance.

I was disappointed not to have seen you all at the ball at Lowbridge; as I had suspected, my business called me away. I hope perhaps I may see you at another before too very long. This same business has now taken an unexpected turn and consequently I must away to Edinburgh, where I will likely be detained several weeks. I do hope I may be permitted to call on you when I return to London.

Assuring you of my continued regard, I remain yours very sincerely,

Quentin Garland

Now I shall surely not see him again for, of the two months Aurelia prescribed I stay at Mulberry Lodge, six weeks have somehow disappeared. I would be happy to pass the remaining precious time quietly, but the Wisters will not hear of me beating a humble retreat from society. I am urged to accompany them on their calls and while it is true that two or three families are frostier than they were, and one refuses to see us altogether, everyone else behaves as normal. Thus time slides by, idyllic and swift.

The weather is fine for the time of year and we pay a second visit to Mr Renfrew, this time with the boys in tow. He has magically coaxed some early fruits in his hothouse and bids us taste them. Hollis particularly favours the peaches and conducts a thorough sampling, juices running all down his chin.

Another afternoon, I take Michael to the river; he confides in me that he does not wish to follow his father into the law. What he likes best, he tells me, is learning, and passing it on. Apparently he is often called upon to help with the younger children at school. His master has told him of an opportunity: the Government has acquired a building in Whitton with plans to use it as a training school for masters who will teach poor children and those with a criminal record. It will not open for two years, by which time Michael will be just seventeen. His master has promised to recommend him for a place if he wishes it.

'I only hope Papa thinks it through,' sighs Michael. 'He'll say I'm young and that there are finer things to be done and that I should go away to university and see the world. But I don't want to, Amy. I want this.'

I think of Henry, who earnestly wishes for a vocation but has not so far discovered one. I wonder – as I often do – if he has made peace with his medical career since we met. It must be a hard thing for a young man trying to be responsible while wishing at the same time to find a tolerable way of passing his life. I hope Edwin will see the beauty of the plan once he understands that Michael is set on it.

Time is moving us forward. Michael is only fourteen yet already in possession of an ambition. Madeleine is about to receive a proposal of marriage, not that she knows it. And I? I am soon to move on to pastures unknown. I spend my private moments dipping into Aurelia's old letters and speculating as to where I might be sent next. I find myself wondering where it is that Henry Mead studies medicine. My fanciful mind dreams up the most unlikely ways in which our paths might cross once again.

Then it comes. The morning I have been longing for, yet dreading all this time.

I am in the conservatory, reading a letter from Aurelia dated June 1844 – from when she was in Twickenham. The weather was so hot, so punishing, week upon week, that the Thames dried up completely. A game of cricket, apparently, was played on the riverbed. All the Wisters went to watch and Edwin was invited to join in. Even Aurelia was permitted to strike a couple of balls – only Aurelia could charm her way into something like that. With her weak heart, the heatwave was a torment. She yielded to the demands of her health when fatigue and dizziness overcame her completely, but still managed to pack in a remarkable number of boating parties and croquet matches and picnics.

I am reflecting on this when Bessy comes clumping in.

'Letter for you, Miss Amy. Just come. You'll be wanting lunch with the others?'

This must be it. It is the last day of March. My time is up.

Dizzy with anticipation, I contemplate the stationery. It is palest mauve, not Aurelia's usual cream. I wonder who has sent it, and where from. I wonder how they knew the time was right. The postmark is a smear so I turn it over, frowning. The ink is black, the hand is flowery and familiar – but definitely not Aurelia's. I drop the letter when I see the return address: Hatville Court, Surrey.

I am flooded with horror. How have they found me? Have

all my precautions been for nothing? Have I let Aurelia down before I am even close to completing the trail? At least it is just a letter. At least they are not here, before me, sneering. I drop to my knees and fish the pages from under the sofa. I do not have the strength to get up again. I read the letter sitting on the floor with my skirts puffed around me in a great cloud.

Amy Snow,

It is with mixed feelings that I write to you, yet conscience dictates that I must. I do not even know if this letter will reach you and I confess a part of me hopes it will not. We ordered you to disappear and you have obeyed. I have been glad of this.

I have questioned the staff thoroughly in case any of them have received any communication from you. They swear they have not. I have gone through Aurelia's old correspondence, seeking the names and addresses of friends she visited that year. She has been extremely vague. She did, however, mention a Wister family in Twickenham and through a tenuous chain of acquaintance I have discovered their address. It is my hope that, even if you are not with these people, they may be in communication with you and forward this letter – or else return it to me. Perhaps it may find you.

I write with a simple request. I wish to speak with you. You may return to Hatville just once more for the purpose. Or, if you prefer, I can meet you in London, at a locale of your choosing. I would require, at most, an hour of your time. If you are unable to comply with my request, then I ask you to write to me, giving an address where a letter will be certain to find you. There are things I wish to say and I shall not confide them to paper if there is any doubt at all that it will reach you.

I had not thought there should be any cause to see you again. However, these are things better said in person, no matter how distasteful such an interview might be.

Sincerely,
Celestina Vennaway

My head is a tumbling, collapsing darkness. Even with all the unpredictability and strangeness of my recent life, I had not imagined this.

For an awful moment I worry that this is the prompt to move on. Is *Lady Vennaway* – knowingly or not – the contact to whom Aurelia has entrusted the next clue? I cannot believe it. Surely this letter from her mother is something unrelated, arrived with uncanny timing. What on earth could she want with me? Nothing pleasant, of *that* I am certain.

Perhaps the secret is that there was some great reconciliation between Aurelia and her mother before she died. Is the trail to lead me in a loop back to Hatville? I cannot believe it and I do not want to believe it. For all that I dread the prospect of any number of unfamiliar places Aurelia might send me,

Hatville is where I should wish to go least of all. I should rather *Africa*!

I stuff the letter deep into my pocket and scramble to my feet. At least she does not know where I am. There will be another clue. It will appear shortly. There must be another clue.

Chapter Thirty-six

And yet the days pass and no further clue arrives. April has come. The meadows of Petersham and Ham across the river begin to blossom; cattle doze hock-deep in clouds of green and budding white. The Thames is greener than ever and there is even a sunny day or two for strolling in the garden, taking tea on the lawns and sitting under the willows at the riverbank, sketching herons and boats.

I wish with all my heart that I could stay. I have never wished so fervently for anything, except that Aurelia might be spared. I daydream, passionately, intensely, as though dreaming might make it so, that the letter comes and tells me the journey is at an end after all, that in fact all the answers are here.

I have spoken to Edwin and explained what I can of my plight. Deeply unsettled by Lady Vennaway's letter, I have asked him if he knows anything of Aurelia's plan for me, of the treasure hunt. I know that in acting thus I am not doing exactly as Aurelia has asked, but the tension of not knowing what is to become of me is unbearable. He knows nothing.

But now he knows that I am soon to leave, that I could be sent almost anywhere when I go. He is deeply concerned.

'I do not like to think of it, Amy! Going off into the world on your own, to who knows where! No one knowing where you are! What was she thinking? This is not what you need. 'Tis a tragedy that she is gone from us, for you more than anyone, but what you need now is a good life of your own. We had hoped that you might stay here. Why not? What's one more woman when I already have five? I should be honoured to count you amongst them, Amy – make it a round half-dozen, why don't you?'

I cry, and he embraces me. For a moment I pretend I am Priscilla and that he is my father and imagine what life would have been with such a man to watch over me. I wonder about my own father, where he is now and whether he ever knew of my existence. I rather hope he did not.

Then I compose myself and tell Edwin that while it seems exceeding strange I must keep faith with Aurelia and trust that there is a very good reason for all this intrigue.

'She had a flair for the dramatic, it's true, but she truly loved me and wanted the best for me, Edwin. After all, she brought me here, did she not? Wherever could I have found better people by myself? I do not want to leave, I want nothing less, but I do believe that wherever I go next will be for good reason.'

'But will it be safe? I suppose I cannot stop you if you are bent on following her wishes, and I can understand that you are. But if you wish me to accompany you, I will. I would ask no questions.'

'I am overcome. That is the kindest offer anyone has ever made me. But I do not know where this quest will take me, nor how long it will be before it is fulfilled. It could be months! It could be years, I suppose, though I hope it will not. Besides, she has sworn me to secrecy. I cannot betray her.'

He sighs, looking deeply uncomfortable. 'Then I must insist on two promises from you, Miss Amy Snow, since you are so very good at keeping them.'

I feel quite burdened down by promises already – they are a heavy sea chain pulling me under – but of course I ask what they are.

'Firstly that you will write to me once a month, even a brief note, even if you cannot write to the others, so I know that you are safe. Even if you will not give an address for me to write back, I must know that you are well. And secondly, that if you need anything at all, even if you are at the furthest end of the earth, you will tell me so I might help you. Promise me, Amy!'

I promise willingly.

'You know,' he adds, 'if you cannot keep contact, Madeleine will be devastated. All of them, of course, but Madeleine in particular. I think you know you will not be the first friend she has lost. She does not deserve it. I confess I feel a little annoyed at Aurelia. Has she not thought of the impact this will have on others? Did she not think how *we* would feel at losing you? Have *you* thought of it?'

'Dear Edwin, only very lately. Before then it never occurred to me that anyone could ever miss me at all, save Aurelia, of course. But no, I never understood that I might inspire the loyalty, consideration and affection you have all shown me, not until the night of the Lowbridge ball.'

He nods gravely. 'That is unutterably sad, my dear.'

Chapter Thirty-seven

For all that I am comforted that Edwin knows something of my circumstances, I am jumpy as a cat as the days crawl by. It is almost a week since I received Lady Vennaway's letter – and still no clue. I worry and fret at the question of what it is she might want with me.

However, there is a consolation. April fifth is Michael's fifteenth birthday and he has decreed that we must celebrate with a boating party to Eel Pie Island. I had not thought I would share this happy event. Usually the good folk of Twickenham save the island for summer, but Michael is resolved – whatever the weather. In the event it is fine, unusually warm for the time of year, and Michael is as smug as if he had arranged the conditions himself.

I know I should have received Aurelia's next letter by now and been on my way; I worry that something has gone awry. Yet I cannot help but rejoice that I am still here after all! I am here to step, giggling and shrieking, into a boat with the girls. I am with them as they float across the water . . . I am with them as we tumble to the daisied grass. Almost at once Madeleine catches my hand and tows me around the island, pointing out the family's favourite landmarks: the preferred spot on the shore where the picnic blanket must be spread; the hotel where summer parties achieve elevated levels of merriment; the oak tree from which Hollis once fell and broke his arm; the willow under which Edwin proposed to Constance.

I am with them as we feast heartily and play boules and cricket and collapse in laughter over family jokes, which I now understand and share. After the picnic, the adults and little Louisa doze; Madeleine and Priscilla make daisy chains. The boys play at being savages on the far side of the island. Their yells can probably be heard in Twickenham. I take myself off to sit quietly for a few minutes beneath the beautiful and romantic willow tree, thinking that *here*, this very spot, is where the family life of the Wisters began. I think of Henry, of course, and imagine him talking and laughing with me here. How I wish he could meet my friends. The thought forms, again: this is what I want. For the first time it forms itself into spoken words and I speak it aloud, in a strong voice, though there is no one but a nodding black moorhen to hear me: 'This is what *I* want.' The wanting of it curls through my stomach like smoke. I have no idea how I might achieve it and still less when I might be free to pursue such a dream, but nevertheless, I have thought it and I have spoken it and it lodges inside me now.

I am with them as we reluctantly pack up and sail home again, tired and happy, breathing chill river air under a waxing moon. I am here when I should not be . . .

And the following day, I wake to find a letter on my pillow next to my face. It is not addressed. The envelope merely bears my initials. Someone at Mulberry Lodge has put it there.

My dearest Amy,

I pray this finds you well, little dove. I trust you are rested and restored, that you are learning your own worth outside of the slanted world that is Hatville. The Wisters love you, do they not? Come along, admit it.

And admit that you like the clothes too. Oh, Amy, that I will never see you wear them. That you and I will never dress for a dance together. Imagine if we had been part of that family, instead of growing up in Hatville. Imagine.

Do you know what we did today, Amy? We went to the stream. It is some time since we did for I have not been able to leave my bed for a long while now and besides, we are too sophisticated now to dangle over fences. But you wheeled me there today and we sat amongst the bluebells, enjoying a small picnic of lemonade – oh Lord, how I <u>love</u> lemonade – and chocolate soufflé – one of Cook's rejected creations. We thought it perfectly delicious but for Cook it was not light enough. She would have thrown it away if we had not saved it from that egregious fate! It was good of us, was it not?

I remember that day. Extraordinary to imagine that after I had gone to bed, unsuspecting, Aurelia had penned these very lines.

But you remember our happy days together well enough, I feel sure. There are other things to say. I have confided in you my parents' glorious plan to wed me to Bailor Dunthorne. Now that you have gathered your strength, or so I hope, I shall shock you further and tell you the rest.

Oh, Amy, this is hard. The forced engagement was not the only secret I was keeping from you in those days. The other goes back even further. It began when I was nineteen and my weak heart was discovered. No, it began when I was eighteen and my parents truly began to insist that I marry. Or perhaps it was even before that! Indeed, I cannot truly tell now when it began.

Heavens, dearest, this is hard to write. Amy, you remember Robin, of course. Dear, gentle, good, handsome Robin. Well, I had always fancied that he was a little in love with me. (Of course, being incomprehensibly vain, I fancied most men were a little in love with me.) The truth is I was right. And as time went by I think I fell in love with him too.

I find it necessary not only to put down the letter but also to get out of bed and stride several times around the perimeter of my room before I can resume reading. Aurelia and Robin? *Robin?* She *thinks* she fell in love with him? I remember the kindly older boy who toted me around like a sack of fertilizer, now recast as 'dear, gentle good, handsome Robin'! *Was* he handsome? Certainly, only I never thought of it before.

I have always thought of Robin as older – he looked after me when I was a little one, he was always so capable and responsible. The truth was that he and Aurelia were the same age, I realize with a shock. I never could quite believe that she was eight years older than me – she was so unruly and fanciful and always seemed to exist outside the normal rules of time.

I get back into bed, pummel my pillows into shape with an energy I cannot quite understand, and return to the letter.

At first, of course, he was just Robin who worked in the gardens. When we were children, before you came, I suppose he was the nearest thing I had to a friend. We both loved the birds and animals and plants. We both felt far happier out of doors. I felt a peace in nature that I could never find in the human world, as you know. He helped me mend and tend things. He didn't say much, as I'm sure you recall, but when he did it was worth hearing. When my mother lost the babies, when she argued with my father, when she told me I had to do something I didn't want to do, I would go and spend time with Robin. But I never thought of him as a <u>boy</u>, we were but children.

Then you came along, Amy! You took all my time and attention and I quite forgot poor Robin. I tended you and spoiled you and it felt quite wonderful to be needed and looked up to. As you grew older, <u>you</u> became the person who soothed and cheered me. When I wanted company, I could play with you. You grew older still and your company was a great deal more satisfying than Robin's, for you were talkative and curious and lively, and those traits are not amongst his attributes!

When I was eighteen, and my parents made it clear that I must marry sooner rather than later, you know how hurt and angry I was. One night, when the pain was too much to bear, I went outside. I sat on the old swing in the rose garden and wept bitterly. I was all outside my body and did not know what would become of me. I was discovered in this tragic state by Robin.

I had not seen him, properly, for a long time. We had not talked for a long time. When he found me crying, he did not say a word – and how wonderful <u>that</u> was, after all those words, those charged, hateful words that my parents and I used to fling at each other. He simply lifted me from the swing, sat down in my place and gathered me onto his lap, held me close to him. We were no longer children.

What I am about to tell you (and I am sure you have guessed it already) would be nothing anyone would commit to paper in the usual way of things. Even if I could tell you in person, how would I choose my words? We are not given a language for it, in our chaste society. But Amy, I will tell you true.

I cried a long time in his arms, my head against his chest, and, Amy, it felt <u>good</u>. With all the talk of marriage and duty, men had started to feel like the enemy to me! How sweet and healing to realize it didn't have to be this way.

He took me to the orchard so that we might be private, hidden by trees. We sat on the grass and he held me again and I found myself smiling, even from the depths of my unhappiness.

Our holding turned to kissing. He looked at me as though I were a rare and precious doll he could not quite believe was his to handle, as though he feared I would break under his fingertips. I felt as though a lifetime's hunger were quenched in me, just by that look.

It was the same for me, the marvelling. His cheek was so soft, despite his toasted skin from working outside every day. On his jaw I learned the feeling of a beginning beard, so alien to me. I felt I were drinking him in through my fingers, palms, absorbing every inch to store in my memory.

Fear not, little bird, I shall not be so detailed about <u>every</u> part of him! I do not wish to embarrass you! I quite embarrass myself! The words look so bald on the paper like that, though what they express was not bald. It was like liquid. It was soft and silky as twilight and luminous as the stars. It felt as though the whole world was reordering itself around me.

I pray for you that you might experience what I felt that night, when you are ready and when the time is right. There was a fever to it, Amy, that was greater than I could have imagined. It felt ancient. It felt sacred. I am still marvelling, years later, at the wonder of it, and that it is so forbidden. Even so, I do not regret it, not for one moment.

There was, of course, never any question of a match between us. In those early days we used to dream wistfully of it – I never heard him talk so much as when he was telling me all he wished for us. But we knew that the dreaming was like our love – an impossible, secret pleasure. We knew we were soothing ourselves with fictions. Stolen moments: those strange times of night when no one else is abroad, the gaps between reality and dreaming, those were the dimensions in which our love could be. If love it was. It makes me sad that all the truly beautiful things in my life, the things I have chosen for myself – your friendship and Robin's touch beyond anything – have had to be snatched and secret.

I lay down the letter again and sink into a reverie for some time. What a confidence to receive! I struggle to adjust my memories to accommodate this new reality. Aurelia was *in love*, all those years, and did not tell me. In all the times that we giggled about her beaux or fretted about the future, she was omitting something – someone – very significant. Robin was her *lover*! I could not be more surprised if she had told me Cook was her mother or Dora her long-lost twin. *Robin?* I think no worse of her for the act, indeed I do not. But that she did not tell me when I had thought us so very close . . . that hurts. Although I was very young then. I suppose I cannot blame her for not telling a ten-year-old about such experiences. Still, when I was older, in her last years, why did she not confide in me then?

I begin to wonder if I am impossibly naive for this is the second great astonishment I have experienced now – the third if I am to count the fact of the treasure hunt itself. Together they make me feel I hardly knew her at all. My memory of Aurelia is as open and frank as the sun on a summer day. But this gives the lie to all that.

Anyway, it continued, this love, this passion, whatever it was, right up until the time that I went away. We knew it had no future and yet we could not stop. For as long as he was there and I was there . . . it was not to be resisted. So there you see, Amy, was yet another incentive for me to go away from Hatville. The feelings between us were not dissipating and no good could come of it. I could not have borne to see him marry someone else. Yet he could not have me, and he was a young man, a good man, in need of a lovely wife. What if they had discovered us? Can you imagine what they would have done to him? He would have been dismissed, naturally. He would have been disgraced. He would not have been able to find another position, my father would have seen to that. What an extraordinary world we live in.

You know the rest of this story, Amy. There was no happy ending for me and Robin. He waited at Hatville while I travelled, to see that I came home safely, which he doubted as anxiously as you, dear, and then he left. Our separation, I believe, had given us both a much-needed perspective and besides, my decline, as you recall, was dramatic. He could not bear to stay and watch me die. I wonder how he does, Amy? I wonder if some perky Gloucestershire miss has now captured his heart?

So now let me return to Bailor. I saw him only once after I agreed to marry him and before I went away. At my parents' invitation, he came to dine. I was pleasant and charming all evening (so he must have been suspicious). My parents left us alone after the meal.

Before he could rustle up his cloying proposal I told him I could not and would never marry him. I was prepared to tell him, if necessary, that I was no virgin. I would have said anything, Amy, but I did not need to. A man like Bailor Dunthorne knows women. He knows weakness and fear, and he saw none in me. He saw determination and dare I say desperation in my face. And he never was in love with me, after all.

I looked him steady in the eye and told him that he could continue to court me and endure the company of my parents if he wished, but that he was wasting his time, that I had lied to my parents and had no intention of keeping my promise. I told him I would make him a perfectly disgraceful wife, make his life a living Hell, and that he was far better off without me. He told me he did not doubt it for a minute. I saw him to his carriage and shook his hand for the first and only time. So much for Bailor! As for how things were settled with my parents, I shall come to that in another letter. When I left with Mrs B, they supposed me engaged.

Little bird, I wonder what you think, I wonder what you

are saying to yourself now, as you read it. I wonder what you would wish you could say to me, if anything.

And now, dear Amy, now to the next part of your journey. I am sure you do not wish to leave Twickenham; I am so sorry that you must. But, my dear, there is more that you must learn and so I send you on. You are soon to meet Mrs X, and for this I can only apologize.

She is an older lady to be sure, and I do have a fear that she will go and die before you reach her, for she is a contrary old bird and that is just the sort of thing she would do! However, she has assured me stoutly of her intention to live for ever so I suppose I shall just have to keep faith, as I am asking you to do. You shall stay with her for three weeks. I have no doubt that it will at times seem interminable.

My heart sinks. This does not sound so very promising.

However, three weeks is not so very long, and there are delights aplenty where you are going. It is a very old and beautiful city with much to stimulate an agile and questioning mind like yours.

I do not include her address with this letter for, together with my revelation about Robin, these are two pieces of information too weighty and important to hide together. I may still be over-cautious and putting you to unnecessary trouble. It is only that as I write, an imaginary scenario plays in my head in which my parents come after you for some reason, stumble upon one of my letters and understand that there is more to my story than they knew. Likely 'tis but fancy and you are cursing me roundly. But I cannot take the risk. Here is your clue, dearest:

> Daisy and cowslip nod side by side,
> Kingfisher blue darts and glides,
> Watches over you when you dream,
> Knots and tangles stitch a scene
> Rural fair and quite serene,
> Green, where lady's secret hides.

'Tis not my best literary effort, I know. But I have quite exhausted myself with the scheming and the plotting. After all, I am only a poor delicate female!

I close tonight with a heavy heart because I have told you a great unburdening, yet cannot see your face. And because I am asking a great deal of you, I know it. And because I am nearing the end of what I must tell you and then there will be no more letters. Although I will be dead and gone when that time comes, you will not, and I miss you already. So be it. This is what life has dealt us. I must be brave, for you are being a good deal braver, I have no doubt.

With great love and affection from your devoted
AV

I throw off the bed sheets once more, for I suddenly feel smothered and snagged by their weight. Aurelia keeping such secrets from me. Aurelia lying to her parents, saying whatever it took to gain her freedom. Aurelia disclosing all that I didn't know before – yet by such a circuitous and mystifying route. A liaison with the gardener is a great and shocking secret indeed – at least it would be considered so at Hatville. But she has told me that now. What more can there possibly be?

At last I rouse myself. I have sat so motionless and for so long that a fly has come to settle on my nose. I brush it off in annoyance and realize it is time to act. I climb from bed, brush my hair, lay out some clothes, everyday tasks that have no meaning and yet reorientate me in my life. My life. I hardly know what that is any more. It was always so bound up with Aurelia's that if one is called into question the other must necessarily be undermined also. And now I am to travel on, into another new and uncertain landscape. I yank a chemise over my head so sharply I hear a small rip. Aurelia is right; I would not choose to leave, if choice were mine to exercise. I must do so only because of her command. A flushed face emerges from the white cotton and scowls at me in the mirror.

I will continue until September, I tell myself suddenly. That will be nine months from Aurelia's death. I will obey her, and go where she bids me and do as she tells me. And then, whether I have learned the secret or not, whether I have reached the end of the trail or not, I will stop. I will go and live wherever I please and do whatever I choose. Nine months is long enough to give up one's life to someone else, even someone beloved. It is not that I expect to stop missing or mourning her, but I am still alive!

Chapter Thirty-eight

Thus resolved, I dress and turn myself to the task at hand. I am surprised to realize that I know exactly where to find the name and address of 'Mrs X'. The canopy above my bed is a tapestry. Its 'knots and tangles' show a meadow scene with, yes, daisies and cowslips and a kingfisher. I cannot believe I have been sleeping for two whole months in such close proximity to the answer. 'Right under my nose,' goes the saying. In this case, it was above my head.

I throw back the bed covers and stand on the bed. I can just reach the canopy.

'Green, where lady's secret hides.' In a long swathe of mossy green I see some loose, loopy stitches with a little white showing through. I lie down again. Now I know it's there, I can still see that tiny, telltale sliver of white. I would never have noticed it before. It is extraordinary how the human mind sees what it anticipates and is blind to anything that could not be dreamed of.

Standing again, I pluck carefully at the note, and it slides out. I smooth the wool back and jump off the bed with a surprising thud. A small piece of paper, folded in half. It is a jumble of letters with a little shovel drawn in the top left-hand corner.

I find a clean sheet of paper and a pencil, then sit at my table with warm sunlight falling onto my face. I study the cipher for a minute or two. It is very easy. Aurelia and I had three codes we used as children and this is the simplest of them. Our crib sheet was to write the alphabet in two columns abreast: A–M and N–Z. The code letter was the letter before that which sat diagonally opposite the real letter. Thus A became Y, B became X and so on. For numbers, we simply reversed double figures and left single figures unchanged. I know the code off by heart, even though it is many years since we used it. I swiftly translate my destination

Mhg Yhqyvlu Hqduhfrkhju
Ryvug Rkegu
43 Huxuwwy Gfhuuf
(lh Ieuul Gieyhu)
Xyfr

as

Mrs Ariadne Riverthorpe
Hades House
34 Rebecca Street
(nr Queen Square)
Bath

Bath. I *should* be pleased: From Twickenham, Aurelia went to Derby. She was not in Bath until the very end of her travels. I had supposed the trail would take me next to Derby and now I feel I am leapfrogging over a great many cities and long weeks of travel. Aurelia did say in her letter that the end of the trail is close at hand. Perhaps Bath, then, is the last place I must go. But I have felt ill-disposed towards Bath ever since those awful months when Aurelia was embroiled there with Frederic Meredith – when I had lost hope that she would ever come home.

A new question strikes me. What part did Mr Meredith really play in her affections, I wonder. Had her feelings for Robin so diminished in the intervening months? Or was Mr Meredith her attempt to steer her inclinations in a direction more likely to please her parents? Did that attempt fail dismally, and was that why she was so reluctant to talk about him when she came home? Perhaps I shall find out in Bath. Even so, I cannot muster any enthusiasm for going there.

Her letters did not paint a picture that held any allure for me. I know Bath to be vastly fashionable and sophisticated. True, it is a 'very old and very beautiful city' but Twickenham is quite old and beautiful enough for me. I do not wish to spend three weeks in a world of balls and beaux and bonnets. These things may be enjoyable with a friend but not when navigated alone. I do not think that elderly Mrs Riverthorpe of Hades House, about whom even Aurelia 'can only apologize', will make a likely ally. After Twickenham, the prospect is a lonely one.

A name and address make leaving real. I have bolted from Ladywell to London and London to Twickenham without any forethought or planning, like a shuttlecock knocked back and forth. I shall handle this departure differently. I shall pen a brief note to Mrs Riverthorpe, alerting her that Miss Amy Snow will follow it in a day or two. Then I shall ask Edwin to advise me about my travel arrangements and help me decide what I can safely say to the others. No matter what tender emotions trouble me at leaving Twickenham, my promise to Aurelia compels me and I remain, besides, vastly curious.

Chapter Thirty-nine

⁂

Edwin arranges everything. I am to leave Twickenham the following day, in the Wisters' carriage. Their coachman, William, is to drive me. He will be accompanied by his brother Jack, so that when I arrive at Hades House there will be two young men to lift the handles of my enormous trunk. I will have nothing to do but wave my parasol and straighten my gloves. I hope Aurelia, if she is watching over me, will forgive this minor violation of her secrecy. I have accepted that things must be difficult for a time; I do not wish them to be impossible.

The journey from Twickenham to Bath is some one hundred and twenty miles, the longest I have yet taken. By road it will be too far to travel in one day. Breaking the journey overnight at Marlborough is the ideal solution; Edwin knows of an excellent coaching inn there.

Edwin also saves me the difficult task of telling everyone that I am leaving. That night, the entire family sits down to dinner together. He has even secured the presence of his mother-in-law, an achievement akin to pinning down a spinning sycamore in an autumn gust.

A veritable feast, served à *la française*, is laid out for us in the plum and fir-green-striped dining room. I suspect that Edwin has alerted Constance (and Constance has alerted Bessy) that something momentous is brewing. The candelabra have been lit, even though it is not dark, lending a festive glimmer to the best china and the copper tureens. The warm colours and soft light, the dear heads bent over steaming bowls, fill me with an unbearable degree of nostalgia before I have even left.

When the soup plates have been passed around and Bessy has retired – and after a decent interval's slurping – Edwin speaks up. Despite being cushioned between mulligatawny and asparagus, the news is received with widespread dismay.

We have agreed to tell the truth but an abbreviated version. It sits easier with me than fabricating a story, or vanishing with no explanation whatsoever. So Edwin announces that I must leave the next day to carry out business for Aurelia – confidential business that I have been asked not to discuss with anyone. He instructs his children not to ask me any questions or demand any promises because I am very sad to be leaving and need their support. My throat fills so that I cannot swallow. I hang my head over my beef, dreading to look up and meet their eyes, though I do at last.

'But you will come back and stay with us again, won't you, Amy?' asks Priscilla, looking so distressed and confused I can hardly bear it.

'Yes, she will, most definitely,' says Edwin. We have not discussed it but he has obviously made up his mind for both of us. Hearing him say it, I am prepared to believe it. 'We do not know when, however.'

'And will you be quite all right, dear?' asks Constance. 'Can we do anything for you? Is there anything you need to take?'

Dear Constance. As if they have not already given me so very much.

If the dinner was difficult, my leave-taking the following morning is worse. Saying goodbye to the girls undoes me completely. Knowing I will not see their pretty, good faces again for an unknowable time is a wrench second only to losing Aurelia. I cannot bear to think that when Madeleine receives her proposal I will not be there to congratulate her. Although we are all very courageous, it is a relief to weep with them a little.

Alone in the carriage, I feel I must be sleepwalking. I hold back my tears to present a brave face as I wave and smile at the Wister clan, who are massed at the gate like lupins. They wave and stand on their toes and their wide smiles are every bit as unconvincing as my own must be. My composure trembles as we roll off and I crane my neck for every last glimpse of dear Twickenham.

As we rattle along King Street, I remember Mr Garland depositing me there at the start of February. If he has returned from his business in Edinburgh I have not heard from him, and I have no address to which I could send a note of farewell. It is another acquaintance rudely severed by Aurelia's treasure hunt and I regret it.

Between Whitton and Windsor I give way completely and sob most heartily. Then I brace myself and acknowledge that the time to be brave has come again. I permit myself today's carriage ride to reminisce about Twickenham and relive my goodbyes. Tomorrow's I must spend preparing myself mentally for Bath. There is only one direction I can go and it is not back.

It was Michael to whom Aurelia had entrusted her letter – so I have learned this morning. I had suspected Constance, Madeleine or Bessy.

When Bessy came to say goodbye, she gave me a handkerchief that she had embroidered with my initials, AS. I take it out now and run my thumb over the silky lilac stitches. She had so little time to finish it, yet they show no sign of hurry; they are tiny and delicate – a clear demonstration of care and friendship.

Society would not approve. Aurelia and Robin, Aurelia and Amy, Amy and Bessy – combinations of people who should have nothing to say to each other, yet with hearts that do not recognize it.

'Was it you, Bessy?' I asked her impetuously this morning.

'Was it me what?' she said.

But as Michael hugged me farewell, he looked troubled. 'It's not too late, is it?' he whispered.

'Too late for what?'

'For Aurelia's business. Only she said two months, and I waited a while longer. I liked Aurelia very much, Amy, and I made her a promise. I didn't want to let her down. I did keep the secret ever so well. So I hope the extra week don't make a difference.'

'I am certain it won't, Michael. Please don't worry. Only, *why* did you wait, if I may ask?'

'Well, I like you every bit as much as Aurelia, Amy. *Every* bit! She went away too soon as well, disappeared all of a sudden, just like you.' He frowns at the memory. 'I wanted to keep you a while longer. Truth be told, I wondered about *never* giving you the letter and keeping you for good, but I knew that would be wrong. Only I did so want you to come to my party on Eel Pie before you went.'

I laughed. I want to keep him too. I also wanted to ask him what he meant about Aurelia leaving suddenly – as far as I knew, she left exactly when she had planned to – but we were interrupted by the arrival of his grandmother. She brooked no nonsense when my brave veneer wavered and told her I never wanted to leave, never wanted anything to change.

'*Life* is change, Amy, and this place is changing as much as anything. It's not the same as it was fifty years ago, or even ten! Houses going up, houses coming down. *Public* houses going up and coming down, though there are more of those going up than closing, to be sure. Later this year the railway will reach Twickenham. Even if you stayed, the Twickenham you love today would be different in a year and in ten years and twenty. We can't hold onto things. Time is like the river. It carries us off, and faster than we would like, most often.'

I know she is right. I know that holding on is a fool's errand; I learned that from wishing with all my heart that Aurelia might not die. Still, I should like to choose my own errand, even if it *were* that of a fool.

The hours pass and we arrive into Marlborough. I look out of the window as we roll to a halt outside the inn and my heart sinks, acknowledging that my pleasant interlude with the Wisters is behind me. How I should like the luxury of trying, and failing, to hold on.

PART THREE

Chapter Forty

The next morning we set off early from Marlborough. William tells me we will arrive in Bath in time for luncheon. I seem to have formed a habit of arriving at new households in time for luncheon.

I have not slept well but already I am a different traveller from the girl who left Hatville, who had never taken a train, nor a coach, nor ever stayed at an inn. Now I am dressed as fine as can be in a gleaming travelling costume of deep claret trimmed with sky blue. I have a fortune of five thousand pounds, which I carry with me (not because I am unaware of the hazards of doing so, but because I lack a viable alternative). I am not bowed by grief and winter, although both are recent memories and both will come again.

But for now, it is spring. It is a beautiful morning. Bath will be a wonderful experience.

I practise saying so, all the way from Marlborough to Chippenham, where we make a brief stop when one of the horses throws a shoe. I cannot restrain myself from sticking my head out of the window and watching the hastily summoned smithy do his work. This is why I will be so transparent in Bath, which is much more fashionable than Twickenham. I am sure a lady should loll in her seat, *intolerably* bored.

Two barefoot little girls on the side of the road point and whisper at the sight of my huge bonnet, with its cascade of pleats and ribbons. When they see me looking at them, they stick their pink tongues out at me and I return the courtesy. They gasp and run away, then come back and sidle closer. Their hair is matted and their clothes don't fit. One hangs back, but one is bold and comes right up to the carriage.

'Please, miss, do you 'ave a penny?' asks the bold one.

'I'm afraid not, not for you,' I reply. Her face draws into a ferocious scowl. 'For you, I only have half a crown.' I watch her mouth fall open.

'Here.' I open my purse and hold out the coin. 'And here is another for you,' I call to the second urchin, who is too petrified to move.

The first girl snatches it and tosses it to her.

'Thank you, miss, oh, *thank you!*'

'On our way, Miss Amy!' cries William, and so we are. The children stand in the street gaping after us and blowing kisses. I should like to take them with me and wash and dress and love them.

★

I had not thought to find the area so beautiful. The city of Bath is built in a circlet of hills, now green-clad and lovely in their springtime garb. The gentle undulations are dotted with farm-houses and church spires. Swathes of sunlight and peaceful pools of shadow define the landscape, carving it into the most pleasing reliefs. Perhaps it will not be so bad, I tell myself as my winding road takes me onwards.

Why then, at my first sight of Bath, am I filled with dread? I cannot explain it, but as my eyes light on the first pale-golden buildings, shimmering in the sunlight, a sharp sense of danger pierces me, just as it did at St Paul's. Perhaps it is the memory of Lady Vennaway's letter; it haunts me. How can I relax when I feel myself pursued? I scour the lanes for highwaymen; of course there are none and the carriage rolls into the city along a smooth, wide road. It is lined on either side with sweeping terraces of gracious townhouses. I have never seen the like.

At least it is not Derby, I comfort myself. If my business concludes here, as I had hoped, I will only be a two-day jour-ney from my friends. It could be worse. I should not have liked to go so far north.

Further into the city we go, past shops and fine homes and a small but sumptuous abbey. We turn right up a steep hill and I feel the horses tug and prance. Now I can see the hills only in snatches between buildings. I am enclosed by limestone and civilization.

A left turn, it transpires, is Rebecca Street. We draw to a halt and I clamber out. The terrace is not so grand as those I saw earlier. The street is not so wide. The air feels closer.

The house at which I am to present myself is the last at the far end. Larger than its fellows, it bristles with turrets and gables. There is even a lead-covered flèche that leans as though it, like me, strains to be elsewhere. A front portico advances onto the street as if intent upon meeting any callers and seeing them off. I am distracted by the words carved into the columns on either side of the door. Heavily leaded, they leap out black and forbidding from the limestone: Hades House.

'Lord, Miss Amy!' says William at my shoulder, making me jump. I have been standing staring, oblivious to all but the house.

'Lord indeed, William,' I agree.

The door is opened by a person so regal that I am entirely confused – she is dressed in the simple grey garb of a house-keeper, yet I have never seen a servant carry herself with such hauteur.

'Are you . . . ? Is . . . ? Excuse me, is Mrs Ariadne River-thorpe at home?'

'May I take your card?'

'I'm afraid I don't have one, but I believe she expects me. Would you be so good as to tell her that Miss Amy Snow is here?'

'Miss Snow, of course. Come in, and have your men bring your belongings. I am Ambrose.'

I hold out my hand. It is not the done thing, I know, but my ladylike demeanour cannot erase my habitual manners. I step inside and stare around me at lofty, ornamental ceilings, a narrow staircase disappearing into shadowy heights and a hall like a river, with three grey stone columns emerging from the depths.

Ambrose waves imperiously at my coachmen, then leads me to a small drawing room.

'You can wait here for Mrs Riverthorpe. I'll have your luggage taken up.'

But I want to say goodbye to the men so I return to the vaulted hall. I am taking my leave of Jack and William when Mrs Riverthorpe descends the staircase.

My first thought is of the Wisters' parrots. Her face is deeply yet delicately lined and the hand that grips the stair rail is hooked and fierce. Her eyes are grey and beady. She wears a deep-purple gown with flashes of emerald green on the bodice and shoulders. It is obviously costly, and looks brand new although the style is some twenty years or more out of date. Her hair is piled high into a crest, which bobs and quivers as she makes her painstaking way towards me, leaning on a cane. She is bent like a question mark.

''Bye, Miss Amy.'

William and Jack duck and disappear into the sunlight. I swallow as the heavy grey door slams shut on my last link to Twickenham.

Chapter Forty-one

The woman looks at me for a long while without speaking and the silence does not seem strange, here, in this echoing, sombre passage.

'So you are Amy Snow.'

I nod. I suppose I am.

'Aurelia's little Amy.'

'Yes.'

Ambrose settles us in the drawing room. The walls are covered with portraits of gentlemen and, strangely, detailed pictures of large, colourful moths. The furniture is old but beautiful. We are served glasses of Madeira, even though I am hungry more than I need wine. I find myself tongue-tied for the first time in a long while. It was one thing to feel confident and at ease when I was surrounded by friends but this cold, dark vortex of a house seems to have sucked away all evidence of my recent blossoming. Here I feel anxious all over again.

'Miss Snow. I had the pleasure of meeting Miss Vennaway four years ago. She has asked me to keep a letter for you and to allow you to stay in my home whenever you should alight here. I take it then that she is dead?'

'Yes. In January. I have been in Twickenham.'

'No doubt. I am sorry to hear it. She was one of life's originals. I do so like an original. Tragedy all round. What is life if not one great long shambling tragedy?'

It takes a while for me to realize that she actually expects an answer.

'Well, I . . . I hope there may be some periods of happiness and stability at least, along the way, Mrs Riverthorpe.'

She curls a lip. She is still waiting for an answer – a better one.

'Um . . . I cannot say it is one long tragedy, madam. Certainly it is shambling. And I'll grant you it contains tragedy and in no small measure. But it contains other things also, I gladly believe.'

'Such as?'

A cold draft blows in through the door, which has been left ajar. I look out at the cavernous hall for inspiration. 'Why, friendship. The beauty of nature. Great literature. Happiness, even if just in small patches and in the oddest places.'

Her eyebrows shoot up. 'You believe in all of that, do you?'

'I must. Why would anyone carry on if not? How could one keep one's spirits?'

'So you believe not what you believe but what you *need* to believe. Would you say that makes you a fool, Miss Snow?'

'On the contrary, I should say it makes me extremely practical.'

She barks a short laugh and I realize I have not had a debate like this since losing Aurelia, although Aurelia was vastly more charming in her delivery. I do not relish Mrs Riverthorpe's manner and yet I remember that she is Aurelia's friend and that she must have qualities beyond rudeness and scorn to recommend her.

'We shall return to the matter at another time, Miss Snow. Let me explain something of what your stay here is to be. Aurelia has decreed that I am not to give you her letter until you have been here three weeks. Today is April eighth, therefore on the twenty-ninth of April you will be free to leave, although you may stay longer if you choose, I'm sure I do not care. This is a large house and there is no need for our paths to cross if we do not wish it.'

I can feel my shoulders slump and I haul them back to the vertical. It would not be mannerly to display my true feelings but my heart sinks at the prospect. I tell myself – not for the first time – that three weeks is not a *very* great deal of time. Only, as I stare around at the pictures of men and moths, at the unlit fire, black with coal dust, at the thin light filtering through murky glass, it feels like for ever.

'That said, I require you to join me tonight – I have people coming for dinner – and tomorrow afternoon for cards. There is a tedious ball on Friday and an archery meet at Tuke's on

Sunday – you shall attend both. Aurelia has charged me with exposing you to Bath and making you a little more sociable while you are here. I can see at once I will not succeed, but there we are. How are you to decide whether to loathe my world if you do not experience it? Beyond Sunday, if you wish to keep out of my way and use my home as a sort of free hotel, you may. Or you may continue to accompany me, providing I have not found you too tedious.'

Between my warm reception when I arrived in Twicken-ham and this yawns a vast chasm that my mind cannot ably bridge. I look down at my hands, clasped in my lap. 'I see. Er, thank you.'

She barks again. 'Oh fiddle, you think me rude and strange; you've travelled a long way and you'd far rather have some kind words, a thoughtful gesture and a soft gaze. But kind words are worth less than nothing in this world so I've grown unpractised at them and as you can see, my face isn't designed for soft gazes. Never stopped men aplenty gazing on it though. And they did a lot more than gaze, besides.'

Her steely gaze is pinned upon me and I look away. The gaping hall, the maw of the fireplace, Mrs Riverthorpe's wicked smile . . . my eyes light on one after another without relief.

'What have you to say for yourself, Amy Snow? What d'you make of it all?'

I hope she cannot read my mind. 'I make very little, as yet, ma'am. I do not know why Aurelia sent me here, so I shall do as you say and wait for my letter. I am grateful to you for any help you have given my friend. Beyond that, I make nothing. I have been here but five minutes.'

'Ah, you're one of those that needs time to make something of something, are you? Me, I know exactly what to make of a thing the moment I encounter it. Take you, for instance: timid, downtrodden, wearing a new frock. Loyal to a capricious friend who's too dead to be much use to you now. Forced to live when you'd rather hide. Too polite to tell me what you think and longing to escape to privacy so you can start the long, arduous process of working out what you make of it all.'

I bow my head stiffly – she is uncanny.

'But you have the advantage of me, madam,' I finally retort, my sense of justice aroused. 'You knew Aurelia, therefore she must have spoken of me. Your instincts have been primed. I never heard of you until two days since and her only comment about you was an apology.'

The moment the words are out of my mouth I long to snatch them up and stuff them back in.

But she barks for a third time and nods. 'That is like her, the minx, and well done, Miss Snow. It's true, I have heard some stories of you. Well now, I expect you'd like some lunch before you unpack, would you not?'

'Madam, I am famished. And I hope I do not upset you by

observing that the offer of lunch seems remarkably like a thoughtful gesture.'

'Haaaaa!' she crows. 'You are wrong, Miss Snow, all wrong. That suggestion required no imagination whatsoever, only a basic knowledge of biology. Do not convince yourself that I am all tenderness under my feathers or you will be sorely disappointed. I shall see you at five for dinner. Explore all you wish, make free of the house. I have no secrets. Or rather I have a great many, but they are so scandalous that everyone knows them.'

Chapter Forty-two

After an awkward repast, spiked with challenging conversation, I escape with some relief to the privacy of my room. It echoes softly, and a little sadly. I try not to think of my room at Mulberry Lodge. This is perhaps more grand but, to my tastes, less pleasing in every particular. It has the strange proportions of an isosceles triangle; the eaves swoop so steeply that even I, short as I am, bump my head more than once whilst I unpack. The colours are sombre – brown and grey and burgundy – and the view is of the street. I do not wish to be pessimistic before my time here has properly begun, but I cannot imagine ever relishing rest or solitude in this pointed prism. I stand my books on top of a chest in a vain effort to feel at home.

Once I have stowed my clothes in a tall, creaking wardrobe, I explore the house as invited, trailing without enthusiasm from room to room. It is a very strange place. Not only is there a tower and a great many cranium-defying eaves but it is dusky and baleful and I cannot relax in it. It feels somehow . . .

unwholesome. Every room is decorated with pictures of moths. There are sketches of men, too, not all of them clad.

One room appears to be a sort of study devoted entirely to moths. Drawn to the bookshelves, as I always am, I find only moth-related titles such as *The Life Cycle and Habits of the Moth*; *Rhoperosera: A Study* and, interestingly, *Moth and Man*. I cannot imagine what could fill so many pages on the subject but doubt I shall muster sufficient curiosity to read them and find out. There is a glass case filled with pinned moths, but strangely they are almost all of the same small, brown variety and so do not present a varied collection. Why *moths*, I wonder, frowning; they strike me as an unusual decorative motif. Perhaps Mrs Riverthorpe has an interest in lepidoptery. She does not seem the sort but then she is surprising in every particular.

At five, wishing I could be almost anywhere else, I present myself for dinner as commanded. Mrs Riverthorpe takes one look at my emerald-green dress, carefully chosen to honour the occasion, and bids me change at once.

'Don't you have anything more . . . ?' She flaps her hand in a manner that suggests my appearance is unbearably dull. She herself is clad in scarlet poplin that clings to her figure or, more accurately, her bones, dipping astonishingly low over a thin and wrinkled bosom. The effect should be disturbing but her iron self-assurance goes some way to carrying it off or, at least, making it clear the dress is here to stay.

'I don't wear these clothes because I am old and unaware that they are out of date, you know,' she says suddenly. 'I kept up with the fashions until they refused to keep up with me. I cannot abide these hideously demure dresses of today, designed to cover us up as if we never had a lustful thought, never had a breast or a shoulder or an elbow. We are *women*, not oranges!'

I had not before considered my beautiful green dress with its round collar and long, full sleeves in quite that light. I wonder if perhaps she is a little mad.

Smoothing down my lovely skirts, I decide that I will not change to please her. 'They suit me very well, Mrs Riverthorpe.'

'Yes,' she sniffs, 'I dare say they do.'

A knock at the door prevents further discussion. There are three other guests, making me an awkward fifth in the party, and they are the oddest combination of society imaginable. As the drawing room fills, I can feel myself shrinking. They all talk across each other, apparently trying to be very impressive and clearly vying for Mrs Riverthorpe's attention.

There is Mr Pierpont, a gaunt, eagle-eyed gentleman of around seventy who speaks endlessly of his glory days as a competitive rower, and Mr Freeman, a flamboyant young dandy who flirts shamelessly with Mrs Riverthorpe all night. His contribution to the wider conversation consists only of tales of his drinking exploits. Since the third guest is Mrs Manvers, active in the Bath Temperance Association, my own conversation is reduced to platitudes as I try desperately not to cause offence to any party.

It is not an enjoyable evening and afterwards I cannot remember what we ate or how the wine was; all I remember is the sensation of tiptoeing over broken glass. To be alone in my room again is an improvement, but not a great one.

I have given up a great deal to come here, I reflect, kneeling on the window seat, shivering and gazing down over the silent street. It was always easy to follow Aurelia's wishes when I had nothing of my own. It is quite another now that I have – *had* – beloved friends with whom to pass my days. And more than that! A gambolling hound, a conservatory, a river and a garden (even if they weren't precisely mine). And hope. From those first shivering February mornings in Twickenham, I felt hope. That is what is most starkly missing here. Mrs Riverthorpe strikes me as too jaded to see hope as anything but a nuisance. I believe she would give short shrift to love, too.

I creep reluctantly into a bed that is almost clammy with cold and stare into the dark, wondering why on earth Aurelia should send me *here*. The most likely explanation I can conjure is that it is to acquaint me with Frederic Meredith. I vow that I will ask Mrs Riverthorpe if she knows him as soon as I next see her. I remain more puzzled than ever about his role in Aurelia's story now that I know about Robin. As my eyelids droop, I think about what I know of him. A gentleman – of course. Handsome – of course. Wonderful dancer. A man about whom she wrote extensively for more than two months, then mentioned two, maybe three times throughout the rest of her life. I shake my head tiredly.

If you wanted to create an enigma, Aurelia, you have done it.

It seems almost foolish to close my eyes and give myself up to sleep in such an unsettling atmosphere. I try hard to remember that I am seventeen years old and do not believe in ghosts or vampires.

Chapter Forty-three

Bath. I arrived on a Wednesday and by Friday morning I am thoroughly miserable. I have been trying to embrace my new position and explore my surroundings in an appreciative state of mind. I *am* trying. But now I miss the Wisters as much as Aurelia and Mulberry Lodge vastly more than I have ever missed Hatville. I am lost in Bath.

Standing dutifully before the abbey in the rain, I stare at the carvings of the men climbing the ladder to heaven, one toilsome rung at a time. I feel a certain comradeship with them. At least *they* do not have to contend with Aurelia's treasure hunt.

Yesterday, tired, irritable and eager to escape the house, I sallied forth to explore the city. As a courtesy I consulted with Mrs Riverthorpe, lest I disgrace her by wandering unchaperoned. She merely hooted at me and did not deign to reply. So I went out alone and was stared at a great deal. As a result I observed a decidedly defiant tilt to my head whenever I caught sight of myself in the glamorous, glittering shop windows.

Then, yesterday afternoon, I dutifully attended the card

party. It was as tedious and tense as the dinner, with a guest list as carelessly assembled. When it was over and the guests had gone, I broached the subject of the ball with Mrs Riverthorpe. I told her that I wished to be excused. I was at a ball just recently, in Richmond, I explained, which left me with no desire to brave another so soon.

She would not hear of it. A Richmond ball is not a Bath ball, she decreed. No one comes to Bath in order *not* to go to balls. If I don't want to go to a second one I don't have to, but she won't hear of me not going to one. And I had better not wear something so tasteful.

Then I asked her if she knows Mr Frederic Meredith, but Mrs Riverthorpe claims never to have heard of him. I should have liked to ask her then whether she might know something of the purpose of the treasure hunt but I had worn out her scant patience with me. She blew off to a supper before I had the chance.

Today I have come out again early, not because I am hungry for more of Bath but because I do not want to spend all day in the house waiting for the ball. By midday I am jaded and drenched, besides. I have admired Royal Crescent. I have stood overlooking Crescent Fields. When I think of how I might have spent a rainy day at Mulberry Lodge, I want to weep.

I have wandered all the way to the river and am studying the weir and rushing water with waning interest when brisk footsteps splash past me along the pavement. Then they slow, and return.

'Excuse me, madam.'

My heart sinks. Have I left myself open to an ungentlemanly approach by wandering around alone? I turn and squint through the curtain of drops that stream from my bonnet.

The blurred figure tips his hat.

'I do not wish to offend or alarm you, madam, but are you quite all right? Seeing you standing there alone in the rain, I merely wished to enquire. Might I offer any assistance?'

Something about his voice is familiar. I put up my hand to stem the cascade; an icy rivulet streams into my sleeve. I stumble, not from the wet but from amazement. Henry Mead reaches out a hand to steady me, then snatches it back at once.

'Beg pardon, madam. Are you unwell?'

'Why, Henry!' I exclaim. 'Whatever are you doing here? How *are* you?'

It is horribly apparent that he does not remember me. I am astonished at the leap of my heart when I see him – and the corresponding plunge when I realize he has forgotten our meeting. I certainly have not been so present in his thoughts since as he has in mine. It is hardly as though I am a memorable sort of a person.

He looks embarrassed. 'Excuse me, madam, I –'

'Oh, please don't apologize, Mr Mead.' I am mortified at having greeted him like an old friend when of course he is nothing of the sort. 'Why on earth should you remember me? We met just the once, at your grandfather's, some months ago. It was only that it was welcome to find a familiar face here in Bath, you see, and –'

'*Amy*? Amy *Snow*? Is that really you?'

Now he is peering towards me through the rain and I suddenly, joyfully realize he has not forgotten me, he simply did not recognize me!

'You look *completely* different! Why, I did not expect to see you *here*! What brings you to Bath? And why are you standing on a bridge all alone in the pouring rain?'

He is shaking his head and shaking my hand and grinning the mischievous grin I remember so well. I find myself grinning too, though I am sure that is another unladylike behaviour to add to my repertoire.

We are both blinking raindrops and struggling to withstand the torrents so he suggests a coffee house and I gratefully accept. Why should I worry? Mrs Riverthorpe doesn't care what I do and I do not expect to impress Bath society in any case. I want to be warm and dry and avoid Hades House. I want to talk to Henry.

Chapter Forty-four

Henry offers me his arm and we hurry back into town, past elegant shops and fuggy public houses glimpsed through a smear of rain. Near the ancient Roman baths, Henry ducks through a narrow doorway, pulling me after him. I find myself in a long, warm room shaped like a letter box, where I am greeted by the snaking, swirling smell of coffee, thick as fog. We find seats in a mullioned window, the rain making fantastical the swirls in the glass, steam veiling the city. I remove my bonnet and with it my own personal waterfall.

'Ah, *now* I see you!' beams Henry, looking more delighted than I could have thought possible. 'Amy, it is so good to meet you again. I confess I was saddened not to be able to further our acquaintance back in . . . January, wasn't it? But you were on confidential business, so what could I do? I confess further, my grandfather *ordered* me not to bother you for a contact address. And now, here you are!'

A waiter brings coffee in a tall silver samovar. He pours the dark, steaming liquid into cream china cups translucent as

petals and I wait until he has bowed and withdrawn to look up
at Henry and say, 'You were? Saddened, I mean.'

'Well, of course! We had a fine night of it in Holborn, did
we not? A warm friendship was born, I think. Unless the pleasure was all mine and the confidential business was a fabrication
to escape a feckless idiot who ruined your dinner by talking
nonsense all night.'

'Oh, no! That is to say, yes, it *was* a fine night, and I wish I
could have stayed to see you and Mr Crumm again.'

'I'm relieved to hear it. Then let's have a toast. To friendship! And to chance meetings in unexpected places!' He raises
his cup, which looks tiny in his large hand. I smile and chink
mine against it. I know I am staring at him but I can't quite
believe that he is sitting opposite me, after all this time. He is
real! Solid and rain-spattered and *real*.

'How is your situation now, Amy? Are you at liberty to
talk about it, or should I stop asking questions? I am not nosy,
only interminably curious. Do tell me to stop talking if you
need to.'

I feel myself stiffen at the mention of the quest, then I shrug.
For those few minutes I had forgotten all about it. 'The truth
is I am no freer, Henry. My time and purpose are still dictated
by the same departed friend. I am afraid I am not at liberty to
explain the details, though I should like to, very much. You
may ask me all the questions you wish, only there may be many
I cannot answer.'

He reaches across the table and touches my hand briefly, sympathetically. I feel like the china cup, dainty and small under his touch. 'I see. But are you *well*? How long have you been here? Is everything . . . um . . . ?'

He takes his hand away and gives a vague gesture somewhere along the lines of querying whether my life makes any sense at all. I experience a great desire to stroke his cheek. I take a sip of coffee instead.

'Thank you, I am well, certainly, and I have found more happiness in the last months than I ever hoped I might.' I look around the coffee shop. I have never been inside one before. I like the steamy air and the brisk, purposeful flit of the waiters. 'I have been in Twickenham, amongst the dearest people. I was very sorry to leave. I came here on Wednesday and I am feeling the wrench very sorely. I have somewhere rather grand to stay in Bath and it is a very desirable city of course, only . . . I . . . I find that it . . . well, to be honest, I dislike it intensely.'

'But how can that *be*? It's *Bath*, my dear!' he gasps. But already I can see he is teasing me. 'No, no, I know precisely what you mean. There is something about being told that one absolutely *must* love a place that makes it impossible to love a place – that makes one quite determined *not* to love the place – true?'

'*Yes!* And Henry, it is an extremely *fashionable* place, and I am by no means a fashionable person. It is beautiful, certainly, but the reasons people come here, to see and be seen, to dance, to flirt . . . well, those things are all very well in amenable company, but I am without friends here and besides, deep in my heart I long for a quieter life.'

'Yet you appear to lead anything but that,' comments Henry, leaning back in his seat and regarding me. 'Mysterious business, travelling alone from one place to the next. It is not the usual thing for a young lady.'

'Yes, I assure you, there is nothing usual about my circumstance.'

'Furthermore I'm not sure you can claim to be an unfashionable person. To be sure, in London you were not –'

It is my turn to tease. 'What? How *can* you say such an ungallant thing!'

'Ungallant it may be, but 'tis true. Whereas *now*, well, no wonder that I didn't recognize you on the bridge. Very fine dress, very large bonnet, your little face quite swallowed up in it. You cut a very different figure now, you know.' He grins and stretches his long legs out beneath the table. They bump against mine, and he pulls them back again hurriedly, sitting up straight again. 'Sorry, Amy!'

'Well, the thoughts in my head are the same, no matter the size of the bonnet that's wrapped around it,' I rush on, hoping to distract him from my flaming face. 'Aurelia arranged . . . many things for me. I am better dressed than I have ever been, but there is still much about me with which society can still find fault. I cannot deny that it is pleasant to dress well and not be looked down upon in the street, but as for becoming a great lady, at the heart of a social whirl, that is not what concerns me.'

'What does concern you?'

'Being true to Aurelia, carrying out her wishes, doing what I must do.'

'But . . . what about yourself?'

I frown and a comfortable silence springs up between us while I think how I can explain it to him. The door behind us opens with a bright jingling of bells. One patron is trying to leave while another enters. My chair is bumped; the tables are rather close together. Henry leaps up but the customer apologizes most kindly and moves on. 'I am fine, Henry,' I smile and he subsides again.

I clasp my hands before me on the table and continue. 'I can hardly think beyond Aurelia; her business determines where I go and when. When I reach the end of this . . . business . . . I know I will need to fill in that blank. I will need to decide where to settle and in what manner to live. I have fortune enough that I do not need to work, and yet I am not a lady, not by birth. I have no wish to constantly pretend to be one, nor do I wish a life of lonely idleness. Having no family of my own . . . well, I will have a great deal to think of, once Aurelia's work is done.' I shrug again, knowing that what I have said is inadequate, but I hardly know what else to tell him – unless I tell him everything.

Henry leans towards me and looks as if he too is thinking carefully of what to say next.

'Your loyalty is inspiring. I can see that you loved Aurelia very much. But does it sometimes feel . . . heavy, carrying out her wishes in the dark like this?'

I sigh. 'It is both blessing and curse.' I pause and Henry watches me patiently. 'While I am thus occupied, I cannot make my own decisions, nor carve out my own way, and that is heavy, yes. When I meet kind friends, I am not free to stay with them. Of course, it is Aurelia who has enabled me to meet them in the first place! But then, I still feel rather lost without her and I am not yet confident, Henry, that a happy future awaits me. Now I am like . . . a carriage. Alone I might flounder but Aurelia's wishes are the horse that pulls me on.'

'I understand. A purpose is a valuable thing. Perhaps soon you may feel that you are both carriage *and* horse.'

'Perhaps. But what about you, Henry? What brings you to Bath?'

Henry stirs his coffee and nibbles a biscuit. Silver grains of sugar fall on his sleeve and he brushes them off. 'Oh, the usual reasons, to see and be seen, to dance, to flirt . . .'

I feel a little crestfallen until I realize he is teasing again.

'Actually, I have been sent away in disgrace. Well, disgrace is a strong word. I have been sent away to reflect upon the error of my ways.'

'Oh! And . . . well . . . are they fruitful reflections?'

He looks out of the window at the rain and the murky street, then turns back to me. 'Honestly, they've turned up little I didn't already know. Just that I am a drifter with no motivation and no direction. I've left my studies, Amy. You remember I was chafing against them when we met? I resumed them shortly afterwards and I was refreshed from the break. I applied myself stoutly to the books, really I did! My tutor was highly pleased with me – for close on two whole weeks! And then it came over me again – that suffocating sense of life unfolding outside my study and I missing out on the parade. My brain stopped working, Amy.' He throws up his hands in surrender. 'It refused to digest one more femur or bacterium.'

'Did it? Well then, what else could you do? Why did you choose medicine, Henry?'

'Well, I wanted to *help* people. I love learning, I hate to see suffering. Medicine seemed an obvious way to address all these things. But instead I found I could not learn, I saw no people, except for in disassembled parts – a skull here, a scapula there, and *I* was suffering! The goal still seems noble to me, but the path to reach it was not one I could tread for one more minute.' He shudders at the memory. 'Now this raises an important question for me and for my father. Does my inability to do what I must for a predetermined period in order to reach a worthy goal mean that I have no character?'

'I see . . . well . . . so you are in Bath to ponder the case.' I avoid answering the question for I cannot tell a man his own character. He does not *seem* feckless or ignoble to me, but I am aware that I may be influenced by his curling hair and tall figure, and by his eyes. (They are of the very darkest, most gleaming brown and currently have a tiny silver raindrop trembling on his uptilted black lashes.) But even I know that hair and figure are not the substance of a man, nor even dark and rain-lit eyes.

'I believe my family think it is youthful high spirits which prevent me from working, Amy,' he laughs, in a way that suggests he can't imagine *where* they'd get such an impression. 'But I do not think parties and young ladies are the answer for me, although I hold nothing against either. I don't *want* to squander time,' he assures me earnestly, settling his elbows on the table and hunching over them. 'I squandered plenty as a young dasher. I already *wish* I had a settled purpose . . . It's just that I don't know what it is.'

Because he is leaning forward and I am leaning forward we are very close. I am flushed with the thrill of sharing sympathetic confidences and I cannot pull away from him; I do not want to. I want to convey so much to him – that I feel privileged he would confide in me so honestly, that I admire his determination to find a course in life that feels right, that I think he has the loveliest eyes that I have ever seen . . . My heart is beating very hard.

'Perhaps some more coffee?' asks Henry suddenly, breaking the spell and raising an arm to a waiter before I can reply. I sit up properly again and look around to compose myself. The coffee shop is more crowded than ever and the door jingles again, announcing yet another customer. My chair is jostled once more. I look up to reassure the jostler but she appears unconcerned. I startle and duck my head almost completely beneath the table, as if my boot laces are in urgent need of adjustment.

'Amy? Hello? Amy?' I hear Henry's voice above me and reluctantly sit up again. I glance to my left but the newcomer is halfway across the long rectangular room. Her perfectly straight back and sweeping skirts are gliding away from me, but still, she is here and I cannot stay.

'Are you quite well, Amy?' asks Henry, leaning over the table.

'Yes, thank you, but I have to go!'

'Truly?' His face falls and he pulls out a gold pocket watch. 'Gracious yes, we've been talking a while. I am late too. But may I walk you home first? I should rather be late than see you disappear into the rain alone.'

But that is exactly what I must do. Like Cinderella – but with both my boots firmly on my feet – I am fleeing. I am already out of the jingling door while Henry tosses coins on the table, grabs his hat and chases after me.

'I'm sorry, Henry.' When he joins me in the rain-drenched street, I turn to him and take his hand, heedless of custom. 'I should love to stay longer but I cannot delay. My hostess is expecting me. I don't suppose *you* will attend the ball at Greatmead Hall tonight?'

He will not. He is staying with friends and they have arranged a dinner for this evening in their house in Henrietta Street.

'I have heard about tonight's event, however. In honour of Miss Genevieve Colt's betrothal, is it not? I'm afraid my friends and I are not sufficiently grand. You're moving in fine society, Amy. Come now, don't look so glum! Half of Bath would give a great deal to be going tonight. And the other half already are!'

I cannot help being glum. To move in circles that would not recognize Henry Mead is no honour at all to me. 'But I will see you again while I am in Bath?'

'Of course you will.' He looks puzzled by my haste and keeps one eye on the street. 'Let me call you a cab if you will not let me walk you. Here!' He gives a piercing whistle. 'What is your address, Amy? Where can I find you?'

'Rebecca Street.' A cab draws up beside us, hooves and wheels splashing through puddles – the door flies open. 'You cannot forget the house. It is called Hades House! My hostess is Mrs Riverthorpe. Do call on me, Henry!' I climb inside and he exchanges a word and some coins with the driver.

'I promise. Tomorrow. Hades House? That sounds like a story for another time.'

'It is. Oh, Henry, it is so good to see you again . . .'

'And you. 'Til tomorrow then! I'll come in the morning.' He slams the door.

I think to ask him one more thing and lean out of the window. 'Oh, before you go, have you perhaps met a Mr Frederic Meredith during your stay in Bath? I believe he was a friend of Aurelia's.'

'Frederic Meredith? Sorry, Amy, no. I'll ask my friends if you like, but I've never heard of him.'

The cab jolts off with a hiss of wheels in rain, leaving me in a shiver of misery. Once again my past has brought a happy encounter to an abrupt end. For an instant there in the coffee house I thought my two nights in Hades House had unhinged me completely.

Aristocratic features – indelibly etched in my mind, proud bearing, long auburn hair and blue eyes. But it was not Lady Vennaway. It was the next worst thing.

Her sister Arabella Beverley.

Chapter Forty-five

By the time I reach Hades House I have persuaded myself that no harm was done. Mrs Beverley did not see me. And although it hurt to be wrenched from Henry again, he is here and I will see him tomorrow. I hurry inside, newly reconciled to Bath. The presence of a friend in the city casts a whole new light on the weeks ahead. That light is dimmed when I find Mrs Riverthorpe lying in wait in the hall. She lurks like a crocodile, patient and deadly in pools of shadow.

'I see you have attempted to drown yourself as a way of evading the ball! I assure you I shall not let you off the hook so easily.'

'I am certain you will not, Mrs Riverthorpe. I have come back to dry off and get ready.'

'It'll take more than drying to get *you* ready, miss! I shall send Cecile to you. She will see you right.'

I do not know who Cecile is but I know better than to argue. I have acquainted myself only a little with the rather odd household that is Hades House so far and have met only

Mrs Riverthorpe and Ambrose. Ambrose seems to occupy an ambiguous position somewhere between housekeeper, lady's maid and esteemed friend. As such, I find myself unsure of how to speak to her, an irony that is not lost on me.

I suppose I should tell Mrs Riverthorpe, who presumably is bound up in Aurelia's secret in some unfathomable way, that Aurelia's aunt is here in Bath. But she is bustling me up the stairway, intent upon the ball. I will tell her tonight, I promise myself; there will be a better moment to speak of it.

Cecile comes to me just after I have laid out my dress and put some curling papers in my hair. I have selected the pink dress again. It seems a shame to wear the same gown twice and I prefer the apricot, yet for this reason I know it will not please Mrs Riverthorpe. Likely nothing will please Mrs Riverthorpe but that cannot be helped.

Cecile, however, takes one look and purses her lips. She hails from France, is very young and very certain of right and wrong. She opens my armoire without asking and leafs through my gowns like pages in a book. She stops at the red dress.

'No, Cecile. I cannot wear that. It is not right for me.' I speak simply in case there is a language barrier but Cecile looks astonished.

'Not right, *mademoiselle*? I think you are mistaken, forgive me. This is the perfect choice for the occasion.'

'No, you see, it is somewhat . . . *racier* than I would normally wear. It was a gift from a friend, a very kind gift, but it does not suit me so well as the pink.'

'It will suit you to perfection. Far better than that one.' She shrugs and pulls out the dress. 'Come, *mademoiselle*, Mrs River-thorpe will want to inspect you before you leave. Let us not waste time.'

'No, truly, Cecile. It's very kind of you to help me but I would not be comfortable. I do not mean that it would not *become* me, but I would not feel *comfortable* in it. It does not . . . express who I am. It does not suit my character. Do you understand?'

'I understand you perfectly, *mademoiselle*, you explain it most clearly, but that is not the point. The point of dressing for a ball is not to express your character, it is to look . . . *comme il faut*. The pink will not do.'

Her English is impeccable, yet it is clear we do not speak the same language.

With remarkable dexterity, Cecile removes my hoop and exchanges it for a larger one, engulfs me with the red dress and pulls the papers from my hair, all in a matter of minutes.

She runs to fetch red roses, bandoline serum and something that looks very much like paraffin wax, then proceeds to work my hair into an extraordinary style. By the time she has fin-ished I look as if I have twice the quantity of hair that I actually do; it is piled atop my head, and I look taller than I am. Flat curls like question marks lay along my cheeks, and there are at least as many roses as tresses upon my head. Because of them, I smell divine.

I murmur that perhaps Cecile has overestimated the self-restraint of my hair, even *with* bandoline, but she shakes her head decisively and I dare to hope that even my hair will be cowed into obedience this evening.

I am equipped with a black fan, a black shawl and a black, beaded reticule. I am turned and turned about for a minute inspection, my bodice is smoothed, my skirts are tweaked and I am at last allowed out of the room.

Mrs Riverthorpe barely glances at me, but I know that in that glance she has taken in every detail of my appearance. 'Well done, Cecile. Good night.'

As we sweep out to the carriage, I catch sight of myself in a long mirror in the hall. I want to weep. It is not only that I feel exposed, uncomfortable and quite unfamiliar. But I do not even look *pretty*! The styling of my hair is not flattering to my face. Roses and hair appear to be engaged in a fight for supremacy and the black trimmings make my white skin look very stark. If I must become someone else for a night, I had far rather become a beauty.

Chapter Forty-six

The most surprising thing is that I impress. With intense concentration, my social graces are impeccable. Of course they are, they are Aurelia's. My dress is admired and my hair even more so. Apparently I am the height of fashion.

Mrs Riverthorpe introduces me with admirable vagueness as 'a young friend from the country'. No one seems to care where in the country — if it is not Bath, it is not interesting. All anyone talks about all night is Bath and no one asks me anything apart from what I think of Bath. I say how fine it is and what an array of diversions it offers, and everyone is happy.

I am continuously surrounded by a great lake of people. Mrs Riverthorpe, although shockingly rude to everyone, appears to be in great demand. Yet at the centre of this little court I feel lonelier than ever. I long for Madeleine and Priscilla, for Edwin and Constance, for Michael. I long for Henry. I long for a familiar face.

And then I see one! For the third time today, I am amazed.

I am starting to feel as though everyone I ever met (which is admittedly not so very many) will congregate here in Bath tonight. As I glance and glance away, I see his gaze sweep the room, measured and methodical. When it reaches my party, it rests on me with some interest, then moves on to Mrs Riverthorpe. I am unsurprised; if Henry could not recognize me earlier, then surely Mr Garland cannot do so this evening. My transformation has gone a stage further tonight.

I still hope to speak with him, however. If nothing else, I should dearly love to hear news of Twickenham and perhaps of my friends there.

Mr Garland excuses himself from his company and moves towards us. He insinuates himself with great delicacy through the throng. I feel some nervous anticipation lest he should greet me, and lest he should not. Upon reaching Mrs Riverthorpe, tonight clad in an outlandish gown of shimmering gold, he seizes her hand and kisses it.

'My dear Ariadne, how splendid to see you, and looking so radiant. How do you do?'

She creaks a curtsey, as though her very bones resist civility.

'Quentin. I do as usual, that is to say still alive, still in possession of my fortune and still vastly displeased with everyone I meet. I doubt you can entertain me any better. At least you are easier on the eye than most. I always think that if a man has no looks to recommend him, he should hide away and not inflict himself on the public. Delicacy demands it. Yet, here we are, surrounded by men both unattractive and dull. What can be done?'

I gasp at her audacity. The gentlemen in question, standing all around, smile gamely as though determined to enjoy Mrs Riverthorpe by hook or by crook.

At my gasp, Mr Garland turns to me with a charming smile. 'Might I have the pleasure, Ariadne, of meeting your new friend?'

'I thought you'd like her. Quentin, this is a young friend of mine from the country, Miss Amy Snow. Amy, may I present Mr Quentin Garland. He's a bore like the rest of them, but he's handsome and rich so it takes people longer to notice.'

'Good evening, Mr Garland.' I make a deep curtsey.

At the sound of my name he raises his eyebrows.

'Good heavens! Why, I do believe we have . . . Miss *Snow*?'

'That's right, Quentin. Amy, have you met this shiny fellow before?'

'Why, yes, at Twickenham. How do you do, Mr Garland? How good to see you again.'

And it is. He looks handsomer than ever – tall and slender, with the light from the chandeliers dancing over his golden hair like sunlight on water. His customary powder-blue cravat has been exchanged this evening for a paler shade, cold and blue as ice.

'I wouldn't go so far as *good*, Amy. It is never truly *good* to see

Mr Garland, with his fingers in pies and his multiple investments. Lord, how he makes one yawn.'

Mr Garland looks genuinely amused.

'I hope that is not your memory of me, Miss Snow, but if it is, I hope I may rectify it tonight. Would you honour me with a dance, if you have any free?'

I consult my dance card, fumbling and dropping my reticule and fan. I duck to pick them up, then remember that I am corseted and hooped in a way that makes doing so impossible. Besides, I am supposed to stand around and wait for eager gentlemen to pick them up for me. As indeed they do. Mr Garland gravely fills in his name in more than one space.

The night passes, unsettling as a dream. Oh, the scene is as pretty as the ball in Richmond: the whirling skirts and twinkling crystal, the beautiful young ladies and enormous bouquets. But it is grander, and Lowbridge was quite, quite grand enough for me. I feel as though I meet the whole population of Bath in one evening, and I dance for hours.

I try to imagine Aurelia here, dancing in this very room before me, too caught up in flirting and fascinating to come home. I keep expecting to see Aurelia, laughing and rolling her eyes at me. When I began this journey, I used to feel this way all the time, but I have not done so for a while. It shocks me to realize that somewhere along the way I must have accepted that she is gone for always.

I dance several times with Mr Garland and it feels very strange to be here with him, particularly after meeting Henry in town today. It is as though the different pieces of my life are reassembling themselves and time has blurred.

I find that dancing with him is an entirely different experience from holding a conversation with him. I feel small and awkward. Where he glides, I scurry, where he dips and sways, I bob and swing. I wish I could feel at ease, I wish I could impress him but I remain convinced that I seem gauche and unpolished next to him. If he receives the same impression, he gives no sign of it and returns for each new dance with as much enthusiasm as the last.

At last an energetic reel defeats me. I cannot keep up with his long legs and he leads me to a seat and brings me a glass of punch, which he delivers with a bow. He has managed to find a quiet spot in a room where I could not have imagined such a thing would exist and sits down with his head inclined toward me.

It is a relief to sit and catch my breath and at last I can ask him about my friends. To my disappointment, Mr Garland has heard nothing of the Wisters since we last met. Apparently, on his return from Edinburgh, he had called and left his card with, he said, a stout red-faced maid.

'Oh, how *was* Bessy?' I cry. He looks at me oddly.

'I did not enquire. I believe she looked . . . hearty.'

Of course, Mr Garland would hardly have passed the time of day with a servant.

The family were all out and I had moved on, he was told – Bessy could not say where. He was disappointed to have missed me but accepted his fate.

'If I am to disappear for weeks at a time, what am I to expect?' he shrugs ruefully. 'I did not like to call on the family, knowing them so slightly, and ask where you had gone. Still, I am very pleased to find you here, Miss Snow.'

I smile. Although we have said nothing of the Lowbridge ball, I still feel certain that news of the scandal with Mrs Ellington must have reached him; it is good to know he has not regretted our acquaintance because of it.

A further surprise is that no one here has met Aurelia. I ask three or four people but the name of Lady Aurelia Vennaway prompts no fond recollections. Neither can anyone tell me anything of Frederic Meredith. I wonder if people go out of fashion here as quickly as headdresses.

Chapter Forty-seven

The hours wear on, my slippers wear out. Mrs Riverthorpe calls me back to her side at intervals to meet someone or to ask my opinion on someone else. I do not know why, for she invariably disagrees.

On one such occasion, she asks me to fetch a glass of punch. I am fishing in the crystal punch bowl – as big as a lake – when I again see someone I know. But unlike Henry or Mr Garland, this is no pleasant surprise. Long chestnut hair, aristocratic features . . . my blood chills and stills. I should have known she would be here. I should have known, and told Mrs Riverthorpe.

'So it *is* you!' hisses Arabella Beverley, Lady Vennaway's third sister.

She is dressed in half-mourning and I feel the red of my dress hot and shameful as blood. Although far less handsome, she has the abundant hair of her eldest sister and niece, the same fine bone structure. It is, quite literally, like being in the presence of a ghost. I move to touch her, expecting that she will dissolve before me, for although my brain tells me it is Arabella Beverley, my heart searches always for Aurelia Vennaway.

She steps back from my reaching hand and I spill the punch.

'I should never have recognized you but that Marianne Hamilton just told me that someone was asking about Aurelia. It made me look and look again. How come *you* to be at Lord Littleton's engagement ball and dressed so fine?' She is looking me up and down. 'I see that bereavement evidently has not troubled *you*!'

I am filled with panic, my head is entirely clouded with it. All I can think is that she must never know that Aurelia has left me a fortune. Her sister has already written to me. She is still thinking about me. If Arabella Beverley returns to Surrey and tells her sister that I am living the high life in Bath society and clearly dripping with money, they will come after me, they will come after me and they will find out that Aurelia had a secret. All those stages of my journey, all those precautions, all in vain . . .

I spin round to run away but her thin arm shoots out to catch me.

'Where are you going, you little hussy? What are you hiding? Should you like me to tell all of Bath what you are and where you come from?'

'I do not care a fig for all of Bath, madam. You may tell them if you like!' I snap, trembling with rage. It is like the last ball, all over again, except this time I make no attempt to avoid the inevitable confrontation.

'Is that so?' she says slowly, still detaining me. 'Why so careless with your reputation, miss, when you have evidently climbed a great way? I wonder how you did that in so short a time. Ah, I see. I *see*!'

I do not see. It is apparent that she has reached a conclusion but I am unsure what it is.

'Amy? Is this person bothering you?'

I am saved by the unlikeliest of rescuers. Mrs Riverthorpe's grey eyes turn black as they gaze upon Mrs Beverley.

'This is Mrs Beverley. She is Aurelia's aunt.'

I mutter the explanation for it seems futile to make a formal introduction and I only want Mrs Riverthorpe to understand that Aurelia's secret is at stake.

She takes my other arm and for an instant I am caught between the two as though they are children fighting over a doll. Then Mrs Beverley lets go and I take a step closer to my hostess. She is narrow as a blade and quivers when she walks but next to me now she feels as solid and strong as an oak.

'Do you know who this *is*?' Mrs Beverley splutters.

'Naturally I do,' says Mrs Riverthorpe dismissively. 'Amy Snow, poor as a church mouse when she left your sister's house, looking decidedly more splendid now. What of it?'

I watch as Mrs Beverley takes in her opponent's plentiful diamonds and bare, wrinkled shoulders, the coquettish feathers piled in her silvery hair. Then she looks at my flashy, low-shouldered gown, at my black net and beading, at the roses tumbling seductively from my hair. I see her draw inevitable comparisons.

'I should like to know how I find her here. She does not belong amongst respectable people. Clearly she was thwarted when Aurelia left her nothing but a modest legacy, and now it seems she has found another means to advance herself . . . well, financially at least.'

Her face is wearing that mixture of horror and delight I saw so often at Hatville. I begin to entertain a creeping suspicion about the conclusion that Mrs Beverley is drawing about me. It is true, I know, that precious few options are open to a young woman alone in the world without protection or means – and really only one that would allow me to have become so fine so fast.

'Respectable people, are we?' Mrs Riverthorpe sneers. 'Your *respectable* sister threw Amy out without a sou, after a lifetime of service to her daughter! Amy has rectified the situation – remarkably successfully. I am proud of her.'

I want to pull away from her restraining hand. I do not mind people knowing I come from the shabbiest of beginnings, but my self-respect chafes at having them think such a thing as this. I want to protest that I am wealthy thanks to Aurelia and Aurelia alone. But this is precisely what I cannot do. And while Mrs Beverley may believe the worst of me, this way she will not ask questions about my legacy.

'I do not know your name, madam,' says Aurelia's aunt, 'for you have not had the courtesy to introduce yourself. I am not sure, however, that what *you* consider a source of pride would be considered such by people of refinement, who *might* see the passing years as a cause to present themselves with dignity and reticence.'

'Ah, courtesy you're after now, is it? Then I shall tell you my name. I am Ariadne Riverthorpe.'

As at the ball in Richmond, a small cluster has gathered at the first sniff of confrontation. I can well imagine Mrs Riverthorpe promises a good show. Mr Garland, I think inconsequentially, will note that I cannot attend a ball without finding myself at the centre of some disgrace.

The name is evidently known to Mrs Beverley, for her pale-blue eyes widen. What little reputation I have is disappearing like rainwater down a drain. Mrs Riverthorpe proceeds, supremely unconcerned.

'Dignity and reticence you want, is it? So a woman should shut herself away the instant she develops a wrinkle, should she? Cover herself in veils and keep quiet? Are *men* made to feel ashamed once they cease to be decorative? Are *men* such creatures of beauty, with their springy hairs and fleshy jowls and sprouting groins? I think *not*!'

A titter runs around the onlookers like champagne bubbles streaming to the surface.

All I can reflect is that I was mortified about saying 'naked' in public at Richmond! At least I never spoke of a 'sprouting groin'. Mrs Beverley's pale cheeks are flooded with colour.

'You are a hypocrite, Mrs Beverley,' Aurelia's extraordinary friend continues. 'You find your refuge in conventions and tell yourself that the bargains *you* have struck are morally sound, because they are socially sanctioned. Only the weak require such a refuge. So go home. Tell them all that Amy has a fortune now. Tell them that all they wished for her – the poverty, the ignominy, the obscurity – has not come to pass. She rejects it.'

Mrs Beverley nods. 'Oh, I shall tell them, you may be sure of it.'

She is joined by a stout, vague-looking gentleman, Aurelia's uncle I presume, and Mrs Beverley turns to him with something like a sob. Puzzled, he glances at the two strangers confronting his wife and guides her away. The little crowd disperses.

Mrs Riverthorpe cackles. 'Ha! Tiny little world, is it not? Inconvenient, but no harm done, I think.'

'Did she . . . did she . . .?'

'What's the matter girl, found a knot in your tongue? Where's my punch, anyway?'

Stunned, I refill the glass I am still clutching and hand it to her.

'Mrs Riverthorpe, if I am correct, Mrs Beverley believes, and you implied, that I am a . . . I am a . . . Now everyone at Hatville will think that I am a . . .'

'Precisely! Ha! You see how useful it is to have people so ready to think badly of you?'

'But Mrs Riverthorpe, people were *listening*! It is not just in Hatville that these rumours will circulate, why, all of Bath . . .'

'I thought you did not care a fig for all of Bath.'

'Well, no, but . . .'

She leans close to me and fixes her beady eyes on mine.

'Amy, do not be such an innocent. It was that or have her think that Aurelia left you a legacy. She has been diverted. That is what you wanted, is that not so?'

'Yes.'

'And you care nothing for Bath society, is *that* not so?'

'*Yes!* But it is painful to have strangers believe of me something so grossly untrue, so vastly at odds with my sensibilities.'

'Pfff, sensibilities. Amy, you were born into disgrace and have been treated as such for most of your life. Everywhere you go people think of you things that are not true, not least that your devotion to Aurelia was a sham calculated to obtain her money! You're a young woman travelling alone in a society that absolutely reviles independence in a woman. You *invite* censure and misunderstanding! You can't *afford* sensibilities.'

I stare at her, lost for words.

'But be honest, Amy. You would not change a thing. You like to think that Aurelia has put you in an intolerable position, but you would not go back to your old life, sweet and dependent and downtrodden as you were. You would not go back!' So saying, she stalks off.

For a moment I stand speechless, watching her go. Then I spin on my heel and storm off in the opposite direction.

I flounce up the stairs towards the grand gallery and the doors to the balcony. I need cool night air to wash away the shame. I cannot bear to think that what Mrs Riverthorpe says is true; I would have Aurelia back at any price. Wouldn't I?

A cluster of guests near the door slows my progress and as I step past them, I see the scene reflected in a huge floor-length mirror with an elaborate gold-leaf frame. Innocent, fresh young girls, dressed in white or cream, are clustered around their mammas, looking as cool and sheltered as snowdrops. And there am I in the foreground, in my vibrant dress, red as wine. My hair has defied Cecile; hair and roses yield to gravity in a dark tumble. My face is flushed, my eyes are burning. I am the same age as those girls but my experience is all different. I falter as I pass them for they look so pretty and pale and safe.

And yet, if the choice were mine . . . For the very first time in my life, what I feel when I see myself is admiration. I am negotiating the world, no matter how clumsily. I am *not* sweet and dependent. I am fierce and free. It scalds me to admit it but Mrs Riverthorpe is right: I would not go back.

Chapter Forty-eight

The carriage ride home passes in prickling silence; I have a good deal of thinking to do, whether or not she approves of it. However, when we step into the hall of Hades House, eerier than ever with a single lamp throwing ineffectual beams along its shadowy length, I follow her to the drawing room without a word being spoken by either of us. We will take a glass of Madeira together.

A small fire burns. Mrs Riverthorpe sinks onto a lumpy green chaise and I suddenly understand that she is old. It seems a foolish thing to remark only now, two full days after meeting her, but Mrs Riverthorpe is brute will and pure life force, all trussed up in extraordinary fabrics. It is hard to see her as elderly, for her every word and gaze and gown forbids it. Nevertheless, it is not every eighty-year-old who would stay at a ball 'til past two in the morning, taking on each and every individual she meets in some obscure battle of her own determining.

I realize that she reminds me rather of Aurelia. True, Aurelia was young and beautiful and charming, but perhaps so was Mrs Riverthorpe once. In sheer presence, determination and brilliance, they are alike.

The thought makes me feel more tenderly towards her as I hand her a glass. I notice that her clawed hand trembles a little in the taking of it.

'Well, and what might Miss Amy make of tonight's interesting events? If it is not too soon to ask such a question. If she does not need a few weeks to work it out.'

Her derision feels perfunctory; she even smiles at me. She must be tired.

I fill a glass of my own and take a seat opposite her. 'I believe I may need a lifetime to work it out. It felt like a dream to me, Mrs Riverthorpe – people from Hatville, people from Twickenham, all the pieces of my life colliding.'

'It is not unusual. One cannot spend five minutes Bath without seeing a dozen people one knows from somewhere else.'

'So I am beginning to understand! My circle of connections is not large yet even I have seen two people I know.' I do not mention Henry. I do not want her mocking me. 'Oh, that Aurelia's aunt could believe *that* of me!'

'You were hardly assured of her good opinion previously. I am sorry to disillusion you, but your association with me alone calls your respectability into question. There are rumours aplenty about me, you know. Never care what anyone thinks, Amy. Or if you must, never let them see it.'

'Are they true, the rumours?'

'Does it matter?'

'No, but I am naturally curious. You were a friend of Aurelia's. I am staying in your home. Yet I know nothing of what your life has been.'

She laughs, not her usual shrewd cackle but wearily, in a way that makes my bones dissolve.

'You could never know what my life has been. Oh, I don't mean to disparage you – no one could understand it. There is a pattern laid out for women in this world of ours, Amy, and Lord help us if we do not follow it.

'But if life throws challenges at us that fall outside that pattern, what may we do? It makes me laugh that women are permitted so few alternatives, and are then punished for resorting to the ones they have. It makes me laugh that women are reviled for using the one true power they possess in a way that benefits *them*! It makes me laugh that we are doomed to a life of obloquy for stepping outside the twisted paradox that nature and training make of us. A good many things make me laugh, Amy, and not one of them funny.' And she rocks mirthlessly back and forth in a grim parody of laughter.

'You sound just like Aurelia.'

Her face softens. 'Once, I was very like her – a lady too, with a great many expectations upon me. I was young, about your age, when I was seduced by a scoundrel who abandoned me. I had run away with him, so my choice was very public, there was no way to pretend it had not happened. A similar thing had happened a few years earlier to another young lady of my acquaintance. She killed herself from the shame of it.'

She rises and stumps over to the fire and jabs it with the poker. It flares up as though protesting, but it does little for the chill. She sits once again on the chaise, facing me very squarely, one arm resting on its mahogany arm, the other stretched out along its back. No demure hands clasped in lap for *her*.

'It was generally acknowledged, then, that she was an innocent victim. Her act of self-destruction, you see, was regarded as a sign of her sensibility and essential virtue despite erring. She did a most excellent job of restoring her good name. The only problem was, she was dead.'

'Clearly you made a different choice.'

'Indeed I did. Anyone who had rather be dead than disgraced is a fool.'

The darkness seems to gather ever closer around us. 'I . . . I agree with you, Mrs Riverthorpe. And are you –' The word 'happy' does not seem appropriate – 'when you look back, does your life please you?'

To my surprise, she looks at me consideringly, as though it is a good question. 'I suppose if God thought my sin was so unforgiveable he could have finished me off himself, but he did not. Amy, that was *five and sixty* years ago now. They have not all been easy, they have not all been pretty and they have been *filled* with trials, but they were *my* years – all mine – and no one can tell me I should not have had them.' She nods decisively and throws her Madeira down her throat.

'I have been talked about, you may believe it. Many of the stories about me are true. And many are not. That is the way of it, once you step outside the cage. But I will not deign to correct a single one of them. So here you find me. Not respectable, but powerful, which is a different thing altogether.'

I am silent a while, digesting her words. I cannot deny that I admire her spirit to live public and proud, instead of hiding away in obscurity. The original parties must all be long departed now – her parents, her seducer, her scandalized neighbours. Yet old taints cling and drift like the smell of onions, as I well know.

I imagine if Aurelia and Robin had been discovered. She would have faced down any scandal head-on, even relished it, had she been healthy. But tired and weak and facing death, well, she had other battles to fight. I am beginning to understand this odd friendship with Mrs Riverthorpe now. I am beginning to understand the great lengths to which Aurelia has gone to reveal the truth of her last years to me and only me.

'What I find incomprehensible is why anyone would *choose* this life,' I say at last. 'I could not bear it. To be always on display, always suspicious of people's motives, wondering what they are saying about me.'

'Do you really think it is different anywhere else?'

I remember Hatville: endless overheard slights and slurs.

I remember London: the cold, affronted glances of the wealthy folk in the Pantheon as I searched amongst them unchaperoned.

I remember Mrs Ellington: 'You presume to name it a friendship? How can such a thing exist between the wealthy young daughter of the finest family in Surrey and one such as yourself?' I feel my heart sink a little more with every reflection.

Then I recall Henry and Albert. The Wisters and Bessy. Above all, as clearly as if I saw her only yesterday, I recall my dear Aurelia, always overjoyed to see me. 'Come on, Amy, it's a beautiful day, let's go down to the stream!'

I blink back hot tears. My throat clogs and I swallow my Madeira in a draught, get up once more to pour another.

'It *can* be different. Maybe not in any one *place*, but in pockets in many places – perhaps *any* place! I have always thought myself unfortunate, Mrs Riverthorpe, but I am not so, for I have known true friendship. Of all the blessings in life, this must be the brightest and best.'

'Very well, child, don't excite yourself. Yes, yes, the world is full of lovely people and true devotion is what makes the world go round. Is that why I was so popular tonight, do you imagine?'

I snort a little into my glass. 'Mrs Riverthorpe, forgive me but I am astonished that you were so popular tonight.'

She cackles. 'It is because I am rich, of course, and better than that, I am alone in the world with no heirs to inherit my fortune. They are vultures circling, Amy, waiting to pick me over when I am dead. Each professes to find me amusing, to admire my determination to live for ever when in fact they find it tiresome in the extreme. I am what you might term an uncertain investment of time and self-respect: they know they *might* pay court to me for years and put up with all my disgraceful ways and never receive a sou.' She smiles a truly wicked smile, her grey eyes bright in the darkness.

I cannot help but share her glee, unkind though it is. I find I am suddenly relishing her company. If I were not wearing a hoop the size of Bath, I should like to tuck my legs up underneath me in this large brown armchair. 'I do not understand you, Mrs Riverthorpe. You profess to scorn society yet you live at its very heart! Why?'

'Bath society is what I know. It amuses me! I could no sooner live a quiet life where everyone stitched and smiled and offered one another hankies than I could fly to the moon. That is the delicious irony of it Amy. I feed off *them*! They who want me dead are keeping me alive.

'Watching Quentin Garland pay court to you, for instance.' She leans toward me eagerly, scrutinizing my face. 'Hilarious! I'll wager *he* does not know your humble origins. I'll wager he thinks *you* look like a sound investment.'

'You're wrong.' I do enjoy saying it. 'Mr Garland met me when I was shabbily dressed and lost. He was as gentlemanly then as he was tonight. *And* I imagine he knows where I come from, for all of Richmond knows it and he is connected there.'

'Is that so? Well, that is interesting. In that case, be careful. But come now, you have me in a mellow mood. Do not waste the opportunity, but ask me the things you really want to ask.' She sits back again and waits.

I am a little unnerved by her comments about Mr Garland but she has hit on the one sure way of distracting me. 'May I have Aurelia's letter and leave?'

'Haaaaa! That bad, eh? You've only been here two days! Oh, you are a tender little thing. No, you may not. You and I both made promises to that girl. I shall not betray her wishes.'

'I knew you would say that. But *why* are these her wishes? For heaven's sake, she cannot *possibly* have thought I would be happy here. Do you know her great secret, Mrs Riverthorpe, the one that she is guiding me towards?'

'I do. I shall not tell you, naturally, but I do.'

I frown at the bent, embattled old woman in front of me. Not only did Aurelia trust her sufficiently to involve her in the treasure trail but she has entrusted her with the outcome too. I look at Mrs Riverthorpe in a new light. Mercy, is the trail indeed to end here in Bath – where everyone now thinks I am a courtesan?

'As it happens, I know the answer to your other question too, and that I can tell you. The reason she brought you here, Amy, is not *about* happiness, it is about choice.' She can read my mind. I knew it. 'That is why I am not to release you yet. Whether you approve of it or not, society, money, a fashionable life, are things that the majority of people in our world covet fiercely. She wanted you to have that choice.'

Now it is my turn to scoff. The proposition seems outlandish. 'But Aurelia knew me better than that. Aurelia loved flirting and being fêted. That is not *my* way.'

Mrs Riverthorpe's face is, as ever, rascally. She reaches out a bony arm and takes my hand. 'Don't dismiss it so fast and sit there feeling superior. You have been here only *two days* – you know nothing! It *wasn't* your way, for how could it be? Aurelia wanted you to make an educated choice. Don't tell me you weren't flattered at being singled out by that shimmerer Garland tonight. Is he your true love, d'you suppose? Do his attentions confer upon you a distinction you never had before – and which you *like*?'

I stutter a little, wanting to defend myself, but she rolls on, still gripping my hand. 'Did you not see the jealous glances cast your way by the other young ladies tonight? If you did, then perhaps you are not averse to being fêted at all costs after all. If you did not, you must be a little stupid.'

'I . . . I didn't,' I murmer. Clearly, then, I am a little stupid. She appears unsurprised.

'Well, there we are then. But consider this, Amy: with Aurelia's fortune and my introduction, if you wanted to stay here and live the life of a great lady, you could. No doubt you could marry some elegant buck like Quentin Garland and have elegant babies.

'Now, I am sure you will not choose thus; nevertheless it remains a possibility for you until you walk away from it. Aurelia knew she had deprived you of choice by keeping you with her. All that is changed now. You can have anything you want.'

She releases my hand at last. I think the late hour and the high drama of the evening have overwhelmed me. 'But I cannot! I cannot have Aurelia back from the dead. I cannot return to Twickenham unless I betray her trust. I cannot leave here tomorrow. So no, I *cannot* have anything I want.'

She curls her lip in disgust. 'Very well, dear, woe is you.'

We lapse back into silence. The fire has dwindled again and it is very cold. I should like to go and fetch something warmer but I'm loath to turn my back on Mrs Riverthorpe in case she vanishes in a puff of smoke. Something else has occurred to me. I take a vain poke at the fire but it promises to expire any minute.

'Mrs Riverthorpe, I find it bewildering that Aurelia would send me here of all places when she has been at such great pains to protect her secret. A treasure hunt! Letters strung across the land! Me travelling hither and thither in complete ignorance of my purpose! But it renders all my efforts at secrecy completely superfluous if everyone I ever met along the way is to converge in Bath.'

'You're quite right. That was a miscalculation on her part. And vastly inconvenient besides.'

'Then why on earth did she do it? Why insist on such stringent measures if only to bring me to the most public place imaginable?'

'Because she did not know.'

'But Aurelia was not stupid. She must have realized there was a good chance that I would cross paths here with at least *someone* I had known elsewhere.'

'No, she didn't.'

'However so?'

'Because, my dear, she never was in Bath.'

I wrap my shawl closer. The hairs stand up on my arms. 'Of course she was! I had letters from her. Do you mean she did not stay in this house? Did she have other friends here? Unfashionable friends . . . servants perhaps? It would be like her. Might that be why you have never heard of Frederic Meredith? Is that why no one tonight seemed to know Aurelia?'

Mrs Riverthorpe stands up stiffly and leans heavily on her cane. I realize with a sinking heart that I have lost her for tonight. 'No, Amy. I was not in Bath when I met Aurelia. I shall say this, then go to bed, for I have more evil-doing to enjoy tomorrow and I need my rest. Aurelia did not know what it is like here in Bath because she never came here. And as for Frederic Meredith, I very much doubt that he even exists.'

Chapter Forty-nine

I wake early on Saturday morning, recent events cavorting into my mind like unruly ponies. It feels as though this should be happening to some other girl; the spirited girl in red I glimpsed in the mirror last night perhaps. No, I cannot deny it; she is me.

Despite all I am learning about myself, what I am learning about Aurelia is yet more perplexing. Since I left London, only weeks ago, I have discovered so much about Aurelia that I never knew. But that is nothing compared with last night's discovery. I am in Bath and she never was. And Frederic Meredith does not exist? Not only did Aurelia withhold a number of truths from me, then, she also *lied*. Is Mrs Riverthorpe making mischief? Is it she who is somehow *wrong*? And if she is telling the truth, then where *did* they meet? In what circumstances did a lonely heiress from Surrey encounter – and apparently form a great bond with – an elderly eccentric from Bath? The possibilities are endless and somewhat overwhelming.

I climb out of bed and ring for coffee. I wrap a shawl around my shoulders and take out Aurelia's letters, not her recent letters, the ones from years ago. I return to bed and decide I will not leave it until I have re-read every last one. Thoroughly.

The letters begin as I remember them, full of exuberance about her time in London. She also sounded homesick for me and for the countryside. There is no mention of her parents. None of this strikes me amiss.

Then she went to Twickenham. The letters are plentiful, detailed, happy. I looked through these old letters just recently, when I was in Twickenham – already I am re-reading with an altered awareness. Different details jump out at me.

In the heatwave of 1844, I read these letters and worried that her adventures would prove too much for her, that she would sicken and die and I would never see her again. Today, with those fears consigned to the past, I read with new eyes. I try to imagine how it really was for Aurelia, after finding love in Robin's arms, after a bitter betrayal by her parents, after fleeing from home. How she must have longed to be well, to relish every chance to enjoy herself without her mother's constant cold-eyed vigilance. How it must have angered and frightened her when her health compromised the freedom for which she had fought so hard.

I find myself returning again and again to certain passages.

May 31st, 1844:

This morning I did not feel strong and felt sure I should have to miss out on the picnic in Whitton, but I was able to eat a little soup at noon and I rallied after all!

June 5th, 1844:

Lady Caulton's dance was highly amusing – the assorted great and good endeavouring to be less serious for an evening. I danced almost every dance, impressive considering how weak and downright shoddy I had felt only that same morning.

June 17th, 1844:

For once my obstinacy failed me. I forced myself to dress only to be overcome with giddy spirals. I passed out, Amy, and lucky I did so with the bedroom door open for apparently Hollis spied my prone form and summoned his sisters with a great many yells. I recovered swiftly, but dear Madeleine would not leave me, not for all my entreating . . .

A strong suspicion comes upon me then, one which makes my own head spin. I wonder if Aurelia suspected it also. I think not, or I do not believe she would have written of her symptoms so frankly. Of course, such references are brief, lost amongst the many passages describing happy times. And all the while she sounded like Aurelia.

Then suddenly, she is in Derby. Here is the never-forgotten warning that the journey would mean a break in our correspondence:

> The journey will be a long one, dear, and there is a great deal to prepare . . . Please do not be alarmed at this delay.

Here is the break in the letters: only three brief notes throughout July, all sent from Derby. As an insecure thirteen-year-old, I was bored by the accounts of this gentleman with fifteen thousand a year and that young baronet with twenty. Today they bore me still but for a different reason: it is because they are not vivid or warm or *real*.

She may have been trying to submerge her doomed feelings for Robin by searching for a replacement. Or perhaps she felt bitter that they had no future, and tried to assuage this by flirting with anything in a cravat. But however I explain it, these pale accounts do not sound like the Aurelia I knew.

In the light of what Mrs Riverthorpe told me last night, I find myself wondering, abruptly, if she was ever there at all.

Surely this is an insane thought. Here is a letter from the August, and another, and another, all written from Derby. But . . . not that many letters, all told, considering how long she was there.

Her sketches are unconvincing too. I do not mean that artistic merit is lacking, but Aurelia's drawings always included deeply personal or whimsical touches. The sketches from Derby are all of the hills, none of people, or animals, or quaint corners. They do not match the letters and they do not contain any little details that had captured Aurelia's attention and that she wanted to share with me. They could as easily have been copied from a book as drawn from life.

I remember what Michael told me the morning I left Twickenham.

'She went away too soon as well, disappeared all sudden, just like you.'

Why should it have seemed sudden to him? She was always due to leave them in June – and come home to Hatville. If she decided to travel for longer, why should that have meant cutting short her time in Twickenham?

I try out a new theory, just for size. *What if Aurelia conceived a child with Robin?*

They would have guarded against it, I am certain, but surely these things cannot be an exact science? It stands to reason that if it could be so easily controlled there would be no unwanted babies. And even though the woman is most often disgraced, men too can be ruined by such a thing.

I am put in mind of Mr Templeton and the maid with the strawberry-blonde curls. Irrespective of the rights and wrongs of the matter, Mr Templeton's standing in the community was compromised along with hers. Their liaison only ever came to light because she fell pregnant. If it had been within Mr Templeton's full control to avoid this, why would he not have done so?

If Aurelia was pregnant – *if* she was – what then? When might she have realized it? What *happened* to her? It would certainly explain her reluctance to commit to paper anything of what she was really experiencing in a letter to me.

And afterwards? During those last years of her life, when I felt we enjoyed a new, mature friendship as two young women rather than small child and big sister, could she really have kept such a vast secret from me *then*? I grit my teeth. They are the same old questions in a new context.

Perhaps, like her mother before her, she miscarried. Perhaps the Vennaway women do not easily bring a baby to term. I do not really know how these things work, I am thinking wildly. But it seems more likely than Aurelia having a child and never telling me. It seems more likely than Aurelia giving birth at all, given her condition. The risks of such a course, Dr Jacobs had told us, were not slight. And she had not come together with Robin just once, in the heat of grief, but repeatedly. *Surely* she would not have done so if she were not sure it was safe? The old Amy cannot think that Aurelia – my clever, bright big sister – could make a mistake so great. The new Amy, who appears to be developing swiftly, can see all too well that Aurelia was fallible and flawed and a little desperate, which does not foster sound judgement. Even so, there is little sense to be found . . .

I continue reading. She stayed in Derby, if the letters are to be believed, into August before travelling yet further north to Manchester and Leeds, promising to return to us by Christmas. Here her letters regain a little of their natural colour and conviction:

> You should have seen the cotton mill at Hatby, outside Manchester, dear: like a never-ending Christmas the white flakes whirl and dance perpetually. But there are no snowmen and there is no cheer; the factory workers – men, women and children too, some as young as six – are red-eyed from concentration and cough insistently, though no one can hear it over the sound of the machines.

I cannot help but recall an article that Aurelia and I had read about this industry some years ago. Was that before her trip or after it? I think it was before. I wonder whether there is a town called Hatby, and whether Aurelia ever really saw the inside of a mill.

> Amy, the countryside of the north makes Surrey look like a pale imitation of the concept 'rural'! Great fells that fall away as if the very winds had cut out great hunks of land, deep bluey-green rolling moors scattered with white rivers that bound over rocks and skip into cascades that come to rest in

glassy pools and fairy glades. Yes! I saw fairies – everywhere – no one can tell me I didn't.

Yesterday, Amy, I went to York! Such a <u>pretty</u> city.

Last week I saw the sea at Scarborough. How you would love to go, dear.

I try to imagine that she is pregnant and understandably preoccupied. Or else that, having miscarried a child, she was weakened and grieving. I try to imagine her moving from place to place to place, throughout the summer, throughout a heatwave. Even if she were never pregnant, with her heart condition it smacks of lunacy. There is no answer that satisfies. After July there is no further reference to her health.

I read on. I read of her decision to extend her trip a little longer and return via Shrewsbury and Bath, in both cases invited by friends of people I had never heard of.

I did not imagine the letters from Bath. They are in my hands, postmarked and full of platitudes about the handsome features of Frederic Meredith, whom Mrs Riverthorpe claims does not exist.

Here the letters end. She did not notify me in advance of her return. It was like Aurelia to make it a surprise.

I look at the pages scattered over my bedcovers. Here is a new puzzle, a treasure hunt within the treasure hunt. I gather what I know for certain. Aurelia was definitely in Twicken-ham. I know this because I have been there, and they knew her, and her letters are convincing and frequent. Aurelia was *not* in Bath, according to Mrs Riverthorpe, and her letters are uncharacteristic and few. Her letters from all the places in between are also uncharacteristic and few, calling the majority of her journey into question. So where was she? And what was she doing?

The idea that there might have been a child is preposterous. If there was, then where is he or she now? It is, however, the only explanation that could conceivably justify her obsession with secrecy, the only secret important enough to warrant sending me hither and thither across the country, although I still do not understand the exact mechanics of her thinking.

And yet Aurelia was *not* always reasonable. She was not always thoughtful. She was anything but predictable. Maybe she *had* no good reason. It is like all the old mysteries – insoluble and cyclical.

I feel close to knowing, so close, and yet I still have to wait nearly three weeks! I only hope that the rest of my time in Bath will not be quite so eventful as last night.

Chapter Fifty

The rest of the morning, at least, is decidedly *un*eventful. Or, more accurate to say, it does not bring the one event I long for: Henry's promised visit. He does not call, he does not leave his card, he does not send a note.

As morning melts into afternoon, I forget my preoccupation with Aurelia's secret and my new, outrageous suspicions. All I can think of is Henry. His absence sits in my stomach like a heavy stone at the bottom of a deep well. I pace the corridors, I slump in my room. I look at every clock a thousand times. At eleven o'clock, noon, luncheon, I tell myself that he has commitments this morning and that the afternoon will bring him, belated and brimming with apologies and smiles.

Although April offers her finest, most convincing sunshine of the year, I willingly confine myself to the grey chambers of Hades House. At three o'clock I worry that Henry's forgotten commitments might keep him busy all day and that I might not see him until tomorrow – or Monday . . . I truly don't know how I might wait so long. At half past the hour, when an almighty knocking thunders at the door, my heart leaps out of my chest. I jump out of my seat before remembering that it is not my place to answer. I force myself to lurk sedately on the stairs while Ambrose goes to the door – did she always walk this *slowly*? My disappointment knows no bounds when she announces Mr Garland.

He seems to make a habit of finding out where I am staying and arriving unannounced. So I reflect churlishly, in my despondency that he is not Henry. Ambrose shows him into the drawing room and Mrs Riverthorpe appears, garbed in purple, a mischievous gleam in her eye. I do not trust that gleam.

He has come, it seems, to establish that I will be at the archery meet tomorrow afternoon and to ask Mrs Riverthorpe and me if we would like to see a new pair of horses he has just acquired. Perhaps we might fancy a bowl around the city in his carriage, he suggests.

Mrs Riverthorpe, already on her feet and halfway out of the door, agrees that she might. 'Was there ever such a boring day?' she demands, glaring at me as though it were my responsibility to brighten it, though I have seen no sign of her all day.

In contrast I linger reluctantly by the fire. 'I . . . I . . . cannot, though I thank you for the invitation,' I stammer, rigid with awkwardness. I will not leave this house and risk missing Henry, but I am well aware I have no good excuse to give.

'Why not?' demands Mrs Riverthorpe, and I am put in mind

of a heron's jabbing beak, skewering a fish. 'Exhausted by the demands of the huge social circle you've acquired in the last three days?'

I force myself to smile. 'Of course it is not that. But I have a great many things to do this afternoon, letters to write –'

'Ah, yes, your wide network of correspondees – that's it, of course,' she jeers.

'Please don't inconvenience yourself, Miss Snow.' Mr Garland, tactful as ever, glides over to me, leaving Mrs Riverthorpe fidgeting in the drawing-room doorwary like an impatient child. 'It was an impromptu suggestion, with no guarantee that I might find you at liberty. I must wait until tomorrow for the pleasure of your company, but would you like to see the horses, at least, before we leave you in peace? They are just outside and I remember you saying you have a great love for animals.'

'Oh, I do! You're quite right, how very thoughtful.' I am flattered that he should remember. 'Very well, Mr Garland, you are most kind.' In truth it is a joy to be distracted from Henry, or the lack of him, for a few minutes and we all troop outside.

The April sun is warm and gentle. Mr Garland has a fashionable little phaeton in sky blue and gold, which is exactly the sort of carriage I would have imagined for him. The new horses are two gleaming bays, identical in height and with strong hocks and finely turned heads. Lord Vennaway would have admired them. I smile as I stroke their smooth noses and hold my hands under their enquiring velvety lips. They duck their heads and butt my chest, disgusted with my failure to bring titbits. I stumble, laughing, and Mr Garland reaches out to steady me. Flustered by the warm pressure of his hand on my arm, I comb my fingers through their silken black manes, perfectly straight and crisply trimmed, relishing the always comforting feeling of horsehair under my hands.

'Come on, come on!' calls Mrs Riverthorpe from inside the phaeton. Mr Garland smiles ruefully and bows.

'Until tomorrow, Miss Snow.' He swings easily into the carriage after her and they move off. I am reluctant to see those beautiful animals go. Horses were a part of my life at Hatville that was never complicated, and always enriching. I watch them trot smartly down the street until the happy sound of hooves has faded and then I go inside to wait.

And wait. Days pass, with no sign of Henry and I am lonelier than ever. When Mrs Riverthorpe asks me whether I will accompany her to this or that occasion, I say yes more often than I say no, simply to make the time pass more quickly. No matter my social obligations, I ensure that I go for a walk each day. Every day I cross Bath to walk the length of Henrietta Street, hoping that I might happen across Henry. Every day I return to the bridge where we met, I walk past the coffee shop where we talked and toasted our friendship. I see him everywhere, and yet he is nowhere.

I cannot understand it. His delight at seeing me again had felt real. Our *friendship* had felt real. He promised to call on me the next morning. My imagination runs wild. He has heard, and believed, that I am a lady of easy virtue . . . or he has simply thought better of a friendship with a woman leading so unconventional a life. I am too unusual, too free-spirited. Even I realize that, considering my fears upon our first meeting that I was too small and dull and dowdy, this is quite a turnaround . . . but I just do not know how to fathom his silence. And I *know* he knows my address – it is not easily forgettable.

Perhaps he has mentioned me to his friends the Longacres and they do not like the sound of me? They are meant to be a steadying influence upon him; they may suspect a roving single woman of no established background.

Or perhaps he has met someone – a lady – and feels our odd little friendship would not foster well a new romance. If this is the case, I will try my earnest best to wish him well with all my heart, for I could only ever wish Henry happy. Only I cannot help but wish I might be the one to make him happy and, as with so many things, I wish I *knew*.

Time passes so achingly slow. With all I have learned about Aurelia, and all I suspect besides, I am wild to receive the next letter. I remain convinced that the end of the trail and all the answers are near. I know better than to press Mrs Riverthorpe to give me the letter early, so it is a question of counting days. If she is happy to have my company, she disguises it well, but neither does she forbid me to join her. The presence of Quentin Garland at most of the functions I attend makes them more bearable.

I saw him, of course, for the archery on Sunday. He then encouraged me to go to a luncheon at a Mrs Rathbone's on the Monday. Later that afternoon, he called in his carriage and took Mrs Riverthorpe and me out for a ride. She is as dire towards him as can be, but he seems at ease in her company. Since I now find myself growing fond of her, for reasons entirely beyond my comprehension, I like him all the better for that. In fact, I like him a great deal. He is always courteous, always reliable and if the impression persists that he is far too glossy and perfect for me, I tuck it away and ignore it, for I have decided he is free to come to that conclusion – or not – himself. Certainly he seems to seek out my company and that gives my heart a warm, full feeling that is new and welcome.

When I have been in Bath, I feel sure, approximately six months, I check the calendar and learn that I have been here a week. Readying myself for another dinner, I pause to rest my forehead on the window pane and gaze at the street. It has become a habit. I see park railings, black and curlicued, an old lady with a small dog taking the air, accompanied by her maid, and pink cherry blossom in a garden. I see a gentlemen walk past briskly. I follow his progress idly, watching as he tips his hat to another gentleman approaching in the opposite direction. I stand up straight and look again. The approaching gentlemen is Henry! It is Henry! For a moment I am unable to move for the joy of watching him walk along Rebecca Street to see me. Oh, the relief! I cannot imagine what has taken him so long but I'm sure there's a good explanation and I will learn it very soon now. I turn to run to the door, then stop and watch him. Ambrose will call me and I want to savour the moment.

He looks taller than ever, dressed smartly for a call and wearing a new top hat, or at least a top hat which I have not seen before. He is not as perfectly turned out as Mr Garland, I note. A little too much shirtsleeve peeps below the cuff of his coat and his cravat is askew, as though once tightly knotted but soon tugged loose. There are dark curls about his face and his walk is a lope. My heart melts. He is exactly how a man should be.

He stops a little way short of the house and I smile. No, it's here, Henry, I telegraph him mentally. But I don't think he has the wrong place, for he is looking directly at Hades House. Perhaps he is put off by its sombre appearance? From this angle I can just see his face and to my dismay he does not look happy. His expression is not that of a man about to call on the woman he . . . well, what was I expecting? But it is not even that of a man about to visit a friend. I have never seen Henry look grim before. He takes off his hat and scratches his head so that all his curls stand up on end, then he jams the hat back on as though he would be happy to break it.

A dreadful thought occurs to me. I do not want to entertain it, but what if he is not coming here to continue our friendship? What if he has come to tell me that it is at an end? It must be the ball – he has heard the talk from the ball and now he wants to tell me that he cannot continue an acquaintance with a woman of such a reputation. Shame washes through me . . . but I can explain! He will say what he needs to say and I will put him right and we will laugh about it . . .

But he is walking away! After a long moment of looking at Hades House, he has spun on his heel and returns smartly in the direction from which he came. My face crumples in horror. At long last he is here, within sight, and I am not even to talk to him? I cannot bear it!

I fly from my room and down the long spiral stairs. I run along the long, echoing hall and heave open the front door, forgetting the curl papers still in my hair. I run into the street just in time to see Henry's tall figure disappearing around the corner. I race after him, as quickly as my wide blue skirts permit, feeling every stone and crack in the pavement through my fine slippers. I don't care. All I can think of is to see Henry, to tell him that whatever he is thinking about me is wrong and see his face break into that easy, melting smile once more.

When I get to the end of the street, he is gone. I cannot see him anywhere on the hill. Other streets cross it to right and left and I look down two or three of them to no avail. People are staring at me. Henry could be anywhere.

Cowed by hurt at the nearness of the thing, I slink back like a dog. Mr Garland's phaeton is at the door. Unable to bear the thought of him seeing me now I run upstairs and tear the papers from my hair. Then I sink onto my bed and cry and cry.

Chapter Fifty-one

———⌓⌓⌓———

I stumble through a numbness of days. I should not quite be able to believe that Henry Mead, who was so kind to me in London and so frank and confiding with me only days ago in Bath, could have come so close to calling yet decided against it. I should not believe it but that I saw it happen with my own eyes. I shed tears over it more than once, but they do not change anything.

By the Friday I am shocked to realize that I have spent a great many more hours in Quentin Garland's company than in Henry's, although I persist in thinking of Henry as a friend and Mr Garland as an acquaintance. In point of fact, Henry is conspicuously absent, having clearly decided *against* being a friend, whilst I could, as Mrs Riverthorpe has so bluntly pointed out, marry someone like Mr Garland if I chose to play up my fortune and my new connections. If I decided to stay.

This life, this fashionable existence of dinners and dances and card parties, still does not feel like the right life for me. And yet I am in it and one day leads to the next without fail.

Existence takes on its own validation and I am weary of looking beyond the surface of things, always looking beyond. I do not have Aurelia's love of the far horizon. I want, still, to settle down, albeit on my own terms.

Is Mr Garland someone with whom I could live on my own terms? Why do I even ask myself that question? Because he is here, I suppose, and he is handsome and attentive and intelligent and everything that is admirable in a man. And it is clear that he is paying court to me now, even in my naivety I can see that. I am excessively flattered and long to write to Madeleine and Priscilla about it. But I still must not. I have written to their father, as I promised, so that he knows I am safe and well. I cling to my hope that the trail is to end here in less than a fortnight and then I will be free to do, be, communicate whatever I will. Besides, although I know the girls would delight in the gossip, my heart would not quite be in it.

Mr Garland remains as he ever was: cool, elegant and so perfect. So *other*. Perhaps that is the way of fascination between the sexes. When we ride together, I notice how his long body sways minutely with the jolting of the carriage, a fluid ability to move as one with the world. When we conduct polite conversation in the drawing room at Hades House, I notice how the light gleams on his smooth, golden side-whiskers. When he holds a door for me or passes me a glass, I observe his pale, clean gloves and his pastel sleeves.

What is it about him that intrigues me so? It cannot be

merely that he is handsome – surely I am not so shallow? It is not as though I have never seen a fine gentleman before, not after living at Hatville. Unlike Mrs Riverthorpe, I do not find him dull; to me his company is intelligent and gracious. Being always with him at social events enhances my sense of inclusion, it facilitates the illusion that that there is no gossip about my mysterious arrival in the heart of society – that I am amongst friends. Certainly he has shown no censure of my outrageous hostess, shabby origins or mysterious background. He has never made reference to the confrontations at either ball, never made me feel unworthy or unwanted. I begin to shed my sense of formal restraint with him and to take pleasure, at last, in his company.

I have never been courted before. In our moments of private conversation, he tells me of his estate in Berkshire, his horses, his many investments. I am aware that he is telling me things that he believes will cause me to think favourably of him. I wonder that he should feel the need to bother, when he is so eminently admirable. I am not sure what it is meant to lead to but I am only relieved that, overall, my time in Bath is passing less painfully than I might at first have imagined.

I am reflecting on this during one of Mrs Riverthorpe's interminable card parties. We are seated in the drawing room, with the rich evening light falling pleasingly into the dusty interior. The guests are Mr Garland, Mr Pierpont, the former rower,

Mrs Manvers, of the Bath Temperance Association, and Mr Gladsby, a fervent campaigner to suppress the education of the lower classes, whom he believes to be corrupt and anarchic to a man.

The conversation is accordingly surreal and I allow my mind to wander on the shafts of light. There it dances, alongside the motes of dust, towards Wednesday coming and Aurelia's impending letter. I have grown accustomed to Mrs River- thorpe's odd little ensembles. My early impression, that she selects her guests purely for maximum potential for torment- ing them, has been confirmed by the lady herself as accurate.

My gaze drifts upwards to find Mr Garland's eyes resting on me. He smiles as though he understands why I have mentally absented myself for a moment. Mrs Manvers has been explain- ing the importance of building public libraries: they give the working man with a taste for strong drink an alternative to a tavern as a place to relax after a hard day's work.

Mr Gladsby responds swiftly that no member of 'that class of person' can ever be prevailed upon to eschew the demon drink and that all they will do with a library is burn it.

Mrs Manvers looks close to tears. Mrs Riverthorpe chuckles silently to herself and Mr Pierpont breaks in with a thinly veiled attempt to steer the boat onto a more favourable current:

'Back in 1803, on the Thames, near Henley, I achieved my greatest triumph when . . .'

At this interesting juncture Ambrose knocks and enters.

'Excuse me, ma'am,' she nods in her usual assured way to her employer. 'Miss Snow, might I speak with you for a moment?'

I am astonished. 'Why, of course! Excuse me please, ladies, gentlemen. I hope I do not disturb your game.'

I lay my cards carefully face down, though in truth it will make little difference; I never win. Mr Garland wins almost every hand with a facility for cards that Mrs Riverthorpe has pointed out a great many times. He told her once that he does not play to lose and she retorted that she knew it very well.

I step into the hall to join Ambrose.

'Apologies for calling you from the game, Miss Snow, only there is a gentleman waiting outside to see you.'

Breath is snatched from me. 'Henry?'

Ambrose looks at a small card, which she then hands to me. 'Yes. Henry Mead. So you do know him. Mrs Riverthorpe would be happy for you to invite him in, miss.'

I can well imagine Mrs Riverthorpe's delight if I lured poor unsuspecting Henry into that nest of vipers. But I want to see him alone. 'Thank you, Ambrose, it won't take long. I shall go out to him.'

'Very good, Miss Snow.'

I run, actually *run*, the length of the hall, determined to catch Henry before he disappears again.

I am overjoyed that I am wearing my beautiful emerald-green dress, much despised by Mrs Riverthorpe. Do not get ahead of yourself, I tell myself severely, he may only have come as a courtesy, to let you down in person. I do not believe it for a minute!

I must be calm, I tell myself, as I wrench open the ponderous door and burst onto the porch. A cream phaeton waits across the street and Henry leaps out, all long legs and dark eyes. He runs across the street and, to my amazement, holds me by the arms and stares deep into my face.

'Amy! You are pleased to see me, I think.'

'Henry? Of course I am! Why should I not be? Where have you been? You said Saturday and I have been waiting and waiting –' I stop abruptly, realizing I have just given away any shred of dignity I might have hoped to maintain. But it seems to me that if there has been some misunderstanding we have wasted enough time.

He lets me go and does not look displeased at my outburst, quite the contrary. He takes my hand briefly, then lets that go as well. All in all he looks as though he does not know what to do with me. 'I'm sorry, Amy,' he says at last, still very serious. 'I had not imagined you would mind. But that is not the point, of course. I promised to come and I should have. I wanted to.'

'So why did you not?'

He rubs a hand over his face and grins at me, but it is not his usual spirited grin. 'Foolish male pride. I did come, in point of fact, although not in the morning as I'd said. When we said goodbye outside the coffee house that day, I was so dismayed that you were slipping through my fingers all over again that I wasn't really thinking. I had promised Gus – Mr Longacre, the friend who is kindly putting me up in Bath – that I would go to Bristol with him on Saturday morning to witness the signature of some important papers. I couldn't let him down so I didn't come to see you until the afternoon.'

'You came on Saturday afternoon? But Henry, I waited in for you all day!'

'You did?' His smile is wider, easier, but a little sheepish. 'Ah, now Amy, I am about to tell you the truth, which is to say I am about to embarrass myself horribly. Are you prepared to like me even if you think me a fool?'

I promise that I shall.

'Excellent. I'm glad you're a forgiving sort, Amy. Considering I'm supposed to be smart, I can be a bit of an idiot. When I came by that day, I found you talking on the street with an extremely handsome fellow, very shiny indeed. It was just the two of you and you were smiling and you looked so happy. He held your arm and you were stroking his horses together. You were both dressed very fine and you looked . . . right together, I suppose. He was obviously very rich and very successful and all the things I'm not –'

'But Henry! It wasn't like that! I never –'

'No wait, please let me finish, Amy. If you've been waiting as you say, you deserve an explanation. He leapt in the carriage and drove off and you spent the longest time, Amy, looking after him, as if you could not bear to see him him go. And I was watching you.'

I am lost in disbelief. 'Henry, where *were* you?'

'Just up the street, just about there,' he points.

'You should have called out! Or why didn't you call at the house when I went in?'

'I lost my nerve and that's the truth of it. I'm sorry. You keep running off, you know, in London and then again last week, and I know you have a great deal to think about other than me. But you went to Lord Littleton's ball that night; you move in the finest circles. That man you were talking to looked as though he belongs in them. And so did you. I thought maybe our friendship was something bigger for me than it must be for you.'

I shake my head, trying to gather my thoughts, trying not to laugh at the absurdity of it all. 'My dear Henry, if you only knew! It isn't like that at *all*! Our friendship is precious to me and I was so happy to see you again in Bath. I wasn't staring after Mr Garland that day, I was staring after the horses! I love horses, Henry. I was smiling that day because the *horses* were so beautiful! Mr Garland is a friend of my hostess and I know him a little from Twickenham, too. And we weren't alone! Mrs Riverthorpe was already in the carriage. Oh, Henry, you *are* a bit of an idiot, aren't you?'

I begin to grin myself. It feels so good to speak so frankly to him, and to realize that I am important to him. He was *jealous*,

I smile to myself. Now he is beaming too, and at last it is the smile I have remembered — the smile that makes everything in the world feel right. For a long while we stand there and it feels as though there is much he would like to say, were we not on a street. I can feel the tension — a delicious sort of tension — fizzing up inside me and making me want to giggle.

I think Henry feels it too, for he turns his attention to the imposing façade of Hades House with an amused expression. 'Lord, Amy!'

'That is just what the coachman who brought me here said.'

'Observant fellow. What a place! No wonder you were looking a little down in spirits when I ran into you on the bridge that day. Who is your hostess? A phantom in a long white dress? A winged night-creature intent on sucking your blood? I hope 'tis not the latter — as an almost-doctor I would not recommend the practice.'

'Henry, you're ridiculous,' I laugh. 'She is neither, although I believe, if you met her, you would find her equally improbable. Mrs Riverthorpe is above eighty years old and she cares for public opinion not at all, yet she knows everybody and is out every night — and most days as well. I cannot work her out. You will meet her, I hope.' And we fall quiet again.

'So, if I were to call on you again soon, you would be happy to see me?' he asks, suddenly a little shy and formal.

I roll my eyes. 'If you actually come, it would be delightful.'

He nods. 'Touché! Thank you, Amy, I'll come. Now I suppose

I mustn't detain you on the pavement any longer. My friends the Longacres are in the carriage there. We are just on our way to watch the sunset from Beachen Cliff. I don't suppose you'd join us? It promises a beautiful spectacle.'

I realize suddenly that apart from my lonely city walks I have been contained within parlours and ballrooms and dining rooms for days on end now. The passing of spring has been reduced for me to the inching of days towards Aurelia's next letter. I have lost all sense of the year turning.

'I should love to, Henry, you cannot imagine how much, but I am detained in a card party. Mrs Riverthorpe has guests; I cannot run out on her.'

'No matter, foolishly sudden invitation. Come and say hello quickly, if you'd like, and then I'll let you get back.'

I cross the street and meet the Longacres, Gus and Ellen. They are a cordial couple a few years older than Henry, who greet me warmly and invite me to dinner the following evening. There will be dancing, they promise; oh, just a few close friends are to attend, but there will be dancing nonetheless!

I accept gladly, shake hands with everyone and run back into the shadows of Hades House.

Chapter Fifty-two

There I bump – quite literally – into Mr Garland, who is standing in the hall. I disentangle myself and lay my hands on my burning cheeks. For some reason I feel caught out – and irritated. This I disguise with copious apologies, even though I could not reasonably have expected to find a gentleman just behind the doorway.

'Please do not excuse yourself, Miss Snow, I was quite in your way. Mrs Riverthorpe sent me to see if all was well with you.'

'Oh! Mr Garland, that was good of you. All is quite well, thank you. Merely an old friend passing by. Shall we return to the cards?'

'Indeed, I look forward to hearing further of Mr Gladsby's enlightened views!' He winks, then places a hand on my arm. 'Although . . . stay, Miss Snow, as we are alone for a moment perhaps I might briefly detain you? I have been wishing to speak to you privately for some days now and it is not easy

when Mrs Riverthorpe does not like to be excluded from anything at all.'

I laugh; this is certainly true. I feel a little flustered that so
attractive a gentleman should wish to speak to me alone, and
only a moment after seeing Henry. He draws me into an alcove
behind a column.

'I had rather hoped for a softer surrounding,' he murmurs.
'No matter. Miss Snow, I must go to London on business
tomorrow. Oh, only for three or four days, but I wanted to
speak to you before I go. I am sure it can come as no surprise to
you to learn that I admire you greatly.'

I look up at him in astonishment. He is wrong! I have come
to accept that he had a certain interest in me, yes, but . . . he
admires me greatly? Why? He looks down at me tenderly.

'Fear not, Miss Snow, this is not a proposal. I am aware that
we have not known each other for very long. I am a realistic
man, not some impetuous youngster, and I believe that a true
connection cannot be formed overnight. I hope that ours will
extend and deepen . . . However, I wished to . . . to *prepare* you,
I suppose.' He laughs gently. 'In case you should wish to silence
me on the matter now and for ever! I should not wish to cause
you any discomfort. But if you are content that we continue to
grow acquainted, knowing that my feelings towards you
include also admiration of a more personal nature, well, that
would please me greatly.'

His solemnity is overwhelming. I become very aware of the

grey stone columns standing around us like witnesses. Together with the vaulted ceiling and the long stone hallway, they start to make me feel I am in church. He takes my hand gently in one of his own and lays his other on top. I must be a little numb from surprise; I can hardly feel it. Suddenly, unbidden, comes a flash of memory. Our early encounters: Mr Garland always polite, always solicitous, ever beyond reproach . . . and me, disconcerted, wrong-footed, wanting to run away. Have I ever been truly comfortable with this man?

'Mr Garland . . . I . . . I hardly know what to say,' I stutter.

Despite all his attentions, it seems so improbable. I cannot imagine what someone like Mr Garland could find to admire in a patchwork sort of person such as myself. Yet Mr Garland himself is looking down at me with the feelings he spoke of evident in his eyes. I decide to be as truthful as possible.

'Mr Garland, I am so very flattered, and surprised, I confess. You pay me a great compliment and I thank you. You have been a good friend to me throughout my time here and you stand highly in my estimation, very highly indeed.' That is all true. I breathe more easily.

'I am happy to hear it, Miss Snow. Am I then to hope that you might look on me with favour as a suitor — in the future, if not immediately?'

'Any young woman would be glad to receive your attentions, Mr Garland.'

'But you, Amy, would *you* be glad?'

Would I? I can hardly tell. It is true that I have a very deep admiration for him. But could that translate into admiration of a more intimate nature? He is extremely beautiful. Sometimes I feel I could drown just from looking at him. But I feel there must be more to a match than looking at a person.

And then there is Henry.

The leap of joy I feel whenever I see Henry feels more immediate and uncomplicated than the gradually built rapport I have with Mr Garland. But . . . now that Henry is not before me, melting my heart with those dark eyes and reassuring me with those beautiful smiles, I remember the loneliness and confusion of this past week. He hurt me. I watched him as he debated whether to call on me, then chose to walk away. And Mr Garland was there, attentive, reliable, every day. He helped me through a difficult time, even if he was unaware of it. I accept Henry's explanation and apology; I know he is sincere. But what if he is to disappear every time he doubts my regard for him and I am to be discarded, again? It is always the most painful thing for me.

I am aware that time is passing. Mr Garland is waiting for my answer, and Mrs Riverthorpe and her motley band of card-playing eccentrics are awaiting our return. There does not seem to be the time to think it all through and I feel something like one of Mrs Riverthorpe's mysterious moths – pinned in place in a glass case. He said this is not a proposal. He is not asking for a yes or no, not now.

'I believe . . . perhaps . . . I might be, sir.' I blush, hearing my own inadequacy. 'That is to say, I had not thought of it before, and you do me too great an honour. But I enjoy your company better than anyone else's in Bath and I admire your courtesy and intelligence very much . . .' I am aware that I am thinking aloud, so I fall silent.

'That is very good to hear, Miss Snow. Perhaps we should return to the others so as not to provoke speculation, but I look forward to resuming our friendship when I return from London.'

'Yes . . . but, Mr Garland, there is something else. I . . . I would not wish to give you false hope and I am not my own mistress at present. It is too long and convoluted to explain, but there are circumstances in my life that mean . . . I may be leaving Bath quite soon and I do not know where I may be sent. It must sound very strange —'

He bows over my hand and kisses it.

'Miss Snow, I am of course aware that there is a certain . . . difficulty in your circumstances. I know that you have been travelling alone and that your fortunes appear to change quite often. And of course I understand that your background places you in a somewhat *ambiguous* position. I beg to assure you that none of this in any way affects my regard for you. Please do not feel that you owe me anything in the way of explanation. The time will come for that. Shall we?'

He offers me a pale-blue sleeve and we return to the drawing room. My feelings are a muddle and I am relieved that I will not see him again for several days. I am a little resentful that this sudden event has occurred to preoccupy me so swiftly after Henry's reappearance. Uppermost, I am heartily glad that neither man has asked me to explain anything.

Then, of course, there is the uneasy pleasure that this gentleman, whom I once gazed upon with wonder as a remote stranger, has asked me to accept him as a suitor. And I can't quite remember what I said in response.

Chapter Fifty-three

After the guests depart, I am surprised that Mrs Riverthorpe asks me nothing about my absence from the party. If she was concerned enough to send Mr Garland after me, I imagined she might be curious.

The following morning I go out. The Longacres are to send their carriage for me at five and I do not know how else to pass the time. It is well that I do, for Henry is loitering under a plane tree outside.

'Amy!' he cries, drinking me in with delight.

I am wearing a pale-blue and white striped dress with large panels cupping the sleeves and a simple scooped neckline. The day is fine and I have dispensed with a cloak. I have dispensed, too, with all thoughts of Mr Garland. I need not deal with him for at least three days and doubtless my mind can undergo any number of revolutions in that time if I am not firm with myself.

'Good morning, Henry!' The sight of him coaxes the broadest of smiles from me, every time. It is like seeing a dog launch itself into a river; you cannot help but feel joyful. 'What are you doing here? Oh! Is the dance cancelled?'

'What a pessimist you are! Of course not. I merely wanted to spend time with you before tonight. We have wasted enough of it over the last few days. But in my eagerness to make up for lost time I had not thought that perhaps it was too early to pay a call. Thus you find me lurking in the shadows as though I am planning a burglary.'

'I am very happy to see you.'

'You are going out. Is this a bad time?'

'Only for a walk. It is a perfect time.'

He offers me his arm and we walk in silence. My head, which was a whirl of excitement and confusion last night, between Henry's reappearance and Mr Garland's declaration, is clearer now. Mr Garland is a tempting proposition as a suitor, of course he is; any young lady would say so. But I know in my heart that it is Henry for whom I have the warmest feelings, I have done so from the start. I promise myself then and there that I will not – indeed, I do not want to – encourage Mr Garland further. I shall have to speak to him when he returns from London, though I dread the prospect. But first I need to have some proper understanding of how things lie with Henry. And then, of course, there is my quest . . .

We walk to the Crescent Fields and sit beneath a chestnut tree beginning to bud with pale-pink candles. He spreads out his jacket to save my dress from grass stains and offers me his hand to steady me while I sit. Then he sits next to me, the breeze ruffling his hair.

'It's good to see you, Amy,' he says quietly. 'I did not act like a true friend to you this week and I want to apologize again. I wouldn't have worried you for the world, you know. I felt unworthy to call on you and you ended up thinking I'd forgotten you.'

I look across the fields. Early slants of sunshine light the grass and show cobwebs beaded with dew. It is early, and the green expanse is mostly empty, but a handful of families here and there are walking, or playing cricket. The chestnut tree rustles above us and I think of Eel Pie Island and Constance and Edwin's willow.

'I saw you on Wednesday, Henry. Oh, I'd been walking all over Bath hoping I'd see you, but the only time I did I was in my room, looking out of the window. I saw you walking down the street and I was so happy, but then you stopped just short of Hades House, you turned around and walked away.'

He grimaces. 'That was not a proud moment. After seeing you with Mr . . . Garland, was it? . . . I'd convinced myself you weren't really interested in pursuing a friendship with me but still a part of me hoped. I hoped we might bump into each other again and I could gauge whether you seemed pleased to see me without taking the risk of presenting myself at your door and making my interest clear. Then I decided that was a coward's way, so on Wednesday I came back, but lost my nerve, as you saw. Anyway, I'm so glad I persevered . . . except that I seem to be very muddled in all I am saying to you, and I should like to be clear!'

He sits up straight and takes a deep breath. 'Amy, in case you should be in any doubt . . . I would like to be more than a friend to you, but I feel just now I cannot, because I have nothing to offer, nor even any prospect of it until I choose my career and get stuck in. And besides, we've only met twice before so it seems more than a little hasty. I shouldn't have said anything really. But now that I've made a mess of things by not calling on you, I have to tell you, don't I, to explain?'

An early bumblebee buzzes past us like a floating powder puff. I can feel the sun on my face, and Henry likes me. I cannot stop smiling.

'You did. And I have said more than sense would dictate too,' I respond. 'I . . . I did think of you often, you know, after meeting you in London. When you appeared here, I was so happy and then I thought you did not care for me after all. I know we are only strangers. Only you don't *feel* like a stranger.'

'Nor you to me. At least now we can continue getting to know each other and catch up with ourselves. Already you have learned that I have my faults, like any man, and pride, of course, is one of them.' He looks troubled. 'I had not thought, though, that pride would make a coward of me. I shall try not to let it happen again. This is a hard time for me, you know, Amy. Turning away from medicine, now this. I always thought myself a rather splendid fellow but now I'm learning that being a man is not always easy. You see? I shouldn't be telling you that! I should be hiding behind platitudes and trying to convince you that I'm perfect.'

'I shouldn't believe you, Henry, not for a moment. But I think you will do a marvellous job of it, being a man, I mean. You are young still, as am I.'

He turns away from me again, smiles at the view. 'Thank you, Amy.'

For a while we sit and watch a black and white dog sport with an immensely fat boy of about seven. When the boy trips and lands on the dog, we both wince. But they untangle themselves uninjured and continue their game, good-natured fellows both.

Henry entrusting me with his confidences is like the sun dispelling shadows. I am so tired of keeping secrets and being guarded. I feel closer to Henry than ever now but I am aware that we may not have much time. I may have to leave Bath in just over a week. I cannot be fully open with him, of course, but I feel a strong desire to tell him what I can, perhaps more, even, than I should. I am reluctant to break the easy silence between us, but at last I do.

'It is not only you who is in transition at the moment, Henry,' I say quietly, stealing a glance at his handsome profile. His lips are curved and very beautiful.

He nods, still staring over the fields, but I can tell he is listening. I untie my bonnet and lay it beside me on the grass, for I want to be able to see Henry clearly.

'The whole mystery pertains to Aurelia, the dear friend whom I lost in January.'

I can tell that he is longing to know. 'The young lady my grandfather knew. You grew up with her, I think?'

'That's right. The bond is greater even than you might imagine, Henry, for I owe her my very life. When I was a new-born, she . . . she found me in the snow.'

'*What?*' Now he turns to me, his eyes fixed on my face.

'Yes. I had been abandoned. I was . . .' I just resist saying naked. 'I was blue with cold and Aurelia, who was then eight and had the most tender heart imaginable, snatched me up and took me home. She was a very great lady, Henry, though she never knew it at that age – indeed, at any age. Her parents did not want me. They saw me as a disgrace, you see.' I tuck my hair behind my ears a little nervously. I am not used to telling this story.

He scowls. '*You* a disgrace? An innocent child? That is not a logic I can understand.'

'I am glad to hear you say it. I felt for many years that they must have been right, else they would not have treated me as they did. They would have consigned me to the orphanage then and there, you see, if Aurelia had not set her heart upon my staying. Their attitude towards me has left its mark.'

'I am sure. Were they *very* unkind to you, Amy?'

I swallow. 'Yes. I think they spent the rest of my life ruing their leniency that day.' I feel tears well up, but I blink them back determinedly, for I want to say this. 'They insisted I be kept out of sight of the family, but Aurelia would not stay away from me. She was spoiled and lonely. She was imaginative too – I think she was fascinated by the mystery of an unknown snow baby.'

'Of course she was. Did you ever learn anything of your origins, Amy?'

I drop my gaze and notice that my knuckles are white; I am twisting my hands in my lap. 'No, I never did.'

'I am truly sorry to hear it. You have seen something of my family. I cannot imagine how it must feel to be without one.'

I don't know how to describe it to him. Where might I begin to explain Cook's impersonal kindness, Lady Vennaway's bitter hatred, the dreary greyness of knowing I was only ever there on sufferance?

Nevertheless I try, in stumbling sentences, for I want Henry to understand. I manage to condense seventeen years into five minutes, then look up to see if I am boring him. He appears anything but bored.

'Amy, please know that whatever your past, assorted Meads and Crumms will *always* be pleased to receive Amy Snow.'

'Dear Henry.' I cannot help myself. I reach out and take his hand. It is quite against etiquette, but once I have clasped it I do not find it easy to release and he does not pull away. So there is

371

an awkward yet brilliant moment in which I find myself sitting in a meadow adrift with pale-yellow primroses, holding hands with a friend who is a man . . . and young, and handsome . . . 'Thank you,' I whisper.

'Amy, you do not need to *thank* me,' he replies, his voice soft.

Slowly I sit back, withdraw my hand. 'Forgive me, Henry, if I am behaving all out of place. I feel as though all my emotions have been stirred like a pudding and risen to the surface like steam. I am not used to telling people things.'

'Do not tell me another word if it upsets you too much, Amy, though I confess I hope you can battle through. I should dearly love to know Aurelia's secret and how it affects you now – your choices, your life.'

'Indeed I will try. I cannot tell you Aurelia's secret, not only because I must not but because I do not know it. I will tell you what I can Henry, but . . . Aurelia has left me several posthumous letters, each containing a fervent plea for secrecy. It was of the gravest importance for her, Henry, and I *cannot* betray her. But it is hard to be so clandestine.'

I had not realized how living a riddle was oppressing me still. It is easy to guard the truth in Bath, for no one requires it. But Henry wants to know me. He is tall and warm and good. If I cannot tell him some of it soon. I shall burst and scatter into petals myself.

Now he takes my hand, and the gesture is not impetuous,

nor is it brief. He holds it firmly and deliberately. Despite the flooding beauty of the moment, I actually find myself glancing around to see if anyone who knows me is watching. Society is a powerful thing.

'Amy, anything you tell me I shall receive in the greatest confidence. I shall feel proud to be your confidant and tell no one. I shall honour Aurelia's secret, whether or not I know what it is. I promise.'

At the end of this solemn declaration he replaces my hand in my lap and I feel relieved and bereaved, both at once.

So I tell Henry about the treasure hunt. I tell him that each letter reveals more and more that I did not know, though I tell him none of the details of her story. I tell him I have more money and fine clothes than I know what to do with but none of the things my heart longs for: security, family, *answers*. I know that I am not following Aurelia's instructions to the letter, but this is the compromise that enables me to feel that my life matters too.

I confess that at times I have cried angry tears for feeling that I am still a piece on the Vennaway chess board. I admit that Aurelia was far from perfect, that I am hurt that she kept so much from me when she was alive. And I conclude with a sigh that, underneath it all, my loyalty to her is as deep and true as it ever was and will always remain thus.

Chapter Fifty-four

I am so happy! I am so achingly, blisteringly, crashingly happy. It is like the sun on my skin and the splash of rain and the scent of orange roses all rolled into one.

He loves me. Henry loves me. And I love him. Of course I do. The past five days have been the happiest of my life.

Throughout my great outpouring in the Crescent Fields, he listened and listened. When I finished, he leaned back with his hands behind his head and closed his eyes. I understood him to be deep in thought, rather than overcome with boredom.

I had not previously had the opportunity to observe him lying down, and so I seized my moment and studied minutely his black, curling hair, the warm tones of his skin, the pleasing curve of his lips. I noticed the way his mouth reposed into a gentle smile, the way his throat grew paler where it disappeared inside the high wings of his collar. His suit was no parlour shade of blue, it was a perfectly serviceable brown and fell open to reveal a white shirt and a red waistcoat, both of which lay snug over a broad chest that I suddenly craved to lay my head upon.

I did not, of course I did not.

I marvelled at the length of his legs. In truth, anyone's legs are long compared to mine, but Henry's appear to me to be particularly fine examples.

When at last he sat up again, I jumped as though caught doing something illicit, although in truth I don't feel there is anything so wrong with a woman admiring an attractive man. Perhaps Mrs Riverthorpe is rubbing off on me. Perhaps that is not a bad thing.

That evening, the Longacres sent their carriage for me as promised. Finally I wore my beloved apricot muslin. I took real delight in attending an occasion for which I could choose my own gown, wear my hair simply, dress myself and, in short, please myself. Cecile would not approve, but I left my room feeling entirely comfortable.

In the hall I collided with Mrs Riverthorpe, who was pulling on a pair of long, black satin gloves.

'Child!' She shuddered when she saw me. 'Are you spending the evening in a nunnery?'

She could not dent me. 'Only with friends, Mrs Riverthorpe. I hope you shall enjoy your evening.'

'I doubt it. I sincerely doubt it,' she muttered as she swept out of the house, in so far as it is possible to sweep when leaning hard on a cane.

I had a brief, rash longing to take her with me and show her a gentler sort of company before rationality returned.

I passed the most pleasant of evenings. The Longacres and their friends made me feel so welcome. The food was simple yet excellent and the dancing was crowded into a small parlour with space for only three couples at once to stand up safely. Everyone danced with everyone else but dancing with Henry was a dream. He was graceful and sure of himself and kept me entertained with a number of witty comments and private jokes.

I returned to Hades House in a warm glow that not even eerie grey corners and mothy artwork could dim. Needless to say, Mrs Riverthorpe was not at home before me.

I spent the next four days with Henry, Gus and Ellen. My world is all tilted on its axis. Appalled that I had not seen any of the surrounding countryside, they took it upon themselves to acquaint me with the views from Beachen Cliff and the leafy lanes of Widcombe. They arranged a picnic in the fields along the river. I believe my memory of that day will always be the sound of rippling water, the brush of ladybirds and a rich warmth of sunlight and laughter.

It is strange and wonderful to be a part of two couples – an altogether new feeling for me. I study Gus and Ellen surreptitiously whenever I have the chance. She is small and fair and feisty, with a great fondness for parasols – she carries a different shade every time I see her. He is not a handsome man – he has a profusion of ginger whiskers and an impressive copper beard – but he is thoughtful and gentle and their appreciation for each other is plain to see. I wonder how Henry and I would seem after a decade in each other's company – if such is to be our destiny.

The city too seems all new to me with Henry as a guide. He is surprisingly knowledgeable about a great many things. I do not know why I should find that surprising, except perhaps that he is so self-effacing. He can take me to the weir and he makes me see, instead of just a rushing horseshoe of water, a sophisticated symbol of modern life. He can explain the series of locks and canals that make Bath a vital centre for travel and trade, not only fashion and flirtation. The splendid architecture of the city comes alive for me when we are together.

I feel the hard shell of my discontent with Bath and my frustration with the treasure hunt breaking open. I am finding the time to pause and delight in life after all; my concerns are all suspended when I am with Henry. He is like a fire on a cold day and draws me closer and closer to him, making me feel treasured and wanted.

We promenade along Royal Crescent but also explore the streets that lurk behind. The backs of those sweeping, smooth houses are knobbly and jagged like teeth. I reflect that society is like that – elegant and flawless at face value, bumpy and biting behind the façade. Henry voices this very thought as it passes through my head. He does that often.

Occasionally we encounter someone we know; it is like being reminded of a strange dream, so caught up am I in these magical days. In the lobby of the Royal Hotel, after enjoying a sumptuous lunch in celebration of Ellen's birthday, we find Mrs Manvers handing out pamphlets about the Temperance Movement. She generously gives us one each (although I already have three) and she and Henry enjoy a long conversation while Gus, Ellen and I go and admire the fountain in the courtyard.

I find Henry informed and reflective, not the light, insubstantial fellow he condemns himself as being. I have had a lifetime of being told that I am worthless and lacking; it has done me no favours. I see no point in Henry inflicting the same anguish upon himself, so I tell him to stop. He seems to take the point.

Last night, after an early supper in Henrietta Street, he told me that he loves me.

We had supped on the terrace with honeysuckle unfolding around us. Gus had excused himself to look at some papers, then Ellen retreated indoors to play the piano. Henry and I braved the chill to stay outside together. Despite the recent sunny days, the evenings have been much cooler. Henry says it is because Bath lies in a basin amongst the hills, a sound geographical explanation for something I had fancied was simply my own disenchantment with the place. We talked of literature and we read a few sonnets to the accompaniment of twittering blackbirds making ready for summer. Then we began talking of our childhoods.

'I wonder what became of them?' said Henry suddenly. 'The awkward little girl running around after her big, bright sister and the scamp of a boy who could not leave the house without getting into trouble. I wonder if they exist anywhere now except in our memories and hearts.'

'I still feel like that awkward little girl much of the time. And in truth . . . I am still running after Aurelia.'

'Much of the time? And what about the rest of the time? How do you feel then?'

I frowned for a long time, pondering his question.

'Like the adult I always wished I had to look after me,' I realized with some astonishment. 'Thoughtful. Confident. And steady. I loved Aurelia dearly but she was not steady. It was like loving a flame. And . . . I *interest* myself, Henry. My path through life is not conventional, and yet I seem to be making my way! I never thought I could. And you, Henry? Do you still feel like the same boy?'

'No.' Henry shook his head decidedly. 'Oh, the mischief is still there, I know, but now there is a great deal more of me besides. I have expanded to include so much more of what I must become. I am definitely a man, not a boy. Only . . .'

I remember my initial shock when I saw him fill the door-frame at his grandfather's place. He is certainly not a boy.

'Only what?'

He looks around the garden and crosses his legs, thinking. Dusk gathers around, soft and lilac grey and chilly. I shiver.

'Only . . . I am not yet the man I *want* to be. I am like the outline of myself. I want to be the full portrait.'

'Do you mean because you haven't settled on a profession?'

'That's certainly a part of it. Some parts of myself are surging ahead whilst others lag behind. The leaders are impatient and they want . . . a great many things. The laggards are doing their best, I'm sure, but they feel very intimidated by what is being asked of them. Does that make any sense?'

I imagine what he means is that he is growing up. I never had the chance to grow up in a gradual progression – I was always dealing with situations that a kinder world would not have dealt to a child. I saw it in Aurelia, though – the struggle and the contradiction. And I could see this was important to him.

'It makes sense. Do you think you might go gently on yourself, show the laggards a little compassion?'

'I'm not sure that I should. I believe I must grow firmer with myself. Do you know what makes me so impatient, Amy? Can you guess what it is that I want?'

He looked at me so very intently that I felt my heart start to drum as if it knew my life was about to change. Suddenly I could not speak, so shook my head.

'Oh, dearest, *dearest* Amy, can't you? Why, 'tis you! Amy, it is lucky I am buttoned up inside this suit for I am coming all undone inside it. I could not bear to cause you a single second's discomfort, yet I must speak. From the first evening that we met, you fascinated me. You looked so very sad, so very alone, yet so determined. I did not want to let you go, indeed I did not, but you and my grandfather made it clear that I must. Then to see you again here! To have the opportunity to get to know you properly, to talk to you, receive your confidences, share my friends with you. Oh, I know we have not known each other very long, and no doubt we still have much to learn, but spending so much time with you these last few days I know this: my life would be so much poorer without you. Amy, if all you feel for me is friendship, then know that I will treasure that always and you must never feel awkward or raw about my declaration. But if you could love me . . . if you could ever, ever love me . . . I should . . . I should . . .'

'What should you do, dear Henry?' I asked softly, drawing his hand towards me across the wrought-iron table.

He looked at me with such extraordinary hope. I will never forget that look on his face. It melted something inside me that I had not known was frozen.

'I should never want to be apart from you, Amy. I should like to build my life with you, if you would have me. I know I am in no position to ask this – at the moment I have very little to offer, except for my unswerving devotion – but one day when I do, might you consider becoming my wife?'

I felt tears spring to my eyes and roll down my face. I made to wipe them on my shawl but he was there before me, his arm around me, softly brushing my cheeks with his handkerchief.

'Tell me these are tears of joy, Amy, please tell me they are tears of joy. It wouldn't do a man's confidence much good to think that the very suggestion of marrying him could reduce a girl to tears.'

Once I managed to stop laughing and crying and to compose myself, I assured him that they were indeed tears of joy. I sat in that garden in a wonderment, my head spinning and my heart singing, floating on waves of heady delight. I wanted to scoop up all his words in my arms and cradle them to me and keep them always; I have been starving for them.

'For me, it began when you laughed at the silly face I pulled,' said Henry. 'I remember Grandfather saying something about you being stuck with just him and me, Mama being in bed with a cold and all that. I made a grimace and your face transformed. I felt protective toward you from the first – but to see that brief glimpse of what it would be like to make you happy – it quite turned the world on end. I had to make some excuse to leave the room, I remember.'

'*Truly?* I *thought* you looked at me strangely! I thought it was because I look so odd when I smile.'

'Odd when you . . .? What on earth makes you say that?'

'That's what they always told me in the kitchen.'

'Well, let me tell you the folk in the kitchen were quite, quite wrong. Dear Amy, you have a laugh that could make a fellow wish to devote a lifetime to making you happy. And you? Did you fall in love with me in an instant, as soon as you saw my manly frame lounging in my grandfather's doorway?'

'Oh yes, certainly the doorway,' I told him, laughing to cover up my embarrassment at just how true this was. I can admit it to myself now. I can hardly believe that I can finally share with him all the times I thought of him across the intervening months, how happy the very sight of him has always made me, how comfortable I feel in his company and how I never dreamed anyone – let alone beloved, handsome Henry – could ever feel that way about me.

Thus we tumbled on, in our dizzy, ecstatic way, never once talking about practicalities, never worrying about the fact that I have no idea where I will be a week from now and Henry has no idea what he wants to do with his life. We might have gone on like that all night but that Ellen came to ask if I wanted the carriage.

Chapter Fifty-five

Today the delightful dream continues. Life is giddy and galloping and lustrous. I lay awake all night, but for none of the reasons that have kept me awake since Aurelia died. My only regret now is that she can never know Henry, nor he Aurelia.

Light-headed and sore-eyed I spring from bed as though I have slept like a lamb, and don my cream dress with the raspberry stripes. Henry has not seen it before. He is coming to meet Mrs Riverthorpe. It is a redundant formality but in our excitement we want to share our joy with everyone and she is the nearest thing I have in Bath to a guardian. I wish he could meet Constance and Edwin and he has promised me that one day soon – when my circumstances are different – he will.

I have warned him, of course, about Mrs Riverthorpe. Now it is time to prepare her to meet Henry.

'Haaa!' she squawks when I tell her I am engaged, or the next thing to it, to the man I will love for the rest of my life. 'Are you engaged or aren't you? Is there a ring or is there not? Oh, child, child, do not bore me with your blustering explanations. I thought you might have had more sense than to add this to your long list of problems.'

Yet meet him she does. He raps smartly at the door at ten o'clock, the appointed time, and I run to answer it, to the chagrin of a disgruntled Ambrose, who lurks in the hall making no attempt to disguise the fact that she wants to see him for herself.

'Lord, Henry!' I exclaim when I open the door. I have always seen him handsome but easy, in serviceable brown town suits that suit his taste for roaming around the city for hours on end. Today he is wearing a dark-grey suit the colour of a November sky and a black waistcoat with a distinguished white pinstripe. His shirt, gloves and cravat are all snowy white and his curls are flattened and combed back from his face, though when he removes his hat they threaten to spring up at any moment. He looks so dashing that I feel an unladylike rush of warmth which bolts immodestly through my whole body, then comes to settle in my stomach, where it spirals distractingly.

'You look beautiful,' he whispers, kissing my hand. 'How well your dress becomes you.'

'You must be a lawyer or an undertaker,' Mrs Riverthorpe observes acidly, coming to the drawing-room door and beckoning us to join her with a clawed hand. She cuts an alarming figure, in an orange gown which would be daring for a soirée, never mind ten o'clock in the morning. 'Amy, are you going to introduce us or just gawp at him all day? Ambrose! I can see through pillars, you know. Stop spying and get back to work.' She shuffles off. 'Eyes in the back of my head too,' her voice floats back to us. 'We shall be needing tea!'

I am horrified, but Henry only laughs. He takes my hand and pulls me after her into the drawing room. 'Mrs Riverthorpe,' he greets her, deducing that I will be little use to the conversation, and kissing her hand. 'I am Henry Mead. I'm delighted to meet you. Amy has told me a great deal about you.'

'None of it good, I'm sure,' she challenges him, jutting her bony chin at him.

'Very little,' he agrees gravely, offering his arm.

She allows him to help her to a seat, then he turns and offers me the same service. Of course I am not stiff and elderly but I am just too appalled by her manners to move.

'So which is it?' she demands when we are all seated.

I throw her a furious glance, which she ignores.

'Undertaker or lawyer?' says Henry equably. 'Neither at present, although I am willing to consider both. I am between professions and in search of a new one.'

'What was your last profession?'

'It was medicine. That is to say, I studied it for a time.'

She shudders. 'Unnatural occupation. Best you dispensed with that one as soon as possible. You should not want a medic, Amy! So you are not between professions, you are in fact a young idler yet to make his mark?'

I wince, knowing what a sensitive subject this is for Henry. What was I *thinking*, bringing him here? But he seems unperturbed.

'That is precisely the case, Mrs Riverthorpe, though I intend to rectify it as soon as possible.' He nods at me and smiles and I smile back, proud of him. I am touched, too, with the effort he has made with his appearance, all for the honour of meeting my hostess and creating a good impression – if such a thing is possible.

'Yet still she seems entranced with you and determined to entertain a romance,' muses Mrs Riverthorpe in a tone which calls my intelligence into question, shaking her head.

'I'm delighted to hear it!' he responds. 'But what of you, Mrs Riverthorpe? I hear you are a fearsome woman who does exactly what she pleases. I am pleased to hear it, though I hope you are not corrupting my Amy, for I should like to bind her to a life of servitude if I can manage it.'

I close my eyes. Mrs Riverthorpe cackles appreciatively and they are off – sparring and exchanging polished jibes as though they had known each other always. I am not sure whether this is a good thing or not.

Ambrose brings us tea in green-sprigged china and Mrs Riverthorpe grills Henry about every facet of his life. She wants to know who his people are and how he intends to make something of himself and what his intentions are towards me (I confess I am interested to hear that myself, I shall never tire of hearing it). She is appallingly rude to him, naturally, but Henry weathers the storm with a great, good-natured fascination. Like Aurelia, he is a lover of humanity in all its quirks and foibles, quick to delight and slow to judge. After a half hour, which leaves me weak with exhaustion, they take their leave with no hard feelings.

I wave Henry off and stand gazing after him long after he has disappeared down the street. He and I are not to meet again until tomorrow. I feel I might not survive the evening, but I am promised to Mrs Riverthorpe tonight for a concert and do not want to break my word.

'Come along then, foolish child,' she says in my ear, making me jump. 'We had better take a glass. I know *I* need one after that sentimental display. Not one to veil your feelings, are you?'

I reflect on a lifetime of trying to hide my hurt and fear, on years of putting my feelings aside to be brave and capable for Aurelia when she was dying, of the last long months of obfuscation and reticence. I cannot find the energy to argue. Being guarded has been my way of surviving the world, but Henry has somehow rendered it utterly impossible.

We have just taken our seats and raised our glasses – 'To love!' proposes Mrs Riverthorpe in an ironic toast – when Ambrose suddenly knocks at the door.

'Mr Garland is here to see Miss Snow, if you will receive him, Miss Snow.'

'Haaaaa!' crows Mrs Riverthorpe. 'Delicious!'

I feel the happy flush she finds so irritating drain from my face. I had quite, quite forgotten about Mr Garland.

'I . . . I . . .' I stutter, wishing with all my heart I could refuse him but unable to think of how I might explain it.

'Tongue in a loop again!' cries my hostess. 'Ambrose, what she means to say is that she wishes she could pretend she is not at home but she don't know how to say it!'

Uncanny.

'But I think she must see him so bring him in, why not, and I shall make myself scarce.'

'Oh no, Mrs Riverthorpe, please . . . I mean, there is no need for you to absent yourself. Mr Garland is quite as much your friend as mine – more so! He will wish to see you, I am sure.'

She shrugs her skinny shoulders. 'But I don't wish to see him.'

She disappears. She can move surprisingly swiftly when she wishes to.

Ambrose shows Mr Garland into the parlour and I feel my face flaming at the memory of our last conversation, so tactfully broached by him, so readily forgotten by me. Will he raise the matter again? Either way I must disabuse him of any false hope at once. But suddenly I realize that Mr Garland will not be accustomed to disappointment. With his favour comes a sense of . . . obligation. How do I tell him that whilst I did not discourage his attentions less than a week ago, I have now consented to marry someone else? Surely this would present a difficulty to any fine belle, let alone Amy Snow, parasite of Hatville!

'My dear Miss Snow!'

He swoops in, all golden and gleaming, looking happy to see me. I had forgotten how handsome he is, but that must not distract me. If he notices that I am twisting my hands together painfully, it does not deter him.

'What a delight to see you again. How well the cream and that pink become you. I am so very sorry that I have been from Bath longer than I intended.' He glides over to me, graceful as a swift, and bows.

I swallow. If he only knew how I had lost track of time in my delirious daze. I actually have no idea how long he has been gone.

'How . . . how do you do, Mr Garland?' I stammer, dipping a curtsey. 'I trust your business in London was successful?' I suddenly feel like little Amy of Hatville again, about to be caught out in some misbehaviour. I feel one of my fingers crack – another moment and I should have twisted it right off. I force myself to put my arms at my sides and bury my hands in my skirts.

'Indeed yes! I am very well pleased. But even more pleased to be once again in Bath, amongst my friends. I trust I find you well?'

'Very well, thank you, sir. In fact . . . very well, yes indeed.'

I cannot meet his eyes and fix mine on his blue cravat. I could swear it winks at me, the fabric is so lustrous.

'Excellent!' He gives his hat a merry little twirl. I seize upon the fact that he has held onto it as grounds for hoping he does not intend to stay long. 'Now I wonder if I might prevail upon you and dear Ariadne to accompany me to hear a string quartet this evening? My old friend Quintus Crace is the viola and I should very much like you to meet him.'

'Is it to be held at the Upper Rooms, Mr Garland?'

'Quite so.'

'Then we are already going. Mrs Riverthorpe knows the cello, I believe. In fact, I expect she knows the entire quartet and the audience besides.'

He laughs. 'Splendid! Then a musical little party we shall be, to be sure. Might I have the honour of saving seats for you both when I arrive?'

'We should be grateful. Ah, Mr Garland . . . I . . . ah . . . '

'Miss Snow! Is something the matter?'

He takes a seat with a look of concern. I wish I had not spoken; he was about to leave, the interview was almost over. Yet I cannot bear the thought of meeting him again tonight with so much unspoken between us and Mrs Riverthorpe brimming with mischief.

'No, that is to say, yes, a little.' I am standing before him, wringing my hands once more. 'I find myself extremely embarrassed to raise the matter but I feel I must . . . it pertains to our last conversation, before you went to London, when you . . .'

'When I spoke of my great admiration towards you, Miss Snow. I remember.'

I nod in relief. 'It is just that . . . I was so very grateful and honoured, Mr Garland, and I knew then of no reason to ask you not to speak, I assure you. However, since then I have become . . . *promised*, I suppose, to another, an old friend who has recently reappeared in my life. I did not want you to . . . I did not want to . . .'

I am, of course, overstating the case by describing Henry as an old friend. Imagining the whole matter through Mr Garland's eyes, if he knew it all, reminds me that I have not truly known Henry very long at all, yet it sounds gentler this way. My face is burning. I truly wish the ground would swallow me up this instant. I steal a glance at him. His head is bowed and I cannot see his face. I have not seen Mr Garland less than poised before. His golden hair gleams. I bite my lip; this is dreadful.

'I understand, Miss Snow,' he says in a quiet voice. 'Matters have progressed and you did not want to let a false impression stand between us.'

'Precisely so, Mr Garland, thank you. I hope we may still be friends. I value your friendship very much.'

'As I do yours, Miss Snow.' He looks up at me at last with a brave smile. There is an unfamiliar expression in his eyes. I presume it to be disappointment and his words confirm it. 'I am disappointed of course, I am a man! But not such a hot-headed fellow, I think, as to spurn a friendship truly given.'

The thing is said. Quite weak with relief, I sink into a chair.

'Are matters quite settled between you and your . . . friend?' he enquires.

'They are.'

'Though I do not see an engagement ring, Miss Snow.'

My head begins to throb. 'We are not yet engaged. Circumstances prevent . . . but the understanding is very clear, Mr Garland.'

'I see. Of course.' He nods and smiles again. There is a little silence. I wonder when he may leave. Then he resumes. 'Your circumstances or the gentleman's, I wonder?'

'Well, both, in truth. I mentioned to you, I think, that I am not currently at liberty to follow my own course, and that is still the case.'

'I remember. And who is the fortunate gentleman? Perhaps I know him?'

'I doubt it, sir. He is not from Bath, merely staying with friends for a time. And he does not . . . he has not been at any of the gatherings that you and I have attended.'

'Oh!' He manages to pack in a world of surprise and mild disapproval into that one syllable. 'But he is a good, solid gentleman? Your equal in every way? He is settled in life and able to make good his hold on your affection?'

Oh, this is horrible. Horrible! 'He is my equal, yes, certainly,' I reply, smoothing out the folds of my skirt with my palms. 'He is not *quite* settled yet but his intention to improve his position is clear.'

He arches golden eyebrows.

'I would not doubt it. It is only that I had imagined, for you . . . well, provided you are confident of his character and he is not some idle young dandy with a great many fine ideas and no decided action . . . provided he is fully sensitive to your needs and all you deserve . . . then I wish you both great joy. And of course this *must* be so or you would not have entered into an agreement with him.

'Forgive me, Miss Snow, I naturally feel protective towards you, though I readily admit it is not my place. I shall take my leave of you now and see you tonight. If we are to be friends, I may still see you tonight?'

'Oh! Of course! Yes, naturally.'

'The gentleman is not accompanying you?'

'No, sir, he is not.'

'I see.'

The look of delicate confusion on his perfect features is plain. This has been the most uncomfortable interview of my life.

I ring for Ambrose, who shows him out, and before I can begin to sort through my fears – of having behaved improperly, of having hurt his feelings, of having answered his questions too fully, or not fully enough – Mrs Riverthorpe is back, pouring herself a second Madeira and settling herself for a good gossip. I am beginning to feel that today is nothing but one conversation after another, in a decreasingly enjoyable sequence.

'Mrs Riverthorpe, might you excuse me please?'

'No, I might not. Come on, Amy Snow. Sit and talk. You don't interest me often. What's happening between you and Mr Garland? I'll wager he's shown his hand and now that you're entangled with your Henry you're feeling very awkward.'

'You are quite right as always, Mrs Riverthorpe. May I speak frankly to you?'

'I am in favour of frank speech, young lady. You may have noticed.'

I close the door, less for privacy than to emphasize the fact that he is gone and comfort myself thus. I seat myself on the chaise. I notice she has acquired a pretty gold and peach shawl which makes her orange ensemble more modest. I feel sure that she met Henry outlandishly dressed on purpose. But that is the least of my worries now.

'I feel very uncomfortable indeed. I fear I have hurt Mr Garland and —'

'Haaaa! If that is all that troubles you, you may rest easy. He is no tender young swain to have his heart broken so easy. But then again, he is also not a man to cross.'

'Why do you say that?'

'You remember what he told us last week? He doesn't play to lose.'

I frown. 'He was talking about canasta, Mrs Riverthorpe.'

'Was he now?'

'Was he not?'

She rolls her eyes. 'Go on.'

I take a deep breath, to gather my thoughts. 'That evening, during your card party, you remember Ambrose called me from the game . . . then you sent Mr Garland after me to see that I was well?'

'I did no such thing. Remember, Amy, I'm in the minority that believes a female is perfectly capable of absenting herself from a room for five minutes without disaster striking.'

'But . . . what? That is what he told me.'

'Did he now?' Again Mrs Riverthorpe reminds me of a heron, neck extended, steely eyes searching for fish. 'No. He excused himself immediately after you left the room. I don't miss much, Amy.'

'*Immediately* after? Then . . . '

I frown. I was conversing with Henry and the Longacres for some fifteen minutes at least. I remember entering the house, colliding with Mr Garland. He was just inside the door. The door has an ornamental glass window next to it. Is it possible that he was . . . *watching* me? That he saw Henry? That the amazing coincidence of his declaration occurring just when Henry reappeared *wasn't* a coincidence? That he wanted to make his interest known as soon as he thought there was someone else? And if so . . . is there anything wrong with that?

'Stop frowning, Amy. You look dreadful. Go *on*!'

'When I came inside, he declared his . . . admiration for me.' Frowning despite myself, I recount what I remember of the conversation.

'He did not wish to make a proposal at that time. He was not some "impetuous youngster", he said.'

Would Henry have appeared to him an impetuous youngster? *Is* Henry an impetuous youngster?

'He wished to ascertain whether I might possibly look upon him as a suitor when we had known each other longer.'

'And did you say you would?'

'I . . . I am not certain.'

Her expression is priceless. 'You don't know what you said?'

'No! That is to say, I believe I was a little vague. I was so very surprised. So very flattered, but *surprised*!'

Mrs Riverthorpe wrinkles her already wrinkled brow and I resist the urge to tell her *she* looks dreadful. Instead I stroke a patch of sunlight on the chaise.

'But Quentin is not a man to be easily put off. Surely he pressed you for *some* response beyond that of an imbecile?'

'Well, yes. I told him, I think I told him, that I admired him very much and that I enjoyed his company and looked forward to seeing him and all that is true! At any rate it seemed to satisfy him – he bade us return to the cards. Then he appeared today, apologizing for having been gone longer than anticipated but I had not noticed! I have spent every day since with Henry. I . . . I had *forgotten* Mr Garland!'

Oh, but I feel terrible. I lay my hands to my cheeks, a gesture I seem to be adopting more and more often lately.

'Haaaaa! That is priceless. Well done, Amy, that is the best thing I have yet heard come out of your mouth. Forgot him! He is not one who expects to be forgotten. Nor one who expects to be set aside. I have known Mr Garland some five or more years now, and every season I see the young ladies fighting over him like magpies with a choice titbit. He is the one who does the forgetting. I venture you will not shake him so easily.'

I fidget uneasily. The Mr Garland she is describing somehow does not match the considerate person I have seen him to be. I watch dust motes shifting in a sunbeam. Reality feels as though it is shifting too. For just a few days, with Henry, I thought I knew how everything was. Now there are questions again, always questions. 'But I spoke to him just now. I was truthful: I told him I have an understanding with somebody else.'

'And he was filled with joy for you and wished you a long and happy life together, I suppose?'

'Well, no, but he was very gentlemanly.'

'Oh, naturally. Quentin is ever the *gentleman*.'

She laughs to herself, an odd little laugh that can really only be described as a snigger. 'And what did he say then? Sow a few seeds of doubt in your mind, did he?'

'I could never doubt Henry, Mrs Riverthorpe. But yes, Mr Garland did suggest that perhaps he is not quite *settled*, was his word. And that I should expect the very best.'

She nods and smiles grimly. 'Namely Quentin Garland, no doubt. Well, he is a great deal better-looking than your Henry, I must say – oh, Henry is pleasing enough in a common sort of way but boasts no real distinction. Though I must say, for a funny-looking little thing you have attracted a decent pair of faces.'

She is wrong! Can she not see that Henry is dashing and merry and alive, while Mr Garland's beauty is polished and gleaming as marble?

'Then you think I should marry Mr Garland?' I ask, puzzled. I had thought she and Henry got on rather well, considering.

'Heavens, no! Marry whomever you please. Or don't marry at all! Or have 'em both! But whatever you do, do it with your eyes open.'

The small brown clock on the mantel strikes noon. The April sun is high and slanting. I have been cooped up in this room all morning and I should like to go for a walk. I stand up and go to the window. The street is golden, and busy. There is a world out there, beyond my complex affairs, bustling away.

'What do you mean, Mrs Riverthorpe? Please speak plainly. It may seem trivial to you but I am not made like you. Do you know something I don't?'

'My dear,' she begins. I turn from the window and look at

her sharply. Is she making fun of me? 'Why do you think I keep pictures of moths in every room of the house?'

I cannot follow her. 'Er . . . because you are a lepidopterist, I have always assumed.'

'Ha! Me, a lepidopterist? Because of my gentle fascination with the small marvels of the natural world?'

I incline my head stiffly. While I have become accustomed to her manners, I have not grown to enjoy her scorn. It is true she is not how one might imagine a lepidopterist. She would be hard to believe at all, but for the fact of her.

'Foolish child. It is because one must always keep the enemy in sight. Those little dusty brown things look so innocent but they nibble my clothes . . . or their young do, I forget which. At any rate, my beautiful gowns get nibbled and 'tis because of them. 'Tis war between us. So I hunt them. I persecute them. When I catch one whole, I mount it in the case. The pictures are always before my eyes to remind me that there are enemies to my happiness *everywhere*, even the small, creeping, harmless-looking kind.'

I am aware that my eyebrows have risen very high throughout her discourse. I had always known her to be unusual. But this is really quite startling. I return to my seat and spread out my skirts, intent upon arranging them quite symmetrically, giving myself time to compose a response.

'Good heavens! I can see that holes in your beautiful fabrics must be . . . um. . . vexing. But interesting though it is . . . I cannot see . . . ah! The pictures of the gentlemen?' I glance up at the portraits covering the far wall, all lit up with pale, dusty sunshine.

'Precisely so, child. The same reason. Always keep the enemy in sight.'

'I understand. Be wary of men, for they can destroy your happiness.'

'Ha! Very good. Indeed, indeed.'

I take up my glass of Madeira. 'Are the portraits of any particular men, Mrs Riverthorpe, or merely a selection to display the variety of the species?'

'They are my former husbands and lovers.'

I spill the Madeira a little in shock. 'What, *all* of them?'

'Don't be silly, child, I should run out of space on the walls if I were to display *all* of them. They are the chief troublemakers, I suppose. Amy, there is no happy ending. Disabuse yourself of that expectation. Even if you marry for love – perhaps especially then. Tall men, short men, rich men, poor men, handsome men, grotesques, grotesques who *believe* themselves handsome . . . I have had them all and they nibble, Amy, they all *nibble*.'

It is a dismaying turn to the conversation. I look all around me. This room has become familiar now, but it still does not feel like home. It is ever the scene of unexpected revelations, difficult questions, unsettling ideas . . .

'Surely not *all* men? Surely there are those who are good and kind and honourable and, and support a woman's right to learn, to choose her way and . . . and –'

'And breathe? How very good of them. I shall be sure to apply to them for their blessing the next time I wish to exercise a basic human right. Well, I assume you think your Henry is one such and you will live happily ever after.'

'Yes, I believe he is.'

'But you will *not* live happily ever after!' She bangs her fist down on the table and I jump. 'You are not even trying! He has no profession, not even a trade. You have been out in the world for all of five minutes and are as green as a sapling. I'm sure his family are good people, but I doubt they have the means to support him in any decent manner indefinitely. Very well, *you* have money, but does *he* know that? Have you even discussed it? Or have you just gazed into one another's eyes and sighed and recited poetry?'

I bristle. 'We have read a sonnet or two, but we have only declared our feelings yesterday. I think we may be forgiven for not having arranged all our worldly affairs to your satisfaction just yet.' My cheeks are beginning to grow hot. 'Remember, we are not engaged; we have not been so very hasty.'

But she appears to have lost interest in Henry and me.

'Then again, I do not think Quentin would make you any happier. I wonder why he has set his sights on you, when there are heiresses crawling all over Bath.'

'You think Mr Garland courts me because I appear wealthy?

But that cannot be . . . why would he need to do that? I am not so very rich!'

'He does not know *how* rich you are, remember. He has seen you impoverished and then, suddenly, dressed like a princess and mixing in the finest circles. You may even stand to inherit my money, as far as he is concerned. He knows nothing of specifics, but you must look like a good bet.'

'I suppose that's true. But *he* is wealthy! He need not marry for money.'

'Well, I'm sure he will not marry for love.' She leans forward and fixes me with a look. 'Amy, I have tried to say this to you before and I wish you to hear me now. Be careful of Quentin Garland. I know nothing specific or I would tell you, to be sure, but I have not spent a lifetime weaving in and out of men's lives without learning a great deal. My instinct tells me he is not what he seems. Be *very* careful of him. And Henry – you love him better, you say?'

'Why, yes. For all that I have admired Mr Garland most highly, Henry is the one I love. I feel instinctively that we belong together.'

'Then be even *more* careful of him. Now, Amy: one final word. Should you ever find yourself in the North Country, do please look up my friends the Caplands. Oh, do not fear, they are nothing like me. I imagine your Twisters, or Willows, or whatever you call them, to be very much like my Caplands.'

This is a change of subject as bizarre as the moths. How will this lead back to the subject at hand, I wonder?

'He is a very good fellow as they go, owns a shop, but for a tradesman he is very respectable. Not that *I* care about that. She is as silly a creature as ever lived, but kind-hearted, and that matters to *some* people.' She gives me a look. 'Shall you remember that name, Amy? Capland? Or will Henry's dark eyes drive it from your swiftly dissolving brain?'

'I shall indeed, Mrs Riverthorpe. But what have your Caplands to do with Henry, or Mr Garland or *any* of this, in fact?'

She rolls her eyes. 'Why, nothing at all, child. I am just so *very* bored of the conversation.'

Chapter Fifty-six

The following morning I attend a small brunch at Henrietta Street. Throughout the feast, Henry seems full of a barely suppressed, gleeful impatience.

After the meal he and I take up our corner of the garden and after he has kissed me in a way that turns my legs to water, he fixes me with dancing eyes.

'Amy, I am brimming with thoughts I must tell you.'

I knew it!

'Amy, we have made a commitment to one another, based on true and loving feelings. I am the most fortunate of men. The past days have been a delight. But I am aware that I have nothing to offer you. I am not in a position to ask you to marry me yet.'

Mr Garland's words flash through my mind, but I push them away and take Henry's hand.

'Amy, I feel that needs to change as soon as possible. So I have been awake at night thinking how to rectify the situation. I need a profession. It needs to be something that suits me and something I can sustain, so that I shall not be the most weary and grouchy of husbands.'

'I could not agree more.'

Henry loosens his cravat. 'I have mentally run through every profession known to man over the last few nights. During those small dark hours I believe I have pursued at least seven careers!'

I smile. 'You must have amassed a very great fortune, dear.'

'Oh, rich as Croesus! And I have found the answer. Now, it is a modest income, it is not a grand profession in the eyes of the world. No doubt many will say, with my education and intelligence, that I could do better, but you do not care so much for finery and fashionable living, I believe, from what you have told me of your own hopes?'

I fidget with impatience to hear his plan. 'Indeed no, and I would see you happy, dear. Tell me at once, what have you chosen?'

'I was thinking about your friends, the Wisters, and what you told me of young Michael's aspiration to teach unfortunate children.' Henry sits up very straight, his eyes shining. '*I* want to do that, Amy. I want to be able to jump into a profession without further study. I want to work with people – help them – right away. I don't know why I never thought of it before, only I suppose I always felt I must have a greater income, that society felt . . . that I would be somehow lacking if I did not.

'But no! I can think for myself.' He detaches his hand from

mine and begins to stride energetically to and fro across the terrace. I watch him as though he is a game of tennis. 'What matters is to make you happy, and myself as well. This will do it, I'm sure, and that is more important to me than earning a vast salary as a fine lawyer and impressing all who meet me. Provided you, my love, are content to be the wife of a schoolmaster. It will be a modest living, I must say so again so that you know what our life would be. If you tell me it must be otherwise, I will do otherwise. If you require a finer living, I will endeavour to earn it.'

I jump to my feet and kiss him. 'Henry, no! You know my heart. I have had enough of great cold corridors and empty rooms. I have had my fill of society and balls and scandals and wealth.'

'I knew you would say it!' he declares, tucking my hand under his arm so that I am pacing up and down with him. 'In that case, I shall ask Elsie to post the letter I wrote this morning when she goes into town. I didn't want to send it until I had spoken with you.'

'To whom have you written, Henry?'

'To a fellow I know in Twickenham, friend of Grandfather's. He is something political, but something educational also. Suffice to say, he's influential in school reform and he will know about this Kneller House and initiatives like it. I have asked him to let me know of any opportunities in that area and to put me forward for any positions he may hear of.'

I stop still and look at him. 'In the . . . *Twickenham* area, Henry?'

He smiles at me. 'You would wish to settle near your friends, would you not, my darling?'

'Oh, I should like that more than *anything*! But, what about you? Where would *you* wish to settle?'

He laughs easily. 'Why, with you of course! No, stop frowning! This is no great act of martyrdom. It's a lovely place, a stone's throw from London and the old one and Aunt Annie. Mother's in Hertfordshire, not so close but close enough – love her dearly but she's got a fierce temper on her. It's not Cardiff. It's not *Manchester*! I think we shall do very nicely in Twickenham.'

I suddenly see all my small dreams coming true before my eyes, and they are exploding, like roses bursting into bloom.

'Henry, do you suppose I might . . . no, perhaps . . . well, do you think I might help you, in some way? I don't know how. Maybe I could read essays if you have too many, or help you research new projects for the children.'

'Amy, I shall depend upon it!'

'And . . . what are your feelings about a conservatory, dear?'

'Entirely favourable, my love, nothing more pleasing.'

'Henry? Do you think we shall have a pony?'

'My dear, we can have ten.'

'One will certainly suffice. Henry, I must tell you –' Suddenly

I remember what Mrs Riverthorpe said and I want to tell him, to trust him. 'I . . . I have five thousand pounds. All left to me by Aurelia, all secret, of course. It is yours – that is to say, ours – to help you set up in your profession, or to buy a house or . . . or . . . in fact I do not know what five thousand pounds can do – I never had one shilling before – but I want you to know that we have it.'

Henry kisses me soundly. Again my head spins and my knees tremble and he sits me back down gently. He joins me, wearing his serious face again.

'I am so glad for your good fortune. But I could not take your money to get started in life – it is my privilege to do that for myself. I should like to be able to provide a home for us. No doubt you will think me very old-fashioned, but taking that responsibility is something I shall enjoy. You must use your money for yourself.'

'But I should like to . . . *invest* it in our life together. You will be working and earning our yearly budget. This could be my contribution to our finances.'

'Then shall we make it our nest egg? In case of any difficulties, or splendid opportunities that may arise. Or, perhaps, for our children?'

Had I allowed myself to be swayed by any of Mr Garland's reservations about Henry's fixity of purpose, my mind would now be put to rest. Over the following week I see a man truly determined. He writes countless letters: to his old tutors, asking for testimonials; to his family, informing them of his decision; to schools in Richmond, Twickenham, Hammersmith and Ham, enquiring about vacancies. He accosts the local schoolmaster, begging to discuss the profession with him, that he might be informed when he secures an interview. He persuades the Longacres to invite local politicians to dinner so that he may discuss education reform at length.

It is a busy, exciting, energetic week and every time I see him he has something new to tell me. I see Mr Garland only twice, at the concert in the Upper Rooms and at a dinner four days later. I feel horribly uncomfortable, and guilty for being so happy, but he is civil, of course, and does not refer to personal matters between us again. It seems that he has accepted my decision and retired gracefully, as I might have expected.

And soon enough, it is the twenty-ninth of April and time to receive Aurelia's next letter.

Mrs Riverthorpe tosses it casually into my lap on her way out, making me jump. I had not forgotten the date – far from it – but I have seen little of her over the past days and have had no chance to mention it. I was expecting she would summon me and present it over a ceremonial glass of Madeira, not throw it at me in the middle of breakfast.

My appetite drains away. I hear the front door bang as Mrs Riverthorpe departs. It is only a rectangle of cream paper but, now that there is Henry in my life, it feels like the sword of Damocles poised above my head.

I leave my kippers half eaten and, telling Ambrose I am not at home to callers, I run to my room. I close the door firmly and tuck myself up in the window seat. I take a deep breath and rip the letter open.

My treasured Amy,

I hope you are well. I hope you are happy. I hope you are finding your way to embrace all that life has to offer.

It has been a bad day today. Mr Clay came to discuss the school but I fainted after breakfast and could not see him. I did not recover myself to any great degree until twilight was all around. What a waste of a precious day.

No matter, I had promised myself that I would write this letter this evening and write it I shall, though in a more sombre frame of mind than I have written previously. I have no spirits to write amusing recollections, nor for emotional unburdening, nor for the commitment to page of my greatest and most valuable secret. Not now.

Your trail is nearly at an end, dear Amy, very nearly. Therefore please, my beloved friend, take one more journey on my account. Go to York. 'Tis a beautiful city and the countryside is wild and wonderful. I believe you will like it.

Dearest Amy, my next letter will be better and fuller. Travel alone, tell no one where you are going and know that my confidence in your discretion brings peace to my poor ailing heart at a time when nothing else could.

With greatest love from your devoted
AV

Chapter Fifty-seven

I rest my head against the window pane. Go to York.

I gaze out over the narrow, quiet street. A solitary carriage bowls along, two black horses high-stepping on air. On a stretch of pale wall, a squirrel dashes and stops, then vanishes in a flourish of tail. The sun is shining. *Go to York.*

My eyes brim hot and a tear escapes. I stare and I stare for, oh, I suppose ten minutes, if not more.

With a sudden deep swoop of foreboding, I hear Henry's cheerful voice planning our life in Twickenham.

'It's not Cardiff! It's not *Manchester*!'

York, I believe, is farther than Manchester.

I take a deep breath and swing my feet to the floor to face into my room. 'My' room. This strange space with its grey walls and its dipping eaves, its framed sketches of moths and an old woman's former lovers. It is time then to leave it. And, suddenly, I come to understanding of what I am feeling.

I am furious! Oh, I am so angry I can hardly bear it! What has my time in Bath been? What have the last weeks achieved?

Well, it has given me Henry, of course, but Aurelia was not to know that. Otherwise it has been time endured in the cactus patch that is Mrs Riverthorpe's home: an onslaught of her merciless teasing, a tedium of stiff social occasions and an awkward entanglement with a gentleman with whom I should never have crossed paths in the first place. I have learned *nothing* of Aurelia's year away, except that she was never here, which only makes it all the more pointless. And all for *this*? Go to *York*! A place she was never supposed to have visited for more than a day or two. If indeed she did! Just when a life of my own was taking shape.

The long-awaited clue, for which I have endured so much, amounts to just three words. I could spit. I am finished. I am finished with Aurelia. I am finished with her ridiculous quest and her demands for my loyalty and her secrets. Finished.

Chapter Fifty-eight

'Are you quite alright, Amy, my beauty?' asks Henry gently over dinner. 'You seem a little quiet.'

I lay down my fork and stroke his hand.

'I am well, only preoccupied by all our happy plans.' Despite myself, tears well in my eyes.

'Well you had better accustom yourself to it and soon enough. As soon as our circumstances permit, we must travel to London and see my grandfather. He will be overjoyed to see you again and to know that you are to be part of our family. We must go to Hertfordshire together to see my mother. And then to Twickenham so I can meet the Wisters. Or Twickenham first and then London, it matters not . . . '

'What's the matter with you, child?' snaps Mrs Riverthorpe over luncheon the next day. 'You look more than usually dull and listless. Not sickening for something, are you?'

'No, thank you, I am well.'

'Hmm, what tiresome melancholies young people in love are prone to. A pity. I was going to ask you to visit Mrs Manvers with me today but I suppose you'll need to stay home and sigh.'

'On the contrary. If you will wait for me to change my gown, I will happily accompany you.'

'Really? You surprise me. Yes, change your dress by all means. Your face too, if you will oblige me. Oh, and Amy? Do not think me more than usually rude, but have you yet formed any plans to leave me?'

I pause, my hand on the doorknob.

'No, Mrs Riverthorpe. Unless you object to my staying.' I brace myself for a cutting response.

'I do not object.'

Chapter Fifty-nine

The days pass. I consider myself, still, finished with Aurelia. I have no intention of going to York. I am going on with my life, and my life, for the moment, is in Bath. The weather favours us with some fine weather as well as Bath's customary selection of rains, fogs and vapours. I am equally well disposed to either circumstance. When it is fine, there are picnics, walks and drives into the country. When it is wet, we visit the abbey or a coffee shop, we play the piano, talk or read.

Henry receives several letters in response to his enquiries, all very informative and obliging. One is particularly thrilling: he is invited to an interview at a ladies' academy in Richmond. It is not precisely the group of students he had imagined, but then a school for girls is in itself something of a rarity. And, as he observes, the education of girls is scarcely a less worthy cause than the education of the troubled or needy.

The interview is not for several days, due to important cricket fixtures in the adjoining boys' academy.

'Why, I am very well pleased with that!' exclaims Henry, laying down the letter.

The simple gesture makes me feel very tender towards him. It is as though, in that movement of his arm, I can see all the letters that will arrive for us in the years to come. Whether they bear sad news or joyful, he will lay them down just thus and his mannerisms will all grow familiar to me.

'It gives me a little more time to spend with you, my love. And I do feel that a place that favours cricket over the appointment of staff must be a very promising place indeed, don't you think?'

I laugh. 'Yes, I do, and I am so very happy for you. You will make the most marvellous teacher.' It is true; he will. And when he secures an appointment . . . perhaps then an engagement will be possible and we will be able to live the life we dream of, instead of sitting in Bath talking about it. 'Mr . . . Merritt, was it? . . . will certainly think so when he meets you too. What a marvellous name for a teacher!'

'What other profession could he have chosen, thus named? Now, Amy, my love,' says Henry, taking my hand, 'when are you going to tell me?'

'Tell you what?' Suddenly I am wary. 'What do you mean?'

'Tell me what has been amiss these last few days. You have not been happy and that's not right.'

I pull away from him a little more sharply than I meant to. 'I *am*, Henry! How can you say that? I told you, I am merely . . . overwhelmed, I suppose, with so much bounty, so much joy. It is hard to accept, to adjust myself, after a life so different.'

'No, that is not it,' he insists gently, watching my face, which I believe may be scowling. 'I have not known you long, I realize, but I have seen you overwhelmed with joy and this is not it. I have two possible explanations; shall I tell you what they are?'

I feel my cheeks flame. Is this what marriage will be like, someone foraging out every thought when you are accustomed to keeping your own counsel and managing your problems in your own way?

'I wish you would not,' I mumble.

He reaches out a hand to tilt up my hanging head.

'I'm afraid I must. I appear easy as a summer stream, I know, but I have a stubborn current that is something fearsome. You may as well know it as you are to marry me one day. My two theories are as follows. Firstly, you may be experiencing reservations about our attachment – though I trust it is not that, for I am a paragon amongst men, as you see.'

I smile. Henry can always, always make me smile.

'Of course it is not that. Though I don't see how you succeed in being a paragon *and* in having such a stubborn streak as you have described.'

'It adds to my charm. Then I believe it is Aurelia's letter that has upset you. Am I right, Amy?'

I am quite amazed. I have said not one word about the letter.

'The twenty-ninth of April, was it not, you were due to receive it? 'Twas the twenty-ninth of April that I first noted the downhill curve of your beautiful smile. I did not like to ask you right away. I thought you needed time to reflect. I did not wish to rush you, my love, but now I am beginning to wonder if you are ever going to tell me anything at all!'

'I did not realize you had remembered the date. That you had marked it. Oh, Henry, I am so sorry!' I cover my face with my hands, then look at him in disbelief. It is inconvenient that he remembered it, for he is interrupting my blithe evasion of the whole affair, but it is heartwarming too.

'Of course I marked it; it is of the greatest importance to you, and therefore to me. And, too . . .' he hesitates and looks uncertain for a moment. I have not seen that look on his face for some time. '. . . I wonder how it may affect us.' He takes a breath. 'If the quest is at an end – as I know you were hoping – why, then you might come to Richmond with me when I attend my interview. I could be your escort on the journey, that would be quite proper, I think, and you could stay with your friends. I had hoped you might write to them.'

I am speechless. I look at his bright, hopeful face, his smooth forehead behind which so many plans and dreams have been spinning night and day, and all revolving around me. In that moment the reality of my dreadful predicament sinks in fully.

'Or, if it is not at an end,' continues Henry, 'you might at least tell me – for then I might prepare myself for a separation. And surely, Amy, if we are to be separated we can correspond? I do not mean to rush you if there are difficult decisions to be made but I am naturally anxious to learn what lies ahead.'

Suddenly his tender expression, his utterly reasonable questions, are more than I can bear. But I have already made my decision – I am abandoning Aurelia in favour of my own life, the one I will share with Henry. It is quite the right thing to do. It is what anyone would do.

'I shall write to Edwin and Constance, Henry. I shall come to Richmond with you. The quest is at an end.'

I see confusion cloud his face. 'What do you mean, the quest is at an end?'

'I should think it perfectly clear. Concluded. Finished. I am at liberty. I shall go on no further senseless, stupid, *desolate* journeys! I am free to go where I wish and when.'

My voice has risen and he tilts his head. 'Then why do you not sound happy? What has happened? I don't understand.'

'Well, of course you don't. How could you? I know a great deal more than you and even *I* do not understand. But we may let the matter rest, for the path ahead is clear.'

Now he looks very grave and seems to consider my request very seriously before shaking his head.

'No, Amy, it cannot rest. I'm sorry. You are unhappy and you seem divided against yourself. You have just said everything I longed to hear, yet it doesn't feel right. It is *not* at an end, is it? There is more, but you have decided to set it aside. Why? I hope you don't do so for me. I want you with me, of course, but I would never ask you to betray your duty to Aurelia.'

I place my hands flat on the table – with some force. 'It is what *I* want. It is what I want more than *anything*! Only, what if I cannot live by my own decision, Henry? I don't wish to do what she asks of me. But can I ever know peace of mind again if I turn my back on it all, as I so *dearly* long to do?'

'What *has* she asked of you?'

Numbly I reach into my pocket and pull out the letter. I have grown accustomed always to keep her latest missive on my person and so I have done with this unpromising document. I hand it to Henry.

'Am I to read it? Are you sure?'

'Oh, believe me, it gives nothing away. You will know nothing you are not meant to know, except my destination. That is, what my destination would be, if I were to go, which I won't.'

He nods and reads the letter. It takes only a minute. 'York?'
'York.'

'Then York played a significant role in her journey?'

'Not as far as I know.'

We are silent for some time and then I start to talk. I tell him of my anger and frustration and how very nearly I had allowed myself to hope that this letter would be the last letter, that it would contain all the answers.

'But it doesn't, and there's no explanation, only that she felt too tired to write more that day! Then why could she not simply have waited to write it another day? The last letter was four pages long, Henry. Four pages! Full of revelations I had never imagined. And now this! I have waited here, endured Bath society, tolerated Mrs Riverthorpe, suffered speculation and insinuation and outright insult. And for what? For *this*? "Go to York." I am finished with her, Henry.'

But even as I say it I know that it can't be so. She is part of me. I am alive because of her.

'I must go with you,' says Henry at last, in a decided voice.

'I'm not going.' My voice is weak. I am saying one thing and thinking another and detesting myself for it.

'Amy, you are not honest with yourself.' He knits his brows together. 'You look as thoroughly miserable as I've ever seen you. It is as you say. You could never have peace of mind knowing you had not kept faith with her. I do not claim to understand this strange quest or what can possibly have gone through her mind when she engineered this . . . this . . . extraordinary plot. It seems to me a preposterous thing to ask of one's fellow man. *Woman*.' He gestures impatiently. 'All I know is that if you follow this thing to the end then, when you say to me, "Henry, I shall come with you; the quest is over," you will do so with a clear conscience and joy in your heart. But you need not do it alone. You have me now.' He looks at me steadily.

'No, she says to travel alone. I could not take you.'

A pause. 'But, my dear, she also says to tell no one where you are to go and you have already done so! And how would taking me with you be more of a betrayal than abandoning it altogether? That is not quite rational, my love.'

'Rational?' At some point I have risen to my feet and begun pacing the room. 'There is nothing rational about any of this. Not the quest, not the position it puts me in, not the way my life is unfolding and certainly not the way I feel.'

Henry watches me in concern while I storm and storm some more. 'Amy! I didn't mean to criticize you, I was merely trying to point out why there is no reason for you to suffer, either by travelling to the north alone or by acting against your conscience. Do what you must! Only, do not do it alone and unprotected. That is what a husband is *for*.'

'But you are not my husband, not yet!'

'Then let us marry at once and take care of that.'

'No, Henry, not like this. Not in haste and expediency, because we have to. I can't take you with me. I can't explain it to you, for I do not fully understand it myself. But I *cannot*, I am quite, quite sure of that.'

The look of hurt on his face strikes me like a blow. There is a tight silence between us and I know he is waiting for me to capitulate, but I won't.

'The revelations of the last few letters,' I say more gently, 'are of the most delicate nature . . .' I am about to say 'for a woman', but I fear even that would give away too much. How could I explain it to him? Aurelia's physical intimacies, outside of marriage, the questions that have been circulating in my mind over the last weeks, are too personal to share. She is a woman and I am a woman and I cannot pass on a confidence like that and especially not to a man.

It was a relief to hand over the letter to Henry, to feel for a moment that my responsibility might be shared. But now I feel cornered. This journey cannot be shared. York will be like London all over again, except with not so much as an Entwhistle's to guide me. There is the possibility that I might find no reason at all, only another clue, another journey. Or that I might fail. These are things I could not bear for Henry to see.

'I . . . I don't know what I will find in York. If I *were* to continue the quest, it would be a highly personal matter between Aurelia and me. If I decide to turn away from it, that too is personal between us. But either way, I must choose alone. To have you go with me would seem . . . I do not know . . . wrong? Unfair?'

Henry shoots to his feet and stalks to the window. I anxiously watch his bristling back. How have we moved in moments from laughter to what may very well be an altercation?

'And your pledge to share your life with me, in all its odd and problematical forms, is *that* not personal, Amy? Is the trust between us not personal? The revelations of the other letters may well be delicate. The revelations of this latest letter, however, are non-existent! Where would you even begin to find a letter when your only clue is the entire city?'

The demands Aurelia is placing upon me do not paint her in a good light. I don't want Henry to think badly of her. Nor do I like to think that she has put me at risk, more than once. So to avoid considering the matter too closely, I snap at Henry.

'This is not what you said ten days ago, Henry. You said you understood my loyalty to Aurelia, you said you accepted that the quest must come first until it is done. You said you supported me!'

'I do support you! That is what I am doing by offering you my protection. Forgive me if I cannot be perfectly sanguine about you crossing the country alone to only a very vague destination! Amy, I stand by what I said. But it's one thing when we're sitting together beneath the trees and the matter is hypothetical. It's far harder when we've admitted our feelings, started planning our future and I am faced with watching you slip through my fingers *yet again*! I am trying, Amy, but I do not see why you must choose between your loyalty to Aurelia and your loyalty to me. You may honour both! *Why* must you turn your back on her in order to be with me? I do not ask it of you. I don't want you divided thus. But take me with you, let me help you; that is what the man who loves you is *supposed* to do! Is it that you don't trust me? Do you think I might disapprove of Aurelia, or of you, or that I would betray your confidence? Whatever it is, Amy, it makes no *sense!*'

By the end of his wretched speech he is glowering at me. I cannot bear it. My smiling, sunny Henry is angry with me. Insisting I do what I cannot as if it were a simple matter to bring together my old life and my new. Asking me to explain the inexplicable. Does he not realize I have been living with impossible conundrums and ambiguity all my life? Of course it makes no sense. Nothing ever has.

'I'm sorry, Henry,' I sob in a great rush. 'I can't be what you want. I knew it was so. I have never fitted easily and my circumstances are too complicated for love and a normal life. I am so sorry.' I race towards the door.

He catches me on the way and wraps his arms around me.

'Let me go, Henry! I cannot bear this conversation. I will see you in the morning when I am myself again.'

But he is strong and his arms about me are gentle.

'Shhh, my darling. It is I who am sorry. Forgive me, Amy. We shall talk of it no more tonight, I promise. You must manage things your own way and not be upset. Please, my love, don't go when you are like this. Let us put this aside for now and be calm.'

And I do grow a little calm. Later, when we bid each other goodnight, we are subdued and affectionate.

But the ache in my heart is heavy and strangling, for I know that I am not behaving as a truly devoted wife-to-be should act. I feel deeply, disappointingly unequal to the role. Perhaps such precious dreams can't come true – not for me.

Chapter Sixty

Over the next two days I learn just how far avoidance can take us – and where it cannot. Its temporary benefits come at a distressing cost. Henry and I are docile and affectionate but there is something lifeless between us, where previously all was flicker and spark. Whenever we are together, we hold hands and we smile. We pass each other milk and sugar when we take tea. We look like the very portrait of a young betrothed couple. But we don't burst out laughing any more. We don't grin or tease. We don't forget ourselves and kiss until we can't breathe. We are close once again, and yet a black abyss yawns between us.

I tell myself he is sulking because he did not get his way, that he does not understand how it has always been for me. Our voices are bright when we talk of the future but our words do not ring true. Our sentences are vague because so much is unknown and so much unsaid. We are in a sort of dreadful half-life. I still cannot feel comfortable turning my back on Aurelia, yet the prospect of leaving Henry is far harder now than if all were well between us. I think I am waiting until we feel like *us* again before I decide – but we seem to grow more stiff and stifled every day and all I am doing is fruitlessly delaying Aurelia's quest. I feel guilty about that. I feel guilty about Henry. I feel, as I did at Hatville, that Amy Snow is a wretched, troublesome creature.

It becomes a relief to spend time away from him. If Mrs Riverthorpe is curious as to why I begin attending her cards parties again, she refuses to show it. And this is how I find myself alone with Quentin Garland once again.

He has arrived early for canasta – I know not why – but Mrs Riverthorpe reacts to his presence irritably; she has things to do before the rest arrive, she tells him, and stalks off, leaving us together in the drawing room. I wrap my thick, mulberry-coloured shawl about my shoulders. It is May now, so there is no fire this afternoon, but the room is especially cheerless. Or perhaps it is my state of mind.

He is, naturally, immaculately turned out, in a jacket of midnight blue and exquisitely tailored cream trousers. The rich shade of his coat accentuates the lighter blue of his eyes, his cravat and, today, his matching pale-blue gloves. These he removes now, delicately tugging at fingertip after fingertip. For something to do, I ring for tea.

For a few moments he and I exchange stiff pleasantries while the tea sits disregarded on its silver tray, then he favours me with a smile.

'Miss Snow, may I speak quite plainly? I fear that recent events have put an end to our former easy friendship and I regret it. I would never have spoken if I had known that the loss would be thus. However, I would like to be your true friend, if I can. May I?'

I do not *remember* us as having an easy friendship, only that I was ever in awe of him, but I say yes, of course.

'Then, forgive me, is all quite well with you? You look tired, a little . . . troubled. If there is aught amiss, I should like to help, if I can.'

Small wonder I look tired. Euphoria chased away sleep when Henry first told me that he loved me. Now I sleep badly for the old reasons. Memories of Hatville reclaim my mind. In skewed snatches of sleep here and there, strange dreams take shape. I have not had a good night's rest for some time.

'It is merely that I am tired, Mr Garland. You recall perhaps the private business of which I spoke to you? The need for me to move on quite soon?'

'Indeed.'

I suddenly feel the need to unburden myself to someone, anyone. 'Well, that time is upon me and the matter is . . . delicate. You're right, I am troubled. I find I'm undecided about my course of action and that is surprising to me.'

'And your gentleman friend, is he content to see you go?'

'There you hit upon the other matter, Mr Garland. Henry wishes to come with me; he does not wish me to go alone.'

'I suppose it is natural he should not want to be parted from you. And it *is* highly unusual for a young lady to travel alone in the manner you have done. Oh, I say nothing of it for myself but perhaps he is the traditional sort?'

'I don't think it's a question of propriety, I believe he is concerned for my welfare. Also, I believe he is hurt that I don't entrust more to him about the business in question.'

'But it is a secret, you said?'

'Indeed it is!' I cry with some frustration.

'Then there is nothing more to be said. A secret must be honoured. Especially, perhaps, a secret between two young ladies.' He smiles fondly. 'If he is the right man for you, Miss Snow, then he will respect your need for privacy on this matter.'

'Thank you, Mr Garland, you are very kind.'

I feel somewhat reassured that I am not being unreasonable. Perhaps I allow him to reassure me so because I need to believe it. I even allow myself to think, for one wild instant, that perhaps Mr Garland is the right man for me. It would be easier, after all, to be with someone who unquestioningly respects Aurelia's secret and does not *press* me. But of course that is not the point. The point is that it is *Henry* whom I love.

One at a time, the other guests arrive and I hope that the game, however tiresome, will take me out of myself for a little while. It does not. I consider the fact that Henry goes to Richmond in two days' time and I still don't know what to do.

The cards are slow. Mr Garland wins every hand. Mrs Riverthorpe grumbles. Conversation is desultory; I know my black mood doesn't help. Outside, an indifferent afternoon has blossomed into a May evening as fine as spun silk so I decide to take the air, pleading a headache. I am glad that Mr Garland does not offer to escort me.

I walk to Crescent Fields, remembering the day I met Henry. Pouring rain and a dripping bonnet. Standing in this very spot contemplating three weeks in Bath and expecting to drag myself minute by minute through the days. Now that time is up and I am loath to leave. I stand beneath a haze of waning sunlight and an early summer moon. Aurelia's quest is suspended, and nothing feels right.

I force myself to breathe, to think. I tell myself I am mistress of my life and even the most difficult decisions are all mine to make. Only I cannot make them. I cannot choose. The guilt of abandoning my quest would surely crush me, shadow every good thing my life might bring. But I *cannot* leave Henry; I can't risk losing him. I want to go to Richmond with him. I *will* go to Richmond with him . . . The prospect shimmers in front of me for a moment like a mirage. And yet . . .

I tell myself I will not return to Hades House until I have settled upon a course of action. The sky grows dark around me.

When a stranger in a slouch hat slips past me from the shadows, fixing me with hooded eyes, I know I am being foolish staying out alone and yield to indecision. Tonight then. I will make my choice tonight.

I walk briskly back, relieved when the house looms up at me, all towers and teeth as it is. But my relief is short-lived. The bent figure of Mrs Riverthorpe stalks up and down, up and down the hall. When she sees me, she swoops towards me with fierce eyes.

'Amy, you must leave at once.'

My hour of reverie is abruptly ended. 'I beg your pardon? Why?'

'You have not seen her then?'

'Seen whom? I have seen no one.'

'Where have you been?'

'At Crescent Fields. Mrs Riverthorpe, what's happened? Why must I leave?'

'You have had a visitor, Amy.'

'Henry? At this time of night?'

'No, not *Henry*. Lady Celestina Vennaway was here at the house, large as life and fine as you please, demanding to see Amy Snow.'

I put a hand out to steady myself. 'Lady Vennaway? Here? What did she want? What did you say to her?'

'Told her I'd never heard of you, of course. Sent her away. Clear she didn't believe me, but that doesn't signify, provided she doesn't get her hands on you, and provided she doesn't

434

know where you've gone. Go on, pack your bags. Make ready. The carriage will take you to London at first light. Oh, you *could* take a train but I want no trace of you. I don't want her snooping around, charming some unsuspecting fool into telling her where you are gone. The carriage can bear you to London – you can take a direct train from Euston to York. I shall send Ambrose with you and she will arrange porters for your luggage. I have sent Cecile to follow Madam Vennaway, to make sure she stays away from the house. I can –'

'Mrs Riverthorpe, *stop*!'

I have never seen her like this. She is babbling, thinking aloud, forming plans, all the while as if I am not there; I, the object of those plans. I remember that she knows Aurelia's secret. It must be momentous indeed if she is so disarranged by the arrival of a Vennaway.

'I am going nowhere like this. Surely a few moments of explanation will not wreak havoc. Please tell me everything that happened and what was said. How did she look?'

I do not know why I ask this, but that she was a part of my life for the longest time. For all that she despises me, I know how it feels to have lost Aurelia.

'How did she *look*? Riven. Pale. Exquisite. Dressed in full mourning and wearing it like a queen.'

Mrs Riverthorpe then consents to tell me that, some time since, there was a mighty rap at the door. Assuming one of her guests had forgotten something, she sent Ambrose to receive the caller, despite the late hour. But Ambrose returned bearing the card of Lady Celestina Vennaway.

Mrs Riverthorpe was at the door in a trice, determined to see her off before I returned. She hobbled out to address Lady Vennaway in her carriage.

'May I come in, Mrs Riverthorpe?' asked Lady Vennaway.

'You may not,' retorted Mrs Riverthorpe.

When she saw that the object of her visit was both determined and aged, Lady Vennaway offered Mrs Riverthorpe a seat in her carriage for the duration of the conversation, which was duly refused on the grounds that the interview would not be long enough to warrant the courtesy.

I permit myself a moment to imagine this mythical interlocking of horns of the two proudest women of my acquaintance; both so haughty, both so accustomed to having their way in every small particular. I do not believe either of them can ever have met with opposition before. It must have been like an exotic dragon facing a prehistoric monster.

Lady Vennaway asked for me. Her sister had seen me, she said, in the company of a lady who claimed to be my guardian. She wished urgently to speak to me and, her attempts to communicate in writing having failed, had sought me out in person.

Mrs Riverthorpe lied outright and said she had never met me, never heard of me and that there was some mistake. She did so with such great energy and such negligent civility that although her visitor clearly did not believe her, she was forced to leave with no satisfaction.

Part of me dearly wishes I could have been there to see it.

But, Mrs Riverthorpe resumes, I must leave the very next morning.

'Would it be so very detrimental, after all, to grant her an audience?' I ask. 'If I did so here, with you, I should feel safer. I am tired of running and looking over my shoulder and always fearing whom I might see. Can I not just stop and face her?'

'No, Amy. Whatever she wants can bode no good and for you to see her would put your quest at risk. You are not an accomplished liar, child, more's the pity. You must go. I am sorry.'

I feel as though I am teetering on the very edge of a chasm. I had never thought I could feel sorry to leave Hades House but now that it is upon me, I find I have developed a strange attachment to the place. While *my* quest is certainly very unusual, Mrs Riverthorpe is a constant, reasurring rebuttal of the conventional. She has seen so much of the world and scoffs at most of it. Although no serene, compassionate mentor, she has been an anchor of sorts. Now I must leave what little stability she has given me to take my longest journey, and with the least guidance.

'Mrs Riverthorpe, how do you know I am to go to York?'

'I know everything.'

'Then please, please, I *beg* you, tell me what I am to do there and what I will find. I have followed Aurelia's trail most diligently, indeed I have, but now there is Henry to think of . . . I have been anguishing over this. Can you not tell me and save me this last step? It would be but a shortcut.'

'No, Amy. It's not that I wish to be obstructive –' she raises her eyebrows – 'but I have told you before, I promised Aurelia. The secret is not mine to tell. I believe you will be better learning it in the way she intended. Henry will wait.'

'Then tell me one thing, just one thing. Promise me.'

'If I can.'

'Is the trail to conclude in York? Will this see an end to it?'

She looks at me for the longest time. I fancy I can see arguments in favour of speaking and arguments for staying silent chasing each other through her cunning brain. Eventually she sighs.

'It ends there.'

Oh! I seize on this slight scrap of certainty. To know this, at last, rather than merely suspecting, or painfully hoping – how wonderful to be able to tell Henry this one thing. Surely then, any separation must be relatively brief; I can reassure him at last. It makes a difference to *everything*, knowing that. It means I can bear to continue the quest after all . . . although, of course, the decision has already now been made for me by Celestina Vennaway.

'I will miss you, Mrs Riverthorpe. Thank you for all you have done for me . . . odd though some of it has been. I truly hope we may meet again, if I do not bore you too much.'

Another pause and I imagine – no, I am *sure* I see a softening in her face. But 'Go and pack, Amy, you must leave tomorrow,' is all she says.

Chapter Sixty-one

I stumble awake to the sound of hammering at my door. It is dark and I search through the tangled strands of my mind for the dark thing I have forgotten. Through the gloom I discern my wardrobe, door open, standing empty, and I recall: I must leave today.

Mrs Riverthorpe bursts into my room and shakes my bedclothes.

'Come on, young lady! Up! Up!'

I tumble from bed like a sparrow chick from a nest, blind and confused. I feel like to be crunched by cats, too.

'Mrs Riverthorpe, wait! 'Tis not light. Give me time.'

She ignores my protests. 'Time we do not have! That woman may call here this morning. You must be gone. I see you are packed, good. Get dressed. I will give you bread for the journey.'

'You will not give me breakfast before I leave?'

'You can eat all the breakfast you like in York. Come, come. Stop mumbling.'

I stagger into my clothes and find myself at the front door, blinking. My trunk is gone before me, the horses are ready, bridles chinking, hooves scuffing at the pavement. A three-quarter moon hangs yet in the sky, veiled by chiffon bolts of cloud.

Ambrose appears in a travelling cloak, holding a parcel of bread. What I really want is coffee.

'Mrs Riverthorpe, will you not accompany me to London? There is still so much I wish to ask you. We have scarce spoken of Aurelia the whole time I have been here.'

There is something else, too; I am strangely loath to part from her. She is old. What if I never see her again?

'Talking won't bring her back. No, if her mother returns, I must be here to deal with her. That woman must never find out the truth. And I shall deal with Henry, too, when he comes sniffing round here, as he surely will. Fear not, I shall be kindly enough.'

'But Mrs Riverthorpe! You cannot expect me to leave without saying goodbye to *Henry*! That is absurd.'

'You don't have time for fond farewells. He will understand, if he is worthy of you. Consider, we do not know where Aurelia's mother is staying. What if you should cross her path just as you go to call on Henry? No, you must get into that carriage and stay in it until Bath is far behind. Besides, it is five in the morning. No one will thank you for a social call at this hour.'

Words of affection and farewell die on my lips. I am trembling with fury, such that I don't trust myself to speak. So I do not. I march down the steps and scramble into the carriage, shaking off the helping hand of the driver. I scoop in fold after fold of my skirts – there seem to be miles of them this morning – and slam the door. She is indulging in senseless levels of drama and she is terribly unkind. Ambrose climbs in and we are off. I don't look back. I don't look at Ambrose either.

We rattle at a great pace through streets more silent than I have ever seen them. Birds fly up at our approach. I fear we will wake the whole neighbourhood, and then anyone who recognizes Mrs Riverthorpe's carriage would be able to tell Lady Vennaway that *someone* was seen leaving that household at first light. And she will know that someone was me. There *is* no safety, does Mrs Riverthorpe not realize that? Lady Vennaway's letter found me in Twickenham; she has found me in Bath. I am starting to feel like hunted prey and I do not favour it.

When we pass very near Henrietta Street, I stand, swaying, and thump the roof with my small fist as hard as I can.

'Miss Snow!' exclaims Ambrose in alarm. 'Sit down. You will be hurt. We must not stop.'

'Ambrose,' I say through clenched teeth, lurching and thumping, still, 'I do not care.'

The carriage draws to a halt, and I am thrown against the opposite wall. Ambrose makes a grab for me but catches only a handful of my infernal skirts. What am I wearing? My claret travelling dress. I do not remember making the selection.

'Do not obstruct me, Ambrose,' I warn. 'You are loyal to Mrs Riverthorpe, I know, but I will not go along with this. You cannot deter me. Wait in the carriage. I shall be but ten minutes.'

I am on the street before she can say a word. I expect she may follow me but she will have to keep up with me to be successful. I am banging at the Longacres' door before half past five in the morning.

At least the servants will be up – I know *that* very well.

A yawning, blinking Elsie is astonished when she sees me. 'Miss! Is everything alright? Beggin' your pardon, miss!' She hops back from the door.

'Thank you, Elsie. No, not quite.' I lean against the doorframe, glad that *something* is solid. The hall within is in shadow, I can feel the upper rooms quietly dreaming. A deep wash of sadness seeps through me. 'I need to speak with Mr Mead immediately if you please; there is no time to lose.'

'Of course, miss. Come in.' She beckons me in and I obey.

I wait in the breakfast room, where I have so often and so pleasantly taken coffee and talked with my friends. The room – the house – is elegant and peaceful. Out there is the garden where Henry told me he loved me. It is another goodbye.

Henry is at my side in moments, a loose white nightgown tucked haphazardly into trousers with suspenders trailing at his sides. His hair is wild – as is my own, I perceive suddenly in a mirror; I must have neglected to brush it. He looks warlike.

'Amy! Is something wrong? Has somebody hurt you? Why are you dressed like that?'

'I am going to York, Henry, now. Lady Vennaway is here in Bath and came to Hades House looking for me last night. Mrs Riverthorpe has sent me away.'

He looks disappointingly uncomprehending.

'But why must you *leave*? Let her come! You will tell her nothing. She can learn nothing to hurt you for no one *knows* anything – besides myself and Mrs Riverthorpe, and we will not betray you.'

His confusion echoes my own. What can I say? 'I know. But Mrs Riverthorpe wants me gone and the time is come and . . . and Henry I *must* do it.' My voice cracks on the word 'must' and I sink into a chair, surrendering to inevitability. I look up at him, silently imploring him to understand. 'Listen to me, Henry, the trail is to end in York. Mrs Riverthorpe told me so. She knows Aurelia's secret. I begged her to tell me, that I might put an end to this, but she would not. But she did promise that York is the end of it. I will come back to you, my love. It will not be long now.'

Henry looks at me as though I am a madwoman. He comes to my side in three long strides, sinks to his knees and seizes my hands. 'Let me come with you. I'll come now. I'll dress in less than a minute. Do not go alone.'

'No, Henry, your interview! You must go to Richmond.'

'Then come to Richmond with me! Stay here, in Henrietta

444

Street, today – she will not seek you here – and we shall go to York together directly after my interview. We will not delay.' He is hanging onto my hands as if they are his last link with common sense. I shake my head miserably.

'No, Henry, you know I will not take you. I am sorry. But I will see you soon.' I am speaking in a whisper.

He pulls away and gets to his feet. 'Amy! You will not leave me like this.'

I feel tears threaten. 'You are giving me orders, Henry? I have orders enough to follow, you may be sure.'

He looks at me in disbelief, clasping his hands behind his head. 'I do nothing of the sort! But I love you. I shall *worry* about you! You expect me to go to Richmond, interview for a post that is to be the foundation of our life together, never knowing where or when I am to see you again? This is madness! Will you not give me an address where I might write to you?'

I feel as though I am shrinking by the minute. 'I don't have one, Henry! I'm sorry, I thought you would understand. Mrs Riverthorpe said you would, if you . . . if . . . '

'If *what*? If I were *worthy* of you? Amy, she has a twisted idea of love and I think you know that. You know the man I am. I am no autocratic husband to insist on dumb obedience. But to ask someone who *loves* you to accept your inexplicable absence for an unspecified time, to accept without fear your taking a long solitary journey to an unknown destination, to proceed without reassurance, to accept being shut out of your life, your business, your heart, as if he were *nothing* . . . I know I said I would support you in your quest, but this – it's too much to ask, Amy. If you think it reasonable, you cannot feel the love that I do, indeed you cannot.'

'I *do* feel as you do. But my circumstances are different. I am not free! You know I am not free!' My voice is so small compared with his.

'I say it again. I do not ask you to give up Aurelia. As strange and secret and dark as all this appears to me, I only ask that you do not cast me aside until it is more *convenient* – that we face it together. That is what a commitment to love entails, Amy! Can you not offer me that?'

I stare at him miserably. My head is spinning. I can barely understand what he's saying to me. He's waiting for an answer. He's glaring at me. I have had enough of being told what I must and must not do. My trunk is packed and sits on the carriage. Ambrose is waiting. And I want to get to York in order to finish this at long last.

I stand. 'Not *now*, Henry, you know that. But you must not say that I do not feel as you do. That is cruel. You know I love you vastly.'

I expect him to try to detain me again but his fury has blown out. He stands apart from me. He looks sad, weary and suddenly ten years older. 'But love is not comprised of words, pretty though they are to hear. It is comprised of the choices you make in every moment. Yours do not seem to include me. You speak of the future, but any future is born of the present: this moment in which we are standing.'

I have grown numb. I cannot feel my own face. 'Henry, I should like very much to debate the nature of love with you but I don't have time for it now – I should not even be here; I was forbidden even the time for goodbyes. But I would not leave you without a goodbye, Henry.'

'Oh! Am I to be grateful for that? That you did not leave the city without so much as a word or a farewell wish, leaving me ignorant of what had become of you? Well, thank you, but that seems to me to be the very merest of courtesies! And in future? Am I to wave you off willingly every time someone tells you where you must go, what you must do? Why must you be so *obedient*, Amy? You are no Hatville servant now.'

I lift my chin. 'I am well aware of it! But this is all I can offer this morning. Truly, Henry, I do not wish to hurt you but I have no choice . . .' I trail off recognizing that this is what I have been telling myself since January – but I know I no longer believe it. I wait for Henry to point out the fact, but he is preoccupied.

'Perhaps it is too soon for you,' he says, 'embroiled as you still are in intrigue and preoccupied with the past. Perhaps you simply do not feel as I do. I have no way of knowing, but I know this doesn't feel right. This is not how it should be.'

He looks heartbroken. His eyes are all darkness and his

shoulders are low. I do not understand what is happening. I take a step towards him but he turns away from me and rests his hands on the mantel.

'Dearest Amy . . . I think . . . I release you from our understanding. I can see you are under a great weight and I do not wish to add to it. I will not place demands upon you when there are already so many. But nor can I live as you expect me to – made marginal, held at a distance. I am not . . . Good God, I am not *indifferent* to you!' He bangs a fist suddenly on the mantel, making the candlesticks jump. 'I wish to care for you. I wish us to have a true and loving partnership. If I cannot have that, I cannot simply be . . . a fool who waits in the wings.'

If I was numb before, now my whole body is ice. 'What are you saying? I don't understand! You are breaking off with me?'

'Don't misunderstand me, Amy. It is not what I wanted,' he shakes his head sadly, 'but I am trying to do what is best for both of us.'

My voice seems to dredge up words from a very great depth. When I speak, I sound strangled and faint. 'But that is nonsense, Henry, *nonsense*! All I ask is *time* . . . and your cooperation . . . to see to certain things . . . to make myself ready . . . *before* you and I . . .'

'Then you have made your choice. Goodbye, Amy, and Godspeed for your quest. I wish you safe and I hope that you will come and find me when you are free to love me as I love you. But I shall not depend upon it, for who knows what other demands might be placed upon you then, demands that you will judge more pressing than our union. I hope I may see you again. But until then I shall continue my life as I see fit.'

He does not move towards me to kiss me, or take my hand. He stands rigid and retracted, as though the slightest touch would burn him. I stare at the floor; all the solidity has drained from me into the carpet. The ice is melting and in its place is *pain*. Our understanding at an end? *A fool who waits in the wings?*

Why can't he understand? I only ever had one person to love before in all my life and that was Aurelia. I do not know how to have more than that. It is not just the treasure hunt, I think bitterly. It is love – *commitment*. I am ill-suited to it. I am unpractised at it. I will need time to make sense of it, to begin to believe that I deserve it, to see my life through its magnifying lens. And I do not have that time. There is no time.

I spin on my toes and bolt from the room. I leave the house, the door banging behind me. I am running again, along a street that is just waking, stirring to a brand-new day.

Chapter Sixty-two

Heedless in my unhappiness, I do not go straight back to the carriage. Tears run down my face until I am half blind with them. I turn right when I should turn left and find myself on Pultney Bridge.

The water calls to me. I hurry down a flight of twisting stone steps without thought. But as soon as the narrow passage of stone has me, I hesitate. It smells cool and damp; the early morning sunlight has not penetrated down here. The steps are slippery and green, as though the riverweed is crawling from the water and advancing on the city. Still I proceed – I have a fancy that to be close to the river will soothe me.

It does not. It will take more than a river to wash away the wound in my heart. Henry has ended our engagement. Well, it was not quite an engagement, of course, but the promises we made to each other – he has withdrawn them! I can't bear it. I can't bear it. Without Henry to come back for, I don't care where I go or how long I may be there. Perhaps then I shall stay in York, far from it all, far from disappointed hopes and shattered dreams. The farther the better.

I grip the rail and stare into the rushing, enigmatic jade. I want to crumple to the ground. I want to go back and beg him to forgive me, but I can't. He is asking something of me that I cannot give and, in truth, that I do not fully understand. This will not have altered in the last six minutes. He sounded so very decided. He looked so very determined.

'I shall live my life as I see fit' – there was the stubbornness of which he has spoken. And the look in his eyes, the hurt I have caused – that stays me above all, for I do not deserve him, I know that.

'Strange and secret and dark.' Once again I feel like a goblin, lurking in the watery shadows. I tell myself it is better for Henry if I don't go back. And I despise myself more than ever because I know it's not true.

Beyond the river's bend I hear the voices of men singing drunkenly, laughing in bursts. I feel a flood of fear. Foolish Amy. Alone before six o'clock on a deserted morning in the secret places at the foot of a bridge. No lady would behave thus. And no one knows where I am.

I start back up the stair, but I slip and bump down three, four steps, grazing my hand and striking my chin. I have just regained my feet when the men burst round the bend and the best I can do for cover is to stand close to the staircase wall, holding my skirts to me. If they climb the stairs onto Pultney Bridge I will be discovered. If they stagger on along the river I may not be.

There are three of them: gentlemen. That is to say, they look rich and are wearing evening dress. I am unsurprised. If a waterman was to be found drunk, it would not be early in the morning with a day's work ahead. These men are returning from a night of revelry.

I shrink against the wall, its touch clammy through my dress. My heart hammers as I watch them stagger and sway. I recognize one of them, a Mr Leaford or Lefton or some such; Mr Garland has introduced us.

I want to steal away, but I fear the movement will attract more notice than staying still. When the last chorus of 'Sweet Molly's Favours' has died away, I suddenly hear a familiar name.

'Old Garland sustained some heavy losses last night!' slurs one of the men playfully. 'Veeeery heavy! He's playing out of his league now, gentlemen. Out of his league. Out of his . . . *league*,' he reiterates, lest his point remain unclear.

His companions guffaw heartily.

'He's not in ladies' drawing rooms now!' observes Mr Leworth — that was it. 'I rather like seeing him taken down a peg or two. Prouder of himself than any fellow I ever met. A veritable peacock!'

I feel indignation on my friend's behalf. Certainly he cuts

a finer figure than any of these three – why should he not be proud of that?

'Down a peg!' adds a short, dark-haired man, jumping up and down, pretending to strike a peg into the ground. 'Down a peg, down a peg! Pound him into the ground!'

'Yes, all right, Whentforth! Steady on or you'll be in the river, and I'm not fishing you out. Leave you for the fishes after you stole Maria Gasby from me last night. For the fishes. The *fishes*! Poxy, sly fellow, you are. Don't know what the ladies see in you at all.'

Whentforth guffaws. 'Don't you, indeed? I'll show you then,' and he starts to unfasten his trousers. I avert my eyes in horror, then look back, curious, but all I see is a flap of trouserfront and a billow of white shirt.

'This is what they like,' Whentforth goes on. 'All the same, women are. Don't matter if they're baronet's wives or waterside whores.' I narrow my eyes. 'I can have any woman I want, you mark me!'

'Any but three, mind you,' cautions Leworth. 'Rhoda Carmichael, Bellatrix Davenport, Amy Snow: all out of bounds.'

Despite myself, I lean forward and frown. *Amy Snow?* Isn't that . . . well, isn't that *me*?

The trio have ground to a halt and stand swaying with their backs to me, looking over the river. Their mood has gone from buoyant to reflective, but still they talk at the tops of their voices, apparently deeply impressed with their own sonorous pronouncements.

'That's true,' bellows the third. 'Garland's placed his bets. Mind you, once he's made his choice, the other two will be fair game again. They'll be fair game. Fair *game*, dontcha know! Wouldn't mind having a crack at that Davenport one, whassit now? Belinda? *She's* a beauty and I doubt she's half so haughty when she's flat on her back with her skirts round her ears.'

I swallow and shrink back again. I want to vanish more than ever but . . . what do they mean, *Garland's placed his bets*?

'Don't know what he sees in that Snow girl,' he continues. 'Snow, you know. The *Snow* girl, you know, the one who's gone from rags to riches and we all know how! The one with the secret business she can't possibly tell him about. My eye! As if he's *remotely* interested! Where on earth did he dig her up from anyway? Funny-looking thing as I ever saw. *I* wouldn't marry her, not for any fortune.'

'Well, you say that, Brazil, but you don't have half a family estate in hock. Besides, I prefer her to the others myself. She looks a feisty little thing and there's something about those eyes, wouldn't you say, Whentforth?'

Whentforth has given up on the journey altogether and is lying on the ground, spread-eagled.

'Pound her into the ground too,' he agrees sleepily. 'Pound all of 'em.'

'Dammee, we'd better get him home,' says Brazil, contemplating him in dismay. 'Which way's quicker, Leworth? River or steps?'

'River, to Whentforth's place.' Leworth gestures extravagantly at the river and staggers. 'Disgrace a fellow can't hold his drink better than that. Speaking of which, d'you think Garland got back all right? Never seen him so laced as he was last night.'

'I think he's cracking under the strain with the net he's spinning.' Brazil leans a confiding arm on Leworth's shoulder and they both lurch a little. 'The strain, you know. It's a lot of *strain*. Serves him right. No fellow ought to have three women on the go when some of his friends don't have one. He asked Rhoda Carmichael to marry him last week, did you know?'

My eyes widen.

'She didn't say no but she didn't say yes so he went back to the other two for another crack, but Miss Snow is still entangled with some *nobody* she's panting for, and Miss Davenport has her sights set on some old European prince so Garland's *her* second choice. He's their . . . *second choice*, d'you see?' He gives a long, loud belch. I screw up my face.

'Quite funny really, you wouldn't think a man like Garland would have so much trouble getting a ring on a finger, you know. Handsome face, manners smooth as glass and all that . . .' Leworth waves a hand loosely about his head. 'Maybe they can sense something's wrong about him.'

Brazil gives an exaggerated scowl of disagreement. 'Doubt *that*, old chap. Don't think women have that much intelligence, to be honest. Suspect he's just on a run of bad luck at the moment. Bad, bad luck. It'll turn around though. It always does for Garland. You know what he's like. By the autumn he'll be married to one, playing it with another and the third one, whichever she'll be, will be carrying his child and he won't know her.'

'Reckon you're right, Brazil, reckon you're right.' He tugs without effect at Whentforth's snoring bulk. 'Come on, let's get this fool home. Think I'll give the brandy a miss for a couple of nights this week.'

Brazil's laugh bounces around the archway. 'You always say that, Leworth!'

Leworth hefts the unconscious man's right arm over his shoulder. 'So I do, so I do. Lord, but he's heavy for a short one. Take his left, Brazil.'

Frozen with shock, I watch them grunt and groan and hoist their friend between them, his head dangling, feet dragging. They begin a slow, painstaking march along the river.

When they have gone far enough, I turn carefully and pick my way back up the stairs on trembling legs. I cannot – *cannot* – think about all this until I am back in the carriage and well beyond Bath.

As I emerge onto Pultney Bridge, another dishevelled gentleman in evening dress comes swaying past me. I shudder in horror. It is Quentin Garland, though not as I have ever seen him. His cravat is loose, his hair is tousled. He has no hat, nor gloves, nor cane. His brilliant blue eyes are shot through with blood.

'Good morning, Mr Garland!' I say in ringing tones. I am astonished at myself, for I didn't mean to speak to him at all.

He staggers to a halt and looks all around him for the source of the address, even though I am directly in his path.

'Here, Mr Garland. It is I, Amy Snow. Do you not know me?'

He squints at me and as he leans closer I smell the alcohol pouring off him.

'Hard night, Mr Garland?' I persist, not recognizing this devil in me.

'By God . . . Amy! Wonderful to see you, Amy.' He sways towards me. 'Hard night? Yes, you could say that. You haven't seen three gents, have you? Think they came this way. Owe me money. Oh, just a quiet game between gentlemen, nothing squalid, you know.'

'Naturally not. No, I haven't seen anyone, Mr Garland. Well, good morning to you.'

'Morning Amy.' He reaches for the parapet of the bridge but misses, and somehow trips over his own feet. He falls heavily to the ground, where he sits and looks up at me, chuckling. His blue cravat has slithered off and landed in a puddle.

Despite myself, I feel embarrassed for him and offer my arm to help. He hauls himself back to the vertical, leaning on me like a cane, breathing heavily. I can smell that he has been sick. I try not to recoil but extricate myself as soon as possible, propping him against the bridge, since straightening his knees is evidently a challenge too much.

'You know, you're looking a little . . .' He frowns and reaches out a finger, prods my scraped chin clumsily. I wince. He examines his finger, and shudders.

'Blood. Thought so. You're looking a little rough around the edges this morning in fact, Amy.' He winks clumsily. 'Well, I won't tell anyone, don't worry. Your secret's safe with me. *All* your little secrets are safe with me.' He nods and grins and taps the side of his nose.

'You're a true friend, Mr Garland. Farewell.'

I run back to the carriage, feeling strangely triumphant. Ambrose's composure has surpassed its limits: I have been a great deal longer than ten minutes. She exclaims in horror at my disappearance and at my wounds but I refuse to explain. Without further delay, the carriage hurtles out of Bath and in moments the golden city is behind me.

I am bound for the north. My Henry is left behind and angry with me and my last memory of the elegant, exquisite Quentin Garland, talk of the town in Twickenham and Bath, is of a debauched chancer sagging against a stone balustrade, sallow-skinned and looking lost.

PART FOUR

Chapter Sixty-three

Two days later, I arrive in York, amidst the predictable turmoil of station and journey's end and conspicuous solitude. I am now more noticeable than ever, for a shabby nobody may have a number of reasons for travelling alone — all of them disgraceful, naturally — but an elegant lady doing so screams for attention. However, my apparent position and wealth allow me to trample over speculation and scrutiny with a haughty hoist to my head and confidently flung orders. It is something I may have learned from Mrs Riverthorpe.

When I step onto the platform, far from anywhere that might ever have been home, I am not afraid; I am too preoccupied by a storm of angry questions inside my head and a heart that seems to be breaking all over again. Under these circumstances the need to hail a porter, ask for a hotel, demand assistance, become trifling.

Thus I am soon ensconced in a large suite at the Jupiter Hotel. 'The finest York has to offer, and very close to the station, m'lady,' the railway porter assured me.

I can barely take in the sumptuous green and cream furnishings and drapes, the thick rugs and heavy lustre jugs of roses. I am exhausted from eight hours on a train today and ten or eleven in a carriage yesterday. My pride is fractured by the discovery that someone I had thought a friend is in fact a profligate, scheming villain. My heart is devastated from the loss of the man I want to marry – either through his stubborness or my own, or possibly both. It is not a pretty state of affairs.

I have no further clue to follow. I am here. I have done as Aurelia instructed. What now?

Sleep must be the first thing. And sleep I do, for even the most troubled soul has its limits. I wake to a fresh summer morning and the tumbling bells of York Minster.

My first sensation is relief that I am rested. Then comes the familiar, weary recognition that I am somewhere all new – I must start again. I no longer doubt that I can do so, but confidence is cold comfort when I'm alone once more.

Then comes the re-establishment of the dreaded mist in my brain: nothing is solved, after all. I decide to get up and explore this new city, for I have fretted and ruminated over my woes for every moment in that carriage and every moment on that train and it has achieved precisely nothing. I am neither reconciled to what has happened nor decided upon a course of action. Naturally, it is too soon to put it all behind me and embrace a new start. In short, I feel wretched.

The worst of it, without question, is Henry. The wrench

from him. The inability to believe that our future has been ruined and the fear that it may be so. I hate it. I cannot yet bear to admit that he was in the right, but a budding suspicion that he may have had a point fuels the flame of my indignation. Nevertheless, more than anything I want to leave York at once, travel to Richmond and put it all right.

But I am afraid. What if he has since realized that loving me was an error from which he has been most fortunately saved? What if his offers to me are all retracted, now and for ever? When he speaks of love and choice, of honouring one's feelings and acting in accordance, my mind can understand him but the dark places in my heart cannot. In those dark places I have ever been alone. There I am always a blight, with a lop-sided smile and grubby hands. And there I have learned that to put my fate in someone else's hands might cost me dear. Since Aurelia died, I have grown accustomed to looking after myself and though it is lonely, it is safer that way. Those dark places whisper always of impossibility . . .

I think of writing to him, but I do not know what to say. Although it feels as though we have been separated an eternity, it has only been two days. He will still be angry – and I am still gone. Besides, he will be in Richmond by now . . . I know not where. And where will he go after that? How might I find him? Any letter must pass through several hands to reach him, even assuming he tells anyone where he is. 'I shall live my life as I see fit,' he told me – he is lost to me. For now, at least.

I have the strangest sensation of being poised on a sixpence, about to bolt at any moment. I just want to take action, *any* action, to change history so that it never happened. But that is quite beyond my power. For now, the precious, damaged puzzle of Henry and myself is one that I must lay aside until I am free of the quest, or at least until I have a better wisdom with which to address it.

In these dark moments of contemplation, I also worry upon Quentin Garland's shameless usage of me – and, apparently, half the other young ladies of Bath. Fortune hunter. Philanderer. Liar. Wrapped up in a shiny pastel exterior with a blue cravat. Thinking about it now makes my skin crawl. I feel so horribly *stupid* when I remember all the moments that my instincts told me the truth and I barely noticed them, so dazzled was I by the elegant figure he cut. I felt honoured, *validated*, by his attentions when I was low in spirits, when I felt like an outcast, when I thought Henry did not love me . . . yet it was all mixed up with a sense that *something* was not right. My instincts whispered to me but my insecurities made me deaf to them. I am angry with myself. And with him, of course – it seems I am angry with *everyone* at the moment.

By what right did he fix upon me as a . . . as a *target*, and decide that *my* life, *my* heart, *my* future might be employed to serve *his* interests? Despicable disregard for humanity! I fume when I recall the clever, subtle ways in which he tried to drive a wedge between Henry and me, the way he sought me out, in

Twickenham and in Bath, having witnessed my dramatic trans-formation. Oh, it was clear that I had come into a fortune and he fixed upon it like a hound with a scent. And I was flattered that such a great gentleman might take an interest in *me*! What a fool!

I feel ashamed when I remember how I allowed myself to imagine that he had my best interests at heart because he appeared to respect my secret where Henry did not. Quentin Garland did not respect my secret – he simply had not the slightest interest in it! He even told his friends about it.

I know it is fruitless to fret this way, yet I cannot stop, not with any effort of will, and this is why I step out into the clear, warm morning and begin aimlessly to wander the streets of York.

'Tis a different world here. The city is old, and beautiful in an altogether different way from Bath. The stone is darker, defensive. The streets are crooked and mischievous. Tiny alleys wriggle from one part of the city to another, with small, silent openings barely discernible to the hurrying passer-by. There are rumours of a second city, older still, buried beneath the very stones on which I tramp, its stories lost for ever. A fitting place, then, to end my quest. The buildings stoop and droop and mullioned windows wink in the sunshine. Despite the golden day, the close-crowding roofs and narrow streets create great tides of shadow, even as midday approaches. I am hope-lessly lost, by then.

In Bath, I found it relatively easy to keep my bearings. Hades House was up the hill. Crescent Fields were higher. The abbey was down and the river a short way east. Here, the streets meander and tease. No sooner have I fixed one landmark – shop, church or garden – in my mind, than it vanishes and I cannot find my way back to it by any means. I must have walked miles, but the unvarying volume of the minster bells as they mark off the hours suggests that all these miles are folded and refolded upon themselves within a contained area, like paths in a maze. It is a beautiful, baffling place.

I return, circuitously, to the Jupiter and write to Edwin Wister again. I tell him where I am, that any of the Wisters may write to me at the Jupiter Hotel if they wish and that I will let him know when I leave. I tell him I am well, for really, what can anyone do to alleviate my particular difficulties? I give my letter to a maid, then time stretches heavy ahead of me.

I could roam the streets again, but what will that achieve? I could try to find some clever solution to the puzzle of York, but my mind is sluggish and slants ever towards Henry and hurt. I could write to Mr Garland and tell him exactly what I think of him, but as there are no ladylike words to frame this, I resist. I am furious that I did not take the opportunity to say it when I saw him on the bridge that morning. Doubtless he would not have remembered it, given the state he was in, but it would have given me such satisfaction to tell him that I despise him.

Henry . . . I want to write to Henry . . . I start letter after letter, even though I have nowhere to send one, until the floor of my room is strewn with crumpled balls of paper and I fling down my quill in disgust. So I sit at my window, staring at pigeons sporting amongst the eaves until dusk draws a veil over this, my first day in York.

Chapter Sixty-four

Heartbreak makes me stupid. I do try, in the days that follow, to set to the task assigned me. I puzzle over letters, speculate theories and try to piece together probabilities. I sit at my window for hours, thinking of Aurelia, hoping that a childhood memory may trigger a clue, as it did in London. But at inconvenient moments I am invaded by the recollection of Henry's lips on mine, of the light in his eyes. I remember the warm, melting feeling I experience whenever I am close to him and touching him is an irresistible possibility. I turn my mind away most firmly, but he follows me . . .

I write to Mrs Riverthorpe, apologizing for my anger when we parted. I assure her of my continued regard – not that she will prize it, I'm sure – and beg her to tell me anything she knows for otherwise I seem doomed to live out the rest of my days at the Jupiter Hotel.

Letters arrive from Madeleine, Michael and Edwin. They each contain glad news and I am reassured that elsewhere, outside my own strange, convoluted life, good things can happen. Madeleine is finally betrothed and her letter glows with rapture.

The elderly Mrs Nesbitt has a beau! Michael reports this with some disgust but, being a boy, gives me no further details, much to my exasperation. However, he encloses a fair copy of his latest school assignment, a critique of John Donne's poetry. It is very accomplished.

And Edwin announces with delighted modesty that Constance is expecting another child! She has also acquired an alabaster statue of Aphrodite for the conservatory.

Between letters and tears I walk. I rattle around inside the enclosure of these ancient city walls, aware that they present a marvellous opportunity for sketching and learning about architecture but, honestly, I do not care.

I am returning to my hotel one aimless evening when something catches my attention and makes me stop.

I look all around me: a winding street like so many others, with a coffee house and a number of shops, all closed now. I consider walking on but no, something snatched at me and I must know what it is. I gaze at the buildings, the doorways, at the cat that tiptoes past my boots, then shoots away down the street. And then I see, really see, the butcher's shop.

'J. Capland, Butcher,' says the sign. What is familiar about that?

A sudden memory of Mrs Riverthorpe: 'Should you ever find yourself in the North Country, do please look up my friends the Caplands . . . Shall you remember that name, Amy? Capland? Or will Henry's dark eyes drive it from your swiftly dissolving brain?'

I force myself not to think of Henry's dark eyes and stare at the shop. Is Aurelia's tale to end in a *butcher's* shop? No matter, it could end in a slaughterhouse for all I care if it means I can complete my charge.

I hurry back to take supper in a newly restored frame of mind. I will say this for Aurelia's treasure hunt: for all its difficulties and inconvenience, the feeling of moving one step closer is uplifting.

I feel optimism for the first time since Bath. I might be able to write to Madeleine in just a day or two and tell her I am coming to Twickenham! She and Constance can advise me about Henry and I will find him, however hard that may be. Seeing him face to face will be better than any letter could be. I will be free at last and he will be able to see it in my eyes. Yes, I will find him and tell him I am so very sorry . . .

I try to recall what Mrs Riverthorpe said about the Caplands. It was a radical change of subject, I remember, and with hindsight it is clear that she was imparting important information to me. At the time, however, it merely seemed typical of her fleeting attention: 'He is a very good fellow as they go, owns a shop . . . She is as silly a creature as ever lived, but kind-hearted . . . Oh, do not fear, they are nothing like me.'

I pass the evening in a sort of fever of excitement. The end of the trail is within my grasp. I have allowed myself to hope this a number of times, but that was wishful thinking; this is certainty. I am filled with such a sense of vigour and energy as I never knew. I curse British trading laws and the need to wait 'til morning. My slumber is fitful, but deep when it comes.

I wake suddenly, to a startled dawn. Something profound has happened. I sit up, pulsing and alert, while the dawn chorus ripples through my room. I have dreamed.

I remember the dream vividly – a parade of faces. I see them still: Mr Clay handing me a parcel in the January dawn; Mr Carlton at the Rose and Crown, with his evangelical zeal for railway travel; dear Mr Crumm, with his books and periodicals and his handsome grandson; Madeleine and her family; Mrs Riverthorpe, with her razor tongue and bristling feathers – all those who have helped me on my journey. I saw Henry. And Aurelia, shining like an angel, laughing in the summertime.

Chapter Sixty-five

It is still too early to find my fate in the butcher's shop. While I wait, I am a-quiver with resolve. The night has changed me. I remember Hatville, I remember it all, and I no longer shrink from the memory. It is what formed me, and this treasure hunt has fired me like clay passing through flame. I will be stronger and better for this, I know that now.

Some things are lost to me for ever: I will never see Aurelia again, nor the place that I grew up, and I know deep in my heart that I will never learn the truth about my parentage. So be it. Other things need not be lost unless I choose to give them up. My love for Henry. My friends. My dreams. My self-respect and determination.

The world commanded that Aurelia and I should not be friends, that the differences between us were too vast. We knew differently. Despite our troubled, prohibitive youth, we found laughter in almost everything. We loved bluebells and snowdrops, horses and stories, good food, mornings at the stream and each other. But I think now that what united us more than anything was that we were both fighters, in our own ways. We both resisted what we were told, preferring to make up our own minds. We chose what was important to *us*.

I had always felt that, without Aurelia, I should collapse. To me, she seemed like the knight in bright armour and colourful array, I her plodding squire. But I find after all that I too am a warrior – I glimpsed her in the mirror at the ball in Bath. I have sensed it every day that I have plodded around London or Bath or York unattended, against rationality and convention, braving condemnation to find my own way, one footstep at a time. I knew it that day in the dining room at Hatville, when I faced down Lady Vennaway and stamped my little foot, just moments before she cut off my hair.

I shall listen to that internal warrior a great deal more henceforth. And as for the dark whisperings in my heart that tell me I shall never be loved? I shall not listen to them. The story of two girls, inseparable and irrepressible, is about to end. Only one story is to continue, and it is mine.

I grow very calm. When the time comes to go to town, I find Mr Capland's establishment without difficulty, even though I have not previously found my way to any one place in York that I have intended. My days of stumbling about in confusion are ended.

I enter the shop and the butcher looks up from his deft and powerful division of a carcass into saleable cuts of meat. I note at once which are intended for a modest family and which for a dinner at a fine household. The smells of blood and fresh meat remind me of my childhood, watching Cook at work in the kitchen. The sight of his cleaver reminds me of Lady Vennaway bearing down on me to slice off my hair. The confusion writ large on the butcher's face at my arrival reminds me that, of course, I look like a lady now.

'Good morning, m'lady,' he says in astonishment. 'I trust you are well? Can I help you wi' owt?'

I remember Mr Crumm approaching me in his bookshop, guessing at once who I was. I remember the Wisters, welcoming me to the bosom. I remember Ambrose's unquestioning acceptance of my appearance at Hades House. In a moment he will understand.

'Good morning, sir. I am well, thank you. Mr Capland, I am delighted to meet you. I am Amy Snow.'

But light does not dawn. 'Beg pardon, Miss Snow . . . ?'

'Amy Snow,' I repeat, for lack of other inspiration. 'I am Amy Snow.'

His bafflement visibly deepens. There is no recognition in his face. Instead I can see him wondering about this eccentric gentlewoman who likes to repeat her own name. He is a tall, broad man with dense black hair and a luxuriantly curling beard. He has peaceful eyes that are at odds with his hulking figure and blood-spattered apron.

'I am sorry, Mr Capland. I am not explaining myself well. I

have come a long way to meet you. I believe that four years ago you met a dear friend of mine. Aurelia Vennaway?'

'Four years ago. Vennaway,' he murmurs, plum-red above his whiskers, poor soul. 'I'm sorry, miss. I don't believe so. Beggin' your pardon, miss, why should you come to find me? What is it you want, exactly?'

'Well, I don't know. I thought *you* would tell me why I am here. Surely you remember *Aurelia*? Aurelia Vennaway!'

He clearly thinks I'm a madwoman. 'I don't understand . . .'

For a horrible moment I wonder if Mrs Riverthorpe's change of subject was just that, and not a clue at all.

'Mrs Riverthorpe, sir, Mrs Ariadne Riverthorpe of Bath. She is a good friend of yours, I think?'

Snow, Vennaway, Riverthorpe . . . I am firing names at the poor man like arrows, but none hits a target.

He moves his head from side to side, ponderous as a minster bell. 'I'm very sorry, miss. I don't know her neither. *River-thorpe*, you say? Nay, miss.'

'Well, for heaven's sake! No, forgive me, sir – my exasperation is not with you but with my predicament. Mrs Riverthorpe is a . . . well, I suppose you may call her a friend of mine. She told me not two weeks since that were I ever in this area I should call on her friends the Caplands. You own a shop, she told me, and you have a kind-hearted wife.'

'Nay, miss. That is, I don't have any wife yet, though I'm hoping Miss Mary Avery will have me come September.'

'Oh! Well . . . I hope so too. But how very vexing and . . . and . . . *disappointing*!'

'Most like your friend meant my brother, miss.'

'Oh! You have a *brother*?'

'Aye, miss. I'm Jeremiah Capland. My brother, Joss, he owns a shop too, a drapery over on High Petergate. He has a wife, and two littl'uns besides.'

'Oh! Thank you, sir, that must be the answer. High Petergate, you say? Is that far from here?'

He directs me and I turn to go.

'Perhaps I will meet you again, Mr Capland, if you see much of your brother?'

'Aye, I see him oft enough. Good luck, miss.'

I stride along the prescribed route with a hammering heart. On High Petergate I see the name Capland once again, etched above the prettiest shop imaginable. It is dark green, and the leading between the diamond panes is painted green too. The door and the legend 'Joss Capland & Sons, Purveyor of Fine Textiles and Haberdashery' are both painted a fresh, gleaming white.

In the window I see a mouth-watering bonnet decorated with peach roses and an array of ribbons, buttons, feathers, hatpins, shoe roses and fine lace, like icing on a cake. They are artfully displayed alongside bolts of fabric stacked in a rainbow of glowing colours. I suspect a woman's touch.

I step inside and the bell sends a merry jangle through the

shop. A man of perhaps forty steps from the back and greets me with a bright smile. I know at once that this is the right place.

'Good morning, Mr Capland. I hope you are well. And I sincerely hope you will know who I am when I tell you that I am . . .' I hesitate. *Who am I?*

'I am Amy Snow.'

Chapter Sixty-six

⟳

Joss Capland resembles his brother in his dark colouring only. He is shorter and slighter and his accent is decidedly southern, though with a slight turn to it that I cannot place. At any rate, it is very pleasing. I have ample time to enjoy it as we rattle through the countryside in his trap. He knew at once who I was and left his shop as promptly, leaving Sampson – a young man of about twelve – to close up.

I asked if Sampson was his son. Joss Capland smiled and bit his lip.

'No, Miss Snow, Sampson is my apprentice. My boy is too small yet for shop work, though his enthusiasm knows no bounds.'

The Caplands live at Fountain Cottage in Heworth, a leafy village situated to the northeast of York. It is a gusty morning – speckling rain alternating with thin displays of sunshine. I have found the north to be noticeably colder even than Bath but this is not what makes me tremble today. I am equipped with my mulberry shawl, my warmest. It is excitement that makes my teeth chatter and my feet feel like blocks of ice within my boots. I am sitting beside the man who can tell me everything I need to know and put an end to my wandering – and wondering. We travel along grassy lanes between fields, under the shade of spreading oaks. The land is flat and the air is green with the smell of sap. It is good to be in the country again and hear the song of thrushes.

Joss Capland chats of inconsequential things and tells me how, when the wind is right, the sound of the minster bells carries even all the way out here. Then he winks and explains that he must tell me nothing of any importance without his wife present or he will face the gravest consequences.

'She will not want to miss a moment of getting to know you.' He smiles.

Sure enough, the cottage has not yet come in sight when a woman in a white dress comes running along the grassy track, a small girl toddling gamely after her, arms flailing.

'Miss Snow!' she cries before the horse has stopped, to my astonishment. 'It *is* you, isn't it?'

'She's found us at last, Elspeth!' agrees Mr Capland, pulling up the trap and leaping off. He kisses his wife, then offers his hand to help me from the cart. I stand before the prettiest woman I ever saw, apart from Aurelia. She has dark hair like her husband, and huge, sparkling dark eyes. The little girl reaches us at last, takes a fistful of her mother's skirt and regards me intently. She is her mother's identical reproduction in miniature. She is so lovely to look at that I cry out in delight and kneel in the grass before her. She lights up – she has her father's smile.

'Miss Snow,' begins Mrs Capland again. 'I knew it was you. I saw the trap from an upstairs window. At this time of day it could only mean that Joss had taken poorly or that Miss Snow had come. When I saw a young woman with him, I knew it was the latter. I am so very pleased to welcome you.'

'Miss Snow, may I introduce my wife, Elspeth, and my daughter, Verity?'

As I stand to greet Elspeth Capland, she shakes my hand and kisses my cheek; I am won over by her expansive warmth.

'I am so very happy to meet you, only please, will you not call me Amy?'

'Of course we will. Now come in and be at home. We have so very much to talk about.'

Elspeth carries Verity and Joss leads the horse and we walk together to the cottage.

'Where is Louis, dearest?' asks Joss.

'I was trying to settle him for a rest when I saw you.'

He laughs. 'Louis, *rest*?'

'I said only that I was trying, not that I succeeded. Ah!' she adds with a rueful smile. 'And here he is. Amy, this is my unstoppable son, Louis.'

I gasp. We are almost at the cottage, which is square and brown and covered in white roses, but I cannot take it in now.

There is a portrait that hangs in the drawing room at

Hatville Court. In the painting, Aurelia, aged around four years old, sits on her mother's lap. It is as if that painted Aurelia has scrambled from the frame and now comes running towards me along the Caplands' flagged path, chestnut curls bouncing and blazing in the sun.

'Papa, you're home! Oh!' Upon seeing a stranger, he falters and tucks himself behind his mother. From behind this safe shelter, he peeps out and regards me through bright, violet-blue eyes. 'Mama, who is the pretty lady?'

Elspeth kneels down. 'Louis darling, this lady is Amy Snow. We've told you about her, remember? She has come to visit us at last.'

Louis's face breaks in a delighted smile. 'Oh! Will she stay for luncheon? Will she see the garden with me? Will she read me a story?'

Precocious, with boundless energy, endless demands and a cherubic face, he is Aurelia all over again, dressed in a dark-blue sailor suit.

Joss holds out his arms, scoops up the boy and swings him around and around 'til his boots are a blur and he squeals with agonized joy that fills the air like birdsong.

'It is as you see, Amy . . .' says Elspeth in a low voice. 'We will explain when the children are occupied.'

My eyes fill with tears and she takes my hand.

'My dear,' she says.

It is enough.

Chapter Sixty-seven

I had suspected, of course, but suspecting had not prepared me for the fact of it. To see this living piece of Aurelia here before me feels like wind filling a sail. I feel taut and tugging with the wonder of it.

His parents make solemn introductions and Louis bows and shakes my hand. I bend towards him and take his little hand as if in a dream. Of all the strange realities in which I have found myself since Aurelia died, this is the strangest. Her *son*, somehow here in Yorkshire. The nodding trees, the stiff breeze that has blown the rain away, and the grassy lane have all receded: there is only Louis. I long to gather him to me and smother him with kisses, but of course I am a stranger to him. So I restrain myself, although I cannot take my eyes off him. He tells me he is pleased to know me and again presses the point about the garden and the story. I am willing to agree to anything he wishes, just so long as I can continue to feast my eyes on him — smooth, plump cheeks pink as roses, determined set to his chin . . . all so familiar, yet so tiny and strange.

'Perhaps Amy might like to come inside first, Louis,' cautions his mother gently. 'She may be thirsty, or tired.' I catch her eye and feel that she understands something of the wonder that I am in.

Louis concedes that I may postpone our arrangement for a little while if this should be the case.

'Unless, of course, you'd rather . . .' Elspeth adds. 'We could take Verity inside if you'd like to spend some time with Louis first. It's entirely up to you.'

Gradually the lane, the breeze, the sunshine creep back into my awareness. I take a deep breath of cool, clean air. When I speak, my voice is not steady.

'It's such a lovely morning. Perhaps I shall see the garden first after all, and then we might sit down together afterwards.'

'That's very agreeable, Miss Amy,' Louis pipes in his high little voice, grabbing my hand. 'Come this way. I want to show you the fountain!'

I wander after Louis, feeling that I've stepped back in time. The garden is exquisite, with a fountain, a dovecote and an abundance of lupins and hollyhocks. The ample lawn is sprinkled with daisies; tall hedges are threaded with honeysuckle. Louis explains to me the significance of every inch and shows me his secret den in the hedge. I am taken back to my childhood as I follow him, rapt and dumb as though I were the toddler, held in thrall to someone more fascinating and adventurous. It is a vastly familiar experience.

Louis is pleased with all my comments. When I explain to him that I know something of gardens, that when I was his age a wheelbarrow was my habitual conveyance, he is rendered briefly mute with awe. Will I push *him* in a wheelbarrow, he wants to know.

A white kitten streaks onto the lawn and I sit on a garden seat and watch, spellbound, while she and Louis play chase. He is Aurelia all over. His laugh, his exuberance, the radiance of him . . .

My poor, astonished brain slowly comes back to life. As it does so, realization floods in. Now, at last, it makes sense – or begins to. If any secret is worth protecting with hidden letters and a trail full of red herrings, snaking back and forth across the land, this is it. He is magical. Already I feel that I would go to any lengths to keep him safe, and I am at peace with every difficulty I have suffered in getting here. Aurelia's extraordinary measures to protect her secret – her *child* – make sense in their entirety now. Louis will not suffer Aurelia's fate. He will not be channelled along roads for which he is utterly unsuited, nor told which friends he may and may not have. He will not suffer his very nature being tweaked and restrained and repressed as his mother did. He will not have every natural inclination of his bright spirit quenched and checked. These are good people, it is easy to see that, a loving, natural family. He will be happy.

Oh, the thought that she will never see her son as a young

boy, going to school, becoming a man . . . Oh, *if the Vennaways only knew!*

'Why do you look sad, Miss Amy? Are you crying?' Louis has climbed up beside me and abandoned the kitten, which is jumping up and down on her back paws trying to swat his shoes. He slides his little hand into mine.

'I was just thinking of a dear friend of mine who died, Louis. I miss her still and I was just thinking how much she would have enjoyed this lovely garden and meeting you.'

He frowns and I wonder for a moment whether I ought to have spoken of death to a child so young.

'I had a frog that died,' he says at last. 'I was sad. His name was Gregory. If I had met your friend, I would have showed her my den too. Would she have liked that?'

'She would have adored it, for she loved secrets and adventures and I always had the most fun with her. When I was little, she used to make treasure hunts for me in our garden, and they were splendid.'

'What's a treasure hunt?'

'You've never done a treasure hunt? Well, Louis, one day I will make one for you and then you will see.'

Chapter Sixty-eight

After some time, Elspeth, Joss and Verity come out to the garden with a jug of lemonade. My eyes fill once again; Aurelia had a passion for lemonade that I have never seen rivalled. It is the little things like that that undo me still, but then it has only been five months since I lost her, though it feels like many lifetimes now.

With the children playing a safe distance away, we begin to talk. Firstly, Joss hands me a thick envelope with my name on it in Aurelia's hand. Like all its predecessors, it disappears into my pocket. This will be the last I hear from her and I want to cherish it. Now, I want to get to know these people to whom Aurelia has entrusted the care of her precious son. I want to know everything.

'The story really begins with Joss's childhood in Wales,' says Elspeth. 'Tell her, Joss.'

He nods. 'Yes, by all means. I was born in Wales, Amy, and orphaned very young. I can't remember my parents. I was from a mining family, I was told, but the nearest orphanage was in

Cardiff and there I was sent at the age of two. I do not suppose it was worse than any other such place, but nor was it a happy one. It was managed without passion or interest by people who did the work for the wage. Friendships were not encouraged and education was rudimentary – counting to ten, writing one's name and so on. We all knew that at the age of eight we must leave – we were furnished with no illusions about the sort of future we might expect. It was a drab existence.

'But when I was six, I was blessed with the most enormous good fortune you can imagine. One of the trustees, Lady Everdene, had a friend, John Capland, who hailed from York. He wanted to adopt a boy. He had lost his wife, you see, and had only one child, Jeremiah. He had determined never to marry again, for he had loved his wife so dearly, but he wanted the very best of everything for his son. That included another boy as a brother for Jeremiah.

'He was visiting Lady Everdene when she suggested he choose a boy from her Cardiff orphanage. She selected four boys who had caught her eye and gave Mr Capland the opportunity to meet us and choose. That was the day that changed my life. Of course, I had no idea of the purpose of meeting this stranger; it was merely a pleasant break from the monotony. If I had known that a chance for a family and a better future was at stake, I believe the suspense would have been unbearable. But I did not know. And he chose me.

'I made the long journey to Yorkshire with my new father

and made his better acquaintance. He was a good man, Amy. He is dead now, which pains me still, even after five years. I met my older brother, Jeremiah, who was then nine years of age, and after demonstrating repeatedly that he could knock me down in a fight – for he was, and still is, three times my size – we became first tolerable friends and then true brothers.

'Two years later, Lady Everdene, who was by then Mrs Hamilton of Truro, sent my father a considerable sum of money to be used for the betterment of his sons. Having instigated the adoption and having no children of her own, it pleased her to have some involvement with our little family. My father was scrupulously fair, divided the money equally between us and offered us the same opportunities. But we were very different. Jeremiah had become apprenticed to a butcher in York and he liked the post very well. Nor did he wish to leave home. I took the chance to go to school in London. I spent every holiday at home but I loved school and devoured my lessons like a plate of grilled trout.

'The years passed and Jeremiah bought the butcher's shop he had begun his career in, for he had been given as capital the equivalent of what had been spent on my education. Like my brother, I wanted a shop of my own, but not a butcher's shop – oh no! I wanted a business that was pleasing to the eye, and profitable, where I might meet a beautiful young lady with whom I could fall madly in love.'

'That's where I come in!' smiles Elspeth. I can well imagine it. 'I was twenty years old and engaged to a boat-builder from Whitby called Sam Perrin.'

'I've never met Sam Perrin,' interjects Joss, 'but I intend to spit on him if I do.'

'I hardly think you need feel jealous now, my love,' she reproves mildly. 'It was a great many years ago. Anyway, Amy, my mother brought me to York for my trousseau, for we had all heard tell of a new haberdasher's that had opened up there. It was run by a dashing young man who had been educated in London, we were told. He had contacts with all the manufacturers, and offered all the fashions of that great city but at a third of London prices. Apparently a great many young ladies passed through those doors that year. A *great many*,' she emphasizes pointedly.

'I intended to make a success of my business and I did,' Joss counters complacently. 'I did indeed meet a great many young ladies. But only one that made me look twice, and then look again for the rest of my life.'

'We married,' concluded Elspeth. 'I broke my engagement, and my mother's heart.'

'And Sam Perrin's, I presume,' I add.

'Oh, Sam. He found someone else within the year so I do not trouble myself over him. My mother has yet to recover, I believe!

'Anyway, I am the happiest of wives and we have a beautiful home, as you see, but, Amy, we were not blessed with children. After ten whole years, that joy was not given to us. We tried hard to remember that if it were always to be just the two of us we would still have a great deal for which to be thankful. But I cannot deny that it was a very great sadness to us. Very great.

'We talked about adopting, but I had a superstitious belief that to do so would be to close the door to conceiving a child of our own. Then one day, almost four years ago, we received a visitor. It was the trustee from the orphanage. Tell her, Joss.'

'Yes, well, the visit was nothing remarkable in itself. The trustee, Lady Everdene as she was in Cardiff, had kept in touch with my father all those years and occasionally came to see how I was getting on. She is a person who likes to interest herself in other people's affairs. After he died, she kept the contact with me. I mentioned that Lady Everdene became Mrs Hamilton, Amy, and over the years she passed through many incarnations as husbands died or disappeared. She was . . . er . . . not a *conventional* lady, but what will I ever care for that? If not for her, I would not have known my father, or my brother or my wife. By the time she reappeared at my cottage door in 1844 she was Mrs Riverthorpe.'

'Mrs Riverthorpe!' How had I not guessed it sooner?

'Indeed. As I say, it was not the fact of the visit that was remarkable, it was what came of it. She barrelled into our house and informed us that we must do her a favour. I agreed, thinking she wanted me to put her in touch with a certain milliner, or perhaps accompany her on a journey, for she was very old by then . . . But no. The favour was that we were to host a stranger, a young lady, in our home for several months. Oh, and the young lady was with child, and we were to oversee the birth, and then adopt the child after it was born . . .'

Both Caplands are quiet for a moment, wearing nostalgic, slightly wry expressions on their faces. I snort with laughter, imagining it.

'It was an outrageous demand, of course,' continues Elspeth, 'and I had something to say about it, as you may well imagine. There was quite a tussle, for she is very used to getting her own way, as you must know. But I was not about to have our entire future commandeered to her whim, for all that Joss owed her everything. It was not that I was unsympathetic to the young lady's plight, but I have told you of my feelings about adoption and I could not just change them for the asking. I don't know if sounds strange to you but it was a very emotional response to a very personal disappointment. In the end, a compromise was reached. We would meet the young lady in question; we agreed to that at least.

'And so, the following day, Aurelia alighted at our door, pale and thin and shaking, but still the most beautiful girl imaginable and with that *heart* burning out of her, lighting up everything around her, drawing us in . . . She told us her story; she was very frank about how she came to find herself in this unenviable situation.'

'When we learned that she was dying,' says Joss, 'we began to see things in a different light. When she told us of her parents, however, it made me very worried. It was not their power and influence that caused me hesitate, it was the idea of keeping a child from its own flesh and blood, of standing between people I had never met and their grandchild. But we spent time with Aurelia. She came to stay with us after all. She got to know us and we learned about her life.'

'I think she felt safe here from the start,' Elspeth continues. I can readily believe it. 'Being so far from home, allowing us to nurture her . . . these things all restored her to some degree. Even so, she was not properly well for the whole of her time with us. Her pregnancy was a strain on her body. Well, her letter will no doubt tell you how we managed things between us, but the outcome is as you see. Louis is as we imagine Aurelia must have been before her illness took hold of her. You will be able to judge that better than we can, of course.'

'And Verity?'

Elspeth laughed. 'It turned out that my superstition was wrong – entirely wrong. Louis was six months old. Aurelia had departed from us some four months previously. And I discovered that I was pregnant. Joss and I could not believe it, though we have heard since that it is not such an uncommon phenomenon, after adoption. Well, Aurelia always believed that we had a great deal to offer Louis. Little did any of us imagine we would also be able to offer him a sister!'

'And now, we hope,' says Joss, looking at me steadily, 'he will have an aunt too. We have told him about our family friend, Miss Snow. He has been excited to meet his Aunt Amy! We should love to know you better, too. Please spend as much time here as you would like. I know this must be a lot for you to take in, but . . . well, we hope this makes you . . . *happy*.'

Happy. Yes.

It will take a long time for me to fit the pieces together in my heart and in my head, but Mrs Riverthorpe is not here to mock me for it so I expect I may take all the time I need to.

I watch Aurelia's son tumbling with his sister on the grass and murmur, 'Aunt Amy.' And smile.

Chapter Sixty-nine

I do not arrive back at the Jupiter until ten o'clock at night. Joss drives me in the cart and Louis demands to go with us, although he has already been put to bed three times. He is refused, kindly but firmly.

At the hotel, a short letter awaits me from Mrs Riverthorpe. In it she graciously agrees to put me out of my misery – as she terms it – provided I burn the information at once. She then instructs me to visit Joss Capland, a draper on High Petergate. She also requests that I continue to correspond with her and allows that I might visit her in Bath again one day at my convenience. I smile as I fold up the letter.

I summon the concierge and beg a plate of sandwiches to be sent up to me. I feel terrible, knowing how the late-night whims of the wealthy can feel to the maids like the tiresome last straw after a busy day in the kitchen. I would be happy to fetch them myself, but of course that would never do. Yet I find that completing a quest, and freedom, and aunthood all generate a fierce appetite.

I sit at the table in my room, still fully dressed, and devour my sandwiches and my letter both at once. The letter is many pages long, and I am glad of it. I have at least a million questions.

My treasured Amy,

This will doubtless be my longest letter to you and I find I hardly know where to begin. It will also be my last – the thought of it breaks my heart. Foolish really, that it feels like farewell when once again I shall see you tomorrow. It is just that I have been keeping so much from you. My letters are the only place where I can shed that reticence. Once this is written, I can share no more confidences with you for the rest of my life.

I wonder if you have been angry with me for not confiding in you. I dare not speak of Louis to you. The temptation to do so again and again would be too great. It would be the same for you, I know it would. We might be overheard. And then, I am quite sure, my parents would stop at nothing to learn whatever you knew. I have to put it all aside and go on as though it had never happened; that is the choice I have made.

At last I can write freely. Joss will guard this letter with his life, I know that. If you are reading it, then you have followed my trail to its conclusion and you will know my whole story. For this one night, alone in my room, I can unburden myself to you fully and fill in the gaps. <u>Then</u> I need only fear its discovery before I post it, but I shall do as I have done with all of them.

I write to you, dearest, last thing at night. I sleep with my secrets under my pillow and rise early to haul myself to the post office, even if it is not a good day, even if I am feeling wretched. I can feel my strength fading fast and I need to finish this before I am altogether incapable. The letters do not stay on Vennaway property for one second more than they absolutely must. I see them placed into the care of Miss Penelope Lambert, postmistress, with my own eyes!

I pause in my reading to laugh at another memory of my old life. To give something to Penelope was akin to placing it in a vault, locking it, throwing it into the ocean and then melting down the key for good measure. We went to the post office whenever there was anything to be posted, even though the servants could easily have done so. We went just for the pleasure of counting how many times in any given encounter she would refer to herself, with consummate pride, as 'Miss Penelope Lambert, postmistress'.

Life is a richness of little details and minute encounters. In losing Aurelia, I have lost somebody with whom I can share a whole history. I should like to tell Henry these inconsequential things. I think perhaps he would understand. I think he might like to hear them.

If you are reading this letter, then you have met Louis. Amy, my <u>son</u>! Of course, he is <u>not</u> my son, not now, he is Joss and

Elspeth's son and yet . . . I cannot help but think of him that way still.

By now (I mean as I write this) he will be nearly a year old. He may be crawling and babbling and chuckling but I have only ever seen him as a babe. Like the both of us, Amy, he was a winter baby. Born in November to grey skies, rain and bare branches. Really, you would think I might have timed it better!

Oh, to be able to write to you of Louis, to be able to share my love for him with my dearest friend! But I must return to Twickenham first. This letter is intended to enlighten you, not to indulge myself (although I never say no to a little indulgence, as well you know).

So there was I in Twickenham, enjoying life with the Wisters to the full. I firmly pushed all thoughts of Bailor Dunthorne from my mind. I felt I was finally gulping down something I had long been denied. I thought it would fortify me to return to my parents. I even hoped, you know, to return early and surprise you. I missed you so.

Well, Robert Burns was quite right when he said: 'The best-laid schemes o' mice an' men an' even Vennaways / often go awry.' (Mr Henley would tell me that I have taken licence with the citation, but I'm sure Mr Burns had a Vennaway or two lurking in an early draft.)

I frequently did battle with my health while I was there, Amy. I tried to make light of it in my letters to you, for I did not want you fearing I might not return. It was bad, and I had not expected that so soon.

I don't think I ever mentioned that Mrs Bolton had left me by then. She had business in London and I would not be torn away from her relations. She returned a few weeks later, however, and took me aside only days later.

'Aurelia,' she said (you know she never was one for pre-amble), 'tell me, is there any way that you might be pregnant?' That is a frank friend indeed!

She was much struck with the change in me, you see, the repeated bouts of sickness, my dizzy spells, and all before luncheon. Yet despite my weakness, she said, I glowed in a most particular way!

Will you think me very stupid if I tell you that it had never even crossed my mind? The biological indications were all there, of course, but I had been too busy to pay them any mind – too busy enjoying myself, too busy gritting my teeth with determination to stay alive and enjoy even more!

I answered her questions with my head spinning and Mrs B suspected her guess was right. I knew it was. From never even dreaming of it, the knowledge rushed in on me all of a sudden. I <u>knew</u> I wasn't ready to die when I left Hatville! Something else was responsible for my malaise.

When I look back at the three-and-twenty years of my life, there are three moments that I remember with a special quality of memory, an extraordinary clarity – moments when I knew <u>absolutely</u> that my life was about to change for ever. The first was finding you. The second was the day I col-lapsed in the orchard and learned I was not going to live for ever, not even close. And the third was standing in the garden at Mulberry Lodge, understanding that I was with child. I put my hand on the trunk of the birch and saw it silver and black beneath my white hand. I see it still.

My dear Amy, you may imagine how I felt! Robin had promised me such a thing could not happen! I can only think these things are a very imprecise art, for he would not have wronged me in that way intentionally. Clearly, I could <u>never</u> go back to Hatville whilst I was pregnant and unmarried.

I remember writing down my options and a dismal little list they made (burned at once, naturally). Of course I might lose the child, as my mother had done so often. Yet somehow, given my body's recalcitrant nature, I knew that would not happen.

I could rid myself of it deliberately. Mrs B assured me that such a thing could be done if you knew the right (or perhaps the wrong!) people. It is illegal, you know, Amy, yet if I wished to do this, she would make discreet enquiries, she promised. Now there was another reason for secrecy, another person to protect. Imagine if my parents ever knew she had encouraged such a thing! But you, Amy, I want you to know everything.

Well, this option was not one I could consider. I can understand how women in desperate circumstances are driven to it. I was terrified, Amy. Yet despite my fear, I could not end the life of my child. You know me, Amy, I cannot kill a worm!

The third avenue then was to carry the child to term, if I lived that long, and then . . .? Abandon it? Impossible. Keep it and spend the rest of my life in hiding . . . well, you know, Amy, there was great appeal in that! I might have sent for you and done just that if it were not for the fact of this infernal problem with my heart. All you needed was to be left adrift in the world with a newborn baby!

Or there was the possibility of giving it up for adoption to a loving family. (I say 'it', my dear, because of course I did not know then that 'it' would be my Louis!) This was the unselfish choice, it seemed to me. A novel choice, then, for me!

It was the first alternative that gave me hope. But it was dependent on finding the right people and I knew of no one; no more did Mrs B. Then again, the <u>secrecy</u> that would have to be involved . . . the length of time I would need to stay away from home . . . ! You may imagine how I stayed awake at night circling over the details and problems and possible solutions . . . All pleasure was at an end and in its place only this obsession with creating the perfect solution.

You might think I resented 'it' for this abrupt termination of my newfound happiness but I did not. Not for a moment. All I wanted was to protect it.

And that brings me to the heart of the matter. You and I both know that if I had come home with an illegitimate child my parents would have raged and roared and the storm would have been vengeful. I imagined it in vivid detail, you may be sure! But then, Amy — and you know this too — they would have been reconciled. Their desperation for a continuance of the line would have done mighty battle with their outrage, and it would have won, I believe.

I would have died and my child would have been brought up by his own grandparents, in the home that his mother knew, and would have wanted for nothing in the world in the material sense. And yet . . .

I was forced to make a most thorough and dispassionate appraisal of my life. You know all my many advantages and all the ways in which I suffered. You know the great rage I had felt towards my parents. Yet I thought then about <u>them</u>, their upbringing, and, above all, about my mother's frequent pregnancies that always ended in tears and bloody sheets.

She lost so many children! While I wrestled with my conscience in Twickenham, I did not know <u>how</u> many – but I knew enough to feel sympathy for her now that I was with child myself. Since my return, I have learned that she lost <u>eleven</u> babies over the years. As well as bearing me! Having carried a child just once, I cannot imagine what she suffered. I believe she has been driven a little mad by it. It makes it possible for me to forgive the wrongs she has done me. And so you see I write with compassion in my heart, not the rage of a wronged daughter.

Nevertheless.

I did not want Hatville – <u>any part of it</u> – for <u>my</u> child.

Imagine had it been a girl! How could I knowingly put my own daughter in that position, after Lord Kenworthy, after <u>Bailor Dunthorne</u>, for heaven's sake? And as for a son . . . Still he might be constrained and inculcated with senseless ideas, still he might suffer if his spirit were anything like mine.

Then again, what if he grew up to be just like them? <u>My</u> son? Oh no, Amy. No.

Weighty decisions, were they not? It was a great deal to consider, and my head was clouded with fear. Whatever I decided, I must act very quickly, for if I delayed much, then secrecy would no longer be an option. I needed medical support too, I knew.

Another choice: to keep child from father and father from child. But Robin was part of Hatville. That he would make a tender, kind father I doubted not at all. That he would bring up a child as I would wish, after I was gone, I could not be sure. Perhaps he would feel his child was better off with a fortune and a bloodline. Was he strong enough to keep it safe from the mighty Vennaways, should they ever find out? Another risk I dared not take.

My course was set. I decided I must live long enough to find the right parents for my child. I must live long enough to give birth. And I must live long enough to return to you and look after you a little longer. And I must do it all in secret. Well, I have never shied away from a challenge!

My decision made, I spoke to Mrs B. She posted a discreet letter and shortly afterwards a reply came back. She informed me we were going to York. I was pleased, for it was far away.

I said nothing of my secret to the Wisters, though I wished to, many times.

Again I remember Michael's remark about Aurelia leaving them so suddenly and another piece of the puzzle drops into place.

I fled from my friends, with a heart full of regret at doing so – yet it was nothing to the regret I felt every time I penned a letter to you.

At first, of course, I could not write a thing. I did not know what to say! So I made up an excuse which I hoped would alleviate your concern. I know now that it did not. It was hastily fabricated and doubtless inadequate. I wrote, too, with a mind to prying eyes. I thought a social whirl, a series of balls, would not overly disturb my parents. As for you, you must have thought I'd taken leave of my senses!

Why did I say <u>Derby</u>? Simply because Mrs B had a connection there whom she trusted to post letters on for me. I have never set foot in that town. In fact, there are a great many places I have never set foot. My grand tour of the kingdom, my exciting, self-indulgent journey from city to city to city, amounted to this: London, Twickenham, York. Then home.

We arrived in York after an excruciatingly long train journey. At least so it seemed to me, vulnerable as I was. From the safety and comfort of my desk, however, I marvel. In just eight hours one may travel the length of our country!

What do you make of the glorious wedding cake that is York Minster? Those endlessly rippling bells that drown out all thought from one's brain? (What a blessed relief <u>that</u> was!) The cunning little streets that look like something dreamed up by the brothers Grimm? I wish we could explore it together. Oh, believe me, I did not appreciate these things upon my arrival – I had much to occupy me without admiring scenery!

We stayed at the Jupiter Hotel. Perhaps by now you know it. There we met an old friend of Mrs B's, the friend to whom she had written, the only person she could turn to in such a delicate situation – the only person who would be able to help. Of course that friend was Mrs Ariadne Riverthorpe.

They had met, I came to learn, a decade or so earlier, at some intellectual gathering in Bath. The young Mrs B, budding bluestocking, was greatly influenced by the old Mrs R and they had corresponded ever since. Mrs R continued to give advice and guidance – no doubt dreadful – to her protegée.

So Amy, I wonder how your time in Bath was? Thinking of it, sometimes I laugh and sometimes I feel very guilty! When I first met Mrs R, I thought her the most arrogant, discourteous, unsympathetic woman who ever stalked our green earth. You may imagine the fireworks in those early days.

Yet the arguments we fought were not like those at Hatville Court. They were not poisonous. They were the necessary sparks caused by the coming together of two very obstinate people with a great many opinions. In the course of these rows, something dispensable burned away and we were left with the core of it. We were kindred spirits, I think (though I am vastly more delightful, I hope).

You may have learned by now that although Mrs R professes to suffer human companionship as a very inconvenient but unavoidable fact of life, in fact she thrives on intrigue and other people's business. Give her so much as a whiff of a situation and she is embroiled in it. She likes to feel useful. I believe she likes to think that the many hardships of her long life have not all been for nothing; that her many connections and experiences enable her to deal with almost anything. If possible, in short, she likes to help. Of course, I did not know all this about her <u>then</u>. In my confusion, all I was aware of was a very determined woman who seemed to swoop down from above and take charge of everything.

The first thing she did was summon a doctor of whose discretion she was utterly sure. That ensured my health would not deteriorate any further unnecessarily. The second, when she had assured herself that I was worth taking the trouble for, was to go and see her friends the Caplands. She had told me that they were very good and warm people with a loving marriage and no children.

'They are boringly devoted,' she told me in her world-weary way. 'I suppose if anyone should raise another child in this tedious, overcrowded, cruel world of ours, it is them.'

Poor Mrs Riverthorpe. First she had to contend with me being difficult and then neither did Elspeth instantly fall into line. Well, you can imagine: a distant acquaintance appearing on your doorstep one day, informing you that you are to bring up the unborn child of a complete stranger! It is not the usual way of things. I did not even realize at first that Mrs R did not live in York, that she had come all the way from Bath as a result of Mrs B's letter about me – a person she had never met. But she was in agreement with Mrs B that it was vital to get me far away from home as soon as possible. So to York we all hastened. And if the Caplands had refused to play their part? It would have been a jaunt for her, she told me once. A jaunt! Two days' journey for an eighty-year-old woman! Amy, she styles herself a loner after all her many disappointments but that woman needs people as fish need water.

Nevertheless, Joss and Elspeth did agree to meet me. And the rest they can tell you themselves. They took to me, thank the Lord, and decided to adopt my child. They are the very best of people, as you will now be discovering for yourself. They cherish Louis. Their cheery openness, their warm hearts, their ideas about rearing a child were all so utterly in accord with my wishes that I am quite sure that angels have the charge of Louis Capland.

Then the questions were all of practicalities. This is how we managed it. Joss and Elspeth have a remote little cottage on the Yorkshire Moors, some hour's drive from Fountain Cottage. Elspeth and I repaired there as soon as matters between us were settled. Thus no neighbours would see the expansion of my form, and the constancy of Elspeth's.

To those few souls I did meet, I was introduced as Nella Cardew; it seemed better to adopt a false name. We agreed, you see, that it should not be known that the baby would be adopted. I never wanted my child to grow up and ask questions about its blood family. I never wanted there to be any chance that he or she could trace my steps back to Hatville Court. And I never wanted the child to feel that its mother didn't want it, not when I loved it more than life, before it had even put in an appearance.

How funny that I had gone away dreaming of the sophisticated world, of salons, lectures, political rallies, dances, flirtations . . . and instead I washed up in the middle of a vast nowhere watching the seasons change over the moors! At first I was too shocked at what had befallen me to feel sad. But now, having found a safe place, I felt my disappointment in all its glory. I wept bitterly, you may imagine. I was restless a great deal – the hand life had dealt me was so vastly different from what I <u>thought</u> I needed to be happy. But when I think of it now, I smile. Remember that I told you I wanted to feel that my life, however brief, should have some meaning. Did I really imagine that soirées and salons could achieve that?

They will take you there, Amy, and show you where I spent July, August, September, October, November . . . I watched blue summer arch overhead, then the mists came and the crackling leaves; the air turned lilac with woodsmoke, the days grew shorter, and then the frosts stole in . . . And all the while my baby grew inside me.

The doctor was a Dr Challis. He was very thorough, very gentle and very dispassionate. He was uninterested in who I was, where I had come from or why two women were alone in a remote cottage with a baby coming. His concern was to keep me alive and deliver my child. He warned me from the outset that if I did not follow his orders to the letter (never my strong suit, as you know) then what Dr Jacobs at Hatville had said would be true – the pregnancy would kill me. You may infer that I followed orders for the first time in my life!

My regime involved a great deal of rest, exceptionally plain food and very gentle walks every day. No fruit jellies, no champagne, no dancing, no strenuous exercise, no excitement . . .

What did I do? I became acquainted with that small corner of the moors in intimate detail. I longed to stride to the horizon and then keep going, but I could not. I never did learn what was over that hill, or round that bend, not there. Perhaps you might take those walks and think of me.

I talked with Elspeth. I rested in bed each afternoon, watching the clouds chase through the window. I read (I was sorely disappointed with Mr Dickens for neglecting to publish a new novel that year! 'Twas churlish of him to leave me without entertainment when I needed it most). I sketched and painted and the Caplands will no doubt show you those 'masterpieces' in due course. Joss visited us twice a week. Dr Challis came almost every day. Mrs Riverthorpe came once, grew bored and went back to Bath. And . . . I wrote to you.

How painfully I remember you confiding that during my absence you had feared that writing to you had become a chore in which I could take no pleasure. You were utterly right, though for none of the reasons you imagined. You thought I was too busy dancing and flirting to remember with any interest my little stay-at-home friend. For shame! The truth was . . . that I could not tell you the truth. And anything else was detestable. Penning lies to you felt hollow, tasteless and sad.

The baby's fate decided, my attention turned to you, dearest. What was to become of you after I was gone? For now it was not just a question of providing for you. I also needed to find some way to let you know the secret after my demise. One day you would know everything – it was how I comforted myself with every bland, made-up letter I wrote.

Mrs B had left to continue her travels as planned and all the imaginary destinations I wrote to you from were places she stayed. I sent my letters to her, then she sent them to Hatville from Manchester, Bath and goodness knows where. My parents needed to believe that I was moving around so much that they could not find me if they tried. Imagine months of letters coming from a remote Yorkshire location! That would have raised instant suspicion. I was exceedingly vague, too, as you may recall, lest I be found out.

When you (and they) wrote back to me, Mrs B again forwarded the letters to me in the north. That is why our letters did not feel as if they connected, Amy. It wasn't that I was uninterested in yours, it was simply that I hadn't read them!

My parents believed my endless postponements were an attempt to evade my engagement to Bailor Dunthorne. But their fury was impotent – they had no way to find me. In fact it was most helpful that there was another plausible explanation to keep them from suspecting the truth. After several months, they grew quiet on the matter, which I thought odd. But I did not want to think of him when I was in Yorkshire.

Despite everything, I found peace during those months,

for the first time in my life. It may sound strange, but a fatal diagnosis had not nearly the impact upon me as carrying a child. The former, you see, did not fundamentally change me. I was still the same Aurelia, hungry to grab at everything and live life in ways that were denied me. But learning how very precious and <u>determined</u> life is . . . well, that did transform me. Death, it turns out, is one thing, but life is quite another. It is altogether more formidable.

I came to terms with my limitations (scandalous, I know, to think I should have any!). The small territory that the doctor had demarcated for me helped with that. I became utterly transfixed by that small piece of the world. The flourish and decay of flowers, the agenda of ants, the depths and directions of rain. The fluffy, staggering development of a young magpie, who grew sleek and glossy as I watched. I came to feel that any more would overwhelm me, so intensely rich is each small portion of land.

Louis Josslyn Capland was born on 18th November, 1844. The delivery was not easy, but it did not kill me, as you have perceived, and Dr Challis was as skilled and calming as I could have wished. Six hours it took, which I understand is very quick for a first baby. Louis Capland was obviously determined to find his way into this world!

When I saw him, Amy, when I held him . . . for those few days reality fell away: the short time I would have with him; the need to leave him behind. There I was with this small being who fit as perfectly into my arms and snug against my heart as if he had always been there, like an arm or a leg. I nursed him myself, just those first days, and feelings flooded through me that were all new.

It was agony and bliss. It was floating on beams of light – the transcendent certainty that when the time came I could give him up because loving him made me so <u>large</u>. It was, too, the black and bitter desire to run away and live on the moors with him and eat berries and die together when the snows came. It was everything, and it was nothing more than it had to be: a brief and beautiful interlude.

After a week, we returned to Fountain Cottage: Elspeth Capland, her new baby and her good friend Nella, who had taken such good care of the mother throughout a tricky confinement.

Mrs Riverthorpe favoured us with another visit. She peered her old beak in at the baby and pronounced him 'a bit crumpled, but likely to grow up fetching enough to cause trouble'. Then she drank a great deal of Madeira and left the next day.

It was February before Dr Challis pronounced me fit to travel. Mrs B returned to escort me to London and we stayed some weeks at Belgravia while I regained my strength. I began the difficult work of leaving behind everything that had happened. My body needed to adjust to being away from Louis and my thoughts needed to turn to the future. I needed to become the fictional Aurelia who had spent a whole year gratifying her every whim and simply enjoying herself too much to come home.

Then I had to go shopping! I have never enjoyed it less;

those months in Yorkshire had changed me. The shops seemed crowded and over-bright; the press and trill of polite society clamouring for possessions exhausted me. Nevertheless, the fact remained that I had spent the last six months in one of two shapeless gowns and a pair of muddy boots.

Shopping in Regent Street one day, whom should I see but Bailor Dunthorne! I had not yet conjured a way to avoid marrying him that would satisfy my parents, but I learned that circumstances had changed, unbeknownst to me. One of his many dalliances had resulted in a child. The woman in question was no one the elder Lord Dunthorne would entertain as a daughter-in-law (she was a chorus girl!). But the unthinkable had happened: Bailor had developed a fancy for her and would not give her up. He could not offer her marriage but he would raise their son. He brought the boy home and though it was put about that he was the orphaned son of a friend, everyone knew the truth. No wonder my parents had stopped writing of the engagement! They would <u>never</u> allow a Vennaway to marry into such a situation. Oh, how this turn of events dented them! Oh, the gratitude I felt then that Bailor's profligate lifestyle had finally caught up with him! I could almost have kissed him (almost, but not quite). That was one problem solved for me, at least.

I returned as Aurelia, but sometimes I miss being Nella, who has borne a child, grown familiar with the rhythms of the earth and lived quietly. However, I feel I have retained something of her consciousness now that I am returned to you. I spend every day grateful that I am alive and every day grateful for you. I watch the light change and the trees turn. Each morning I send a prayer and a kiss to Louis, then I put him firmly from my mind. I turn my attention to the life that is at hand: Hatville Court. I tell myself that it is all surprisingly simple. In truth, it is not always so simple. My heart and body ache to hold him in a way that I cannot describe and of course there are those dark moments of the night when I imagine how it might have been. If I might have married Robin and brought up Louis myself, if it had been my happy family living at Fountain Cottage, if you and I, Amy, might be enjoying the countryside and playing with Louis together . . . But I am dying and I would not want him to lose his mother. So every time these thoughts and feelings invade me, I grit my teeth, I do nothing, I hold my course and they pass, they always pass. So I shall continue to weather these gales for however long I might live.

Another thing that is not simple is this treasure hunt! Amy, please forgive its inevitable imperfections. I am calm about leaving Louis with his parents, but I am not calm when I think that if I figure this wrongly you may never find him.

I am trying to grapple with a clandestine past, a present that is full of obfuscation, a fictional journey and an unknowable future. The surest thing would have been to let the secret die with me, yet I could not have you ignorant of all this, never knowing my son, nor he you. So I must take the risk of engineering this outlandish scheme after all. I must bring together the two people I love most, or die trying.

By the time I came home all the puzzle pieces I needed had

appeared in my life; they needed only to be ordered so that the treasure hunt was transparent enough for you but too cloudy for anyone else. And as I contemplated the pieces, I realized that it would not only be a means to obscure the truth about Louis. Somewhere along the way of planning it, it acquired a further purpose. By the time I began planting the clues I knew the treasure hunt was for you, as well as for my child. Money was not enough to give you, nor even friends. I wanted you to have choices. Experiences. Freedom. I want you to meet the people I have met, have your horizons expanded as mine have been, and share everything as you could not do at the time, so that you might benefit. No doubt it is presumptuous of me, but I have been changed and strengthened by all that has occurred. I want the same for you.

And so it took shape, gradually, like a piece of clay becoming a pot. A crucible, in fact, from which you can emerge phoenix-like – wealthy, travelled, strong and free to choose any life you want. I pray that it is so. I pray you will derive the benefits I dream of, and not merely think yourself inconvenienced in the extreme. I pray so many things for you, Amy.

Eventually the final shape was before me. I wrote to beseech the various parties and when I had received the agreement of each and every one, I wrote your letters, one at a time. I have worked swiftly, Amy, never knowing how long I might have. At least my rapid decline has dissuaded my parents from attempting to find me another husband. I no longer look hale and hearty and marriageable.

And so the treasure hunt is at a close. This last letter goes to Joss tomorrow and his part is very easy. He need only stow it away until the day that Amy Snow comes walking up his garden path. I have asked a very great deal of you, Amy – perhaps more after my death than I ever did alive. You understand why, now. Henceforth I request nothing of you.

I do not ask you never to speak of this to a living soul, for I trust your discretion utterly. I know you would never share it with anyone I would not also trust. You may certainly tell the Wisters all you wish, for I should like them to know why I left so hurriedly and kept in touch so little.

I hope that you will be a joyful part of Louis's life and he of yours, wherever you may find yourself. I know that you will love him, for his own sake and for mine. Please look after him, Amy, in whatever way you see fit and the situation allows. Make sure that he is happy. He has wonderful parents, I know, but how it comforts me to imagine you, with your loving heart and staunch loyalty, also watching over him like a fairy godmother.

Having a child must be the most commonly occurring miracle there is – just one small life – it is not as if I have changed the world. And yet the world is changed indeed, because Louis Capland is in it. In this I feel satisfied in how things have turned out in the end. He will do great things, I feel sure, but that he is happy is all I desire.

This is goodbye at last, little bird. In fact, I can call you 'little bird' no longer — you are flown. You have become a woman, and the world is better, too, for having you in it. Just as my life has been the better for you. You know how I love you. I shall be watching over you, Amy Snow, you may be sure.

Now and for ever,
AV

Chapter Seventy

A week after my walk in the garden with Louis, I depart the Jupiter to stay with the Caplands for an unspecified time. The hotel has kindly agreed that I may continue to receive my post there; I shall call to collect it once a week. It is no doubt an unnecessary precaution but the habit of covering my traces is not so easily shed. I am heartily glad that I am no longer obliged to be secretive in all I do, but there is still Louis to protect. Aurelia's decision to keep him from her family I applaud with all my heart. Perhaps I should have more sympathy for the Vennaways, kept from the one thing they have always wanted with all their cold hearts, unaware that it even exists, but I have been a child in that house. Not for any reward would I see Louis grow up there.

Now I am settled as one of the Capland family, an arrangement enthusiastically welcomed by Louis, who has identified me as an easy source of stories, games and every indulgence. I believe, as 'Aunt Amy', close family friend, that is my prerogative.

It is a little like being at Mulberry Lodge, except more far tranquil. I have that same feeling of soaking up friendship, rest and laughter like a thirsty summer garden. But now I have all the answers I need and the relief of knowing that if and when I move on, it will be my own decision.

The days are delightful and varied. Mostly I stay with Elspeth and the children. Sunny days pass in the garden or fields. Rainy days confine us to the house but are filled with chatter and music, congenial visitors and the acrobatics of cats. Sometimes I go to the shop with Joss to learn about the business. I find it fascinating: the sourcing of different textiles, the lengths to which suppliers will go to command the highest prices, Joss's tales of his eccentric London contacts. Best of all are the free samples of ribbon, buttons and lace that arrive like sweets, and which I am very happy to appropriate.

When Elspeth can pry Louis and Verity from my side, I spend time alone with Aurelia's sketches, paintings and poems from her time in Yorkshire. When I compare them with the generic sketches and missives I received four years ago, I have to laugh. Here at last are the impressions and details that she would have sent to me if she could. Beautifully detailed sketches of Elspeth and Joss, of Mrs Riverthorpe (frightening in their likeness), of the wildlife on the moors. As I leaf through sparrow and jackdaw, squirrel and stoat, briar and pinecone, I feel her with me, turning the pages, pointing things out.

Then come sketches of Louis as a tiny baby, sleeping and cherubic, or wide awake and screaming, with flailing fists and gaping mouth. Aurelia has captured the beautiful innocence and tyranny of a newborn with equal degrees of love and fascination.

The only empty space in my landscape, the only cloud to cast a chill, is the absence of Henry. If I had thought I loved and needed him when I was unhappy and anchorless, it was as nothing compared with how I miss him now. Since I arrived in York I have been dreaming of the time when I will find him and put everything right. The possibility has enabled me to move through the days. Now that there is nothing to stop me going to him, I am frightened; what if I cannot find him, or worse, find him and cannot put things right? What would my life be then?

Chapter Seventy-one

In the evenings, after the children have gone to bed, I sit with Joss and Elspeth in their snug sitting room and they tell me everything they can remember about the time they spent with Aurelia. I recount every detail of my journey to find them. It is good to tell my whole story at last, to honour and complete it by giving it voice before sympathetic listeners. Inevitably this brings me to Henry. At first I am reticent to mention him but soon I find it is a relief to speak his name.

When I come to that last morning in Bath, I grow hesitant. It remains a very difficult memory. Mrs Riverthorpe pounding at my bedroom door and our last, curt words on the threshold. The entire overheard conversation between the drunken revellers. The mad flight from Bath. And the argument with Henry . . .

'He said that he released me . . . that our understanding was at an end and he was going to continue his life as he saw fit. He said he would not be a fool who waits in the wings.'

'And you have heard nothing from him since then?' Elspeth frowns.

'Not a word, although . . . he would not know where to write to me.'

'So . . . you have not been in touch with him either?'

'Well, no! I could not write. I did not know what to say! And I did not know where he was. But most of all, I am afraid. His words *haunt* me. I long to go and find him, every day, but what if it is all spoiled now? What if he looks at me the way he did before?'

Joss and Elspeth exchange glances.

'Let me be clear on this, if I may,' says Joss. 'He insisted that you choose there and then between your loyalty to him and your loyalty to Aurelia? He wanted you to give up the treasure hunt for your new life together?'

'Oh no! Not at all. He was very clear that I must do nothing of the sort, that I must honour my loyalty to Aurelia. But he wanted to come with me –'

'And you did not want that?'

'Oh, I did! Only I felt I must not . . . I had begun to suspect, you see, that there was a child. I already knew there had been . . . a lover. He did not know Aurelia and it is such personal information. So easily judged or misconstrued.'

'Did you feel Henry would think badly of Aurelia?'

'In truth I did not know what he might think of her. Our

upbringing always taught us that such behaviour was utterly reprehensible in a woman.'

'And yet such things happen every day,' Elspeth smiles, rather as if she is glad that they do.

'And if Aurelia had not acted as she did, I would not have a son,' Joss adds with a shrug. 'And what if Henry had felt differently, if he did judge Aurelia for her actions, what then?'

I bite my lip. 'Well, then I would feel badly for her. And I would worry, I suppose, whether his regard for me might be so easily lost in a . . . um. . . similar situation.' I blush and shake my hair back from my face. 'And I wish to protect Aurelia, her memory, that is. Henry did not know how her life was – how *our* life was – and it would not be right to judge.'

'So you did not give him the chance to prove himself either way?' Elspeth reaches over and squeezes my hand. 'I do not blame you, of course. These are delicate matters and you were quite without a confidante – Mrs Riverthorpe is hardly given to gentle guidance! Nevertheless, if you plan to marry the man, it would be as well to know what his thoughts are on such things, true?'

I look down at my lap. It sounds so simple, put like that. At the time, it did not feel simple.

'But let me be sure of the situation,' Joss presses, with a man's taste for fact. 'Was it also that you did not trust him with the confidence? I mean, did you not trust him to keep Aurelia's secret?'

'No! Henry would *never* betray me that way, even if he did not approve. I trust him completely.'

'And you love him?' Elspeth verifies.

'With all my heart.'

'So you love him, you trust him and you want to marry him. He did not tell you to abandon Aurelia's quest for him, but he wanted to share it with you and help you?' persists Joss, inexorable as Cook's rolling pin.

'Yes. I have made a terrible mistake, haven't I?' I ask in a small voice. 'Henry was blameless and I have treated him shockingly and now I can't find him and I will never see him again!' My voice has risen by the end and I am breathing heavily. Guilt and heartache threaten to smother me once more. Louis and the Caplands have been balm and distraction but I cannot hide from my feelings any longer – I can't further postpone looking for Henry and discovering my fate.

Behind me, a little voice says, 'Aunt Amy? Who's Henry?'

Joss stands, scoops his son up and removes him, but not before pausing in the doorway to shrug, bewildered. 'What do women *want* of us?' he demands to nobody in particular, before leaving me alone with Elspeth before the open window. A jasmine-laden breeze blows in and an owl calls somewhere outside. I laugh shakily.

'I love him still, Elspeth, heart, body and soul. No other man will ever be like Henry. What have I done?'

'Amy, Henry was not blameless. Not blameless. It was not a usual circumstance in which you found yourself and he knew that from the outset of your acquaintance. And don't listen to Joss! Only consider – men and women *never* truly understand one another, for we are different creatures. That is part of the adventure! If you imagine you may find a husband with no faults, and never a misunderstanding between you . . . well, you will not. It is intention and the orientation of the heart, I think, that matters.'

'I see,' I say, but only after I have given it some serious thought and hope that I really do see. 'It makes sense, of course. He told me he was stubborn, I know he is impetuous. He is not given to compromise. Yet I love him, for all of that. He said that he never wanted to be parted from me, and that if I loved him it would be the same for me. But we ran too far along the road of our dreams while I was still bound up in the past.'

'Of course you did, for you were young and falling in love. That's what falling in love *is*, Amy – an ecstatic departure from any kind of sense or circumspection! But *after* falling in love, actually *being* in love – marriage – those things require thought and sensitivity and patience. Henry was impatient, and that impatience was one burden too many for you at a difficult time, so you fled. You may be forgiven! Only his impatience came from loving you and caring about you, I think. Perhaps, then, *he* may also be forgiven?'

'Oh, I have already done that. I forgive him with all my heart, Elspeth. With all my heart!'

'Well, that's lovely, dear. Only, might *he* not want to know that too?'

Chapter Seventy-two

That night I write a very long letter to Henry. When I have finished, I copy it out again. I address one copy to Albert Crumm and the other to the Longacres in Bath. I put a brief note in each envelope begging that if they know where Henry is they will forward the letter to him without any delay at all. The following morning I rise early and travel to York with Joss.

I go to the post office and see the precious letters into the hands of the postmaster, thinking of Aurelia as I do so. I have not committed Aurelia's secret to paper but I have committed all else that is precious to me: my feelings, my regrets, my love, my hopes. I have told him that if he wishes me to come to him he need only tell me where and I will be at his side as soon as is humanly possible. I have told him that when I see him I will tell him everything, and exclude him from nothing, not ever again.

Despite this, I feel desolate. I feel I have wronged him by agreeing to share my life with him and then, at the first test, insisting that I manage things alone, running out on him at only a moment's warning. In my mind's eye, I see him rumpled and bewildered in his nightshirt, running his hands through his hair, watching me slip through his fingers.

'You will not leave me like this, Amy.' It was not a command, I realize now; it was a plea. The memory is almost enough to make me lose hope, except then I remember Elspeth's wise words: we were both at fault, both only human. Perhaps he can forgive me, love me *despite* my faults, as I do him.

I find myself feverishly calculating dates. When might I hope to hear from him? If he is with the Longacres or his grandfather, I might receive a reply in just a very few days. If he is not, but they can send my letter straight to him, it will be a little longer. If they do not know his whereabouts, it may be weeks before my letter even finds its way into his hands. It may be months! How might I be patient so long?

I have never been in love before. I do not know what is forgivable and what is not, but I do not hold out any great hopes that I can reasonably expect a reprieve. Still, I have promised myself at least to *try* to believe that love and happiness can be mine, even if precedent suggests otherwise. I have done what I can for now, and if he does not reply, or if he is still angry with me when he does, then I shall go to London and speak to his grandfather. I shall ask him to persuade Henry to listen to me, just once, out of the goodness of his heart.

But if he no longer loves me, if there is someone else who

can make him happier or if he simply does not wish to take the risk that is Amy Snow, I shall let him go, indeed I shall, and wish him well at all times from the bottom of my heart. But not until I have done everything in my power to win him back.

So I vow, as I set off back to Fountain Cottage. I did not intend to walk; I had thought to ask Joss if he might spare his apprentice for a short while to drive me. But, lost in my ardent ruminations and silent, fervent promises, I have somehow missed the shop altogether and passed beyond the city walls. I hesitate, then decide to walk. It will pass more time and the way is a pleasant one. I realize how sweet solitude is when it is not enforced, how contented it is possible to be in one's own company when it is not the only possibility one has.

The day grows warm, so I take off my bonnet and swing it as I walk. I am surrounded by green and there is no one to see. Besides, I could not spend so long with Mrs Riverthorpe without coming to relish flouting convention even a little.

By the time I reach the lane that leads to the house I am warm and no doubt a great deal flushed. I can feel my rebellious hair hovering about my head like a cloud of bees and I promise myself a seat in the shade, a book of poetry and a comb, when I return. I feel a little embarrassed when I see that Elspeth has had a visitor in my absence.

Whoever it is strides from the cottage in the direction of York. In a minute our paths will cross and I think briefly of hiding before remembering that anyone is free to think me a fright if they wish; I care not. It is very liberating. I squint, wondering if it is anyone I have already met. It is too slender for Jeremiah, who would be at work in his butcher's shop now anyway. Indeed, it looks a little like Henry from here, but I see five-and-twenty Henrys on any given day, such is the extent of my preoccupation. So I keep walking and swinging my bonnet.

My bonnet flies from my grip; the ribbons are satin and my fingers are slippery with perspiration. Now I look even more preposterous, flinging my bonnet about the countryside. Thanks to a sudden, stray breeze it bowls towards the walker as though eager to meet him.

He snatches it up with a large smile, a smile I see a thousand times every day, and so I still do not realize, even when I am standing directly in front of Henry Mead, that he is truly here in Yorkshire.

'*Amy Snow*,' he says, looking at me in wonder, as though I am rare and precious and marvellous. I see anxiety and determination do battle behind his smile. 'My God, it's good to see you. I can't be without you, Amy, so don't ask it of me.'

Chapter Seventy-three

'Henry?'

All my self-castigation, all my fears for the future fall away. In that moment I am so happy just to see him that I feel I shall never want anything else, ever again. We look at each other for a long, charged moment and then I run into his arms.

'Oh, Henry!'

As if my words were the cue he needed, he picks me up and swings me around and around.

'I love you,' he murmurs into my hair, the words muffled and gruff.

I am weak with love and relief. I feel as though tides are rolling through me. All I can say, over and over again is 'I love you,' and 'Henry'. For five months now my life has been governed by words. The clues, the letters, what I could say and all I was forbidden to say. Now at last I can lay it all down and follow my feelings; I can surrender.

When he finally sets me down, I refuse to let go and stay

clinging to him, my arms ecstatic to be reunited with the breadth of his shoulders, my face determined to stay buried in his neck.

This way is better than words.

Chapter Seventy-four

The words come later, after we have returned to the cottage and Elspeth has supplied us with lemonade. She takes the children off to the fields and they protest mightily at being removed from this interesting stranger with the mischievous eyes.

'However did you find me, Henry dear?' I ask, kissing the hand of his that I am clutching in both of mine.

'No thanks to you, my love,' he supplies cheerfully.

'I am so sorry. I was afraid to write to you and I did not know where to reach you. What if you had fallen out of love with me? What if you were too angry with me? I'm afraid I am not at all experienced in these things, which of course is why I have handled it all so badly. But I have written to you at last. Two copies! I have posted them this morning.'

He laughs. 'I look forward to reading them, my beauty. Not in love with you? Foolish girl, that could never be. When you left, I was furious. But it was only because I was hurt, and feared I'd lost your affections. I did not know I could be such a boor, Amy. I am sorry!

'I went to Richmond, for I did not know what else to do. I thought I did us a better service by securing an income and acting in faith than by chasing after you to York, with feelings still running high between us and you still perfectly unreasonable, my love.'

'*Henry!*'

'Yes, yes, perfectly unreasonable. And I still impatient and indignant and completely lacking in comprehension. Does that sum us up, do you think, Amy?'

I ruefully agree that it does.

'It was hard to concentrate, you may be sure, for I wanted to bolt at every moment and leap onto a northbound train. But I stuck to my purpose and I secured the post!'

I kiss him in delight. 'Well, of course you did! Oh, congratulations, that is splendid. And did you like the school?'

'Very much. Mr Merritt is an amiable gentleman and the docile young ladies I saw hard at work in the schoolroom no doubt have a barrel of their own ideas tucked away behind their ringlets, which I long to hear and encourage. I shall be as subversive as possible, you may be sure! The building is very well appointed, and you know Richmond of course – a delightful place. I think I could do very good work there, although I shall give my firm acceptance only if you approve. I realize a great many things may have changed with you since last we spoke.'

'Only that I am surer than ever that I want to be with you, Henry, and that at last I am free to be so. But carry on, please.'

'From Richmond, I returned to Bath. I went straight away to Mrs Riverthorpe and demanded she tell me where to find you.'

I laugh at the very idea. 'Lord, how brave you are! What happened?'

'Well, she told me.'

'Henry, no! That cannot be. She would *never* tell you! She would not tell *me*!'

'I was exceptionally fearsome, my dear!'

I look at him sceptically.

'Oh, very well, it was not quite that simple. I wore her down – I bored the information out of her, quite literally. I told her I refused to leave her house until she told me. Then I proceeded to talk – on and on, about how much I love you. You know how she hates that. She left the room. I remained.

'She swept past an hour later, changed into one of her gaudy costumes – in truth, I have never seen anything like it – on her way out to a ball. I was still there. Oh, her *face*!' He laughs helplessly. 'I wish you could have seen it. Anyway, I followed her out to her carriage, talking all the way, and she slammed the door and rattled off leaving me halfway through a sentence. No matter! I had plenty more sentences! I knew where she was going – you know Mrs Riverthorpe, she won't go to something that isn't the talk of the town – so I went too.'

'You had an invitation?'

'Of course not. But this is where a history of mischief-making comes in exceptionally handy. I got myself all dressed up – you should have seen me! You would have swooned, I expect. I shimmied in through a window, swaggered about the place until I happened on Mrs Riverthorpe and made a great many more protestations of my love for you. Oh, she was not content to have her evening of grand company and salacious gossip interrupted, you may be sure!'

'I *am* sure! You were lucky she did not have you thrown out.'

'Oh, she did! I was there but five minutes before they flung me through the front door and threatened me with arrest. No matter. I was waiting for her at Hades House when she got back.'

'And I can imagine what sort of time of night that was!'

'Indeed. I believe Gus and Ellen thought I had taken leave of my senses for the duration, but I had the bit between my teeth. Mrs Riverthorpe is a stubborn old bird and tough as nails, but I am in love, and that gives me the upper hand every time when it comes to irrational endurance. Anyway, the long and the short of it is it took me a week to wear her down, and I am not sure she will ever be glad to look on me again, but I am here and we are together again at last, and I want to tell you that I am sorry, heartily sorry for everything I said before you left.

Do you forgive me, Amy?' He looks at me so solemnly, and lifts my hand to his lips.

'Henry dearest, I forgave you the instant I had left you. I'm sorry too. I am so long accustomed to secrets and solitude that making you part of my life just then suddenly seemed impossible – and I ran away. But now I will tell you everything, if you will also forgive me.'

'It is already done and never was needed. So . . . are you really free now? You have learned Aurelia's great secret?'

I nod, my eyes shining. Freedom at last.

'You need not tell me, Amy, if it does not feel right. You need *never* tell me if you do not wish to.'

Bless him. I can see how he burns to know.

So I tell him.

We sit and spin dreams together, just as we did in Bath, except that now I need not censor what I say. Now I will not be sent off to some strange city at a moment's notice. It is as though a vast purple thundercloud has moved off from above me, taking with it all the tension from the air and a headache I hadn't known I suffered.

We sit close, heads bent together in the sunlight, until we hear the grassy thrumple of Joss's cart in the lane. He sizes up the situation in a glance.

'Amy, have you dispatched my wife and children so you may entertain your lovers again?' He leaps to the ground and throws the reins over the horse's head. 'I jest, of course! Sir, you must be Henry.'

'No, sir, I am Randolph Boniface,' replies Henry with a worried expression.

I swat his arm. I am sure there will be no peace when these two become acquainted.

Chapter Seventy-five

Before we leave York, I light a fire in my room, even though it is June and so hot that every window in the cottage must be open else we could not breathe. I have known for some time that I must do this. I take all of Aurelia's letters and I burn them.

First of all, those early letters, full of desperately constructed lies – the anxiety they concealed and the anxiety they caused. I watch them blaze, blacken and vanish. And then the clues in the treasure hunt, one by one. I read Aurelia's final words to me for the very last time.

> This is goodbye at last, little bird . . . I can call you 'little bird' no longer . . . I love you . . . Now and for ever . . .

It seems impossible, still, that the immense part she has played in my life is at an end. Yet so it is.

'Goodbye, Aurelia,' I murmur. 'I love you too. Thank you, dear friend, for everything you have given me.'

I watch as all her words and all her secrets turn to ash, taking with them as they crumble the truth of Louis Capland's parentage. It is the story of one small life – so cherished, so loved and so vital – obscured for ever.

My own chronicle, too, I set alight. I take the pages that I have covered with heartache and memory, and a sizeable sheaf they make. It is all here, my life to date: nights in a scullery and days by a stream; a great friendship and a painful loss; exile and a quest. My history, my hopes and my heartache. Questions – some of which have been answered and some of which may never be. They flare and flourish. And suddenly they are gone.

I say my farewells not only to the treasure hunt, not only to Aurelia, but to this whole part of my life: seventeen years, begun in snow and ended in flames. I shed my misfortunes in the fire; they do not define me. And in this way I claim another blank canvas on which to paint my identity – and my future.

For it is as Aurelia said: death is one thing, but life is quite another.

Chapter Seventy-six

Twickenham, April 1849

An announcement appears in the *Twickenham Herald* that Mr Henry Mead of Hertfordshire and Miss Amy Cardew of Twickenham are to be married on the twenty-ninth of that month. And duly we are.

I am married from Mulberry Lodge, where I have spent the intervening months. I wear a striking gown of bridal silver with a stole of pale-green silk, embroidered with forget-me-not. The reception is held in the garden, from whence guests may easily stroll to the river. Edwin Wister gives me away in the local church and Madeleine is my matron of honour. Little Louisa, now five, does sterling service as flower girl; Michael is an usher.

The ceremony is attended by assorted Meads and Crumms, by the Caplands of York, by Mrs Ariadne Riverthorpe, resplendent in saffron silk and yellow diamonds, and by the entire Wister clan, of course. The number of Wisters at Mulberry

Lodge remains unchanged; Constance gave birth to Caroline Aurelia in January (a month I am determined to learn to love), by which time Madeleine had already left home. She became Mrs Renfrew in the autumn. My joy at being there for both events may be readily imagined.

And now I am Mrs Amy Mead. It seems that my wintry identity has thawed altogether, from Snow to a name I am pleased to fancy invokes summer – for who ever thought of a winter meadow?

When it came to placing the notice in the *Herald*, we chose a name that ensured there would be no written record of Amy Snow. Anyone who ever knew aught of my parentage could never find me now. But I am long reconciled to that.

I have, after all, obliged the Vennaways. Amy Snow is quite, quite lost, vanished like a melted footprint.

Epilogue

❧

Hatville Court, May 1848

The road back to Hatville is long and straight. It strikes me as
laughably symbolic. My daughter was right about one thing.
Women may be reared to be virtuous, innocent and pleasing
but there is no reward for it in this life.

I do not know why I went to Bath to find Amy Snow. At
any rate, it was fruitless, like so much in my life. I return still
burdened with my secret. It is not such a sensational secret: the
world is not transformed for the keeping or the sharing of it.
'Tis merely that loose ends chafe.

The roofs of Hatville are visible on the horizon above the
trees, although some miles remain of this road that does not
curve or yield. I remember the Bible story about walking the
straight way, the narrow way, never deviating nor meander-
ing; it is what I have done. All my life.

It is what I tried to teach Aurelia, but she would not learn. I
am as mystified as ever about my daughter. I do not know how

she came to be born of Charles and me, for she was nothing like her father and, except in appearance, nothing like me. I was a very great beauty.

Once, the fact gave me such pride and pleasure. Of all my sisters I was the brightest and best. The eldest of seven girls, all born within a year or two of one another. I scarce had time to draw breath and look into my mother's eyes before a sister came screeching into the world, then another and another . . .

When I married, I never doubted that I would produce a brood of children. Charles and I were both awash with siblings and I was young, strong and healthy. 'A man's dream,' he told me on our wedding night. As he ripped open my corset, I turned my face towards the wall.

My first pregnancy, seventeen months after marriage, was the most wonderful thing that could possibly have happened. When I told my husband, he snatched me up and whirled me around in a boyish, joyful way. He looked at me with a tenderness I had never seen before.

Parents, his and mine, rained congratulations upon us and I could feel the collected sigh of relief. There would be an heir to Hatville after all.

Perhaps no child could survive such a mighty weight of expectation. At any rate, mine was lost two months later in a flurry of blood.

There are no words to describe what I felt then.

It was scarce a month before Charles resumed his conjugal visits, though the doctor bade him wait longer. My body and spirits were ravaged and sagging. Four months later I was again with child. This one stayed with me only four weeks. In any case, I could not feel for it what I had felt that first time.

Then a new possibility suggested itself to me, a new life to dread. Instead of worrying that I would never conceive, I worried that my body would be put through this endless cycle of hope and loss, hope and loss, on and on throughout the years. Even if I did birth a child, one would not be enough and so it would begin again. That was the first time I started to feel that my life, perhaps, was not a bearable thing.

Two more years, and two more children vanished before I could grasp the reality of them. One stayed for two months and one, cruelly, for five. Four sons or daughters, but I never saw one face. Vanished. Melted away as though they had never been and I thought my suffering heart must break.

And then, the miracle. It happened six years after my marriage – six years during which the Vennaways senior believed their line was fatally compromised. I conceived again and *this* time, month after month after secret, silent month crept by; Aurelia was born. My child!

Charles despaired that she was a girl but I would not change one thing about her, not even that. As a baby, she was a true cherub: ruddy gold curls, a mouth as pink and sweet as a kiss and wide violet eyes that never changed colour or faded.

She looked just like me. In her I saw all my second chances. She was so lively, pleasing and merry that she reconciled her grandparents to her sex to some considerable degree. Despite everything, I had succeeded in changing our situation. A girl, at least, could be married, and a girl such as this could be a treasure indeed.

Yet we continued trying. I conceived again and again, as if my body had learned, from Aurelia, that it could indeed do this thing. The day Aurelia brought Amy Snow to the house, mewling, blue and hideous, my seventh pregnancy since Aurelia's birth had recently ended.

When Amy was laid before me on the Indian rug, wrapped about in my daughter's sky-blue cloak, I was already weary, wretched and stretched taut to the utmost degree. Perhaps that is why all I could think as I looked at the babe was, 'My son would not have been so unappealing. Why is that child here instead of him?' I could find no compassion in my heart. I believe it was all wrung out of me. After all, small lives, dead before they'd begun, were commonplace to me.

Amy Snow was a thorn in my side in my side from the beginning, contaminating Aurelia with her unsavoury birthright and the offensive ease with which she slid into the world. Marriage, love, duty, within the best families, are not like that. They are hard. Hard fought for, hard come by and *hard*.

I knew the fact that she was found on our estate prompted

talk. The gossip was all that she was Charles's love child, placed on Hatville snow to shame him, but I knew the truth. The shame was intended for me.

Everyone speculated about Amy, my fanciful daughter most of all. But the truth was that no one knew where Amy came from apart from her mother. And me.

During the long years of my suffering I had, as befitted the lady of Hatville Court, visited the poor: handing out baskets, dispensing trite courtesies and so on. I cannot say I enjoyed it. My manner with those people has never been easy. I believe they could sense my discomfort and scorned me for it. The differences are so very great.

However, I was able to make a connection with one young farm girl. She looked forward to my visits and for my part I found them not so uncomfortable as the rest. I believe she admired my beauty and refinement, and had some aspiration towards improving herself.

I knew I must not encourage her in that, for her father was a dairyman and her mother likewise an ignorant nobody. The world would never favour her. She was not especially lovely to look at, although she had an open, frank manner and an unruly thatch of beautiful golden hair the colour of corn. Her name was Sophy.

One day, in May of 1830, I found the girl alone in her cottage in bitter distress. Through her tears she spilled out her sorry tale, one snuffling fact at a time; she was, of course, with child.

The father was a gentleman who had been staying near Enderby that spring. He happened upon Sophy driving cows from one pasture to another. He told her that her hair in the sunlight put him in mind of an angel; he professed himself enchanted with her smile. I sincerely doubt that he was. Sophy's smile was exactly like Amy's – too wide, too clumsy, unrefined. However, he had clearly had designs upon her in that moment and the silly girl believed him.

It sickens me to hear such tales. What a fiend he must have been to debase himself with someone so greatly inferior to him.

This gentleman – she knew him only as 'Bradley', and whether that was a Christian name or a family name I cannot conjecture – stayed for a week and sought her out more than once.

I felt some sympathy with Sophy, knowing the horror of such an act. But no! The girl told me I misunderstood her tears. She was not crying with horror but with heartbreak that he was gone. She could not believe it, for he had told her they would marry.

She had loved every moment with him, she told me. More than anything she had loved their coupling – in the hay loft behind the dairy! She felt her soul flood with light, so she said. I stopped her there. I would not listen to more. I had some extensive experience of these things, after all, and the suggestion that it could be enjoyable was obscene. Profane.

It was too late for Sophy; the act had taken place. But perhaps it was not too late for her soul, that soul of which she spoke so lightly. I urgently explained that this was an act only to be sanctioned within marriage, that taking pleasure in it was as grave a wrong as a woman can commit. It was difficult for her to understand, naturally, for she had not been educated at all. I insisted that the resulting child could be naught but disgrace and shame.

I made her a gift of a cast-off dress. This was seen by her family as a great kindness; in truth its size and unaccustomed style hid her steadily altering shape. When her time was near, I offered her a place at Hatville, that she might carry out only the lightest of duties without raising her family's suspicions. When the child was born, I would take it to the nearest orphanage and Sophy could resume her normal life as soon as possible. She said she wanted to keep it, but I insisted. She need not be marked by it. It would be as if nothing had ever happened.

Then I lost my last, longed-for baby and I was very ill. Some of my children slipped from me like an involuntary sigh. Others struggled and fought to stay with me – that's how I understood it anyway. This little son (I was convinced that this child was a boy) fought harder than any and I was told that I was very near death with it. I would have died, to bring him to life, but yet again it was all denied me.

When I was able to dress and take to my feet again, my sisters had arrived and Sophy had vanished.

I never learned what happened to her. I did enquire once. She had not gone back to her family and was never heard of again. It was, indeed, as if none of it had ever occurred. Or would have been, but for the appearance of a baby girl, naked in the Hatville snow.

I do not pretend to understand. Sophy loved her child enough to run away with it, ill-considered plan though that was. And then she abandoned it.

I imagine that a sort of nervous lunacy descended upon her. Even I have felt the pull to madness that comes with the terrible experience of loving and melding with a child when all was impossible. Likely she simply lost all sense of what she was doing – she had been distraught over the preceding weeks.

At first I wondered whether the child Aurelia named Amy Snow was in fact some other unfortunate's baby and the timing of the thing was merely malign circumstance. But as Amy grew, there could be no doubt. Every time I saw her clumsy, ugly smile, I saw Sophy accusing me. Her thatch of hair, too, and the way it parted in the centre of her brow, was all Sophy, though its dusky colour must have come from the father.

I even wondered, in dark moments, whether Sophy deliberately left her own child to die before my eyes, as a direct reproach. There are a number of possibilities, I suppose, and I cannot claim to have the energy to spare for their consideration.

The fact remained that this child, this small girl, who should never have been conceived, who should never have been born, found her way into *my* household to live a full and healthy life under my very nose. The timing was so cruel, just days after losing my sweet Samuel, as I thought of him in private. At each sight of her, grief clanged loud within me. I told Cook I must never see her.

It worked well enough for a time – I thought the solution imperfect but functional. But then Aurelia – recalcitrant, contrary Aurelia – made a pet of her, and then a sister, and the rest makes for a very sour history.

Now Aurelia is gone and so is Amy. Her departure is the one good thing to come out of Aurelia's death. I breathed my first full breath in seventeen years when her obstinate little form finally vanished into the grey gloom of a January day, months ago. I believed I should have peace of mind at last.

But the memories of Sophy grew strong; I remembered details I had not considered in years. She chose names – Flora for a girl, Nicholas for a boy – even though I told her the orphanage would do as they pleased. Why should I remember *that*? She told me the father came from Devon and rode a white horse. Well, of course he did. She would sing to the baby inside her sometimes, when she did not know I was near. Should I have sung to mine?

Perhaps I hoped these shreds of someone else's story would leave me if I passed them on to Amy. Perhaps she *should* know her history, after all those years of gypsies and princesses and Charles Vennaway's bastard child. I told myself many times that I owed her nothing, that her survival was due to my condescension. But I know the truth.

When Arabella returned to Surrey bursting with news that she had seen Amy Snow glittering like a ruby pendant at the heart of a Bath society ball, I knew I must chase her, just this once, and tell her what I knew if I could.

Arabella's certainty as to how Amy has gained her fortune I believe not at all. My sister is a fool. I am certain that Aurelia left her a great legacy; doubtless she went to some extraordinary lengths to hide the fact. It was well that she did, for Charles would have fought it. Deprived of a bloodline, he grows closer than ever about money. I could not care less.

I have not seen Amy Snow. I know, I feel it deeply, that I will never lay eyes on her again. Quite as I have always wanted. The life I face is barren and burdened – but thus it ever was. The chapter is closed.

I am returned, yes, with the knowledge unshared. But really, it is such a very mundane sort of a tale; as secrets go it is hardly original or interesting. What is it, after all, but the story of one small life, obscured for ever?

Acknowledgements

I'm tremendously grateful to all the amazing and talented professionals I've 'won', thanks to the *Search for a Bestseller* competition. I couldn't have wished for anyone better to work with, or to bring *Amy Snow* into the world for me. So a BIG and heartfelt thank you to ALL at Furniss Lawton, Quercus, Plank PR and WHSmith for their expertise, support and the warm welcome they've given me. Special thanks go to my truly inspiring agent Eugenie Furniss and my very brilliant editor Kathryn Taussig. And, of course, to Richard and Judy.

Also, thank you, Therese Keating, for being the first of the competition team to read and love Amy.

Huge thanks and love to my own readers, who were my cheerleaders through the writing process and have blessed me with priceless enthusiasm and feedback: Wendy Hammond, Ellen Pruyne, Marjorie Hawthorne, Andy Humphrey and Jane Rees (a.k.a. Mum).

Likewise to the other friends in my Swansea and London

posses who have supported and encouraged me in so many ways over the past year. Lisa Mears, Cheryl Powell, Karen Wilson, Patsy Rodgers, Lucy Davies (Research Associate!), Kathryn Davies, Sarah Cole, Anna Hunt, Stephanie Basford-Morris, Rosie Stanbridge, Ludwig Esser, Jacks Lyndon and Bethan Jones: your friendship and general amazingness make my world a better, richer place and make it possible for me to do what I do.

I would like to thank York Writers, a truly talented and motivated writing group, for supporting my literary dreams and for being the first to comment on the opening pages of *Amy Snow*.

And last but very definitely not least, thank you to my wonderful and ever-supportive parents, without whom I would probably never have seen the competition flyer at all and *Amy* would still be six pages long.

The following books have been invaluable resources in helping me to understand the context of Amy's life and times:

Judith Flanders: *The Victorian City*. Atlantic Books, London 2012

Ruth Goodman: *How to Be a Victorian*. Penguin, London 2014

Michael Paterson: *A Brief History of Life in Victorian Britain*. Robinson, London 2008

Acknowledgements

David Turner: *Victorian and Edwardian Railway Travel*. Shire
  Publications, Oxford 2013
*The Railway Traveller's Handy Book 1862: Hints, Suggestions and
  Advice for the Anxious Victorian Traveller*. Old House,
  Oxford 2012

The World of *Amy Snow*

Tracy Rees writes about what it might really have been like for a young woman like Amy living during the Victorian time

Was Hatville typical of a grand estate in the Victorian era?

Yes, I would say that Hatville was a typical early-Victorian estate. One of the things that really impressed itself on me when I started researching the period was how much change there was throughout the Victorian era. Of course, it spanned more than sixty years. Amy's early life at Hatville is set in the early years of Victoria's reign when Regency tastes and customs still pervaded Great Britain.

The inside of a house then was often sparsely decorated, partly because it was customary to dedicate time and attention to the outside of the house instead, so as to impress visitors with a display of wealth and status. This attitude would definitely have influenced the Vennaways, and so I was able to take great pleasure in creating the wonderful grounds of Hatville, with streams and orchards and rose gardens, all lovingly tended by Robin.

Another reason was that furniture – carpets and the like – were terribly expensive at that time. Of course this wouldn't have been an issue for the Vennaways, but even the wealthy people of the time preferred a rather severe interior. Given the Vennaways' cold, joyless personalities, this was perfect for my story. I really couldn't see them taking pleasure in creating a warm and welcoming home! By the time Amy reaches Mulberry Lodge in 1848, times and tastes were changing. Constance Wister represents the modern Victorian, purely delighted with all the novelty and variety newly on offer.

What sort of food would the family be eating at Hatville?

Because of their wealth, the family at Hatville would have been able to enjoy elaborate, rich food that the poorer people of the time wouldn't even have been able to imagine. Even to modern tastes the meals seem rather lavish! Meals typically had many courses and were devoured in rather large quantities. Even the servants at Hatville would have eaten well, thanks to being able to eat the same hearty breakfast as the family (though not at the same time, of course!). Dinner menus were often presented in French, and consisted of soups, fish, different meats (roasts, chops, etc.) and desserts, all accompanied by the correct wine. Madeira wine, so much enjoyed by Mrs Riverthorpe, was one of the correct choices to accompany dessert.

What were clothes like in the Victorian era?

As with everything else Victorian, clothes varied a great deal between the classes and also across the decades. Early and late Victorian fashions were relatively unfussy – everything in the middle was pretty lavish! In Amy's time, balloon sleeves and high collars were very characteristic features, and shawls and bonnets were essential! Hair would typically be worn coiled and braided and piled on the head, so Amy with her shorter hair would have been quite unfashionable. For girls like the young Aurelia, skirts were shorter and long frilly bloomers were worn. For servants, like the young Amy, the emphasis was of course on practicality. My next book will be set a little later in the era, in the 1850s, when the crinoline made an appearance. I'm sure I'll have some fun with that!

For gentlemen, costume was less sober in the early Victorian years than it became later. Top hats, waistcoats and gloves were all mandatory, and interesting colour combinations were often seen! Quentin Garland's penchant for pastels was quite usual for this time.

What was travel like in Amy's time?

OK, I'll admit it. My choice to set Amy Snow in the 1840s, rather than any other decade, was completely random. I said to a colleague, 'Give me a year in the nineteenth century', and she said '1848', then walked off, without even knowing why I was asking. I then discovered that I had unwittingly plumped for the most interesting time in the whole era in terms of travel. It was the cusp – the time when the battle between coaches and trains was at its fiercest, the time when, in retrospect anyway, transport was poised between past and future.

I got carried away on a massive railway tangent when I was doing my research – it was absolutely fascinating! In the 1840s train travel wasn't new but it was developing at an unprecedented rate. People wanted to invest in it, speculate on it and generally get involved. As a result, management companies formed and reformed about every five minutes! Amy arrives in London at Bricklayers' Arms but a few years later this terminus had fallen into disuse and London Bridge was used instead. I learned that building a railway line and station sometimes meant razing whole residential neighbourhoods, which is quite staggering!

As with every social change there were those who were skeptical and those who welcomed it. The Begleys, whom Amy meets on her train journey from Ladywell to London, embody these attitudes.

A Quick Interview with Tracy Rees

What's your comfort food?

Oh, food in general is pretty great, isn't it? A chocolate orange or creme egg can never be a bad thing – aside from the sugar jitters I get because I EAT TOO MANY! But when I'm on the straight and narrow, I really love: brown rice with veggies and halloumi, Pad Thai, brown toast with peanut butter and banana. I'm hungry now . . .

What's your favourite tipple?

A glass of really nice red – probably from Chile or Argentina – or champagne! Or both. Why not? But not in the same glass.

Dog or cat?

Dog. I love cats too, but I long for a dog. My living arrangements don't allow for one at the moment but when that changes, how will I choose between all those gorgeous breeds? To the special dogs in my life – Skip, Ruffles, Romeo, Billy, Tasha, Kelvyn, Tom and Jenny – lots of love and hugs.

What keeps you sane?

Whatever finely balanced and precious degree of sanity I possess is due to: amazing friends (truly, no-one could have better); writing at least half an hour of drivel first thing every morning (in the hope that writing later in the day will be less drivel-like – let's not examine that one too closely); exercise (it's a fact, though not a welcome one); being out in nature, and green tea.

What would people be surprised to discover about you?

The secret world inside my head maybe . . . in it I'm a rockstar, performing spectacularly with any number of music legends, regardless of whether or not they're actually still alive. In this other universe I'm be-sequinned, adored . . . oh, and I can sing!

Town or country?

Both! I am a penny-and-bun girl. A have-my-cake-and-eat-it girl. I've spent much of my life moving back and forth between London and Wales trying to decide exactly that. After many years and a lot of angst I've decided that I need clean air, space, coastal walks, my family AND the buzz of London. So I'm based in Wales but visit London a lot.

What's your favourite holiday read?

Oh so many! Isabel Woolf, Rosanna Ley, Patricia Scanlan, Marian Keyes . . . and WHY did the *Twilight* saga have to end?

What scares you?

Just life! Seriously, I don't have any of the usual fears: spiders, snakes, rats, the dark, heights, buttons . . . I love them all. But that's not to say I'm never afraid, quite the contrary. Life can be difficult and painful and we humans are tender little souls. But I like to focus instead on the things that help me rise above anxiety (see sanity question above!). I used to be scared of spiders but I conquered that in 2000.

Sweet or savoury?

Sweet by natural inclination. Savoury by sheer, iron-willed, *extremely* impressive determination and strength of character.

Read the book or watch the film first?

Read the book. Always, always read the book.

Night in or night out?

Totally, totally depends on my mood. If I had to pick a ratio . . . it would be 5:2 in favour of nights in. I do love to curl up in peace and quiet with a book, DVD or sketchpad. A blanket and a glass of red wine in winter; a glass of rose in the garden in summer. As for nights out . . . anywhere my friends are is good for me!

What are you currently reading?

I have finally, finally got around to reading *Stardust* by Neil Gaiman. The film is one of my absolute favourites – I adore fairytales – so it's a joy to devour the original that inspired it. I've just realized . . . I need to go back and amend my book or film answer! There's an exception to every rule.

. . . and finally!

Henry Mead or Quentin Garland?

A million times Henry! Dark, handsome, funny and slightly disheveled. What's not to like? Quentin is definitely not my type. I mistrust anyone with very tidy hair.

Twickenham or Bath?

In Amy's day? Twickenham. Nowadays, well, I lived in Twickenham for a long time and it was great. Bath is fantastic for a day out. So both. Again!

Pretty day dress or the low-cut silk evening one?

Low-cut silk. The brighter the better. I absolutely loved writing Amy's *Pretty Woman* transformation when she unpacked Aurelia's trunk. But the reservations about the flashier items were all her own!

www.quercusbooks.co.uk

Join us!

Visit us at our website, or join us on
Twitter and Facebook for:

- Exclusive interviews and films from
  your favourite Quercus authors

- Exclusive extra content

- Pre-publication sneak previews

- Free chapter samplers and
  reading group materials

- Giveaways and competitions

- Subscribe to our free newsletter

www.quercusbooks.co.uk
twitter.com/quercusbooks
facebook.com/quercusbooks